D0934127

CHILD OF SHADOWS

CHILD OF SHADOWS

JOHN COYNE

WARNER BOOKS

A Time Warner Company

Warner Books, Inc., 666 Fifth Avenue, New York, NY 10103

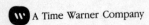 A Time Warner Company

First printing: October 1990
10 9 8 7 6 5 4 3 2 1
Library of Congress Cataloging-in-Publication Data
Coyne, John.
    Child of shadows / John Coyne.
        p.   cm.
    ISBN 0-446-51555-8
        I. Title.
    PS3553.096C47   1990
        813′ .54—dc20
Book design by H. Roberts

90-50289
CIP

For Anita

"I have always believed evil does not go unpunished."

*Annabel Markov, on hearing that
the killer(s) of her husband, Georgi I. Markov,
exiled Bulgarian writer and critic
of the Communist regime, will be
tracked down by the Bulgarian Politburo*

PROLOGUE

DETECTIVE NICK KARDATZKE stepped carefully through the sewage water, the filth and garbage that had found their way into the tunnels under Grand Central Station. It was a cobweb world of intersecting and interchanging rails that disappeared into dozens of dark tunnels, vast switching yards that spread out under the city, in the midst of midtown Manhattan.

A dozen yards ahead of him was the crime scene, lit up like a movie set. The police photographer was working and the bright explosions in the darkness of the tunnel hurt the detective's eyes. He glanced down in time to see a foot-long rat scurry across the tracks and disappear into the darkness.

"Shit," he said out loud, surprised by his voice. He hated being underground. The truth was, the subways frightened him, all the noise and violence, all the unwashed of the world. No person in their right mind rode the subway. He wouldn't let his kids use them, not with what he knew happened under the streets.

He pulled his shield from his breast pocket and hung it on his suit jacket, then he pushed himself into the circle of cops surrounding the body and called out, letting his voice bounce off the wet walls, "What have we got?"

Several of the plainclothes cops moved aside, spotting him.

"We got a real cute one, Lieutenant," one of the men said, and moved himself so Nick could see the naked body of the small boy.

"Jesus H. Christ," the detective whispered, staring ·at the victim. The naked boy was curled up, as if seeking warmth in the wet corner of the concrete beam.

"Sex?" he asked, staring at the child and thinking of his son, as he always did when he came on a dead kid.

"Sex and drugs, what else is there?" the same cop said, grinning, and squatted down beside the boy.

Nick saw the cop was wearing surgical gloves and he watched as the man shoved his hand between the boy's bare cheeks and pulled a thin six-inch plastic tube from the boy's rectum. "You could say the kid was shitting a hundred thousand of the white stuff."

Kardatzke caught his breath. This was new to him, and he had seen plenty.

"Anything else?" he asked. He didn't like the other cop.

"You want more, we got more," the cop said. He shoved the plastic tube back up into the boy, then reached over and turned the stiff body so Nick Kardatzke saw the boy's chest. "You want more, we got more," the cop said again and moved aside so Nick saw the bloody mess of a hole in the boy's chest.

The deep wide gash in the teenager's body puzzled the detective. He stepped into the harsh shadowy light cast by the emergency equipment.

"What happened?" he asked, sounding innocent.

"They cut out his heart, Lieutenant," the cop said. "That's what they done."

The detective took a flashlight from a uniformed cop and pointed it into the cavity. The boy's small body was drained of blood, and the exposed muscles and tissues swarmed with maggots.

"It's been ripped out!" he exclaimed.

"We've seen it all now, haven't we, Lieutenant?" The cop laughed, glancing around. "Seen it all," he said again, for emphasis.

"That's not a knife cut," Nick went on, thinking out loud.

"No way," the young cop agreed. "The paramedic says the same thing. The fuckin' guy, or whoever, ripped out this kid's heart!" His voice grew excited.

Kardatzke stood up.

"Are we done here, Lieutenant?" another cop asked, and Nick nodded. The young cop let go of the stiff corpse and the body fell back, face smashing against the rocky base of the underground wall.

"Yeah, we're done," Nick whispered and stepped away, walking through the crowd of uniformed cops and transit workers who had gathered at the crime scene.

In the darkness of the tunnel, beyond the emergency lights, he looked back up the track, to the dim lights of the Lower Level of Grand Central Station. He was wondering how the boy had gotten there, deep underground. They had called him in, he realized, because of the drugs shoved up the boy's rectum. It was another twist in the world of crack trafficking.

He knew what would happen next. They'd ID the body, go to the FBI with prints, and do a computer run, see if they could find a match. All of that was routine. What wasn't routine was what happened to the kid. Who in God's name had ripped out the boy's heart? But he knew even as he asked the question what a mutilated murder like this meant. He had seen it before. Another serial killer was loose in the city.

SOMEONE HAD GIVEN THE homeless boy a piece of hard candy from the jar Sara kept on her office desk. He held it in his open palm, staring at the bright yellow paper. One of the cops standing around the edge of the room told Greg to unwrap it, that the kid didn't know what it was, and Greg had done that, and placed the candy back in the boy's palm. The boy looked from Greg Schnilling, who was telling him it was okay, to the candy, and finally the child sniffed the small yellow piece. Another cop, a short, beefy man, exclaimed, "Oh, shit, did you see that? The kid doesn't know what it is!"

Melissa Vaughn left her corner cubicle at the rear of the office and walked up front, where Sara, the receptionist, told her about the kid, how the cops had found him in the tunnels under Grand Central, living on rats, she whispered. Sara's brown eyes widened.

Melissa kept moving forward, passing through the crowd. Because of who she was, the others let her slip through quickly, telling her more information about the boy. He wouldn't speak, someone said. Or couldn't. Maybe he's autistic, Sara added, then told them all again about her cousin Ralph.

Melissa said nothing, not responding to their questions of why the police had brought the child to their offices, to them of all people, and not the precinct. They all sounded offended, as if their world of work had been somehow breached. Yet it was a question, she, too, wanted asked. This wasn't standard procedure, bringing a homeless child to the offices of the city's human resources agency.

She was watching Greg, seeing him sitting on the edge of Sara's desk. He was leaning forward, still encouraging the boy, smiling and whispering, and had taken a second piece of candy, unwrapped it, and popped it into his own mouth. The boy looked from him back to the small round yellow ball of candy in the palm of his dirty hand.

Melissa reached the edge of the circle and saw the boy, and smelled him, too. Now she realized why everyone was giving the child such room. The boy smelled like shit.

He had no hair or eyebrows. His head was perfectly round, smooth, and glossy white. He looked like someone from a freak show. There wasn't much to him. Sitting, his feet didn't touch the floor. He was dangerously thin, and she thought of the children she had seen on television, all the starving children of Africa, with their swollen stomachs and polelike legs. He was twelve or thirteen, she guessed, though she had learned that homeless children were often older than they seemed.

He was wearing a torn shirt, torn pants, both filthy and beyond recognition. She glanced at this feet and saw he had attempted to wrap his left foot in bits and pieces of rags, all tied together. On his right foot was a man's black shoe, too big for him, but he had used thick twine to tie the old shoe to his bare foot.

My God, she thought.

Greg looked over and said something.

Melissa shook her head, indicated that she didn't catch his question. She couldn't take her eyes off the boy. He was sniffing the candy again, leaning closer to his open palm. Take it, she said to herself.

The boy did. He licked the hard round ball off his palm and popped it into his mouth where it momentarily bulged his thin face. His face brightened and around her she heard everyone laugh.

She knelt to be at his eye level and waited for him to respond to her, to look over, and when he didn't, she snapped her fingers to catch his attention.

He shot a glance at her and there was a flash of terror in his eyes. She was sorry now for what she had done, and she smiled at once to reassure him, but the fear remained. It was in his gray eyes, on his face. He drew back his lips, like a snarling dog.

"Jesus," the beefy cop said, and several others moved, as if getting ready to rush and subdue the boy. She raised her hand at once, and kept her eyes on the boy, kept smiling.

He was a beautiful child behind the grime and soot of the city. His face was perfectly formed and his gray eyes were clear and very bright. He did not have the look of defeat that she always saw on the faces of the homeless.

He had been hurt, too, she noticed. There was blood caked on his forehead, and a large black swelling under his left eye. She guessed the cops had done that, catching him. She held out her hand with her open palm up, as she might with a strange dog, and the boy recoiled, bracing himself.

"Watch it," one of the cops said, warning her.

"He might bite you," another said, and then to the other cops, "remember what that kid did to Keefer?"

"You could get AIDS from a kid like this," the first cop said.

The circle widened around the boy.

Melissa blocked out what the cops were saying, but did not take her eyes off the boy. She was watching to see if the child might respond to the voices, to see if there was any reaction on the boy's face or in his eyes.

She reached up and slipped her hand into Sara's candy jar and pulled out another yellow sucker and unwrapped it, doing it all without taking her eyes from the boy. He was watching her now; rather, she saw, he was watching the candy, seeing what she was going to do with it. She saw him moisten his lips and swallow. She saw how his eyes brightened as they focused on the candy.

She placed the hard piece in her palm and held out her hand. He swatted it off her fingers and popped it into his mouth in one quick grab. Then he curled up again on the wooden chair, like a small dog who had stolen food from the dining-room table.

Behind her, one of the secretaries complained how awful it was to have a child like that brought into their offices, and the anger in the room shifted toward the cops, and several people asked why the boy had been brought to them in the first place.

Melissa let the argument swirl above her. She stayed kneeling at the edge of the desk, within arm's reach of the child.

Greg asked her what should they do, call Bellevue? Send the kid to a center? It was already five-fifteen and several of her employees, glancing at the clock, started back to clean off their desks and get ready to leave work.

She kept watching the homeless boy.

He had finished the hard candy and was staring at the large jar on Sara's desk. When Greg reached for another piece, Melissa spoke up.

"Don't!" she told her deputy.

The swat of fear in the boy's eyes shifted to rage. He would kill her, Melissa realized; he was that hungry.

"Go downstairs, Greg, please, and buy a couple of hot dogs, chips, whatever. This child is starved." She stood and turned to the cops, asking why the homeless boy had been brought directly to their offices.

"We got a couple of transvestites down in the holding pen. They went after each other pretty bad," the beefy cop told her, shrugging his shoulders and grinning. "That was no place for this kid."

"Okay," another cop spoke up, "what do you want done with this one?"

"Leave him with me. I'll handle him."

"Melissa," Sara asked, standing beside her reception desk, "do you want me to call the shelter on Forty-second?"

Melissa shook her head and, without answering the woman, said to the boy, "Come with me." She reached over and picked up the jar of candy off Sara's desk and moved through the crowd, back to her office. She knew, from the way the others were scattering, that the child was obeying, that he was following her.

"Look!" the fat cop exclaimed. "The kid's like a goddamn dog."

Melissa wished now she had gotten that cop's badge number.

In her office, in the close confines of the corner cubicle, the child smelled worse. She broke open the window and took a deep breath of the cool late April afternoon. The days were longer, and it was still daylight at five o'clock. She could see the Hudson River and soot clouds hanging over New Jersey.

When she turned away from the window, the child was emptying the candy jar, stuffing the hard yellow pieces into his pockets, working furiously. He didn't pause when he glanced up, nor did she try to stop him.

Instead, she sat down and waited, saying nothing. The boy ignored her. He wasn't frightened and that pleased her. She could see in his eyes that the fear was gone. Now he was obsessed with eating. He kept popping the hard yellow balls into his mouth, bulging his cheeks as he sucked on the hard candy.

He ate like a barnyard animal, she thought, but was not offended by his slovenliness. She could only guess how he had been finding enough to eat in the tunnels.

"Here!" Greg announced, rushing into the room. He had two brown bags full of deli food. Setting them down on Melissa's desk, he said, "I got something of everything." He took out hot dogs, cans of Coke, a small package of chips, and a container of coffee. He dumped the packaged condiments onto the small coffee table, and the boy jumped up and seized the tiny packages and began to stuff them into his pockets.

"Hey, wait!"

"Let him alone," Melissa whispered.

"Jesus, what is this?"

"Never mind. Unwrap the hot dog, please."

The boy took everything that Greg gave him. He stuffed his mouth with food, licking the mustard and sauerkraut off his cheeks, tearing open the tiny plastic packages of ketchup and sucking out the insides. He was kneeling beside the office table, gorging himself.

"What do you want me to do?" Greg asked, watching Melissa. He had moved over to stand by the open window.

Melissa shook her head. She kept watching the boy.

"You want me to call Berdock?" Greg asked next. "I can take the child directly down to Bellevue."

"That's okay. Why don't you go. It's late. I'll handle him. He's just hungry, not crazy."

"We don't know that," Greg said quietly.

The boy did not look up from the food.

"I think he's okay."

Greg watched her a moment, then he glanced at the groveling

child. When he looked again at Melissa, he knew what she was planning.

"You're not thinking of signing this kid over to yourself, are you, Mel?"

Melissa shrugged, not looking at her deputy.

"Jesus Christ, you can't do that!" He ran his hand through his short hair. It was something she had mentioned to him. She was always saying she could take better care of a homeless child than their city agency. "Melissa, I won't let you! You're violating procedure."

"Greg, it's late. Helen will be wondering what's keeping you." She glanced at him, smiling.

"Melissa, you're breaking the law!"

She shrugged again.

The boy had stopped eating and had slumped down beside the table, leaving a wreckage of garbage, bits and pieces of food, wax paper, and empty ketchup and mustard packets.

"I'm not going to let you do this," Greg insisted. "You'll be breaking the law."

"It's stretching the law, not breaking it."

"Honest to God, Melissa, I just don't believe you!"

Melissa didn't take her eyes from the child. He had quieted down and was silent, overwhelmed, she realized, by all the food. The hostile glint was gone from his gray eyes. He was sleepy, and nodding his head. She felt a pang in her breast, an emotional tug, as if he were really her child.

She wondered when the poor boy had last slept in a warm and safe bed, and thinking that, she felt another plunge in her body, as if a dagger of motherly worry was piercing her heart, causing her guilt.

She reached down into the bottom desk drawer and pulled out a set of city forms and fed them into her typewriter.

Greg had approached her, circling the boy and coming around so that he faced her and the typewriter.

"Melissa," he whispered.

"Go home, Greg. This isn't your problem."

"Melissa, why in God's name are you doing this?"

"You know why," she told him, banging the keys.

"This isn't going to solve the agency's problem, Mel."

"No, but it might solve mine!" She looked up at him, her eyes glassy.

"Where is he going to sleep? You have a one-bedroom!"

"I'll work it out."

"Mel, you're not thinking straight. I know we've talked about this, but..."

"There was a man on the train this morning," Melissa said calmly, staring off. Her eyes were too blurry for her to type. "He had his little girl perched on his shoulders and was telling everyone that he had just lost his job, lost his wife, and he had no money to buy Pampers, nor anywhere to live but the city shelters. He kept telling people he was afraid to sleep in the shelters with his daughter. He was afraid what might happen to the little girl. He didn't want her raped, he said."

Greg reached for Melissa, held her gently by the shoulders, and kept saying, "Okay, okay, don't cry."

"I can't keep doing this, Greg," she said, sobbing. "I sit up here in this high, safe office and shuffle paper, dispatch these people, my 'clients,' from one shelter to the next. And what happens to them? Little girls get raped!"

"They don't all get raped! And besides, it's not your fault."

"Then whose fault is it?" she shouted back.

"Goddamnit, I don't know!"

She pulled out of Greg's grasp, telling him, "I'm just one person, Greg. A single woman living in Brooklyn. I'm thirty-three and I have two college degrees, and I can't help these poor suffering people. Some days I hate them all."

"Mel, we all get like that, sometimes." He was close to tears himself, kneeling beside her typewriter. He wanted to reach over and take her back into his arms, to squeeze all the pain from her body.

"Greg, I can do something. I can take this one little boy and help him. Save him. That's right! Save him." She stared at Greg, the tears gone from her eyes. "You know what will happen to him in a shelter! He'll be abused. Look what those cops did to him when they grabbed him! If I let him go, he'll end up a whore, or a thief, or worse. No," she announced, shaking her head and resuming her typing. "I'm not going to let that happen to him."

"Melissa, what's going on here?" he asked, whispering.

"I've made up my mind, don't talk to me." Her fingers banged at the old machine.

Greg looked from her to the boy, then back to Melissa. Tears had begun again to slide down her cheeks. He wanted to lean over and kiss them off her soft face. He thought of Helen, waiting for him at home, and remembered that they were going to his mother-in-law's for dinner.

"Melissa...?"

"Leave me alone," she begged.

"Okay," he said, pulling himself up, stepping away. His legs felt weak. He should just walk out of the office, he thought. He should resign, get a transfer, get away from her. It couldn't stop himself from thinking that this was all his fault. He was driving Melissa to such an extreme.

"Do you want me to help, you know, with him?"

"No, it's okay." She kept typing.

At the door, he stopped again and said, "You can't just leave him alone all day at your place. If you want, I could talk to Helen about day-care. What's available in Brooklyn."

"I think I might just take a leave of absence," she answered back, having just thought of that solution. She paused in her typing, staring at the form. She had enough accumulated leave, she knew. She could sublease her apartment, take off, leave New York. The city was no place to spend the summer. She could go off somewhere and get to know the child, spend all her time with him. That might be what she really wanted out of life.

"Mel, you can't! I mean, who's going to run this place!"

"You!" She turned to look at him, smiling at the wonderful simplicity of her idea. It was a solution that had come full blown to her and made perfectly good sense, not only for the homeless child, but for her.

Greg started back into the office. He had raised his hand to make another point, and then the homeless boy stood and reached for Melissa, as if to grab her, but instead he uttered a growling belch from deep in his body and retched up all of the food, the hard candy, the ketchup and mustard, and deli sandwich and hot dog, everything that he had gorged down. He vomited it all onto her desk, spraying her with the green and yellow vomit of his stomach.

The boy looked helplessly at her, helpless in his sickness, and Melissa reached over to motherly caress his flushed face, saying at once to calm him, "It's all right, child. It's all right. I'll take care of you. I'll take care of everything." She reached for her phone, deciding at once how she would arrange to leave the city and go someplace safe to raise this homeless child.

2

THEY REACHED THE WESTERN edge of the state at the end of the second day, driving up through the Piedmont region of North Carolina and into the green mountains at the southern end of the long Blue Ridge range. They had left the interstates and were on the narrow back roads, twisting through hills of tall spruce and pine. There was no traffic and only a few houses, most of them built close to the road, nothing more than tar-paper shacks and broken-down farmhouses.

But occasionally Melissa began to spot bigger and newer homes built back from the road and nestled in groves of trees, or higher on the mountainside with clear views of the long pine valleys that looked south, into Georgia.

The modern houses were all new since Melissa had last come into the mountains eight years before to take classes at the crafts school. It had been summer then, too, and she had stayed three weeks, studying pottery. She had a vague hope of dropping out of her graduate course in social work and setting up a studio in the mountains and making a living by creating one-of-a-kind ceramic pieces.

She soon realized, however, that she didn't have the talent nor the steely devotion to become a studio potter, but she still clung to the romantic notion of living a simple life off somewhere in the mountains, far from New York City.

It was this secret dream, more than anything else, that made her decide to bring Adam here, deep into the Appalachian Mountains. She remembered how wonderful the brief period had been for her at the crafts school, where all her troubles seemed far away, and where it seemed everyone just forgot about the outside world, forgot about time itself, and just let the warm summer days slip by.

She thought again how much she hated life in New York, hated her job at the agency. She knew, too, that she had only stayed because of Greg. She hadn't wanted to give up seeing him. But New York City wasn't where she wanted to live out her life.

She glanced over at Adam, thinking that she could raise Adam safely here, away from the crime of New York, away from the dank and dangerous tunnels under Manhattan. She would use the money she took out of her retirement fund to keep them going for a year. Next year, she'd worry about what to do next. But for the moment all she cared about was seeing that Adam got better.

Melissa didn't even know what Adam's real name was. She and Greg had guessed it must be Adam when they found "Adam" stenciled in the child's old and torn underwear. Still, Greg had notified the police and they did a missing child search. No boy with the name of Adam matched his description. Melissa had come to love the name, thinking of Adam as being God's "first born." And if not God's, she thought secretly to herself, then hers.

It had rained earlier in the mountains and now there was a fresh sparkle to the late spring afternoon. Melissa opened the side window and smelled the clean breeze. She grinned with pleasure. For the first time in years, she felt free of New York's dirt and soot, free of the tension of her work at the city agency. She glanced at the boy and said, "We're almost there!" She reached out instinctively and stroked the child's cheek with love. He jerked, ducking his head away from her touch.

Melissa remembered the doctor's advice; don't rush the child. Let Adam find his own way of trusting her. And she remembered again how much he had warned her, saying, "You don't change a damaged psyche just by removing him from the city. In fact," he had also warned, "all of those woods and rural life might be worse than the tunnels from which he came. The truth is, Ms. Vaughn, we don't know who this child is. I do know, however, that there is no medical reason why he can't talk. But until he decides to talk, well, we'll never know who he is."

Melissa turned a sharp corner of the mountain road and spotted the school about a mile ahead. It stood at the head of a shallow valley of pine trees and open fields, flush against a small hill called Miller's Knob. There were a half-dozen white buildings clustered together, hidden in a grove of towering spruce pine.

The sun spotlighted the buildings and made them shine in the yellow glow of late afternoon light. Melissa pulled the van off the mountain road and pointed ahead, showing Adam their new home, the Blue Ridge Crafts School.

She took out a crude map that Connor Connaghan, the man whose house she had rented for the summer, had sent her. She opened it as she drove by the school, circling the buildings and Miller's Knob, and going deeper into the hills.

When she glanced at Adam, the boy was passively watching the scenery, which reminded Melissa of a rain forest: a heavy wet canopy of trees, and yellow and orange sunlight filtering through the thick branches. It was beautiful and cool after the long day of driving on the turnpikes, but she feared using this road at night, coming back from school, and not having the comfort of city streetlights. She remembered how dark it could get in the mountains.

They came out of the trees. The van abruptly reached another hilltop curve and below them was the town of Beaver Creek, built on both banks of the high mountain stream. It was a lovely hamlet of two dozen houses nestled in trees, and Melissa smiled, responding to the sight, and then she saw out of the corner of her eyes that her excitement had caught Adam's attention. He glanced at her, suddenly frightened.

"It's okay, Adam," she whispered, downshifting and smiling at the boy. "Isn't this a lovely place? That's where we'll be living." She kept smiling, kept speaking slowly, as if teaching English to a foreign child.

The mountain road came into town at the western edge, descending directly to the main street. According to Connor Connaghan's map, their rented house was at the other edge of town, past the post office and general store. She had to turn left at the only stoplight and go a few blocks.

As she drove slowly along the main street, called Store Front, she remembered having stopped once in the town when she had last been at the school. She recognized a restaurant called Bonnie & Clyde's where she'd had a hamburger. She smiled again as she passed the sign in the general-store window: IF BAUER'S DOESN'T HAVE IT, YOU DON'T NEED IT.

Well that is exactly what she wanted. She was going to reduce all her needs, she promised herself, to whatever was available at the general store.

She turned at the light and headed up Creek Drive, toward where Connor Connaghan had drawn a rough sketch of a house and labeled it Ship's Landing.

There were several big, rambling houses on the first block. They were southern gothic places, Melissa thought, noticing the screened wraparound porches, the high second-floor gabled windows, and the telltale widow's walks on the roofs. Each house was set in the middle of a huge lawn with small barns in back, and John Deere tractors and other farm equipment. All of the houses had large gardens, planted to one side of the house and protected by high fences. The fences, she guessed, were to keep out the deer.

There were houses with children, she realized, spotting rope swings hanging from huge poplar trees and crudely built treehouses. She smiled with anticipation. There would be kids here to play with Adam. And nothing, she knew, would be better for Adam than other kids. Normal kids who hadn't been abused by parents, cast away by society, or forced to grow up on city streets.

At the end of the first block, the pavement ran out and the van bounced over the hard ruts, and went through the empty crossing, and Melissa slowed, but kept driving, realizing she was headed out of town again.

There were no cut lawns here, no ancient shade trees, and no gabled houses. The corner lots were vacant fields gone to seed. The unpaved road crested another ridge and dipped sharply down toward the creek. She looked ahead, over the tops of the long yellow grass. Melissa spotted a metal roof and brown shingle siding and a patch of grass.

That must be Ship's Landing. She looked across the fields searching for other houses, thinking at once that they would be isolated at the end of Creek Drive with no neighbors even within shouting distance. She had a vivid memory of the black nights of the mountains, and she imagined being alone in the woods with only Adam and the howling wind.

"Oh, shit," she whispered and, downshifting, descended the steep drive to the river and swung the van into the yard of Ship's Landing. How could she have rented this house unseen? Then she needed to veer to her right as another car, a small VW Bug, shot out of the yard. She saw the thin faces of two young women in the front seat.

The house was across an open, bare yard. It was small, much smaller than the rambling gothic places up on the ridge, but perfect for her and Adam, Melissa thought, seeing it.

It was also, she realized, a handmade house. One of those places that a craftsman had carefully constructed with odd pieces of hard wood. The house was an art form, a craftsman's statement.

It looked weird and wonderful, Melissa thought, driving slowly ahead across the yard. Melissa couldn't stop grinning at her good fortune.

Ship's Landing resembled the bow of an eighteenth-century schooner, placed in the yard to resemble a sailing vessel plowing into shore at the bank of Beaver Creek.

"Of course," Melissa said out loud, "ship's landing!"

The "bow" of the house appeared to run aground on the rocky shoal. From the narrow front door, cut into the flank of the ship's side, there was a cobblestone patch spreading like an open fan to create a small terrace by the creek's edge, shaded by black willows and cottonwood trees.

On the high side of the house, the grass had been cut, trimmed, and well tended. A smooth green lawn grew in a wide area around the ship-house and swept up the sloping lawn, only to disappear and die out in the thick outcropping of shale boulders that framed the shallow river valley.

Melissa thought of Beaver Creek, and wondered how safe the house might be in a flash flood. But no one, she hoped, would have built such a house and maintained it so meticulously in the face of flooding.

Melissa moved to stop the van and Adam seized her arm, holding her.

"What, Adam?" she asked, remembering to be calm with the child.

He wasn't watching her, she realized, but was staring up at the house, frightened by what he was seeing.

She turned to the house and saw a man had emerged at the top of the house, in the bow of the ship. He turned to wave as if Melissa's new home really was a ship. A safe, snug, welcoming ship from sea, here to this inland shore.

"It's okay," she told Adam, "that must be Connor Connaghan. We're renting his house."

The boy beside her would not stop trembling, nor take his eyes off the man in the bow of the ship, high up on the second floor of the weird-looking house.

She shut off the engine. The man had disappeared from the second-floor porch.

"We're here!" she said to Adam, taking a deep breath and feeling her own fatigue sweep through her body. She glanced over at the boy, grinning.

Adam had not taken his eyes off the house, and when she looked again, she saw the man had appeared at a side doorway and was coming quickly across the yard toward them.

"Wait," she instructed Adam, feeling protective, and jumped from the cab to meet Connor Connaghan, and realizing, too, that she wanted to keep him away from Adam, to put a buffer for the moment between the boy and the owner.

"Hi! I'm Melissa Vaughn. And you're...?"

"Connor. Connor Connaghan." He smiled.

His smile was warm and bright and big as all outdoors.

Seeing him smile, Melissa knew Connor was a good man and someone she could trust. She stuck out her hand, saying, "It's great to be in the mountains, and this," she added, feeling good about saying it, "is Adam. My son." She looked back to where the bald-headed boy still sat in the front seat, silently watching them with his big, blank gray eyes.

3

BETTY SUE YATES RAN. She ran down Store Front Street, dodging the few people on the sidewalk and sang to herself, sang out loud, "I've seen the boychild...I've seen the bald-headed boychild." People were jumping out of her way, swearing and calling her name. The old woman kept running.

The words sang in her mind, running together as fast as she ran. Her sneakers were light as air. Her legs were flying. She was grinning, happy. Even though she'd peed in her panties, she didn't care. "No, sir, I don't care!" she sang out, hearing her voice sail away like a kite.

At six feet two, she was all long arms and legs. A skeleton of a figure weighing less than one hundred fifty. She wore jeans under a flower sack dress, and two tattered homemade sweaters over her shoulders. One sweater was pink, the other red, and both were too much for the hot afternoon. However now, even in summer, Betty Sue was always cold, and shivered in the slight breeze.

Just before Stan's Mobil Station, she cut across Smith's vacant lot, followed the worn path through the high wild grass, and ran for Simon's Ridge, toward the New Land Tabernacle Church and Reverend Littleton.

She knew her little brother Rufus was behind her, running as fast as he could on his little legs, but she outdistanced him, climbing the hillside, knowing, too, that he'd be there again, watching her, once she reached the churchyard.

At the edge of the ridge, she stumbled and tumbled forward into the soft earth. She was panting for breath and her head hurt, oh, it hurt something awful, like it always did when she was real excited and real nervous. That's why Nurse Peele said to her, smiley like, "Oh, Betty Sue, don't you go getting yourself all excited now, you all hear me, honey? You're pushing sixty, gal. You're only a child in your mind, hear me? Your body is done wasting away."

That silly little bitch, Betty Sue thought, grinning to herself and licking the tip of her nose with her long, thin tongue.

She pulled herself up and kept walking. Her whole body was hurting. She gasped for breath walking into the church graveyard. She couldn't think. Her eyes were dizzy with pain. She thought, I'll die right here, crossing through the graveyard, right down there between the slabs, the Grayson clan. She saw, reading slowly.

Douglas Grayson
1912–1985
REST IN THE LAP OF OUR LORD

The horse's ass, she thought, remembering how he and Dubby Arnold, the Yowells boys, and Stan Turner had taken her over to Peppertree Fontana Village, made her drink Doc Clark's whiskey, and then fucked her like a cow in the woods, off the parkway. Good and dead and good riddance, she thought, with a nod of her head. She gave his tombstone the finger.

He was always grabbing her teat when she came into his drugstore, she remembered next. And she spat in his face, given the chance, until her daddy boxed her ears once, told her he'd lock her away in the fruit cellar.

She spotted the small church through all the white birch. She saw the tall spire of a tower, and the weathervane. She saw Reverend Littleton and grinned, happy again.

The preacher was in the backyard, working in the garden. He had flowers in his hand. A bunch that looked like a red torch. He was bending over, picking more flowers when she came thrashing out of the underbrush, too exhausted to speak, stumbling on the thick rosebushes, but still rushing and all her breath gone.

Littleton bolted back, surprised by the sight of her in the flower garden. His tiny pinched face was white behind his bulging glasses and his mouth went slack.

Close your mouth, Betty Sue thought, or bees will fly in and bite your gums.

"Betty Sue! What are you doing, girl?" He came stomping from the flowers, his high black boots covered with red mountain clay. He was wearing black trousers, a white shirt with full sleeves, black suspenders, and a bow tie. Dark patches of sweat stained under his arms.

She had fallen to the ground to smell the cut grass and she closed her eyes, smiling, thinking how she loved the smell of clover and wished she were a cow again. It wouldn't be the first time she was a cow. Or other animals. She had been a marsh hawk and had broken her leg jumping off the town's water tower. She was younger then, in her thirties, her daddy told her. She didn't know what thirty meant. She couldn't count but ten.

"Betty Sue, my child, what are you doing?" The Reverend reached down and seized her forearm.

She was frightened at once, trembling from the rage of the tall man's voice, so she spoke quickly, before he could scold her, "I've seen him, Reverend! I seen him."

The words began to singsong in her head and she shut her eyes to keep from singing. She knew people didn't like her singsonging. But sometimes she couldn't stop, no matter how hard she tried. Or how much they hit her.

"Betty Sue, what are you talking about? Coming all the way up here. Thrashing through my cemetery." He waved his bunch of flowers, thrashing the air with his red dagger.

"...seen him," she whispered, keeping her distance from the reverend's flaming knife. "Boy. Bald-headed boychild..."

"Betty Sue, Betty Sue!" The minister pulled her upright, straining to lift her weight.

Standing beside him, she was nearly as tall, but she wouldn't straighten up. She stood hunch-shouldered, ducking her head, and kept her thin arms wrapped about her body.

"Now, Betty Sue, no one will hurt you. Seen who, child?" He spoke softly, gently, and took her by the shoulder, moving out of the red clay flower garden and over to where there was a pine bench in the shade of several water oak trees.

"Evil all around. In the hills. On the street. Right beside you in your seat," she said, squinting at the thin preacher. It was what the reverend always told them in church.

Rufus, her brother, had come to sit with them on the bench and he was grinning at her, making faces. She paid him no mind. She knew the preacher couldn't see Rufus. No one could see Rufus, no one but her, not since she had dunked him in the barn well.

"Boychild," she said again. She glanced around, thinking: He doesn't believe me. He'd tell Aunt Mary Lee and she'd beat her for bothering the preacher, talking about the boychild. The bald-headed boychild.

Betty Sue cocked her head, listened a moment to the words singsonging in her mind, listening to them twirling wildly around until they made her dizzy. She shook her ears to silence her brain.

Brains were a terrible thing, she knew. Her daddy had said as much.

"Betty Sue, you go home to Aunt Mary Lee's. She'll be lookin' for you."

Reverend Littleton, leaning forward and bracing his bony arms on his thin legs, frowning, watching her, looked like the man on a nickel.

"Boychild," she whispered, defying him, and then, in spite, as her daddy would say, she stuck out her tongue and with its tip licked her left nostril. Behind him, Rufus rolled off the wooden bench, laughing, holding his sides, kicking his short legs in the air.

"My Lord, aren't you a loony tune, that's for sure."

Betty Sue grabbed the minister, pulled him into an embrace and whispered in his ear, grinning now, "Boychild. Boychild. Bald-headed boychild." She kept grinning, listening to the word *boychild* sing through her mind like a hawk flying off, higher and higher into the clear sky. She glanced up and through the branches of the oak trees and spotted the word sailing in the wind over Simon's Ridge.

"Damn it, girl!" The minster jerked free, and stumbling a moment, he raised his hand and thought to himself, Dear God, what am I doing talking to this loony child? I am going to have this creature put away in Lenoir before she causes harm.

"I done seen him, boychild!" Betty Sue shouted.

"Go on home, Betty Sue! You tell Aunt Mary Lee to come see me, hear? We got to do something about you, Betty Sue. You're too old to be running through these streets like a wild child. Frightening people the way you do." He shook his head and walked back to his muddy flower garden. His boots stomped through the wet grass. His hand clung to the bouquet of red flowers.

Rufus was screaming at her, telling her to jump the old man. It was the first time, Betty Sue thought, that Rufus had told her what to do.

She sprinted after the minister and jumped onto his back, saddled him with her muddy legs. She wrapped her arms around his neck and caught his Adam's apple in her grasp.

Choking from the attack, the preacher dropped the red church flowers and wheeled around, stumbling under the weight of the old woman. He tried to free her arms from his thin neck, but she tightened her grip and fought him.

They fell together into the flower garden, onto the blooming dragonroots and roses. Momentarily he pulled loose, choked up a mouth full of blood and spit and tried to speak. Betty Sue grabbed him again. She was mad at him for not listening and she shouted, "Evil all around us. In the hills, on the street, right beside you in your seat."

The preacher kept fighting. He kicked his legs, he tried to roll away, but Betty Sue wouldn't let go. She was stronger and she wasn't afraid. She kept squeezing until he stopped struggling, as Rufus had once, long ago, and before she had dropped him in the well water.

When he stopped fighting her, Betty Sue rolled off the preacher and found her feet. Grinning, she thought of what Aunt Mary Lee had said, saying she was as quick as a cat, quick as a cat. The little singsong verse ran at once through her brain and she slapped herself hard to keep from going silly, as Aunt Mary Lee always said she did.

Reverend Littleton hadn't moved. The preacher lay in his flowers. His long body sprawled out like a broken toy. Rufus came over and the two of them kicked the preacher's legs, leaving a muddy smear on his black trousers.

He's dead, Rufus told her.

"Reverend?" Betty Sue asked, jumping forward to shake his

hand, then jumping away, circling the fallen man, trampling through the flowers, afraid to edge up close enough to touch him again.

He's dead, Rufus said matter-of-factly, moving off.

Betty Sue saw Reverend Littleton's face when she circled around once more. He had lost his glasses. They were jammed up beside his head, as if he might be seeing with his ears, and she grinned at that, thinking how silly that was, watching TV with your ears.

Then she forgot about Reverend Littleton and went chasing after her little brother, Rufus, tried to catch him in the cemetery as he dodged away, ran wild through the old fallen-down tombstones. Shouting after her dead little brother her new singsong words, "I've seen the boychild! I've seen the bald-headed boychild."

4

CONNOR CONNAGHAN WAS TALKING softly, telling Melissa how he had come to build the house, Ship's Landing, there at the edge of the creek. "Money really didn't have anything to do with my decision. It was the quality of life that mattered. It was this"—he gestured around—"having a great place to live." Now he smiled, showing he didn't really take himself all that seriously.

Melissa kept herself from staring at the man.

She kept looking around the house, which didn't make any sense at all, not as a house, nor as the cabin of a sailing vessel. But Ship's Landing was somehow livable and Melissa felt deeply connected to the place.

She felt the old barn-board floor underfoot, saw the wood-burning stove in the corner, the handmade ladder that hung against the far wall, and went up to an open second-floor loft. (She would sleep there, she already decided, spotting it when she first came through the slant door built into the ship's side.)

"Course it won't pass inspection"—Connor was laughing, standing against what he used for the kitchen counter—"and when the guy came out to wire the place for the electric, I told him it was a pottery studio."

"You throw?" Melissa asked, turning to him, looking quizzical, and then she remembered the director of the crafts school said that Connor Connaghan was on the faculty.

"I teach a couple of courses, yeah. Got one in 'bout an hour, in fact. You're into crafts?" He kept smiling, watching her. The secret with women he had learned was to never let his gaze falter. One woman had told him once she felt as if she were drowning in his gaze. He liked that.

"Well, yes, I mean, I did once. I took a course here, years ago." Melissa shrugged and kept talking fast, aware, too, that she was sweating under her arms. "What's this?" she asked, pointing, shifting his attention away from her.

"A sauna. I built it just this winter. What I did first was start here, you know, with this kitchen. And I lived in this space for a couple years while I made some money, and gradually I built onto the main frame as fancy and inspiration struck me. A room here, another there, nothing much planned, guess that part shows." And now he laughed. "First this place did look like a pottery shed, to tell you the truth, and then I made some serious mistakes, you know, and I looked at it one day and thought, Hell this is a ship! a two-masted schooner, and I set off in that direction, made it seem as if the damn ship had plowed itself right into the bank of Beaver Creek."

"It's wonderful!" Melissa smiled, turning to him. "It's perfect! It's beautiful." She kept looking directly at him, wanted him at that moment to be swept away by her charm and enthusiasm, and, she wished, her breathtakingly good looks. She felt a rush of sexual excitement and simple success when she spotted a faint puzzlement in his dark eyes. She had made a connection.

"I don't know." Connor shrugged his shoulders, still glancing around. "It's sure funky enough, and that's what I wanted." He began to ramble on, telling her more about the place, why he had done this, why that, and then he sighed, showing he was pleased she appreciated the house.

To keep the conversation going, floating on over what she knew was the sexual wave that was cresting, Melissa said, "I think I'm going to feel guilty, living here. I mean, I'm sorry you had to rent it out and all." She stopped talking, fearing she was making assumptions about him and what money he might have.

"Oh, I'm building another place on the other side of the ridge." He gestured over his right shoulder. "I have to live down in the dust and all to get anything done." He pushed himself away from the marble kitchen counter, which Melissa realized was just an old tombstone. "What about your things? Can I give you a hand with your luggage. Your boy?"

"Adam!" Melissa shouted out, startled that she had forgotten the child. She raced to the window, a small triangle of clear glass in a larger stained-glass montage. She spotted Adam below the ship-house at the edge of the small creek. He was sitting cross-legged on a boulder, casually flipping pebbles into the shallow water.

"He's okay," she announced and was suddenly impatient to be with him, responding to her need to care for him, and feeling guilty that she had forgotten him while talking to Connor. She was so new at being a responsible mother that she didn't really know what was the right thing to do at all times.

"He's fine," Connor told her. He had come up behind her and was also peering out through the triangle of glass. "Has he been sick?" he asked.

"Yes," Melissa said, slipping away from the man's towering proximity. His closeness made her tense.

"Nothing serious."

"No, thank God," she answered vaguely, and wondered from the tone and concern of his voice if he had children, or was even married. She thought then of Greg and asked at once, her words escaping before she could think, "Are you married?"

"Once. I've been divorced maybe ten years. I married a girl in college, and..." He shrugged. "I don't know, we went our separate ways, as they say. I've never been lucky when it came to women. You've got to be lucky with women to stay married." He stepped away from the stained-glass windows and was leaning casually against the thick trunk of a tree set in the middle of the open front room to support the second-floor loft.

Everything about him was casual, almost deliberately so, she thought, or maybe it was the way people were in the south, up in the mountains. There was no edge to the man. He just glided along, easy, never raising his voice. It was as if he had all the time in the world to talk to her. Then she remembered this was the way all people were, once they were outside of New York City.

She stood at the windows with her hands in the pockets of her orange Land's End jacket and looked back at him.

He braced against the thick tree, his fingers wedged into his front pockets. He was wearing a T-shirt with a drawing of the schooner-house painted across his chest, which was wide and muscular, as if he had spent a lifetime lifting weights.

His dirty blond hair was combed back and tied into a short ponytail. It made his thin face seem even thinner, and drew attention to his soft blue eyes, the color of a china glaze.

Her eyes scanned his body, and then, when she realized he had noticed, she said quickly, "I think I better go check on Adam."

"He's okay. The only trouble a city kid can get into up here is good trouble. Are you, by the way?"

"Am I what?"

"Married?"

She shook her head. "I've never been, actually." She nodded toward the creek. "But Adam is mine." She moved away from the windows and went toward the side door. Say no more, she told herself, leaving the house.

He was a strange one, Connor thought, watching the bald-headed boy. Something was wrong with him, Connor knew. His attention shifted to the woman, watched as she approached the kid, sitting high on the big boulder. She was keeping her distance, slipping around so she was in front and below where he was perched. She reached out to brace herself against the rock as she stepped around, but she didn't touch the child. She kept her distance. She was on guard, Connor saw.

Connor couldn't hear her voice. He saw only the tight, worried expression on her face, the concern in her eyes.

Outside the schooner-house, she seemed younger, more like a kid herself. It was because she wasn't dressed right for the weather, wearing jeans and a cotton top, and over that just her vest. It was cooler in the late afternoon. The sunlight had left that side of the ridge.

The wind blew her short black hair into her face, made her tighten her shoulders and hunch over. She looked sixteen, he thought, younger- and meeker-looking than her boy.

And she looked like a potter. She wore the same sort of earth-tone colors that potters favored, and had the same sort of hard nut-brown skin and sharp features. There wasn't anything soft about her, but she wasn't burned-out either. She looked like a runner, he guessed, trying to think of how he might describe her, and not fragile like the other city people who came up into the mountains for a crafts course.

No, she was self-contained and strong. Someone, he guessed, who spent a lot of time alone. There was an attitude about her, as if she were her own best friend. She wasn't one for lots of close friendships. She drifted, Connor knew.

And having seen so many women come and go through the mountains, Connor had learned that these women were the best lovers. They had a fierceness about making love, built, he guessed, from a lot of lonely hours. He never learned whether it was deep unspent emotion, or simple horniness, but he always appreciated such women.

She was gesturing to the child, motioning the boy to climb down off the boulder, and he thought how the child had not spoken, not even to complain, since they arrived. Maybe the kid was mute. He watched Melissa, saw how she stood directly in the child's line of vision so the kid could read her lips.

He wasn't sure if the kid was deaf, or mute, or what, but he knew for sure that the boy wasn't her child. She wasn't the child's mother. No way, Connor thought, and turned away from the windows.

5

She was crying. Crying because she knew it was wrong. Crying because this was her private part and he was making her do it. She was crying because he told her if she told her mother, if she told anyone, then he would cut out her tongue with a kitchen knife.

She was crying because when he did it, she hurt. Her whole body hurt, and there was always blood that made her ashamed, and she was afraid her mother would see and ask her about the blood on her underwear, and then she might slip and tell, and he would kill her.

She knew he would kill her. She knew he wanted to kill her. She could see it in his eyes when he grabbed her and pulled down her panties and made her do it to him.

It was wrong, she know. It was evil. He was evil and he was making her do evil things, and she was evil, too, for doing them. And she couldn't stop crying.

MELISSA DID NOT KNOW where she was when she woke. She sat up, grazing her head against the slanted ceiling joint.

"Ouch," she cried, seizing her forehead.

She fell back into the loft bed, tears coming to her eyes, dizzy with excruciating pain. She held her forehead, realizing that her skin was nicked, but she was okay. She took a deep breath, feeling weak and helpless, and thinking how stupid she was, crashing her head.

She had forgotten where she was, forgot that she was sleeping in the tight loft of Connor Connaghan's hand-built schooner-house. She flashed onto her nightmare. It was a familiar one, and she had trained herself not to dwell on its significance, the meaning for her life. She concentrated on where she was, in the tiny, tight loft space of the strange schooner-house.

*She moved again, this time onto her elbow, and peered over the edge, across the length of the kitchen/living-room space, and through the open doorway of the downstairs bedroom where Adam lay sleeping. She had left his door open and the light on in case he woke in the night. Also, she wanted to be able to see him at all times. She was still unsure of how much leeway she might give the boy. At home, back in New York, she was afraid to let him out of her sight.

The first few nights in the apartment in New York, Melissa also couldn't sleep because Adam constantly thrashed in bed and cried out in his nightmares. She had lain awake in the next room, straining to hear what he might say, what pieces of information about his secret life might emerge from his trouble dreams. Perhaps in his dreams, he would talk. But the boy raged incoherently, moaning and crying out with piercing shrieks.

Now, watching him from her loft perch, she could see only his bare head, the smooth round dome of his skull. She wished he would begin to grow hair, and she thought that perhaps she might try and fit him with a wig. He would not attract attention, she knew, if he could grow a little hair, if he looked a little less like an alien.

She turned from the boy and looked out the small porthole window. The view showed hillside and part of the back lawn. Deer grazed on the dewy grass and Melissa smiled, thrilled by the sight of them. She reached up to open the porthole wider and the tiny noise of the metal window alerted the animals. One, startled by the slight sound, stood stiff and poised, listening. Melissa knew that deer had faulty sight, but she stayed perfectly still and waited until the small herd went back to grazing.

She would write Greg, she decided, and tell him how wonderful it was to have deer grazing outside her house in the early morning mist, and not some poor homeless person scrounging through her apartment building's garbage. She studied the scene from her small window. She was like that. She wanted to have the details clear in her mind when she wrote later, and also, she wanted to commit it to memory just for herself, as if someday she might need to recall the view for some life examination.

What she saw was the steep hillside on her left. The trees were in full bloom and created a rich green backdrop, sweeping up to the sky beyond her small porthole window and out of sight.

Looking directly ahead and through the thick foliage, the creek ran fast and white, bubbling over rocks down the steep hillside in a tiny cascade, emptying into the eyeglass pond located between the woods and the schooner-house.

The night before, Connor had told her to watch out for the pool. It looked placid enough, he said, pointing it out, saying you might think you could wade across since the pool wasn't four feet wide. But he didn't know, Connor told her, exactly how deep the sinkhole was. He had dropped a cement block on a fifty-foot rope and never felt bottom.

Connor had pointed the hole out to Adam, too, speaking slowly and loudly, as people always did with a mute child. Adam had simply stared at the black water, then at Connor, and then he had gone back to tossing brown pebbles at the swift mountain creek.

Looking right, away from the pond and the steep hillside, Melissa could see most of the flat and smooth back lawn, shiny with dew. The whole yard was about the size and shape of a football field, bordered at the far end by mounds of earth and boulders, overgrown with shrubbery and evergreens.

Connor had told her the mounds dated from when the valley was excavated to mine for gypsum. Once a railway line ran into Beaver Creek, and over a hundred trains a day came and went, linking Beaver Creek to the outside world and carrying off the valuable gypsum.

But the trains all stopped in the early fifties when roads were finally cut into the mountains, connecting the isolated villages with each other, and ending the need for a rail system. When the gypsum mines played out, Beaver Creek lost its only industry, and with it any importance to the rest of the country.

This had all been in his father's time, Connor said. Growing up in the mountains, he told her, all he knew was that when he finished school, he had to get out of Beaver Creek; there was no future for him in the hills.

"But you came back," she told him, smiling.

Connor had managed to return her smile and gazed off toward the town itself, which was partially visible high on the ridge, and said softly, sadly, as if it were some kind of failing of his, "Well, I've been all over, I guess, but I never was really happy anywhere but in these hills."

He seemed hurt, admitting it, and that tugged at her heart. She briefly envied Connor, and felt a sudden sadness that no nurturing hideaway existed for her, a home where she could find her roots. She didn't even know where she might call home. She couldn't identify a hometown on any map nor in her memory.

Her childhood years were full of moving. She went to six schools before finishing high school. When she went away to college, she had come home for freshman Christmas vacation to find her mother had remarried again and lived in a mobile home, traveling from state to state selling household appliances out of the trunk of her new husband's car.

Melissa had stayed with them long enough to exchange presents on Christmas morning. She took a bus back to her empty college dorm room late that day, and spent the holidays with the foreign students stranded on campus. She never went back to see her mother, and heard only once from her stepfather. He wrote to say her mother had died of a heart attack in Florida, while they were traveling south from Gainesville to Ocala on Route 75.

Her remains had been cremated, "as was your mother's request," the stepfather wrote, adding only that Melissa's mother was at the wheel of the JetStream when she suffered the attack and had "damn nearly killed them both" when the trailer flew off the highway and crashed into a culvert. Close doesn't count, Melissa thought, crumpling up the letter.

The deer bolted, drawing Melissa's attention back to the lawn. She watched them pivot and charge into the green hillside, their dark bodies slipping through the trees. She heard a brief moment of branches crashing and then the morning was silent. She glanced around to see if Adam was awake and saw his empty bed.

"Oh, shit!" Tossing off her blankets, she slipped between the loft railing and climbed down the straight wooden wall ladder, barefoot and wearing only her red flannel pajamas. When her feet touched the barn-board floor, she jumped at the sudden cold and pulled on her sneakers, hurrying after Adam.

The schooner-house, she realized, had few back windows, and those few were oddly shaped and mostly stained glass, leaving beautiful mosaic patterns of light on the floorboards and against the interior cedar walls, but were useless otherwise.

When she opened the side door and stepped into the morning sunlight she spotted him at once. He was standing in the middle of the lawn, his bare feet marking a clear path through the dew. He was wearing only khaki shorts, the ones she had bought him at the Banana Republic in the SeaPort mall the night she had taken him home from her office.

Adam's chest was bare and he looked away, toward the mound of boulders at the edge of the lawn, or perhaps at the skyline of the town. Melissa approached him slowly, swinging wide so he would see her out of the corner of his eyes before she came too close.

She spoke to him, softly calling his name as she crossed the lawn, for she could never be sure if he heard her.

"Adam, what is it?"

He didn't respond or take his eyes off of whatever caught his attention. He stood like a garden statue, all white and shiny, the bright morning sun shining on his alabaster skin.

"Is everything okay?" she said, holding down her fear and thinking: How did he get out of the house so quietly.

He pointed then, and she saw with shock that he was holding a long, black-handled kitchen knife.

"Adam, what in God's name are you doing with that knife?" She moved closer, fighting the urge to rush and grab the weapon from the child. The shrink had warned her about being too aggressive, of crowding Adam's space. He told her. "This is a boy who has been living by his wits, keeping himself alive and unmolested, and maintaining his personal space. What he thinks of his 'space' is what you and I might call our home or apartment. It's our sanctuary, our castle. Well, so is the physical space around this boy. Don't wantonly violate it or you might get hurt."

Adam turned and did look at her. His face a blank, white canvas. He gave off nothing. His hard gray eyes shone like chunks of flint.

"Adam, please come inside. You have to dress, and we have to have breakfast." She kept smiling. "Here, give me the knife, please." She held out her hand with her palm up and the boy glanced off again, toward the rise and underbrush, and then handed over the knife, doing it carefully, giving her the handle first.

"Thank you," Melissa whispered, feeling the breath go out of her. She took the knife and brought it down by her side, tucking it into the folds of her heavy flannel pajamas and out of sight.

Adam followed her obediently back to the house. She wondered if it was the deer that had frightened him. Maybe he had never been read childhood stories of Bambi and forest animals. That realization momentarily crushed her spirits and she remembered reading how orphan babies in Mexico were never touched or handled, so when one was picked up from the crib, the baby wouldn't bend in one's arms, or respond to an embrace.

Then from behind her, from the other edge of the property and in the direction that had held Adam's attention, Melissa heard a crash of branches and both of them spun at the sound. Melissa raised the kitchen knife, as if to defend herself, and quickly shaded her eyes from the bright morning sun, but she saw nothing in the bright light. Then to her surprise, Adam seized her arms. It was the first time he had touched her. His sudden, desperate reaction pulled her eyes away from the boulders at the end of the property. She turned to the boy, touching him in return, calming him with her voice and her arms.

He kept staring at the boulders, startled eyes in his blank face. Touching his bare skin, she gently massaged the back of his neck and the width of his thin shoulders. She could feel his pounding heart.

"It's okay, Adam," she told him, thankful that he was having such a human reaction, that he had shown fear of the unknown, and turned to her for trust. "Come on, let's go inside, get dressed and drive to town for breakfast. We have a busy day!" She filled her voice with anticipation. "We have to check in at the crafts school!" She tried to make their daily chores sound like a great adventure.

She followed Adam through the slanting doorway, pausing to glance back across the lawn to the mounds of boulders and dirt.

The bright sun clearing the ridge shone in her eyes and made it impossible to see anything at that distance. Even the mounds and the small evergreens were blurred beyond distinction. Nothing more than a deer, Melissa knew, had crashed through the underbrush, fleeing the boy. She turned and followed Adam into the schooner-house, knowing she was right and knowing, too, that she had nothing to fear. This was not New York City.

6

CONNER ROLLED AWAY FROM the woman, wakened by her gentle snoring and the bright sun. The sun lit a patch of the bed on his side and, even at seven A.M., burned him with its heat. He moved slowly on the waterbed, knowing the shift of the mattress might wake the woman and he didn't want to talk to anyone, especially her.

He glanced back as he stood and saw the woman roll over, seeking his body. He held his breath, but she settled into the warmth of his pillow. All he could see of the woman was her tiny brown face, and one hand, which she had tucked up to her mouth, as if she wanted to suck her thumb. Her hand was hard and callused, the nails dirty with clay. He resolved again not to go to bed with another potter.

The weavers at school were the cleanest craftswomen, but he had never found one of them that gave him a hard-on. They were such soft, mushy people, he thought, and then he did a quick review of the women he had slept with last summer, counting them not by name (he couldn't remember most of their names) but counted seven potters, two photographers, one glass worker (he did remember her!), and three jewelers.

It had been a busy summer, he remembered, thinking how he had, during some sessions at school, gone from bed to class and then back to bed with a different woman. He had been sleeping at times with two or three women at a time, more for the sport, than sex.

This summer, he realized with some surprise, he was growing tired of all the work it took just to get a girl in bed, to get her excited, and to bring himself to a climax. Some mornings, he knew, it just wasn't worth it.

Like this morning, he thought, glancing again at the young girl as he bent to pick up his jockey shorts. He braced himself against an exposed beam and slowly pulled on his underwear. His whole body ached, not from lovemaking, but from cleaning the schooner-house the day before.

Thinking of the house and his new woman tenant stirred his spirits and pricked his interest. He buckled his jeans belt and left the bedroom, going barefooted downstairs to the kitchen, which he was thankful was on the other side of the old house, where he knew he could run water and make coffee and clear his head without waking the sleeping potter.

He stepped between tools and power equipment that he had left on the stairs and went downstairs, closed the door between the floors of the farmhouse, and walked into the bright sunlight of the kitchen.

Connor took a deep breath and grinned, feeling as if he had escaped punishment. He knew if she had woken she might have wanted to have sex, and the thought of mustering up such energy and excitement depressed him.

He shook off that thought as he filled the kettle with water and set it on the stove. He thought again of Melissa Vaughn, realizing that there was someone worth getting excited about.

He was happy about her for a half-dozen reasons. First, she had express-mailed him three months' rent. He overcharged her on the house, getting more than the place was worth, and having met her, he did feel a bit guilty about it. She was a good person, he realized. Though her kid was weird, and that puzzled him. He wondered how the boy was retarded. And he wondered, too, if he might be able to use the kid. Someone like Adam, a deaf-mute, would be a natural.

Connor moved over to the kitchen cabinet, which was still

unfinished and had no doors. He took down a pound of ground Mocha Java coffee and filters and went back to the sink.

Standing still for a moment, he looked out the kitchen windows at the uphill road to the crafts school, a mile away. He glanced at his watch, which he had left on the counter the night before.

It was earlier than he thought, not even seven o'clock, and he wasn't due at the school until after ten. He wondered if he had time to go downstairs and cook up another batch. In two days he had to make another run north. He thought again about Melissa's boy, wondering if it was possible. Nothing could be safer than sending a deaf-mute courier into New York with the shit.

He picked up a butane lighter off the window shelf and debated with himself about taking a hit. He never liked messing with the stuff, not when anyone was in the house. Nor did he keep the glass vials where he lived. That was one convenience of having two houses. He thought about Melissa again, let his mind speculate about making love to her, then he glanced at the wall clock to check the time once more.

She would be at his ten o'clock class, he knew. He had seen her name on the registration form. He wondered what she planned on doing with the boy, where she was going to leave him back at Ship's Landing. He didn't want the kid in his class, that was for sure.

Kids were always trouble, he knew, even when they were useful. He grabbed a cigarette and lit it with the butane lighter, and went to sit down at the kitchen table while waiting for the water to boil. He stared at the clutter of dirty dishes, tools, and several thick books on home improvements. He had had the books out the night before, showing them to the girl while they sipped wine and shared a joint. He told her what he was going to do with the old house, and the improvements he had planned, while all the while trying to decide whether he really wanted to sleep with this potter or not.

It wasn't even a decision to make. When the woman came back from taking a pee, she sat down on his lap and slipped her hand beneath his shirt and began to knead his breast while asking him in a small, southern voice if he had ever read *Centering* by M. C. Richards.

The next thing he knew the girl's clothes were off, and they were making love on the mattress he kept downstairs in case anyone crashed. It was after midnight, after he had fucked her twice, that they finally went upstairs to fall asleep on his waterbed.

Now he yawned, shook his head, and felt the sharp pierce of a red-wine headache. He had to stop drinking red wine, he told himself. He was getting too old for red wine. He debated about going down into the basement for a smoke to clear his head, but decided against it.

The kettle hissed and he picked it off the burner and poured the steaming water into a cone filter. His hands were trembling.

"Shit," he swore, angry at himself for drinking too much. He had to quit drinking, he told himself again. He had to get back in control of his life. He was letting too many people run him, get what they wanted.

He let a pure and simple wave of self-pity smooth the raw edges of his mind and felt momentarily better, thought again of all the work that he had to do, what with rebuilding this tar-paper farmhouse, teaching his classes, and doing his own pottery. He hadn't fired a kiln in two months, and there was still a couple thousand dollars of unfilled back orders for gallery work.

Not that he needed the money. He had enough money buried in the basement to take care of him for the rest of his natural born life, he reminded himself, and felt immediately better.

He shifted his thoughts. He looked out the kitchen window, watched two deer in the distance move slyly through the misty morning.

He did not respond to the deer. They were common as groundhogs in the mountains, and about as interesting. Connor didn't hunt, nor did he find them beautiful to look at.

Instead he thought about Melissa Vaughn, who did interest him, and who, he thought, was very pretty. He liked her, he knew, because, like him, there were secrets about her. The kid was one secret. And there had to be others. A single woman didn't get to be over thirty without collecting lots of secrets. He always liked women with secrets.

He filled his coffee cup and picked it up, letting his fingers feel the warmth of the mug, and aware that his fingers were still trembling, and that every morning now he had to warm up his hands, get his fingers loose, just like an old lady suffering from arthritis. Shit, that was all he needed, he thought, turning from the window and spotting the young girl coming into the kitchen. She was barefoot and wearing a Yale University sweatshirt and nothing else.

She wiggled her fingers at him from the kitchen doorway and yawned as he tipped his steaming cup of coffee to her and said, "Good morning, honeybun." At that moment he had no idea in the world what her name might be.

7

MELISSA WANTED ADAM TO wear the blue wool cap, using as her excuse the fact that it was still damp in the morning.

"It will keep you warm," she told him, pulling the schooner-house front door closed behind them, and thinking again how she wouldn't have to lock doors up here in the mountains.

Adam had held the cap loosely in his fingers, not putting it on, but when they both got into the van, and Melissa had turned over the engine, she noticed he had stuffed the cap down behind him in the bucket seat. He wouldn't wear it, she realized with a sigh, and angry, too, that she couldn't get him to do what she wanted. She thought of how she used to always get upset at mothers when she saw them screaming at their children. Now, she was beginning to understand their problem.

She wouldn't push him, she told herself again, though she knew his baldness would attract attention, especially at Bonnie & Clyde's where she planned to have breakfast.

Well, she thought, she'd have to live with it. He'd have to live with it. His baldness. His silence. The town, she had decided on simple faith, would have to accept them for what they were. She wasn't going to be able to spend the summer in the mountains and keep Adam hidden away, especially, she thought, if in the fall she decided to stay in the mountains and send him to school.

That thought was a little unnerving. She knew how brutal school kids could be on the playground.

She shifted into first and pressed the gas pedal and the van, with its engine still cold and sputtering, rolled out of the yard and up the gravel mountain road, cresting at the top of Creek Drive. Melissa drove the few blocks into town and parked on the main street, directly in front of the small town diner.

She had been talking to Adam as she drove, telling him what she knew about Beaver Creek, which, she realized, wasn't that much. But she couldn't tolerate the silence between them. She found she had to talk, filling in the silence as if it were a blank canvas, building up little pieces of an ongoing story, as if they really were a mother and child with a life to share.

She told stories of what had happened to her growing up, of what she knew or had learned in school. She tried her best to put a twist on each event, to someway make it sound exciting to the boy. And she kept glancing over at Adam to include him, to make eye contact, to watch his face and search for any hint of response in his empty silvery gray eyes.

"Okay," she announced, turning off the engine, "let's get a big breakfast—I bet they make terrific pancakes at a place like this!—and then we'll go up to the crafts school. I have a pottery class at ten and we'll talk to the director about your taking classes, or something. Would you like that, Adam? Wouldn't it be fun to learn how to make pots?"

Melissa didn't wait for the response she knew wasn't coming. She masked her disappointment by activity, jumping from the van and going around to Adam's side to open the sliding door. The boy sat there, perched up in the front seat and staring ahead, as if his interest had been caught. Melissa turned to see what might be attracting his attention.

The Store Front Street was empty of people, but there was some traffic. A few pickup trucks and vans moved by on the main street as people went off to work. The cars' exhaust hung over the town in the early coolness of the mountain morning.

She opened the side door and waited for Adam to hop down as he always did, obedient as a trained dog. But he didn't move.

"Adam," Melissa said, "let's go have breakfast." She said it nicely and moved away from the van. She saw the smooth back of his head, and realized that something had caught his attention.

Stepping around the front of the van, Melissa looked across the street at the stores that filled the block. They were all closed. There was no one in sight this early in the day. Nothing moved. At the corner of the big red-brick Bauer department store, Melissa spotted a skirt and a woman's leg.

She walked away from the van and down the deserted street to get a better angle on the corner. She saw a patch of grass as well as a small alleyway between the two-story building and a yellow frame building, which she saw from the sign out front was the office of a lawyer. No one was hiding. Someone, however, could have circled out of sight behind the store.

Melissa turned back to the van, thinking this was the second time this morning that Adam had been startled by something or someone. It was a good sign. But then she thought: What if there was someone out there watching him at the schooner-house, and now, here, in the middle of town? That made her apprehensive. When she reached the open van door, she told Adam to get out of the cab quickly and rushed him into Bonnie & Clyde's, as if deciding it was safer inside the town diner.

Stepping inside, Melissa realized the diner was smaller than she remembered, and crowded with men. There was a row of ten stools at the counter, and facing the windows and the street were six booths. Only one table was available, a back booth near the rear wall.

The booths had overstuffed green vinyl seats and speckled Formica tables, and on each table was a small jukebox outlet. Faintly, behind the noise of conversations, Melissa heard country music.

The floor was gray linoleum tile, and on the walls between the windows were hung battered stuffed heads of deer and brown bears. Melissa smiled. She was tired of all the shiny clean Howard Johnson restaurants they had eaten at driving south. She remembered now the funkiness of this small diner and was grateful it had not changed.

She directed Adam toward the back booth and was immediately aware that people were glancing up, staring at them. She spotted one or two nudging another person beside them. Still it wasn't until she slipped into the last seat, giving herself the view of the whole diner, that she realized how silent the place had become. The country music was suddenly loud and intrusive.

Melissa looked back at the room full of customers, challenging them with her brown eyes. No one flinched, no one looked away self-consciously. There was no anger or hostility. They simply appeared startled by the sight of them. Or was it just Adam? She spotted a waitress standing at the counter, the only other woman in the place. She, too, was staring at them.

Perhaps that was the cause of the silence.

Melissa nodded at the skinny blond waitress with the bouffant hair, and the woman jabbed out her cigarette and reached for her order pad, saying something to the counterman before stepping quickly across to them.

When she approached, Melissa watched to see if the woman would look at Adam first, and she did. Adam had curled himself into the corner of the booth, had his hands tucked between his legs, and was staring intensely at a plastic container of honey shaped like a brown bear.

"I think we'll have pancakes," Melissa said at once, ordering for both. "And a glass of milk"—she nodded toward Adam—"and coffee, please."

"You want grits?" the blonde asked, her eyes darting from her pad to Adam.

"Yes, please."

"He's a bald-headed boy," the waitress said bluntly, nodding toward Adam.

"Pardon me?" Melissa leaned forward to catch what the woman was saying, remembering how hard it was to understand these unschooled mountain people.

"You've got yourselves a bald-headed boy," the waitress told her, raising her voice.

"Yes," Melissa answered, staring up at the woman. She had promised herself she wouldn't shy away from inquiries about Adam, that she'd face them without apology. She would shame the person for even asking the question, for drawing attention to Adam's looks. The waitress surprised her. She looked at Adam and then to Melissa as she tucked her order pad away, and she smiled, as if she were grateful that Adam was indeed a bald-headed child.

Melissa's face lit up, thrilled by the unexpected response. The woman said she'd get their breakfast right fast, and though her voice was harsh and the words uttered with the sharp twang of the hill people, Melissa knew the woman was someone special: she had been friendly to Adam.

Melissa looked over at him, wanting to share her pleasure, and was amazed to see Adam smile. His smile overwhelmed his face, brightening it. Melissa realized this was the first time she had ever seen him smile. Her spirits soared.

Connor spotted Melissa Vaughn's blue van as he came through town. He pulled over and parked his pickup in front of Bauer's. None of the downtown stores were open and the parking places were empty on that side of the street.

Beside him, the young potter looked at him. Her mouth formed a perfect "O" with her lips. She did not speak.

"I'll be right back," Connor said, hopping out of the truck and slamming the cab door. The door on his side was out of line and when he slammed it, the crash of metal echoed along the empty street, disturbing barn swallows in the trees in front of Garrity's law firm. The birds burst out of the green trees in a tight pattern, as if they were buckshot.

Connor spotted Betty Sue Yates then, saw her crouched behind the old barrels Doug Bauer used as planters at the front of his store. Betty Sue was watching the diner.

"Shit," he swore, already upset and knowing Betty Sue and the others up at the church were going to complicate his thing with Melissa Vaughn.

He went straight for the old woman, ready to flush her out of hiding and get her away before the woman and kid finished breakfast. He didn't need Crazy Sue causing trouble.

"Hiya, Betty Sue!" Connor shouted, rushing the old woman and wanting to startle her.

She didn't react. She didn't look away from the diner.

The old bitch, he thought. She had heard him, he knew, and he was tempted to step forward quickly and kick her dumb ass. Connor spotted Doug Bauer turning the corner and coming up the sidewalk toward his store.

Connor spoke quickly, "Betty Sue, I want you leaving those folks alone, hear me?"

Betty Sue didn't budge.

Bauer had reached the store and nodded hello, saying as he pulled a ring of keys from his back pants pocket, "I got those special order nails you wanted, Connor. You goin' be around your place later? I'll have Sammy drop them off sometime after one. He's pretty busy this morning. You hear about the reverend...?" He stopped speaking, spotting Betty Sue squatted behind the barrel. "Betty Sue, don't you go pissing again in my plant!" He reached to grab the old woman, but Betty Sue recoiled like a cornered cat and hit back, knocking the small man off balance.

Connor caught Bauer before he fell against the store windows, then stepped forward to shield the small man. He was edgy himself at the idea of subduing Betty Sue. She was over fifty, he knew, but he also knew, from seeing her running through the woods down by the house, that she was stronger than most men; and her craziness made her dangerous.

"Okay, Betty Sue," he said gently, "run on home to Aunt Mary Lee." He didn't approach her.

Betty Sue hugged the wide brown barrel, had her face pressed against a metal band. He wouldn't get her away now, Connor knew, without a struggle.

"Go call Perkins and have him send over one of the sheriff's cars," he said to Bauer, speaking loud enough for Betty Sue to understand. The old woman, he guessed, wasn't as crazy as everyone suspected. She wouldn't want to deal with the sheriff, Connor knew.

Looking beyond Doug Bauer, Connor spotted the young woman he had slept with the night before get out of the truck and come over, her curiosity getting the best of her. On the street, and with clothes on, she looked smaller and younger, young enough almost to be his daughter. Jesus, he thought, distracted by the sight of her, he was sleeping with kids.

Then he saw Melissa and Adam. The two of them stepped onto the sunny stoop of the diner. Melissa was pulling on her vest and Connor was momentarily distracted, watching the fabric stretch over her breasts. She had a better body than he realized. The boy was ahead of her, standing on the sidewalk. He had crossed his arms, standing stoop-shouldered and glum as he waited for Melissa. Where did she find him, Connor wondered, puzzled by the couple, puzzled by her. Maybe he just wanted to sleep with the woman to find out what made her tick. Perhaps this kid was her younger brother and she was taking care of him. But why wouldn't she tell people? He shook his head, and than he spotted Betty Sue.

The old woman was getting up from her crouch. She was growling, staring at the boy. Oh, Christ, Connor thought, knowing he couldn't wait for the sheriff, and knowing, too, old man Bauer wouldn't be of any help if Betty Sue went crazy on him.

"Betty Sue!" Connor shouted, trying to frighten her off.

She bolted then, ran onto the sidewalk, ran for the boy, just as the little potter approached, puzzled by all this commotion at the entrance of the store. Her brown face was frowning as she glanced at Connor.

Betty Sue ran over the girl, knocking her back against the side of Gerry Miller's red-paneled truck. The young potter screamed. In her fright and panic, she lashed out at Betty Sue and hit the old lady before Connor caught Crazy Sue and pinned her arms down against her sides.

But even he couldn't hold the wild woman. She reached down and seized Connor's testicles and squeezed them. He cried out in pain and let her go as he slumped to the sidewalk, reaching with both hands for his painful balls.

Betty Sue was off, running not for the bald-headed boychild, but around the side of the brick building and into the open fields that swept uphill to the small cemetery and yard of the town's New Land Tabernacle Church.

8

WHAT MELISSA LIKED BEST about the crafts school was that she didn't know anyone and no one knew her. The anonymity made her feel safe. Crafts people, she knew, were much more tolerant than most. Adam's strangeness, she hoped, wouldn't put them off.

The school's director had arranged for Adam to take a class in art, taught, he assured Melissa, by a qualified professional, a woman with a masters in art therapy. Adam would be under good supervision while he wasn't with her, the director promised. And Melissa planned to speak to the woman later that day about doing additional work with Adam, perhaps back at the schooner-house.

She had already decided she would use the money she had taken out of her retirement fund to pay for Adam's medical treatment. Now that she had taken over the foster care for the child she had to tend to all his needs. Especially his psychological ones.

She took a deep breath, thought again how overwhelmingly expensive and time-consuming a child could be. She hadn't really thought about that when she had made her swift decision in the social agency office.

And she wasn't getting much back for her investment, she thought wryly. Not even a simple gesture of thanks from Adam. That hurt her. Then she remembered the smile, the single bright, if fleeting, smile, and felt better, thinking of better times to come.

She flushed the school's toilet, washed her hands, then went back to the office where she had left Adam with the school's director.

Adam hadn't moved from where she had instructed him to sit on the tall stool in front of the waist-high counter that divided the office. The director was behind the counter, holding a dozen brightly colored forms, and when he spotted her, he said at once, "Melissa, why don't you go ahead to the pottery studio and get set up, find yourself a wheel. I'll take Adam up to the art classroom and have him meet Carol Scott. How's that?"

He glanced back and forth between the two of them, smiling and shuffling a stack of forms in his thick fingers.

"You can do all these when you finish your class. Okay?" The man patted his stomach.

He was enormous, both heavy and tall, and his immense size crowded the office on the ground floor of the crafts house.

Melissa nodded, and asked Adam, "What do you think? Go with Mr. Martin and I'll see you in an hour. All right?" She paused, inviting his response, but as always he didn't indicate he understood, just slipped off the stool, ready to follow orders.

Gene Martin took Adam away, going out of the office and up the stairs to the top-floor art room, talking all the while. His voice kept rising, as if he felt the need to shout to get the mute boy's attention.

Watching from the doorway, Melissa waited for Adam to look around, to show some hesitation about leaving her. They hadn't been apart since he was brought into her office. She had done everything for the boy, with him, and now he didn't turn around or wave good-bye, or show any sign that he was leaving her and going off with someone strange.

She felt a sharp pang of resentment, then rationalized, as she always made herself do, remembering that the boy had lived on his own in the subways of New York. Why should he suddenly feel a strong attachment to her, regardless of all her kindnesses and what she had done for him. It was her failing to need such reassurance. How did he know she wasn't going to desert him, as his mother must have done at some point in his young life?

How could a mother do such a thing, she thought next, and then to stop herself from growing angry, she turned from the doorway and the sight of Adam, and headed for the pottery studio, focusing on seeing Connor Connaghan, and admitting to herself that she did feel a slight twinge of excitement thinking about him. She smiled to herself at her own infatuation, and never heard the office secretary say into the telephone receiver as she passed out of the office, "They think the poor man had a heart attack, but you never know, do you? Why we're in a state of shock over all of it, ain't you, Willa? Dear God, I was just speaking to the reverend yesterday afternoon, and..."

Connor had saved her a wheel. It was by the windows that looked across the long, shallow valley. She could see Miller's Ridge beyond it, a smooth knob of hillside, all covered with spruce pine and evergreen.

"How's Adam?" he asked, coming to stand by the windows as she adjusted the seat of the potter's wheel. She was nervous, she realized, at the idea of throwing pots again, especially with Connor around.

"Okay, I hope. I'm not sure." She shrugged. "Gene Martin took him away. He's going to put Adam in the open painting class. It's taught by Carol Scott. Do you know her? She's an art therapist, Martin says." She was tense with Connor standing so close, and she sat down hard on the small seat of the potter's wheel.

"Take it easy," Connor whispered, stepping by her, "everything is going to be okay." He gently, friendly, touched her shoulder, let his hand slide down to the small of her back before he dropped his arm away. "I want to say a few things to everyone, then we'll get some clay and have you wedge up a ball."

He moved briskly into the center of the large room and clapped his hands, calling everyone's attention to himself.

Melissa took a deep breath and looked out the windows at the sunny morning, calming herself with just the sight of the mountain range and the long valley. There were a few horses grazing on the hillside and their wet coats gleamed in the sunlight. She took another deep breath, smelling the flowers that grew wild below the windows, smelling the pine needles and new hay being cut in the field. A tractor mounted the hillside, cutting a wide straight swath through the long grass.

It was simply a beautiful mountain morning, she thought next, realizing how lucky she was to be out of New York, away from the crime and grit of the city. So, then, why was she so frightened? Her hands were trembling and she couldn't get enough air to breathe. It was silly, all of this hypertension. She wondered whether it was Adam, her anxiety about the boy? But then she allowed herself to admit Connor was the cause. The man excited her, and she thought it must be because of how she had to deny all of her true sexual emotions about Greg. Now she was just out of control. She smiled wryly at her own silliness, and then from behind her, she heard Connor speak.

"Let's talk a little bit this morning about centering," Connor began, speaking up and addressing the room full of potters, scattered as they were around the open studio, all of them sitting attentively at their wheels.

"You know, it took me over three years before I could center a piece of clay on a wheel," Connor confessed, smiling shyly, moving as he spoke, turning slowly, as if he were on an invisible wheel himself, pivoting on the heel of his left cowboy boot. He was wearing old jeans that were tight on his thighs and patched crudely in several places. A woman hadn't done the sewing, Melissa noted with satisfaction. And he was wearing another T-shirt, this one from the 5K Thanksgiving Day Trot in Red Rock, North Carolina. The T-shirt was blue and fitted him closely.

Melissa watched the way his forearms bulged, the way his chest muscles expanded as he spoke; she followed with her eyes the tight flatness of his abdomen and the way the T-shirt slipped beneath his heavy, broad handcraft belt, until she realized she wasn't breathing and she looked back out the window at the pastoral scene that stretched to the horizon, and forced herself to count slowly to twenty.

"How many of you could center the first time you sat down at a wheel?" Connor asked, spinning around and watching for raised hands.

Melissa raised her hand. It wasn't true. She was not sure if she could even center a wedge of clay today, but she wanted, with the simple gesture of raising her hand, to have Connor notice her. She glanced around and saw the way at least half of the women were looking at him, and knew instantly they were her competition.

She forgot to listen to Connor. All her attention was taken up with watching him move, seeing the movement of his hands as he gestured, watching the way his neck curved and disappeared into the neck of his T-shirt. She watched the thickness of hair on his neck and back and wondered if all of his body was that same dark hairy mass.

She heard him say, "You are crafts-artists all of the hours of the day, not just when you are here in this studio and sitting at this wheel. Your wedge of clay is not your signal to think, 'Yes, I am a potter now!' No," he whispered, stepping closer to the group, rocking on the high heels of his boots, "the creative urge flows from your very being like blood itself, like life itself!" He cupped his hands together and lowered them to his crotch, then slowly drew them up, saying, "Pull the energy of your body, the need of your sex, from here deep in your body, from the source of your creativity, and let your heart speak to you, tell you how to bring up, and smooth out, and center this wedge of clay, yes! But more importantly..."

He had raised his hand, indicating another point, turning slowly in the midst of them like a statue himself, gaining all of their attention and heightening their anticipation with his waiting, then saying softly, so they had to strain to hear, "You must learn to center your life. If you are not centered as a person, you will never throw a perfect pot. Oh, yes! You'll be praised and honored perhaps for this vessel or that, but I tell you, the cylinder will know. It will not breathe. It will die."

He stood up straight, pulling himself together. Melissa watched the way his chest expanded, his muscles jumped beneath his tight T-shirt. Then he said softly, as if telling a story to a child, "In ancient China a noble rode through a little village and saw a potter working. Stopping to admire the pots of this anonymous artist, he saw they were of great beauty and grace, and he said to the old man, 'How do you make pots of such beauty?' And the potter replied, 'Oh, you are looking at the shape. What I am forming lies within. I am interested only in what remains after the pot has been broken.'

"It is not pots that we seek to make in this class. It is the beauty that lies within the cylinder. It is this cylinder," he tapped his breast. "We seek to make the cylinder of our lives live in perfect beauty."

He stopped talking, lowered his head. Melissa could hear others in the class draw in their breath. Her own hands, she realized, were trembling, and the classroom of students was stunned into silence.

Then Connor looked up and smiled.

"Okay," he said, challenging them, "let's go to it!" And he immediately stepped forward and touched the young woman closest to him, ruffled her thick head of black hair, then moved on, giving a high-five to one of the men, and continued around the large studio, as gradually everyone shook off the moment, and was swept up with his enthusiasm and the excitement of his challenge. There were quick bursts of laughter and shouting from the young people.

Melissa heard wet clay being slapped onto potter's wheels. She sat perfectly still. Her knees were weak. She doubted if she had the strength to even kick her wheel. Connor was coming closer, still circling the room, laughing with everyone, becoming more exuberant as he fed off the class's excitement.

Melissa lifted her hands and set them palm down on the flat wheel, aware of the coolness of the turning surface. She could not look up. She was afraid to look at Connor, though she knew he was approaching. She could already feel his body, smell his skin. Staring at her motionless hands, she realized she was dizzy, and she thought as calmly as she could how silly all of this was, how totally immature of her. Why was she reacting so to this man? She wondered if it was solely because she had not been with anyone for a while, and this primitive raging in her was nothing more than lust. It frightened her, the power of this emotion, and made her feel helpless to her passion.

"Hi," he said, approaching from her blind side, stepping so close she felt his breath on the nape of her neck. It was as if the man had slipped his hand down her blouse and fondled her breast.

She lost her breath.

"Easy," he whispered, circling her, coming to stand before the wheel where both of her hands were planted, palms down.

He said something else, another whispered remark, and she shook her head, not understanding. She would not look at him, though she was instantly aware that others in the class were aware of them, and she guessed, too, that the women would hate her now. It wasn't fair, she thought. She had not asked for any of this. She was overwhelmed already with Adam and his problems. She had new responsibilities. She didn't need a love affair.

They were interrupted by Gene Martin. The big man swooped into the room, his hands flying, his voice booming, and Melissa, startled by his sudden appearance, saw the director look first at Connor and then at her. At that instant, seeing the look in his eyes, seeing how he seemed to consume Connor, to suck the man into his sight, Melissa realized the school's director was in love with Connor Connaghan.

Then the director said to her, "It's Adam. Would you come!"

Hearing him, seeing him, Melissa couldn't decide whether the director was frightened or only excited.

She found Adam in the fine arts studio on the top floor of the crafts house. The other students had formed a loose semicircle around him, and he was painting, using the wide white back wall of the large room.

"He was given paints and a small sketchbook, and the next thing Carol knew he was using the wall, using oils on the white wall."

"He's incredible," a woman said, slipping up beside Melissa. She had come over to them when they appeared at the studio door, but she did not take her eyes off Adam and what he was doing.

"This is Carol Scott," the director said, whispering. "She's the instructor of our open painting session. Carol is the art therapist I mentioned to you."

"Do you have any idea of what he's painting?" Carol asked Melissa.

"The tunnels under Grand Central Station." Melissa recognized the scene in the vividly etched surreal painting. The dark, dank tunnels were ones Melissa knew but had never seen. It was in this world that the police had tracked down Adam, cornered him, and brought him up into the daylight and her office.

The painting was cool and clinically rendered, with even the closest details carefully etched, rendered with the perfection of a photograph. Yet it was so strange to have it being drawn there on the white wall of the studio, larger than life and more terrifying to Melissa than the actual tunnel.

It was as if Adam had not escaped New York. It was as if he had carried the secret memory of his past life to these green mountains and needed to re-create his nightmare world for all of them to see and for him to remember.

"Look!" Carol whispered, leaning closer, excited by the art. "See the rats!"

Melissa did see them, dozens of huge rodents hidden in the dark corners of the huge painting, hidden high above the steam pipes, the network of metal ladders and tunnels of the ancient system. Melissa felt as if she could step from the warm sunlight of the crafts house into the dark interior of this underground, deep under Grand Central Station.

She wanted to reach out and stop Adam. She wanted to pull him away from his painting, away from the nightmare world, but there was such a fury in his painting, such a need to painstakingly etch the scene, drawing it all in perfect proportion, and with such speed, that she could only stand and stare into the depths of the work, follow the tunnels with her eyes, as the tunnels went deeper and deeper into the black hole. The painting overwhelmed her. It felt like a physical force pulling her into the hidden world. She broke off her gaze.

Gene Martin was staring at her. His glassy blue eyes sparkled, and there was a shine of sweat on his smooth cheeks.

"The boy's an idiot savant," he announced.

"No, he isn't," Connor answered immediately. He was standing beside Melissa, had slipped himself between her and the school director.

Melissa sighed, thankful that Connor was there. She did not want to defend Adam in front of all these people. This was what she had feared the most, that some wild rumor might start about Adam, the way he looked, or the fact that he couldn't speak.

"The boy might have some psychological problems," Connor admitted, "but who doesn't. Right?" He smiled at everyone. "Why he doesn't speak has more to do with a severe personal trauma, not any mental illness. Right, Melissa?" He looked down at her, still smiling.

She nodded, and realizing not everyone could see her, she spoke up, "Adam will be just fine in a few more days."

She went on to say that the doctors felt Adam needed to be away from New York for a while, and then, expanding on Connor's deliberate falsehood, talking about the boy's severe personal trauma. She liked the inclusiveness of that phrase, its medical vagueness. It was an expression she could use to camouflage Adam's real problems.

"Let's see if we can move him?" Connor suggested, lowering his voice. "Do you want me to try?"

"No," she said at once, fearing Adam might become violent. "Let me."

She stepped out of the semicircle and approached the boy,

doing it as she had that morning on the lawn, swinging wide so her movements would not seem threatening. She gave him the chance to see her and hear her voice.

He was still intent on his painting, working frantically, chased by his hidden obsession. She waited a few moments more so he could complete the wall, to paint with his somber colors, the deep blues and purple, the deep greens, the last edges of his overwhelming vision, a wall canvas that, she guessed, was over twenty feet wide and ten feet high.

She was struck by the energy that had gone into the work. He had been gone from her less than an hour, but had enough time and strength to paint the entire wall.

Melissa spoke to him, asked if he was finished. He didn't respond, but he did look over at her, and his eyes for the first time showed some anguish, and a new sadness.

She was elated by his response, realizing that his show of emotion meant he was returning to the world of feelings. This morning he had smiled at her, and now in his eyes there was a glimpse of his tragic life. He was trying, she realized, to communicate with her. He was finally telling her what he felt and how he had once lived.

Melissa kept smiling. Her encouraging smile enticed him closer and she reached out and touched his thin shoulders, still wary and fearful that he might jerk away. But he did not resist her. He understood what she wanted and he carefully set down the paintbrushes and came to her.

Taking a risk, she slipped her arm around his shoulders and drew him into a soft embrace. For a moment, his slight body nestled against her. She looked up, beaming at the classroom of students, at the director, and at Connor. She had never felt happier in her life. It was as if she had overcome a great hardship or instantly learned how to speak a foreign language. She had reached the child. Her life with Adam, she knew for certain, would only get better.

9

"I FORGOT JUST HOW dark the mountains could be," Melissa re-marked. They were out on the lawn, all three of them, Melissa, Connor, and Adam, though Adam had gone back to the boulder. He was playing there, more sitting on the high rock and tossing brown pebbles at the swift dark water of the creek.

Melissa had given up trying to guess what it might be that fascinated him with the simple routine of tossing pebbles into the mountain stream. She was pleased that he enjoyed it, though she had already decided to go out the next day to Bauer's and buy some art supplies, and to provide space at the schooner-house where he might paint, now that he had displayed such an interest and a talent.

"You get used to the dark," Connor answered, setting his beer can on the top of a boulder. "It actually becomes your friend, this darkness. Once you've been here in the mountains, you find it is a great comfort."

They were just beyond the shadow of the house and the floodlights. They had left the schooner-house ablaze, Melissa real-ized, and she was pleased by that. The house looked warm and inviting with its pretty stained-glass windows, and the little odd-shaped portholes and wedges of glass. Melissa thought again how lucky she was to have found this house and be up in the mountains. If she were back in Brooklyn, she would have been locked up in her place at this time of night. She took a deep breath, inhaling the smells of the grass, the cold stream, and of the pine woods that stretched the length of the lawn and framed the property.

Over the tops of the trees at the far edge she saw a thin bracelet of lights from town, and occasionally she could hear a semi pulling up a distant hill, but the outside world seemed very far away, and that made her feel wonderfully secure.

She smiled to herself.

"A lot of city people can't take this kind of life," Connor remarked, picking up the conversation. "They come here for a few weeks, you see, and say how great it all is, living close to nature, that kind of bullshit, but then the silence gets to them. They can't take our laidback ways."

"I can," Melissa answered, feeling she needed to defend herself.

"Well, it takes some working at."

"And it's good for Adam," she added, lowering her voice, nodding at the boy. They were separated by a dozen yards, and speaking softly, but Melissa had become aware of how far her voice carried in the cool evening, in the silence of the mountains.

"And it's good for you, too," Connor said, smiling down at her.

He was standing close with his elbows set against the boulder. She was aware of the size of him, though in truth he wasn't that big, less than six feet, shorter than Greg, she realized, but there was a sense of strength about him that she had never felt with any man from the city. It was his rough ways, she guessed. She liked that he wasn't smooth and slick, like every other man in the city. And then she thought of Greg, who wasn't a yuppie either, and then she forced herself not to think of Greg at all.

"In a couple of days," Connor went on, "you'll be as laidback as the rest of us."

"I'm not at all tense," she answered, knowing she was lying.

"You are so, but that's okay." He shifted his weight.

Melissa could hear the pull of his jeans, the way the leather of his boot stretched.

She glanced at him. She was weak in her knees, and in the insides of her thighs. She felt a surge of blood flood her vagina. This is ridiculous, she told herself, her heart slamming against her chest.

Her face was inches from his chest. He was wearing a red plaid shirt, and under that another T-shirt. It stretched tight across his chest. She glanced up, hoping he might be grinning, or that he might not look so gorgeous in the darkness. He was staring at her, but all she could see was the strong outline of his chin and jaw. Everything else was lost in the darkness.

"Is it for Adam or yourself that you left the Big Apple?"

She shrugged, thankful for the question. She calmed down, explaining herself. She told him about her job at the agency, of how she shuffled papers all day, and made decisions about other people's lives, and never once saw them or knew them by name. They were just statistics, that was all. Overwhelming numbers, she told him, and she got so that the numbers didn't mean anything to her, she was just matching shelters with bodies, that was all.

"Then I tried to do something more," she told him. "I decided I should work in a soup kitchen or something, you know, actually do something for the homeless. Well, I tried to do that. I went to the local church in Brooklyn one Saturday morning to volunteer, but I couldn't do it. I mean, I couldn't even help those people.

"I saw all those homeless men and women standing in line waiting for the church doors to open so they could get their miserable cup of coffee and stale donut. The line went around the block. It was cold and rainy and miserable. Yet they stood peaceful and silent, huddled up, you know, in blankets and dirty overcoats, wearing layers of everything. Some had all their belongings with them, grocery carts stuffed with plastic bags, cans, God knows what."

She began to cry, remembering that Saturday morning, but she kept talking, needing to tell someone. She had gone to the church over a year before and had never told anyone at the office. She had never even told Greg. She was ashamed that she didn't have the courage to help the homeless.

"I couldn't do it," she told Connor. "I couldn't even work in the soup kitchen of the church. I walked around the block a couple of times trying to build up my courage. I walked to the other side of the street and I stood looking at the homeless people. I started to cry. Not for the poor homeless, but for myself, for my lack of guts. I couldn't help another human being. It made me feel like shit."

She was sobbing. She pressed her forehead against the cold boulder, tried to press the pain of her memory from her mind.

"Hey," Connor whispered, reaching for her. He took her easily into his embrace and smothered her with his arms. He saw Adam stand on the high boulder, not to come to them or help Melissa, but rather to jump down, fly off the high perch, and scale the small brook, then crash down into the trees and go loping off like a forest animal, disappearing like a deer.

"What's that?" Melissa asked, pulling up.

Connor felt a rush of fear race through her slight body.

"It's nothing. It's just Adam."

Melissa pulled out of his embrace, her own problem slipping away.

"Adam! Where did he go?" She squeezed Connor's forearm.

"He ran into the woods," Connor tossed off, making light of it. "He's a boy, Melissa. That's what boys do. They go out tramping in the woods."

"In the middle of the night!" She stepped at once to the edge of the creek, stood staring into the darkening trees.

"Melissa, it's not even nine."

"Why would he do this...?" she asked out loud, her worry making her need to talk. "...go running off?" She was immediately sure it was her fault, that he had seen her embracing Connor and crying in his arms. Oh, Christ, she thought, what had she done?

"Do you want me to find him?" Connor offered. He was afraid she might say yes and he didn't want to go tracking through the trees. He knew, too, that he'd never catch the kid.

"I don't know," Melissa sighed. "Dammit! I should have..."

"Melissa, you shouldn't have done anything. Look, he's a boy. He'll be okay. What's going to happen to him out there?"

"I don't know!" She waved at the black woods. "I don't know what's out there! Bears! Tigers! Crazy mountain men!"

Connor laughed, saying, "If he can handle himself in the tunnels of New York, then he can handle these hills."

She had told him earlier, after Adam's huge painting on the studio wall, who the child really was, and how he had been found in the tunnels under the city.

She began to cry again and Connor stepped over and slid his arm around her shoulder. She let herself be held. She was cold. Her body was trembling and she knew it wasn't because of the cold, but rather her fear of what might happen to Adam, and her more basic fear that she really couldn't take care of this child. She had been reckless and crazy to take him out of New York, to think she might be a mother to a teenage boy.

"Hey," Connor whispered, "let's go inside. I'll make you a cup of coffee, okay?"

"I need a drink," she told him, "and I don't have any liquor."

"That's okay. There's booze in the house. The county is dry, so I keep a supply."

"I didn't see any..." She was letting Connor direct her across the lawn, back inside the schooner-house. They had come out of the shadows and into the lights from the house, the floodlights Connor had installed and that shone over the backyard, down to the edge of the creek.

From a distance, from where the boy watched, sitting high in a branch of a sugar maple tree, they looked like a dark, hunch-shouldered monster moving around the ship, moving from shadows into a misty light. The night brought fog and the mist coming off the cold creek water moved across the lawn and shrouded the house.

Then the two-headed monster disappeared around the bow of the house, and the dark mist filled the lawn, swept up to the edges of the schooner-house. The boy waited to make sure they didn't follow him into the woods. The man especially. He was right about the man. He had smelled it on him when they first drove into the yard, when he caught the scent of him, there on the bow of the house.

The boy swung loose from the tree, dropped softly onto the bed of forest underbrush and sprinted up the hillside, running effortlessly, like an animal of the woods, deep into the night.

The second glass of red wine made her enormously sad and talkative. Or perhaps it was just Connor who made her talk so much. He was so open with her, telling her stories of his upbringing, sharing his feelings about being a mountain kid as she sat on top of the butcher-block counter watching him make what he called his "extra-famous" spaghetti. "Handed down from one cookbook to the next."

He grinned when he offered to make them dinner, and then went ahead anyway as she weakly protested, though she was thankful he was cooking. She was hungry and she felt helpless. Also she didn't want to be left alone, not with Adam gone from the house.

She had felt a deep physical pain when she realized she couldn't run after Adam, realized there was nothing at all she could do but wait until he returned, if he returned!

It was only after she had finished the first glass of wine that the pain in her heart eased somewhat. Now she just felt sad. Still, it wasn't such a bad feeling.

She liked thinking of herself as helpless, of being abandoned, of having life turn another cruel corner.

In the misty haze of her gaze, with her head dizzy with the drink, and her body warm from the oven heat, from the drink itself, she was content to just sit on the counter and watch Connor be busy in the kitchen, moving with ease from one chore to the next, finding pots and pans, cutting up vegetables, browning meat, while listening intensely to her story, to what had first brought her to New York City, and now here, to the mountains, where she hoped to escape the crime of the city and save Adam's life.

"You know, some girls are lucky," she told Connor. "They're lucky in love; they're lucky in life. I've seen them. I knew them when I was growing up. I was never lucky. I don't know why, really.

"I guess I do know why. It was my mother. I mean, my mother really fucked me up!" She was teary again but she kept talking, wanting to tell him about her mother, Alice Gross.

"I never knew my father. I have this dim memory, which I guess is true, of him stepping to my crib. I don't know if he kissed me or not, but I want to believe he did, and I did see his face before he left me.

"Let me tell you about his face!" She sat up straight on the counter, seized with the desire to explain herself to Connor. She realized she had been acting like a fool, crying, carrying on, and now talking too much, but it was all understandable, she told herself.

"He was the most handsome man I've ever seen. His face filled my whole vision at that moment. I could see his eyes. He had wonderfully blue eyes. And very dark full eyebrows! But it was his mouth that I remember most. His lips were thick and his mouth was wide and smiling. Warren Beatty has the same sort of wonderful lips. And when he smiled, his whole face beamed. He was smiling at me.

He was taking such pleasure, you know, in looking at me, his little girl. And then he was gone from my life."

Melissa sank down on the counter, suddenly exhausted.

Connor came over and leaned against the counter, his hands framing her body. He moved so his face was directly in front of her, less than a dozen inches away.

"And what happened?"

"They got divorced. We were living in Tulsa then. I was almost three. Mom was married briefly there, and Stephie was born."

"You have a sister?" He seemed surprised.

"I did. She died of meningitis."

"Jesus," he whispered.

"And I have a brother. An older brother who I never see."

"What does he do?"

"He serves time. He's in jail somewhere." She shook her head. "When I was living in Texas, this was after Kansas, he was doing time in a reform school. Mom just turned him over to the state, saying she couldn't control the kid. And she couldn't."

Connor's eyes widened. "How did you escape?"

"Some days I don't think I did."

"You escaped," Connor told her.

He sounded impressed and that pleased her.

Connor had returned to the stove. He was holding a large wooden spoon in one hand and his other was deep inside a padded cooking glove. He kept glancing at her as he held the pot steady and stirred the thick meat sauce.

"I built up this history," Melissa continued, "a fictional past. I started to put it together when we were living in Kansas. This was when Mom was living with a man named Davis. Roland Davis. He drove trucks long distance. Mom was working at the expressway diner then. That's where they met. It's such a cliché, really."

Connor had stopped stirring the sauce and was staring at her with his mouth open. She knew, too, that he was a bit afraid, and that for some reason pleased her.

"What did you do?" he asked, impressed by her, seeing her for the first time as another kind of person, as someone he really didn't know at all.

"I became Melissa. That's not my real name. My real name is

Mary Lee Gross. I changed it myself. I took on an identity I got out of magazines, from books, wherever. I created Melissa Vaughn from nothing." She was smiling.

"But you were in college! How did you do that?"

"Oh, that was easy, actually. I used school to escape from the trailer. I spent all my life in the public library, just to get away from the trailer. There was a wonderful woman there, a Mrs. Butterfield, who for some reason took an interest in me. She helped me fill out scholarship forms. I had very good SATs." She shrugged again.

"Once I got to college, I had a home, and another life. And I had legally changed my name. It was actually pretty simple. People disappear all the time. All I did was reappear as another person. As Melissa Vaughn." She smiled again, pleased with herself for impressing Connor.

"And I thought I had an interesting life, studying in Africa," Connor said, setting out plates.

"I thought you went to the Rhode Island School of Design?" Melissa slipped off the counter and steadied herself before going to help with the silverware. Her head was dizzy, but she knew she was okay.

"I did later," Connor said quickly, "but when I was an under-graduate I lived in Africa."

"You did?"

"When I left the mountains, I went down to the coast and got a job working the shrimp boats and ended up in Key West when I was about eighteen. Some guy there needed a crew to sail a sixty-foot sailboat to Europe. I got a job, but when we pulled into Africa, I decided to stay and hitchhike around. I ended up in Africa working in Rwanda for Dian Fossey. You know, the woman who got killed? The movie, *Gorillas in the Mist*."

"You're kidding me!"

"No!" Connor was grinning. "I worked for her about a year. I mean, I could have gotten a Ph.D. in anthropology."

"You mean primatology."

"Yeah, well, whatever." He had gone back to the stove and turned the fire on under the water. "Do you want to wait, or go outside and call for Adam?"

"Oh!" Melissa stood up straight, realizing that she had forgotten about Adam. "I'm sorry," she whispering, as if to herself, "I guess I should, shouldn't I?"

She went to the front door and then decided against that. She would call for him from the small second-floor porch in the bow of the schooner-house. She took the circle staircase upstairs and, going through the tiny sitting room, opened the small door in the bow of the house and stepped outside onto the deck. The deck was only large enough for two chairs, but there was a narrow passageway that did circle the house, like the deck of a sailing ship.

She edged herself around the house to stand at the back where the odd-shaped building faced the creek. She thought Adam might have returned, that he would be sitting again in his favorite spot, but the boulder was empty and the night was quiet.

Scanning the backyard and the dark woods, she was going to call out his name when she saw a shadow on the lawn. Someone was running across the backyard, just beyond the arch of floodlights. It was Adam, she thought, and then realized the shadow was too large for the small boy. It must be a deer, she thought next, and she saw a flash of clothes and realized it was a woman out on the back lawn. A tall, thin woman had run soundlessly across the yard, leapt the rocky creek, and plunged like a wild animal into the dark woods.

Melissa's heart jumped to her throat. She spun around and ran back along the narrow walk to the small balcony space that overlooked the main floor of the house and called down to Connor, "Someone's outside, Connor! A woman, I think."

Connor was standing at the table, forking the steaming pasta onto two thick plates.

"She ran into the woods!"

Connor paused, holding a fork full of pasta above the blue glazed dinnerware.

"It's Crazy Sue," he said, unconcerned, and dropped the pasta on the dish. "Let's eat."

"Who's Crazy Sue?"

"She's the town's loony. Come on down before everything turns cold." He set the plates on the table and reached for the red wine bottle.

He was totally unconcerned, Melissa realized. He was not even aware of her fear until he glanced up and saw her standing above him on the landing, clutching the railing.

"Melissa," he whispered, setting down the wine bottle. "What's the matter?"

"She was out there, Connor. She was watching us!"

"Melissa, she does that to everyone around here."

"I didn't know that!"

"Jesus, I'm sorry." He walked toward the hand-built stairs, going for her. "Melissa, come on down, please. Would you like a glass of wine?"

Melissa shook her head, stepping toward the circle staircase. She couldn't hold the glass, she knew. Her hands were trembling, and she tucked them under the waist of her jeans. "I went upstairs," she said, explaining herself. "I'm looking for Adam and out of nowhere I see this shape tearing around the back lawn. It scared the shit out of me, that's all." She stopped to take a deep breath, then added, to sum up her feelings, "God, what a day."

"Hey, easy," Connor whispered. He went up the tight stairs and knelt below her. She was terrified. He saw the fear on her face, in the wilderness of her eyes. It made her incredibly sexy. He wanted to make love to her, at that very moment, and on the stairs.

But instead he stayed kneeling beside her, and continued his story of being in Africa with Dian Fossey. He told Melissa of tracking through the misty mountains at her campsite and being startled by a gorilla.

It was all untrue, his story, his being in Africa, of seeing a gorilla. He had seen the movie of Fossey's life, seen also dozens of nature films, and had even, when he was in high school, done a research paper on Africa. He knew a few facts, and he could tell a good story, imagining the cold morning in the African mountain, the sudden sight of the enormous black beast. He saw she was listening. He saw her brown eyes widen. His story had taken her mind off Crazy Sue. She did believe he had been with Fossey in Africa. It made him suddenly reckless with his story. He stretched the incredible tale and told her more, making it all up in his telling, like someone performing a reckless trick.

"I knew I couldn't seem frightened. That was the key. Dian had told me that much. I stood perfectly still and made some gorilla gestures. I made as if I was scratching my head. And the gorilla—Dian called him Uncle Bert—turned away from me, from the both of us, because Dian was behind me on the trail. Anyway, the animal simply turned and disappeared into the wet, thick underbrush. You couldn't even hear him moving through the jungle as he walked away."

"And what did you do?" Melissa asked, holding her breath.

"I crumpled. And I realized I had wet my pants."

"And Dian Fossey?"

"Oh, she just laughed at me and said Uncle Bert was too used to humans. He wouldn't have even been upset if I had jumped into his arms."

Connor stood, and sipped his wine, then he stepped off the stairs and announced, "Okay, let's eat!"

Melissa followed him off the stairs and took a deep breath of the rich sauce. It immediately made her feel better.

"Thank you," she said to Connor.

"Thank you for what?" He smiled at her, being charming.

"Thank you for understanding that I'm, you know, your basic New York neurotic person, and that I shouldn't be let out of Brooklyn."

"Hey, you didn't know about Crazy Sue, that's all." He gestured. "No problem."

"Well, what should I do about her?"

"First off, she's harmless. She's a little off. Touched, as we say here in the mountains. She's about, I don't know, maybe fifty-six or -seven. My mommy told me Crazy Sue was in school with her when they only had a one-room schoolhouse over on Simon's Ridge. She lives with an aunt of hers across town. The aunt is a little peculiar, too, I'd say. The family is called Yates. They're a big family up here in the hills.

"Anyway, she finds this schooner-house incredibly interesting." He was gesturing with his fork, talking to her. "I'll have a word with the old lady if you want." He dug his fork into the thick plate of spaghetti, then cut the pile with his fork.

Melissa looked away. "No, don't do that. I don't want to frighten the woman." She began to slowly swirl a mouthful of spaghetti onto her fork.

"You've got another problem besides," Connor said next, softening his voice.

"You mean Adam? Yes, I know he's strange-looking." She was tired already of making excuses for the boy.

"It's more than that."

Melissa stopped her fork.

Connor paused in his eating, and deliberately set down his knife and fork and sat back. He picked up his wine glass, doing a small performance before he answered. Melissa had not realized he could be so theatrical, and now she resented it.

"There's a church up here, over on Simon's Ridge, called the Church of the New Land Tabernacle. It's one of those fundamentalist places that years ago broke away from the main Baptist church over in Banner Elk. I don't know when it started off on its own, but it was years ago, and the place back here was pretty isolated, and over the years, you know, they got to doing their own thing, snake handling for one."

"Oh, no," Melissa sighed. She briefly closed her eyes anticipating the direction of Connor's story.

"There's an old story, a folk legend, or superstition really," Connor went on, "that goes with this church saying 'into their midst,' that's the way they put it, 'a child will come.' A pure spirit who will prepare them all for the end of the world. A John the Baptist type, you know."

He was watching Melissa. Watching the way the frown gathered across her forehead and darkened her face. She was not pretty, he decided, when she was concerned. Her worry tightened her mouth and pinched her face like a prune.

Melissa was only aware of Connor's voice, and what he was telling her in his own sweet, dramatic way. She was furious at him for making her wait, and her heart, beating against her narrow chest, felt like a ball being battered about by racquets.

"Not everyone in town, you see, believes this bullshit. But those in the church. The old folks for sure. They believe it."

"Believe what?" she demanded.

"They believe a boy, a 'chosen child,' as they call him, will come into the mountains one day as a forewarning of the day of judgment.

The end is near. That shit." He settled back in his chair and turned his attention to the steaming spaghetti, forking a mouthful.

Melissa sat away from the table. She couldn't eat now.

"And they think Adam is this chosen one because of how he looks?"

"He's mute," Connor added.

"I don't believe it," she whispered, feeling totally helpless.

"Well, it's not so bad," Connor said, reaching for more bread. "Look, you're going to get great service in this town. Everyone is going to be incredibly nice to you, thinking that Adam is the one, God's disciple." He smiled.

"It's not funny," she told him. "Adam isn't going to like having people gawk at him."

"They're already gawking."

"Yes, but..." Melissa stopped. She remembered the incident at the diner that morning. Now she realized why the place had suddenly gone quiet, and why the waitress had been nice to them. "Oh, God," she whispered.

"It's not so bad," Connor told her, continuing to eat. "Look! It doesn't matter to you what they think, right? I mean, they won't touch you. My God, you're the one who is suddenly revered. Adam is the wunderkind, right?" Connor was grinning. He kept forking his food as he talked. "Adam's going to be treated special by just about everyone in town. It will be great for his self-confidence."

Melissa nodded, understanding what Connor meant. It might not be so bad, she thought next, trying to think of the pluses. It certainly would be easier than having the town treat him like some freak show. She nodded, smiled, warming to the notion.

"Maybe you're right," she admitted, picking up her fork.

Connor was wiping his plate clean with a chunk of whole wheat bread, and still concentrating on his food, he summed up the situation, reminding her that at the crafts school Adam was already tagged as a prodigy, and now, in town, he was seen as the "second coming, for chrissake!" He kept grinning at Melissa, telling her, "Hey, you're golden! This is going to be a great summer!"

Melissa nodded, kept trying to convince herself that she was better off, that Adam being seen as the fulfillment of the mountain prophecy actually wasn't so bad.

"What about Crazy Sue?" she asked.

"I'll give her a little talk. I'll tell her Adam is going to send her to hell, or something."

"No, don't do that! Don't frighten her." Already she was feeling bad about wanting to have the woman kept away from the property. If she were so harmless, what difference did it make if she came around the schooner-house, Melissa asked herself.

Connor had finished his meal and was slouched down in the high-back chair. His legs were crossed and he had shoved his chair sideways so his left arm rested on the tabletop. His eyes were glassy.

"Look, Melissa," he said, speaking very deliberately, "you got to get a few things straight, okay? You're not dealing with a totally civilized society up here. I mean this ain't the Big Apple." He grinned at her.

"Who said New York City is civilized?"

"Right! Well, you know what I mean." He waved away her objections.

He was drunk, Melissa saw with disappointment.

"What I'm trying to say is that here in these mountains the locals can lack the usual civilized behavior we know about in proper society. Okay?" He stared at her with his wet eyes.

Melissa nodded, deciding not to be argumentative.

"You get people up here and after a while they go a little crazy. It's subtle at first, but what with all the inbreeding and all, well…" He shrugged and looked away, his head nodding.

For a moment Melissa thought he might just nod off. He was still holding the glass of red wine in his right hand. She watched it tilt and sway, like a toy boat at sea. She debated lifting it out of his hands before he did spill the wine, and then Connor roused himself, sat straight up, and leaned forward, focusing himself intently on Melissa.

"We're not that way," he said defensively, as if she were the one attacking the mountain people. "We've had some great people come out of these hills. Rhodes Scholars, basketball players, poets, golf pro, the whole works." He gestured with both arms, waving them wildly in the air.

"Connor, I haven't said a word!"

"I know! I know!" He grandly waved off her protest and said quickly. "No, they aren't going to harm him. Jesus Christ, no." He whispered, "They want him." He stared at her, his eyes glassy bright, his face flushed red.

"Want him?" Her heart leapt to her throat.

He started to nod, and then said, "You heard about Reverend Littleton?"

Melissa shook her head. He wasn't making any sense now, and at that moment, she felt another surge of fear. She could not handle a drunken Connor if he decided to make a move on her.

"He died yesterday up at the church on Simon's Ridge. Heart attack, maybe. But those Tabernacle people, they think old Littleton was summoned by God Almighty! Shit!" He kept shaking his head, having forgotten the point he was trying to make.

"What, Connor?" she asked, pressing him.

"He croaked up there on the ridge just when you and Adam were spotted going through town, that's what. People talk, you know."

"No, I don't know." Melissa kept shaking her head, refusing to accept any connection between their arrival in Beaver Creek and the death of the minister.

"The talk in town, you see, is that Adam, this bald-headed boychild, as they're calling him, summoned old Reverend Littleton to his just rewards, and that they're next, all the good people of the New Land Tabernacle Church."

She thought again, in a sudden flash: What had she gotten herself and Adam into? Why had she come to this lonely mountain place? She had thought it would be safe, an idyllic retreat. But it wasn't. It was as crazy and dangerous as the streets of New York.

And then she thought Adam was in trouble. He hadn't come home because something terrible had happened to him. She jumped up from the table just as the front door banged open and Adam came running inside, out of breath, his eyes wild in his head, his arms smeared with dirt, and his hands dripping wet with blood.

10

DEACON MACCABE MOUNTED THE small platform at the front of the New Land Tabernacle Church and scanned the congregation. It was Saturday morning in Beaver Creek and the people had come up onto Simon's Ridge to bury their pastor.

These were folks he had known all his life, family and friends from the town and the two hollows that converged at Beaver Creek. There wasn't a man or boy in the church who didn't come to his shop for his haircut, and most of the ladies, too, those women that didn't go down to Elk Pine and the fancy new "beautician," as she called herself.

He raised his arms and waited for the crowded congregation to recognize him, to settle down and pay attention. He found a moment of sweet pleasure in this, having all their attention, and in his strongest voice he sang loud and clear, "Hallelujah!"

"Hallelujah, brother," a chorus of voices answered him, and at once he shouted out the response, "Praise ye the Lord!"

"Praise ye the Lord," the people sang back.

He was moving now, he could feel the divine spirit seize his soul.

"Jesus, Lord, has taken our good friend from our midst but God Almighty has not forsaken his children. No, sir! He has not left us alone in a bitter world. He has sent us a sign. A sign of his everlasting judgment. Of Kingdom Come!"

The big man paused. He had both of his hands gripped to the

thin pinewood pulpit, was leaning forward, pushed up on the toes of his cowboy boots. The plaid leisure suit he wore was loose on his frame, sagging around him like a deflated truck tire. The suit was ten years old. It was the only suit he had ever owned. He had bought it when his daughter, Mary Sue, had married the Berger boy.

"You know what I'm talkin' 'bout, don't you?" He paused, scanning the church, taking them in with his shiny eyes, smiling, grinning like he had the secret, the eternal secret of their lives.

"I've seen the boy!" he shouted. "You've seen the boy!" He stepped away from the thin pulpit, stood balancing at the edge of the plywood platform. "I was at my place, cutting Spike's hair. Remember, Spike?" He grinned at the oldest Crawford boy. "I looked out the window onto Store Front Street and seen that van, saw his face there, bright and sunny and smiling at me as they drove by, and I said to Spike, 'God Almighty, it's him. It's him!' Ain't that right, Spike? Hallelujah!"

The spirit had taken him over. The words were singing through his mouth, and he wasn't thinking of what to say next, how to say it. God's graces were pouring from his soul.

"Jesus, Lord Almighty," he shouted. His voice boomed off the high arch of the New Land Tabernacle Church. He swung around, crouched low, sweating now, and with one quick motion, like a cheap trick, he pulled off his plaid jacket and let it sail away.

There were dark, spreading pads of sweat under his arms. More sweat rolled across the folds of his pink face. His eyes were bright and glassy and he was very happy. He felt the people watching, felt their obedience, knew that they were caught up in his rapture.

"My people," he told them, "why did our good friend Reverend Littleton die out there in his flower patch? Die in the prime of his saintly life? I ask you, my people, why did he die? He didn't die but for one reason: to tell us! To show us! His death was a heavenly sign. A godly sign of the coming of our bald-headed boy. Ain't that right? Ain't that the truth?"

He paced the stage, thumping his boots. He liked the authoritative sound his cowboy boots made, stumping the platform altar. This is where he belonged, he knew. This was his true calling. They didn't need no other pastor, pay some outsider good money, not when he could do better than the next fellow. He'd preach on Sunday mornings, handle the snakes, marry the young.

"Who else seen him?" he asked, halting his pacing.

A few hands tentatively rose from the attentive congregation.

MacCabe kept nodding, encouraging other witnesses.

"You are all blessed. I'm blessed! Hallelujah!"

The congregation roared back its response.

MacCabe took another deep breath, reveling in his power. Yes, he thought, this was where he belonged, here in front of these people, his people.

He raised both arms, drawing the shouting chorus to a close. Then he told them in hushed tones, "I will bring the bald-headed boychild into our midst. I will deliver him to our bosom. But, folks, I ask you. Are we ready to meet our Maker? Have our souls been washed in the river of salvation. Can we go to Our Lord with a pure heart, a forgiving soul, without lust for our neighbor's wife, without the sins of pride and avarice? Remember what good Reverend Littleton preached to us, 'Evil all around us. In the hills. On the street. Right beside you in your seat.'"

They sang back a chorus of "yeses," as he called out renouncing sin. He pulled them together with the power of his chant, with the strength of his voice. They were declaring to God, to him, that they were prepared for the long journey to the other side. A journey, he shouted, that Reverend Littleton was already on, crossing the wide river of life. "Wider than these puny Appalachian Mountains," he sang, gesturing toward the rising sun. He held his arms up, spread his thick fingers, and standing with his legs apart, he told them, "We know our testament. We know our salvation. We know the Word of God."

A single chorus rang in his ears, and when the sound echoed through the tiny wooden church, wafted off into the sunlight and the bright, beautiful summer morning, Deacon MacCabe broke at once into song, singing out:

"Love lifted me
Love lifted me.
When nothing else could help,
Luuuuuhhhhhhve lif–ted meeeee."

Hiding in the graveyard, Crazy Sue lay inside Reverend Littleton's freshly dug grave, six feet deep in the red clay, stretched out and playing dead while she listened to the singing from the church.

The singing reminded her of Reverend Littleton, and remembering him, she thought of how her brother Rufus had jumped his skinny bones and knocked the old man down in the flower garden.

Remembering that made her nervous and she climbed up out of the grave, using the cut roots of trees to pull herself from its depths. When she got to the opening, Rufus was there, grinning at her.

"What you want, boy?" she demanded of him, and swung her long arms at her little brother, who was dead, long dead, as people said, but won't lie down, "like a normal person," she told her aunt Mary Lee.

She had a brief flash of remembering how she had hung Rufus upside down over the barn well when he was just a little boy. He wouldn't give her the new shiny coins he had found on the road. He had screamed at her, cursing her out, she had told him it was a sin, swearing like that, and when he wouldn't listen, she just let go of the skinny boy. He had splashed, hitting the water of the deep, dark hole.

"You get!" She kicked dirt into his face.

Standing in the bright sunlight of the cemetery, she could see into the open windows of the white church, see the people, see Deacon MacCabe on the platform, singing away.

She hated Charlie MacCabe. He had made her fuck him when she used to live at her uncle Billy's place, before Aunt Mary Lee came home from South Carolina to take care of her.

She remembered how he would catch her out back behind her uncle's barn, pull her into the shithouse and fuck her there, standing up against the wooden walls. She stuck out her tongue at Charlie MacCabe as he paced back and forth on the high platform.

"Fat ass," she said out loud, shouting to the trees, and then, liking the sound, the ways the words ran together, she sang again, "fatassfatassfatass." The words ran off her tongue like warm honey and made her feel better.

She left the cemetery, jumped the stone wall, not troubling herself with the metal gate, and when she landed on the other side, her feet hit the ground hard and another spike of pain shot up her leg.

"Ouch," she cried, stumbling. The pain brought tears to her eyes and she sat in the gravel parking lot rubbing her legs, wondering why she hurt. In the morning when she got up from bed, some days she couldn't open her hands or squeeze her fingers. She'd sit by the wood fire huddled up in a blanket until the warmth of the stove eased her pain.

Aunt Mary Lee sucked her mouth, then clicked her teeth, saying, "Betty Sue, you're gettin' on, child. You'll be pushing up flowers soon enough."

Betty Sue stared at Reverend Littleton's flowers. She could stamp them down, she knew, and not push them up. And just for spite, just to get back at Aunt Mary Lee, she did just that, until she forgot why she was jumping up and down in the garden, and then remembered the people in the church and ran to the rear exit of the building, next to the water pipe, where she had discovered a small hole in the wall, and where she could, spying, watch the people, watch Charlie MacCabe, and her own aunt Mary Lee, watch all the people, looking up at MacCabe as he pranced and danced on the platform, waving his hands, shouting down at all of them, sweating like a pig.

That turdface, Betty Sue thought, listening.

"I will bring our bald-headed boychild into our midst. I will deliver him to our bosom. But are we ready, folks? Are we with Our Lord? Have our souls been washed in the river of salvation?"

Betty Sue pulled her eye away from the peephole and screwed up her face. Why did Charlie MacCabe want the bald boychild?

"Ain't got no hair," she said out loud, speaking to Rufus.

"He's goin' take us to Kingdom Come," Rufus told her. He was barefoot on the sunny morning and wearing a pair of overalls frayed at the knees. He wasn't wearing a shirt, Betty Sue noticed, and his skin was nutty brown.

Betty Sue eyed him with her good right eye, thinking that Rufus might not be crazy after all, as Aunt Mary Lee always said.

"He looks like E.T.," she told Rufus. They had moved away from the white church and gone into the yard where a rope swing hung from a sycamore.

Betty Sue sat down on the wooden seat and kicked herself up, still talking to Rufus, who was now sitting on top of the cedar picnic table.

She kicked her feet under her and sailed up, trying, as always, to swing above the church and see the town beyond the cemetery trees. She felt like a bird.

Thinking about E.T., she remembered how Aunt Mary Lee had taken her to Blowing Rock on a Sunday after church to see the movie, telling her first that it was just a movie, that there weren't no E.T., that it was all make-believe, but when she saw him, saw the little space boy, she knew it was true, and now she knew E.T. was the bald-headed boychild and he had come to save her from the devil and take her up to Kingdom Come.

Betty Sue grinned and let her tongue hang out the side of her mouth the way she liked, even though she knew it drove Aunt Mary Lee, "just crazy," as she was always saying. But Aunt Mary Lee wasn't in the churchyard as she swooped down, feeling the rush of wind on her face, then she went soaring off, higher and higher. One day, she thought, she was going to just let go when she was as high as the church top and go flying off over the cemetery, fly down to town.

She knew she could fly. If she got up high enough, up where the birds were swooping and turning and sailing away to sit up in the thin branches and look down at her, laughing to themselves 'cause she couldn't.

"I know who the bald-headed boychild is," she told Rufus, swinging low.

He cocked his head waiting for her to say, and when she swung low again, passing the picnic table, she told him how the bald-headed boychild was really E.T., the little space boy, and he had come to get her, to take her up to Kingdom Come, and she wasn't going to live in Beaver Creek no more.

Thinking of that, and knowing she was going to leave Aunt Mary Lee, she started to cry. She didn't want to leave Aunt Mary Lee, she told Rufus, and she stopped the swing, dragging her heavy boots across the bare earth until the rope swing slowed and twisted, and finally stopped with her clinging to the rope and crying hysterically, holding the rope swing tight so the bald-headed boychild couldn't steal her away.

*   *   *

Connor Connaghan, stopping at Stan's Mobil Station at the end
of Store Front Street, heard about Royce Brother's sheep before he
reached the crafts school.

Glen Batts was telling Johnny Druke, shouting to him as they
stood at the gas pumps filling their tanks. Glen had been there, he
told Johnny. He had heard about it on his CB that morning and
swung by Royce Brother's farm.

"Sheriff from Marion came up himself to take pictures," Batts
added, pulling the gas nozzle from his pickup and shoving it into the
pump. Then he went over to Druke's side, lowering his voice as he
got closer to the farmer.

Connor moved to the other side of his pickup to hear the
conversation and busied himself with cleaning the front windows of
his truck.

"Sheeps had their throats cut?" Druke asked.

"Nope, that's the goddamn weird part. Animals were butchered,
all cut up in pieces." Batts was grinning, enjoying the telling.

The CB in his cab cracked and he popped his head into the cab
to listen, and then called to Druke, "That's the old man. Says for me
to get my ass up to Logan's." He was already moving around the back
of his red truck. "Catch you later, Johnny." And then, seeing Connor,
shouted out, "How's it goin', Connaghan? How's that new pussy
down at your place?"

"Not bad, Batts. Not complaining." He didn't look at the man.

"Finger lickin'?"

"Yeah, finger lickin'." Connor kept busy with the windows until
Glen Batts gunned his truck out of the station, and then Connor,
watching him leave, said softly, to himself, "Asshole."

They had been in school together at the old Consolidated High
in High Point. Batts had been an asshole then, Connor remembered,
and he still was. Nothing ever changes in the mountains, Connor
thought, and not for the first time.

He tossed the used paper towel into the can and shoved his
hand into his tight jeans pocket to pull out a clip of money. Walking
to the station, he passed Johnny Druke and stopped the farmer,
"What's up Batts's ass?"

"Someone butchered ten of Royce's Alpacas." The tall man
pushed the bill of his John Deere cap up off his face and revealed his

pale forehead. "Pretty soon a farmer goin' have to sit in his fields with a shotgun." He nodded good-bye, saying, "You take care, Connor."

Connor paid for his gas, then lingered a few minutes inside the station talking to Jessie George about the early summer, the hot days they had already in the mountains. He was listening to her CB monitor, trying to catch mention of the sheep killing. But the radio was silent and he grew tired of watching the scanning light.

He glanced at the station clock and saw he was due at school, said good-bye to the fat woman, and went back to where he had left his truck parked. He was hurryin', and worried, too, thinking about the blood on the boy's hands and wondering if the kid had gone over to Royce Brother's field and killed the sheep.

It was possible, Connor knew, starting the engine and pulling away from the pump. It was possible to cross the ridge behind Ship's Landing and come up onto Brother's bottomland. He had done it himself during deer season. He guessed it was less than a forty-minute walk.

"Shit!" he said out loud, letting his own voice roar over the engine. "That goddamn kid killed those fuckin' Alpaca."

He banged his palms against the steering wheel, scared at once, not for the woman, but for himself. Then he reached beneath his seat and felt the slight bulky shape of his .38. It made him feel better knowing the pistol was in place, and then he touched the brake and swung the truck off the highway onto Wilkins Road and took the back way up Miller's Ridge to the crafts school.

Gene Martin, taking Adam up the three flights of stairs to the artist's studio, kept touching Adam's smooth, small shoulder, kept feeling the soft flesh of the boy. He bit his lower lip, suppressing his pleasure.

Already, as he took Adam upstairs, he began to think how he might get the little boy off by himself. He was talking fast, excited about the possibilities, telling the child that he could work whenever he wanted, for as long as he wanted, and that if he needed a lift from down in Ship's Landing, well, by golly, he should have his mommy just give him a call. He'd run right over, he told Adam, encouraging the boy with a smile, and playfully, he tucked at the small boy's thin shoulders, hugged him briefly as they came into the upstairs studio where already on the bright Saturday morning a half dozen of the summer art students were at work.

The director managed to avoid looking at any of them, though a few tried to catch his attention and call him over and ask some technical question. He knew they only wanted him to glance at their work and say something encouraging, like that their oil was the finest composition he had seen since Gauguin.

The director steered Adam back to his painting, to the far wall of the barn-loft studio, and stopped before the expansive work, which now, in the bright morning light, did not seem as depressing.

Martin stood a moment and evaluated the work with a trained eye. It was reminiscent of Edward Hopper, of his bleak and bold contrasts, though Martin now saw that there was a softness to the painting, a surreal element suggesting perhaps a spiritual world beneath the subways and railway tunnels.

He wondered if the boy was religious, if he was another one of those fundamentalists. But for the most part, he marveled at the technique, the boy's wonderful skill with a brush. This was not an unschooled artist who just happened to pick up a paintbrush. The boy had been taught at some point of his young life, and he had mastered the art.

Adam stepped away from the director. He walked over to the brushes and paint, and was immediately busy.

Martin watched him, thinking that there was nothing to him but skin and bones. Yet he wasn't misshaped. The director liked his cleanliness, even the fact that he was hairless as an infant.

This morning he was dressed in a blue T-shirt, cutoff jeans, and a pair of new sneakers. The child wore no socks and the sneakers seemed loose on his feet.

Martin settled down on a stool to watch the boy, to watch the way his young body moved, and immediately one of the art students approached. She was worried about the perspective in her piece, she told him, and Martin, annoyed at the interruption, kept it to himself as he turned away from Adam to walk back through the open studio and look at the woman's small drawing of still-life objects, flowers and fruits arranged in a ceramic bowl.

He told her what to do, how to handle the depth of field, and, concentrating on her problem, showed her with quick brushstrokes how to create the illusion, and when he glanced up again, it was only because a few students were whispering, making a fuss. Martin looked across the long studio and saw that Adam was wiping away his huge painting. Using white paint and a wide roller, he had painted over the dark, dank world of the New York subway underworld.

"No! No!" Martin shouted, rushing to seize Adam's arm. "What are you doing?"

Adam spun around and hit the director in the face with the wide wet roller of paint. The paint sprayed off the roller and hit a half-dozen students, who screamed and shouted, jumping away from the shower of enamel white.

Martin was blinded from the splash of paint that crossed his face like the center stripe on a mountain road. He stumbled back, cursing the boy, trying to escape, but Adam pursued him.

He dipped the long roller into the pan, and grimly chased the director, reached him, and swatted Martin again, this time painting down the width of his back, blotting out the photo of the school on the T-shirt. The director ran for the door, ran to escape.

The other students were with him, toppled their easels as they fled the loft studio and stampeded down three flights of wooden stairs.

Adam didn't chase them. At the top of the stairs he halted, listened a moment to the screaming women, then went inside the classroom and locked the door.

Alone, he looked like a ghost of a child. The paint had splashed his face, left white stretches on his cheeks and forehead. He wiped his arm across his face, smearing the wet enamel, then turned his attention to another stretch of bare wall.

The glassy grayness of his eyes was gone. He looked in pain. The pain came from deep within him, a deep remembered dark memory. He pressed his hands against his forehead, pressing against the pain. His jaw tensed and tightened, drawing his mouth into a tight rope.

Stumbling to the wall he seized another brush, jabbed it into a bucket of orange, and in quick, frantic strokes swept the orange paint over the clean plasterboard between the high windows of the studio north wall.

As quickly as he finished with the orange, he grabbed another brush and plunged it into a bucket of sapphire blue, then returned to the wall, working fast and seemingly without a notion of symmetry or any concern for what he was depicting.

He turned away from the work only to seize a new brush, another can of bright paint to throw against the wall, and in a rush kept adding new colors to his expansive work, filling the long white wall with his nightmare vision.

Gene Martin came running up the flights of stairs with keys to the art studio. He had wiped the paint off his face but now was sweating from his exertion. His T-shirt was soaked with paint and perspiration. As he fumbled with his keys, he kept swearing about Adam, telling Melissa he wanted the "goddamn boy off school property."

Connor snatched the jumble of keys from Martin's hands and unlocked the double doors, pushing both open so they all saw at once what Adam had created on the north wall of the studio.

The massive work silenced them.

Before she even comprehended the significance of the nightmarish painting, Melissa was stunned that Adam could have so swiftly produced it. She thought of her humble attempts to throw a pot, and realized again, as she had when she saw his painting of the tunnels, that the child was a genius.

"What is it?" Carol Scott asked, following them into the studio, but watching the boy.

Connor thought of not saying anything, or saying he didn't know, but then another student, one he had slept with earlier in the week, announced to everyone, "It's Connor's place! Ship's Landing."

Of course it was Connor's place several more added. They had been to Ship's Landing for parties, and they began to recognize the abstract painting of the schooner-house, as well as the lawn and creek. They saw, too, that the bald-headed boychild had painted a half-dozen realistic human figures on the bottom lawn, all of them slaughtered in one way or the other. Some with their throats cut, others decapitated, many more were missing limbs, hacked off and scattered on the lawn. One very young blond boy was missing his heart.

The heart had been plucked from his chest, leaving a bloody mess of tissues and bones, all of it clinically rendered by Adam. He had also painted the mountain creek a violet red, bloody from the blood of the massive murders.

"Dear God," one older woman whispered. She put her hand to her face and spun away from the wall of art, leaving the crowd of students pushing into the studio.

Adam backed away from his painting. Everyone gave him room. A large brush soaked with red paint hung from his right hand. He was staring up at the painting, studying it, as if deciding to add a final touch.

Melissa approached him, saying softly, "Adam, I think we should go home." She watched the child, not daring to look at his painting.

Adam did not respond to her, but he did set the brush down.

Melissa wanted to touch Adam, to try with a simple physical gesture to pull the poor tormented boy into her arms, but she realized she was afraid of him. Adam looked up into her eyes and smiled. His face was calm. His eyes silvery gray quiet. He was again at peace with himself.

11

MELISSA TELEPHONED GREG FROM the schooner-house shortly after eleven o'clock. She stood in the kitchen, using the long extension cord to move around, to keep track of Adam, who had gone outside to play in the yard. She didn't want him surprising her on the phone, or hearing her talk to Greg at the agency. Also, she wasn't sure what Adam might do next, and she wanted him in her sight. She really didn't know anything about the child, she was increasingly realizing, and that thought, which once had only depressed her, was now frightening.

She had promised Greg she'd keep in touch, but she didn't want to, hoping that being away from him would help her forget him. Now, unfortunately, she needed his help.

She told him about the paintings on the crafts-house walls, and about Adam coming back to the house late at night with blood on his hands. She told him, too, about the folklore in town that a bald-headed boy signaled the end of the world.

"Jesus Christ, Mel, you've got to get away from that place. Get that kid out of there," Greg told her as soon as she stopped talking.

He sounded so frightened for her that Melissa began to cry into the phone. She had called for reassurance, to have Greg say that everything wasn't really that bad. Instead he had only frightened her more. She slipped down into the corner clutching the little receiver and sobbed as Greg, five hundred miles away, tried to calm her down, to talk her back from the edge of her hysteria.

"I'm all alone," she whispered, trembling with fright, "and I don't know what to do."

"I do!" Greg told her. "Leave those fucking mountains. Get out of there, Melissa! Listen to me! I don't know what's going on, but he might hurt you. I mean, what do you think he was trying to tell you in those paintings?"

In the tight corner of the schooner-house, Melissa kept shaking her head, not wanting to believe any of it.

"I can't leave," she whispered into the receiver, knowing that was true. She had subleased her apartment in Brooklyn and given up her job at the agency. She had nowhere to turn, no home to run to where she might be cared for by loving parents. She was all alone in the world and she started sobbing again, and this time Greg let her cry herself out before telling her, "Look, I've got some vacation days. I'll speak with Helen and fly down for a few days, help you get matters straightened out, okay?"

Melissa shook her head, still sobbing. She pulled a tissue from her pocket and blew her nose, then took several deep breaths to pull herself together. Finally she said, "No, Greg, I can't have you throwing a wrench into your family life just for me. I got myself into this, and I'm going to make it work."

"Helen would understand," he told her. "Don't be a goddamn martyr."

"I am not a goddamn martyr, Greg." She was immediately angry, and then softened at once. Realizing how much he had done for her, how much she cared for him, she said quickly, "I'm sorry, but you have the new baby. I'm okay, really. I mean, I can take care of this myself. Besides, there is a guy down here, the man I rented this place from, and well, he's been really nice." She tried to sound confident, for his sake and hers. "But you can do me a big favor."

"How? Anything at all."

"Call those cops? The ones that brought Adam up to our office? Ask them if they found out anything more about him. Maybe, you know, some of the homeless people down in the tunnels might know him, where he came from, or when he showed up in the tunnels. I know from a class I took at NYU that networks of support develop among the homeless."

"I can do more than that," Greg answered. "I have his files we worked up. His fingerprints. I'll ask the FBI to do a computer search and see what they turn up."

"We did that!"

"Just the missing children. Maybe Adam was never reported missing, see what I mean?"

"Yes! Of course! He might be from some institution."

"A juvenile institution."

"Yes, an institution," Melissa whispered, realizing that was probably true. Adam might have escaped and found his way to New York. She heard his footsteps on the gravel path and knew he was circling the bow of the schooner-house and coming inside.

"Greg, I've got to go. He's coming and I don't want to be on the telephone. Call me as soon as you hear back from the FBI."

"I'll ring you tomorrow and make sure you're okay. And call me at home if you just need to talk."

"Thank you, Greg. You're wonderful! Tell everyone I said hello."

Melissa hung up as the front door opened and Adam came into the house. She smiled across the kitchen at him, asked immediately if he was hungry, and could she make him a peanut butter sandwich or something? She kept talking, afraid of a silence between them.

Adam had mud on his sneakers. Melissa wanted to tell him not to track dirt through the house, but she was afraid of disciplining him.

She glanced over to see if he recognized her suggestions, to see if he was nodding okay. She saw he was coming at her across the open living room, and that both of his arms were hidden behind him. He was concealing something, and he was smiling.

Oh, dear God, she thought, backing off, backing up against the kitchen sink. She reached behind her to brace herself and her fingers touched the wooden handle of the kitchen knife.

"Adam, what is it?" she asked, controlling her voice and keeping her eyes on him.

Adam stepped onto the tile of the kitchen floor. The sunlight reflected through the stained-glass windows, casting blue and red squares of color across his head and down the length of his clothes. He was wearing his stonewashed jeans, and a tie-dyed T-shirt with an image of Madonna. It was another one of her hand-me-downs.

"What are you hiding, Adam?" she asked quickly, forcing a smile, trying to seem amused by his action. Her heart pounded against her chest. This child is going to kill me, she thought. She wondered if she had enough strength to defend herself. Was she stronger than a thirteen-year-old?

She thought of when she was his age and had been attacked by her stepfather, and how she had tried to fight him off. All of her suppressed fear swept her body, paralyzing her.

"No!" she whispered.

Still grinning, he whipped his arm around and lifted up a bright bouquet of wildflowers. He had pulled them from the woods behind the house and there were roots and dirt clinging to the stems.

"Oh, no! Oh, dear God!" She fell against the kitchen counter, weak with relief. "Oh, Adam!" she cried out. "Aren't you wonderful! Aren't you just wonderful." And for the first time she leaned over and kissed the top of his head.

He responded at once. Wrapped his arms tightly around her. For a moment the two of them swayed together in the colored sunlight that beamed through the stained-glass window, high on the western side of the odd-shaped house.

She remembered another morning, another day long ago when the sunlight beamed through the bright window, remembered how she had crossed the small bedroom to get her sister, to go after the little girl. She was thirteen then, Adam's age. She remembered the rage in her small body at having her stuffed toy taken from her. She was blinded from the bright sunlight, blinded by her uncontrollable rage. Her whole body shivered again, remembering, and she clung to the silent bald-headed boy in her arms.

The two insurance salesmen from Winston Salem who had been college roommates at Duke put their fifteen-foot aluminum canoe into the Toe River above Bandana, and were drifting southeast through Yancey County, drinking Coors beers and sunning themselves in the early June morning.

It was their yearly rite, as they described it. They were happy to be off alone in the mountains, just the two of them, running the rapids twenty miles downstream to Buck's Landing, where their current girlfriends, Sally Pierce and Patti Cally, were to meet them with a picnic dinner, by the edge of the swift-moving river.

The girls had wanted to come along, wanting to share the experience as a way of proving their worth, and also to show themselves that they were really special in the eyes of these guys, who were famous for the women they had dated at Duke and in the three years since graduation.

The two women kept it to themselves that they didn't like each other, didn't really approve of each other's life-style, and the two men, meanwhile, kept it to themselves that they were lovers, that the women were just convenient to hide their secret relationship.

Sally Pierce was frustrated that her man, Chase Hanes, didn't really seem all that interested in having sex with her—they did it, but it wasn't very exciting, and Chase kept suggesting that all four of them should, "you know, get in the sack."

That made Sally jealous and she just knew it was Patti Cally he wanted and not her, and she was furious about that, but she kept it to herself, mulled over it, and did not say anything until the two of them, she and Patti, were driving southwest on Route 80.

Patti had made an off-hand comment, a tiny admission that sex with Billy Joe Ridgeway wasn't all that great, and Sally had said quickly, before she lost her nerve, that Chase had suggested maybe they should all sleep together that night in the tent, because, he had said, he could only get just one, and if they weren't sleeping together, well then, two of them were sleeping outside.

Sally Pierce had glanced over at Patti Cally as she weaved Chase's big station wagon through the tight turns on Route 80, and the two women caught each other's eyes, and they knew, both of them knew the truth. And Sally just blurted out, "Oh, shit, Patti, they're gay!"

Patti began to cry, and started screaming that she was going to get AIDS from sleeping with Billy Joe Ridgeway, and she pounded her small fists against the leather dashboard of the Chevy station wagon.

Sally pulled the car off the road and into a small parking area where there was a picnic table set out, and both of the women cried into each other's arms, telling each other, over and over, that it wasn't their fault, that they didn't know, no one at Chapel Hill knew.

Finally, when they stopped crying, they opened the cooler, took out two cans of Coors, sat in the front seat of the Chevy, and really talked to each other for the first time.

Patti told Sally that when they had sex, Billy Joe liked for her to put on his cowboy boots, that's all, and also to hit him a little tiny bit on his behind with his western belt, and the first time she nearly died, doing it, but actually it was kinda fun because Billy Joe got so excited, and it got to be a lot of fun afterward, and Billy Joe was nice to her, though when she thought about it, she had never come when she had sex with him, but she had always blamed it on herself, that it was her fault, somehow.

She started to cry, hysterical with fear that she was going to get AIDS, and once more Sally Pierce had to calm her down and get her to think straight.

What were they going to do, she asked Patti, and then she told Patti that it was her opinion that they should really fix them good for being queers masquerading as good old boys.

Patti kept nodding, drying her tears, trembling with fear.

Do what, she wanted to know.

Sally didn't know, right off. She started the car again and pulled back onto the mountain road, kept driving south toward the meeting place at the boat landing.

She hadn't told Patti what Chase made her do when they made love, nor would she. Sally didn't really trust Patti Cally, and she didn't want her spreading stories all over Greensboro about her and Chase Hanes and what Sally Pierce had to do to make the man come. She, herself, couldn't believe that Patti Cally had worn boots and whipped little Billy Joe Ridgeway's ass with a leather cowboy belt when they made love.

When Sally reached the junction of Route 80 and 19E, she knew what they should do, how they could fix the two men, and she told Patti her idea. Both of them started giggling and screaming again, all excited about the plan and anticipating what the men would say when they came out of the water and found out what was waiting for them inside the tent.

They drove straight into Beaver Creek and found Bauer's store. Sally ran inside and asked the pimple-faced clerk if the store had any of those "anatomically correct" blow-up dolls.

The clerk shook his head, staring off, saying he didn't know what anatomically meant, but they had full-size party dolls all right, if that was what she meant. And she told him yes, yes it was, and when he pulled out the plastic package, she saw with glee that the dolls were anatomically correct. She bought two male ones and a small bike pump, then went outside into the bright sunny afternoon and held up the package, grinning in triumph.

They left the packages in the car and went across the street to Bonnie & Clyde's for lunch. It was cool in the air-conditioned diner and the hamburgers, Patti said, were the best she had ever had. She was also ravished, she told Sally. Getting upset and crying always made her hungry. They finished their meal, ordered coffee, and had cigarettes, sitting in the window booth and watching the street.

It was Patti who spotted the bald-headed boy and motioned to Sally to look, whispering across the booth that wasn't he a weird-looking one. Sally said, yes, but that was to be expected back here in the hills. At least, she thought, his mommy was nice-enough looking, if she did something with her hair.

When the two of them came into the diner, Sally saw how solicitous everyone was, especially the thin bouffant-haired waitress, and she thought to herself that the bald-headed boy and his mother must be somebody important in town.

Leaving, she heard the young woman talking, asking the silent boy what he wanted, carrying on this conversation, as if the child couldn't talk or anything. Sally could tell by the woman's voice that she wasn't from around there, she wasn't even southern, and she wondered what the mother and boy were doing up here in the mountains.

When they were outside, in the heat of the midday, Patti started to whine about the weather, and her plight, and she got teary again, and morbid, talking about having sex with Billy Joe, and here he was a homo and everything. Sally let her cry as she drove through the town, went down the mountainside, and circled around to the river at Buck's Landing. It took her less than ten minutes to reach the campsite, and it wasn't yet two o'clock.

They parked in the shade and watched the swift-running water. The river was high and brown and filled with logs and floating debris, even whitecaps. Chase had said earlier it would be a good day for white-water canoeing, what with the overnight storms. Sally sat watching the water, thinking of Chase, of him grinning back at her, waving, as the two boys set off by themselves, swinging into the swift current above the town of Bandana.

She began to cry silently, still sitting behind the wheel of Chase's station wagon. She felt like shit. She felt humble and humiliated, and she worried, not like Patti, that she would get AIDS from sleeping with some gay guy, but that she had invested over nine months of her life in Chase Hanes and it had turned out to be a complete bust. Well, by God, she would make him pay for it!

They took turns pumping up the dolls, laughing at their own naughtiness. They were half drunk from drinking in the hot sun, and exhausted from the long day of driving. When they finished, marveling at the fact that someone actually made male blow-up dolls with gigantic erections, they took the blow-ups into the hot tent and stuffed them inside a sleeping bag, fitting the slippery plastic dolls together so the two appeared to be wrapped in each other's arms, "fucking doggy-style," as Patti put it.

They labeled the dolls next, printing Chase and Billy Joe on each forehead, debating which one they thought was the "male," and which the "female." When they finally figured that out, their moods shifted. Patti was angry once more and depressed, saying if she had AIDS she was going to personally kill Billy Joe Ridgeway, but first she was going to cut off his "little-bitty prick."

They heard noises outside the tent, like someone walking around the campsite. Sally told Patti to hush up as she listened hard. It couldn't be the boys. They would have shouted from the river, had them come running down to the landing dock with cans of cold Coors.

It was nothing to worry about, she knew. The park area was in view of the road, and there were ash-wood picnic tables a dozen yards away. All afternoon people had been stopping to have their lunch by the edge of the river. Still, she didn't want anyone to see them, two women, inside the hot tent with life-size male blow-up dolls. She motioned to Patti to go outside when the flap of the big tent opened. They were both briefly blinded by the bright sunlight.

Sally thought first, What in the world is that person doing here? She started to say hello, friendly like, when she next saw the kitchen knife, saw the sun flash off the bright steel blade, saw how swiftly the knife was raised.

She screamed, cowering behind her small hands, and thought of the movie *Psycho*, and the bloody shower attack on poor Janet Leigh.

Billy Joe and Chase had their shirts off and were barefooted in the silver canoe. They were also an hour late to Buck's Landing, having pulled onto shore several miles back. They had gone into the thick woods to have lunch and make love on a mossy patch of level ground. Afterward they had gone for a swim naked in the river. There was no one else on the Toe, not this far downstream.

Chase guided the canoe around the concrete slab, pointed it toward land, and dug at the back paddle. The light metal boat sailed through long cattails and shoreline weeds and thumped up against the muddy bank just in front of the campsite, where the women had set up the tent.

"Hey, Pat!" Billy Joe shouted from the front of the canoe. He jumped from the boat, waded to dry land, and pulled the front end of the light canoe up onto shore as Chase hopped out.

"Where are those bitches?" Chase asked, lowering his voice. He scanned the parking lot and the half-dozen picnic tables set in a grove of trees. "Gone for a walk, you think, Billy?"

"Shit no! Patti Cally ain't walked a mile in her life, 'cept maybe around the Greensboro Mall." He glanced around himself and shouted, calling toward the silent green tent, "You got a couple cold ones in there, girls?"

The two men stood staring at the tent, higher on the bank. the flap was open and blew loose in the breeze. There was no sound from the insides. A car went by on the highway, then a truck, the sounds of the engines faint in the warm day. Chase was aware of silence. It didn't seem right, he thought, what with the tent and all the camping equipment set up, the car parked under the evergreens.

"Bitches," Billy Joe said out loud, climbing the slope, angry at the women. He kept talking while approaching, complaining that they were playing games with him and Chase, and the two of them dog-ass tired after their long day on the river.

He didn't pause at the tent flap. He stooped low and slipped through the dark opening.

Chase looked down to throw the short tow line into the canoe and spotted the footprint in the muddy shore. The print of a small boy or a woman, he wasn't sure which. The print was fresh, and looked so curious, a solitary perfect impression in the wet red clay. He was wondering where it came from. Was it one of the girls? Had they gone for a swim? Or were there other campers here that morning? A kid maybe, fishing bullheads in the reedy shores. Then Billy Joe screamed.

Chase spun around and saw him stumble back out of the dark entrance, tripping over the tent peg as he scrambled away.

"Jesus Christ, Billy Joe!...what the fuck...!" Chase yelled, knowing something was terribly wrong. Knowing too that something god-awful had happened to the girls.

He seized Billy Joe by the shoulders, trapping his lover, who kept trying to escape.

"Goddamnit, Billy Joe, what is it?"

Billy Joe's skin, blistery red from the day's sun, was now as pale as churned milk. His eyes were wild in his head.

"It's them, Chase! It's them," he said, before turning his head to one side puking up on the green grass of the picnic site.

Chase ran to the tent opening. He could hear Billy Joe behind him, warning him about going inside, saying they had to get the cops. He glanced around and saw Billy Joe on his knees. He was trembling in the late afternoon sunlight.

Chase stepped closer to peep inside and he smelled the women.

It was a sweet smell at first. The sweet smell of ripe fruit in a closed room. It reminded him of the tropics, of papaya and pineapple, and he thought of a trip he took to a Club Med in South America with Billy Joe, of warm mornings lying in each other's arms, and the pungent odors of wild fruit.

Then the sweet smell reminded him of Sally's cunt, of the cunts of all the women he had to sleep with, for one reason or the other, mostly to prove to other guys that he wasn't queer after all.

And then he smelled the dead bodies of the two women. The smell curled into his nose, choking him like oven gas. Chase backed off, moved to one side trying to escape the reeking stench that followed him. He wouldn't have thought death smelled so, but then he realized the closed tent had baked the bodies. It was as if the two women were loaves of bread left on a kitchen windowsill to rise.

He needed to see them. He had to know what had happened. Stepping closer, he clamped his nose with his thumb and forefinger and, crouching low, edged around the open flap. He reached out and pulled back the thick canvas to expose the dark hot interior.

The dolls distracted him at first. Where had they come from? And then he saw the backs of Sally and Patti, saw how the two women, stripped naked, were spread out on the sleeping bags, and how the killer had arranged the life-sized dolls so it seemed they were performing cunnilingus on the butchered girls.

Connor Connaghan, circling back to Beaver Creek after seven o'clock with a load of ceramic supplies, spotted the convoy of highway police cars at Buck's Landing and slowed down, making the sharp turn below Miller's Ridge. A half-dozen more pickups and cars had also pulled off onto the highway shoulder and were parked haphazardly in the long grass and dry weeds by the side of Route 80.

Slowing, he looked ahead and searched for the accident, some overturned car or truck, but the highway was empty, and no cop directed traffic. Then he saw the cops standing near Buck's Landing, and the county hospital ambulance backed up against an army tent.

He braked and pulled off the road, up against the steep rise of Miller's Ridge. He cut the engine and hopped from the cab. Crossing the highway, he went down the slope and into the grassy corner where a dozen men stood together.

He knew most of them by name or sight, and nodded hello. Then adjusted his John Deere cap and nodded toward the cluster of police and county sheriff men.

"What happened? Drowning?" he asked everyone, but glanced at Glen Batts.

"Some yuppies got themselves all cut up," Batts said, grinning. "Two women from down in the Piedmont, they say. Got that Marion sheriff runnin' his ass off; first Royce's sheep, now this." He gestured toward the tent and in the same motion unfolded a pack of cigarettes from the tight sleeve of his white T-shirt and picked one up from the loose pack, doing it all with one hand, as if he were performing a sleight of hand, a small time trick.

Standing among the others, Batts looked small; a little runt of a man with long, loose hippie hair, and a bill cap that advertised Bauer's General Store. Connor pushed by him and the other farmers without another word. He spotted Bobby Lee Clemente, who drove the county ambulance, and who had once rented a house from him, when Bobby was split from his second wife.

The ambulance driver recognized Connor and nodded, saying nothing. He, too, was cupping a cigarette inside the hollow of his yellow-stained fingers.

"What the fuck's goin' on, Bobby Lee?" Connor asked, resting his boot on the picnic table and leaning forward, one arm braced on his knee.

"Double killing. Two girls. That there's their boyfriends." The chubby driver slicked back his oily hair with one hand and nodded across the park site, to where the two men sat together, talking to a county detective who looked familiar. The detective wore a leisure suit and green tie that was too wide and too long. He kept tugging at his tight suit jacket as he sat questioning the men in the dark shadows of approaching night.

Connor studied the detective and the two men while Bobby Lee explained how the boyfriends had driven up to George's place and called the sheriff's office. He told Connor, too, what he had seen inside the tent. Told him how the women had been mutilated with pine cones.

"The bodies still there," Bobby Lee said, glancing at his watch. "I'm off in one hour, too. There ain't no way I can get back to Marion, not with the FBI here."

"FBI?" Connor shot a look at Bobby Lee, made nervous by the information. The local cops he never worried about, but it was always scary when the feds came into the mountains. There was always a danger of what they might pick up.

"Shit, I don't know why, neither." Bobby Lee shook his head. "Some fuckin weirdo, that's for sure." He mentioned the life-size dolls again and how the women were positioned, "...sucking those rubber pricks." But the worse, he added, warming up to describing what had happened inside the tent, was how the women had been cut up. "Took out their goddamn hearts, for chrissake."

"Hey, easy," Connor protested, shifting his body. "I've seen the movie."

"You ain't seen this movie!"

Two men emerged from the tent wearing surgical masks. That impressed Connor. He watched them peel off the white cups and stuff them into their suit pockets as they stood together, talking softly. One of the uniformed cops called out to Bobby Lee, waving him toward the tent.

" 'Bout fuckin' time," Bobby Lee swore, dropping his cigarette. "See you, hear!" he told Connor, striding off.

Connor moved, too, but kept his distance from the green tent. He circled around so that he might be able to glance into the opening flap, and found himself on the other side of the picnic table, where the two men were still talking to the sheriff's detective.

He could not hear the men, but he watched them. They were sitting across from the detective, with their backs together, and Connor saw, watching them, that they were holding hands under the table. He wondered who they were, and what it might mean that two women, out camping with two gay guys, had been murdered in the middle of a bright, sunny afternoon, hacked to pieces at Buck's Landing.

He tipped his cap up and swept the sweat off his brow with his forearm, then flipped his cap back on and thought immediately of Adam. "Shit," he said out loud, "no way!" But even as he said it, the notion took hold, caught at the corner of his imagination. It was possible. Anything was possible.

Connor shuddered.

He moved, made nervous by what he was thinking, and walked away from the campsite, toward the highway and where he had left his pickup parked in the long grass.

Bobby Lee, with the help of two of the state troopers, had brought out the first of the bodies, all wrapped up tight in a black body bag.

Connor stopped and looked back at the boyfriends still sitting at the picnic table. They were watching the bodies being carried to the ambulance. The two men were staring at the black bag. They were no tears, no hysterical crying.

They had done it, Connor knew. They had come downriver in their little silver aluminum canoe to meet the women, then murdered them in the tent, making it look like some crazy killer loose in the hills.

Or maybe it was worse than that. Maybe they had been into some rough afternoon sex, there in the tent, and perhaps it had gotten out of hand. The girls might have objected, started to protest.

His mouth watered and he realized he had a slight erection. He turned from the scene, turned away from all the other men, and stepped across the hot tar, moving fast, sweating, knowing he had to get away from this place, and feeling the tightness in his jeans, the bulge of his cock, and terrified someone might spot his hard-on, might guess the truth about him.

"Shit!" he said out loud, angry at himself, and frightened, as he always was, by his own secret thoughts, his hidden life.

12

MELISSA WAS UP BEFORE dawn, dressed, and downstairs in the kitchen making breakfast. She didn't bother about keeping quiet. She wanted to wake Adam. She had decided after midnight, when she couldn't sleep, that she would confront him about the new painting on the crafts-house wall.

But first she needed to eat. She was so wired by tension and black coffee that her hands were trembling. A solid block of pain was locked in at the corner of her forehead.

She took the coffee and muffin out onto the downstairs patio that Connor had built off the kitchen. There were wrought-iron chairs, but Melissa didn't sit down. The chairs were wet with dew and Melissa felt a chill go through her body. She shivered and clutched the warm cup of coffee with both hands. The sun did not reach that side of the house until late afternoon, and the patio faced the mountain stream and the green hillside, both of which gave off the dampness of the long night. Melissa felt as if she had stepped into a cold green diorama, not a bright sunny June morning.

She debated about going around to the other side of the house, to where the sunlight first cleared the hills and reached the property. But there was no terrace on that side of the house, and she wondered why Connor had built his strange place without taking advantage of the morning sun, and then she guessed it was because the schooner-house was situated to take advantage of the winter sun to fuel his homemade solar-heating system.

Finally, when the cold from the stream became too uncomfortable, she circled the house to stand for a while in the bright warm sun. She was wearing jeans and a wool shirt, and clogs. She knew she would have to change before she went up to school. She could already tell it was going to be a warm day in the mountains.

Melissa began to plot out what she needed to do that day, from shopping to making some sort of arrangements for Adam while she was at school. She was determined not to take him back there, but she was beginning to worry about leaving him alone at the house. She sighed, wondering what he might do next.

She should leave the mountains, she realized, and do what Greg told her; go back to New York with Adam and turn him over to the city. But where would she live, since she had subleased her apartment. And what would she do for a living? Just thinking of the fix she was in made her nervous. She paced around the front yard of the house, into the cul-de-sac driveway where she had parked the van, and where Connor had hung a rope swing from the high limb of a black walnut tree.

She sat in the swing to finish the muffin and the rest of her coffee, then she set the mug on the ground beside her and swung back on the long ropes of the homemade swing. For a moment the new motion made her dizzy, but then she closed her eyes and enjoyed the warmth of the sun on her face.

She stopped worrying about Adam and her problems. She thought of when she was living on Benton Place in St. Louis. She had been seven or eight then, she wasn't quite sure which, and her mother was between men. She was working nights at the hospital, taking care of old people.

She remembered that it was one of the happy periods of her life because she had her mother all to herself. After school they would go up to the park and swing on the big swings. Her mother used only one hand to push her higher and higher while she smoked her cigarettes and talked with the other mothers in the park.

She was never afraid. When she was high up, above the treetops, she'd pretend she could fly, that she might, if she wanted, fly away and find her daddy. And one time, when she was flying high over the tops of the trees, she thought she saw her daddy walking by the big park, thought she saw him watching her and waving from beyond the high iron fence that framed the park. She started to scream, shouting to her mother to stop the swing, to let her down, to hurry because her father was there, beyond the playground.

Her mother caught the swing and brought it to a stop, swearing at her for making a crying fuss, and when she tried to slip out from under the chain seat guard to run after her daddy, her mother slapped her across the face, telling her to mind herself, to stop "fibbin'" and "lyin'" because, "your daddy done run off, girl, and he ain't coming back again."

She had stumbled away from her mother, crying from the slap and her humiliation, and ran to the high iron fence. Her daddy wasn't there waiting. She saw a man crossing the street, moving down the block, and she screamed after him, went running along the inside of the iron fence, trying to shout over the busy traffic of the intersection, but the man never looked back.

Her mother came and grabbed her a second time, told her to mind her and come on home. She grabbed her arm and pulled her out of the playground and across the street to Benton Place, where they lived in two rooms on the third floor of Mr. Montesi's rooming house.

Melissa was crying, exhausted from the long night and the tensions over Adam, crying because of the vividness of her sad memory. She still kept a secret hope that her father would someday return to her. And when he did return her whole world would be better, and she would be happy again.

She stopped the swing and wiped the tears from her face with the back of her hand. She pulled the tissue from her jeans pocket to blow her nose. She was looking down, staring at the hard bare soil under her feet, still wiping her nose and eyes, cleaning up her face and getting herself under control when she saw the heavy black brogues and two stout legs. An old lady's legs. She had not heard the woman approaching and she tumbled back on the wooden seat, catching herself at the last moment.

"Yes?" Melissa asked, looked up, bracing herself against the tree.

The old woman grinned at her.

"Who are you?" Melissa said, softening her voice, realizing she didn't have to be afraid. The thin woman in front of her was over fifty. She had the unkempt and dirty looks of a New York City bag lady. But this wasn't New York, and this woman wasn't homeless. Also, she could see from the hard, wild look in the woman's face that she was clearly crazy. Then Melissa knew who the woman was.

"Rufus says you're the bald-headed boy's mommy," the woman said.

It took Melissa a moment to decipher the high twang of the mountain accent, and she answered back, speaking slowly so the woman would understand.

"His name is Adam."

The old woman continued to grin at her.

Melissa stepped away from the swing and moved toward the house. The old woman tagged after, bouncing up to her toes, like a girl at play. She seem to be all legs and arms, gesturing and moving quickly, with the awkward, jerky movement of a string puppet. She was not weak, Melissa realized, and there was even a healthy glow in the tautness of her tanned face.

"You the Mommy?" the old woman asked, pointing toward the schooner-house.

"Yes," Melissa said, making it simple. "And who are you?" She smiled, but kept her distance. She noticed the woman's fingers were crippled, making her hard brown hands resemble chicken's claws.

"I'm Crazy Sue," the woman said proudly, clutching the hems of her cotton dress and delivering a quick, awkward curtsy.

Melissa smiled. "Why, hello, Crazy Sue! It's nice to meet you."

"He done killed Glen Batts," the old lady said at once, hushing her voice, "last night." She gestured again to the imaginary boy behind her. "Rufus done saw him."

Melissa had reached the door of the schooner-house and stopped. Her hand was already on the copper door handle, but she didn't open the door.

"Adam hasn't hurt anyone," she answered, not knowing what Crazy Sue was talking about. She looked back at the old woman. The smile was gone from the face.

"He killed him, Rufus told me. He done seen it." The old

woman squeezed her lips together. She had no teeth and her gums sucked up her mouth, making a cavern of her hawkish face.

"You better go home, Sue," Melissa told her, opening the door.

"Rufus and me, we want to play with him." The old woman's eyes darted from Melissa to the open doorway. She had scurried around to get a glimpse inside the house.

"Go home!" Melissa ordered.

"Where's the boy?"

"I told you to get!" Melissa demanded, gesturing, treating the old woman like a child. "I'll call the police."

"I ain't done nothin'. Rufus, he ain't done nothin'."

Melissa squeezed her eyes closed, feeling the pain push against her temples. She was going to scream at the woman. She was going to get hysterical, and that would only make things worse.

"Please go home!" Melissa ordered, raising her voice, speaking sternly, but knowing, too, that this woman wasn't afraid, that she had spent her whole life being run off other people's property. Melissa dug her hand into her back jeans pocket and asked, "Sue, would you and Rufus like some ice cream?"

The woman's smoky eyes brightened and fixed on Melissa.

She had her, Melissa realized, and said quickly, "Go to town and buy some ice cream." She took a folded five-dollar bill from her jeans and held it out, not giving it yet to the retarded woman, but telling her, "You take this money and go to Bonnie & Clyde's. Hear me? Go get some ice cream and go home. Do you understand?"

The old woman nodded, her eyes on the folded five-dollar bill.

Melissa handed her the money and held her breath. She had no idea what the woman might do, whether money even meant anything to her simple mind. Crazy Sue snapped the folded bill from Melissa's hand and bolted away, went running across the bare lawn, out onto Creek Drive, and uphill toward town. Her long legs kicked up the dust as she ran.

"Dear God," Melissa whispered, pushing open the door and stepping inside the coolness of the schooner-house. She paused long enough to lock the door behind her, thinking that it was getting as bad as New York. But at least in New York she knew how to keep crazy people out of her life. Now in the mountains she wasn't sure if that was possible. Also, she thought wryly, she wasn't sure who was crazy, and who wasn't.

Driving through Beaver Creek, Connor spotted six white highway police cars lined up in front of Bonnie & Clyde's and he pulled over and parked his pickup at the end of the block, then walked back to the diner. Something was happening.

The inside of the small restaurant was packed with the morning regulars and the state police, who had taken over three of the booths and half of the counter stools.

He slid onto the last stool near the waitress station. It was hot in the diner, too early for the air conditioner, but the smell of bacon and grits and hot bread made Connor feel better and also hungry.

"What have we got here, Clyde? A crime convention?" he asked the counterman, grinning and already aware that being so close to state cops was making him edgy.

"It's Glen Batts," Clyde said softly, pouring Connor a glass of water while tossing down a small red plastic menu on the marble counter. "Looks like that little prick butchered up his family last night, then blew a fuckin' hole in his chest with his shotgun."

Clyde was leaning forward on the counter with his arms crossed so Connor had a close look at the tattoo on his right forearm: Christ on the cross, set in a wreath of thorns.

"Batts!"

Clyde kept nodding. "These guys have been down at his place all fuckin' night." The big man still wore his hair clipped short, as he had it cut when he came back from Korea and took over his mother's diner.

"Who'd he kill?" Connor asked, picturing Glen Batts's family, recalling seeing them sitting on the front porch of their old farmhouse. They had set out three stuffed sofas, all bought by mail order from Sears, and still with the clear plastic on the colored pattern.

"Eleven. Sally, she's the only one living, 'cause she was over at Grubb's place. She and Grubb been carrying on something."

Clyde pulled himself up and adjusted his apron, then shifted his attention to the waitress who had come back from the booths, still scribbling on her small pad. "What 'ya got, Lucy?"

"Give me two over and a side, couple slices of wheat toast, and grits all around." She slid her pad into her waist pocket and reached at once for the plastic pitcher of ice water. "How you doin', Connor?" she asked, not looking at him. "Hear what your good ol' buddy did to his kin?"

"Ain't no buddy of mine, Lucy, and you know that well enough."

The two of them caught each other's eyes and Lucy nodded, knowing what Connor meant. They had been lovers once, back when Connor was in high school. She had broken off with him during his junior year and taken up with Glen Batts. The romance between Batts and Lucy had lasted just that fall, in football season, while Connor played wingback for Consolidated and didn't have time to take out Lucy, who had already quit school and was working in Bauer's shoe department.

"He was always a mean little son of a bitch, weren't he, Connor?" Lucy said calmly, confessing the truth about the man they both disliked.

Connor looked away, down the length of the counter crowded with state cops, all alike in their bright green uniforms and shiny-brim hats. Connor hated cops. He hated the very idea of them. He said softly to Lucy, "A lot of mean sons of bitches in this town, Lucy, but they don't go and blow away their folk."

"Ain't that the truth." She popped her chewing gum.

Clyde turned away from the stove and grabbed two heavy white plates with one hand and said confidentially to both of them as he flipped eggs off the grill, "Little Batts didn't kill his kin, no way!" He turned around and slid the plates to Lucy, using the iron grill spatula to make his point. "He's a mean cuss, all right, and he ain't no good. But he ain't got the balls to hack up his family." Clyde shook his head and turned back to the grill, saying over his shoulder, "Something weird's goin' down around here, Connaghan."

"How's that, Clyde?" Connor leaned over and picked up Lucy's pack of cigarettes, and dipped one into his hand without asking the waitress, who had finished buttering the toast and lifted the plate of eggs and bacon in one hand and grabbed a pot of coffee with the other.

"Help yourself, Connaghan," she snapped, but without resentment.

"Thanks, I will."

"I thought you quit?" she said, leaving the service station for the front booths.

"I quit lovin', Lucy, not cigarettes."

"That will be the god-almighty day when that happens, not with all those young gals coming up every summer to the school."

"Hear 'bout those two gals down at Buck's Landing?" Clyde asked, disregarding Lucy's banter. "Hear 'bout them?"

Connor nodded, lighting up.

"Know what happened?" The big man's eyes widened and there was a slight and undeniable moment of pleasure showing on his face as if he possessed secret information.

"I happened by there, but didn't see much, didn't want to see much, from what I hear." Connor sensed that the highway cop nearest him was listening hard to Clyde's account.

"Girls had their pussies cut out," Clyde whispered.

"Jesus H. Christ!" That news stunned Connor. He leaned back on the stool, thinking of the two blond guys holding hands under the picnic table.

"Some fuckin' madman done that, you know yourself." Clyde straightened up, tucking his white shirt into his belt, then he hitched up his pants. He glanced down the row of highway patrolmen, and announced, his voice carrying the length of the counter, "You boys are looking up the wrong asshole." he grinned.

Connor lowered his head, staring at his coffee, the dark liquid in the thick white cup. He tried to distance himself from the exchange that suddenly swirled around him. He knew what Clyde was about.

Clyde was the only one of the Barnes boys to return to the mountains, to start working for his mommy, Bonnie Barnes. It was after he had been rejected by the sheriff's office, told he wasn't smart enough to be a cop, and now he was getting back, sticking it to the neatly dressed highway patrolmen.

Clyde moved slowly along the counter, asking the cops about Royce Brother's Alpaca sheep, telling the men that wasn't it kinda odd about Reverend Littleton up at the Tabernacle Church? He kept jabbing them with questions, grinning, like he knew the answer, something hidden from them, something that they were too dumb to understand.

Connor concentrated on his coffee cup and the thick diner

plates, thinking about the ugliness of utilitarian dinnerware, and wondered if he should try to sell Clyde some good-looking pottery from the school. They might offer him a deal, a cut-rate discount for leaving pamphlets about the school around for the tourists.

Connor did not let himself ponder the nightmarish thought that swam around the back of his head. Still he couldn't stop thinking about the bald-headed boy, remembering the blood on his arms, the wild look in his eyes as Melissa rushed for him, worried that the boy had somehow cut himself, ripped his veins crawling through brush, or under barbed wire, but the boy wasn't injured. The blood wasn't his.

"Ain't no one askin' me what's going on, no, sir!" Clyde Barnes declared, standing behind the counter with his legs apart, his thick arms folded across his chest, challenging the cops.

"That's right, Clyde," one of the men said, dismounting the round stool. "Ain't no one asking you." He had a toothpick pressed between his teeth and was holding his brown wide-brimmed hat in his hands. It was their turn. "We know who killed the females at Buck's Landing," the cop said, tossing change onto the counter.

Connor waited for the cop to continue. The room had calmed down, even the other men of the sheriff's office seemed surprised by that announcement.

"Who's that, Jake?" Clyde asked, stepping to the end of the counter, to where the cash register was positioned.

The room was quiet.

"Ain't at liberty to say," the man replied. He was using both his hands to fit on his brown hat.

"Sheeit!" Clyde said, hitting the register keys and popping open the cash drawer.

Connor, looking dead ahead, grinned over his raised coffee cup.

The other highway patrolmen were standing, grabbing their checks off the marble counter. Connor glanced over and saw that several of the men in the front booths were also cops. He saw the detective from Buck's Landing.

"We got ourselves a crazy kid up here in these hills," Clyde told everyone, upset that he was being ignored. "He's not even human."

"Who's that, Clyde," the cop asked, grinning back at the big man, "one of your kin?"

All of them laughed, tossing more coins onto the marble counter.

"Shut your fat mouth, Clyde," Lucy ordered.

Connor could not see Lucy behind the row of cops, but her voice silenced the laughter.

"You stay out of our business, Clyde, hear me!" she told him, appearing at the service station.

"Those crazy folks up there at that church, they got themselves a bald-headed boy. He ain't human, that one." Clyde was talking fast.

Beside Connor, Lucy slammed down her dishes, swearing at Clyde, and, without pausing, slipped under the counter, saying to Connor as she went for Clyde, "I told that fucker not to mess with my people." And then she shouted, "Clyde, you shut your mouth, hear me!" and grabbed a thick black-handled knife from the cutting block.

"Lucy! Hey, what the fuck!" Connor jumped up and ineffectually grabbed for the thin woman.

Clyde was still talking, laughing, too, telling the cops who the bald-headed boy was. "Those church people think he's a goddamn alien! An E.T.! And Lucy Webster here, she done sign up to take a flight with the bunch of them. Gave them a week's salary, too. They're all goin' up to heaven on a goddamn chariot of fire!"

They were lovers, Connor realized. Lucy was sleeping with big Clyde, and he thought of Sally Barnes, who had been a friend of his mother's, and who still lived on Church Street, in the red frame house that Clyde's mom, Bonnie, had left him. And he remembered when he was thirteen and making love for the first time to Lucy Webster, and how she had showed him, with great seriousness, how he should stick his dick into her.

"Goddamnit! Clyde, watch it!" Connor shouted, jumping forward again. He shoved the pie display tray off the counter as he grabbed for Lucy.

Clyde never saw the kitchen knife. She held it down at her side, flat against her white starched uniform, partially hidden in the folds of her skirt, and when he paused long enough in his ridicule to grin at her, she was already so close that she simply stepped forward, as if she wanted to wrap her arms around his big, fat waist and hug him to death, only this time, she swung her right hand and brought the thick blade up underhanded and plunged it into his side, just above his belt. She pushed eight inches of blade halfway home before breaking down into screams and letting go of the knife and pounding Clyde's startled face with her small fists.

The cops never saw the hit, not until they were sprayed with Clyde's streaming hot blood. He was dancing behind the narrow counter, trying to pull the black-handled kitchen knife from his left side.

One cop jumped the counter and dove at Lucy, knocking her over, and slammed Clyde and Lucy down into the tight corner under the cash register. There was blood everywhere. On Lucy, on the cops, on the marble-top counter, but all Connor could focus on was the blood that had begun to bubble up out of Clyde's startled mouth.

The sight of that pushed him back from the counter. He stumbled into the wall and the other cops started yelling, swearing, rushing to get at Lucy, trapped on the diner floor.

Connor grabbed the doorknob of the rear door and stepped into the back hallway, crowded with boxes of food and supplies. He stumbled through the boxes, knowing there was an exit here, having used it himself when he parked behind the diner. He pushed open the door and took a quick deep breath of fresh air, feeling the bright warm sun on his face.

"Jesus H. Christ," he swore, tripping on the wooden steps and stumbling into the gravel parking lot. He saw Crazy Sue coming across the street, running for the diner.

"Betty Sue," he shouted, "no!"

She paused, puzzled by his command.

"Where are you going?" he asked, unable to concentrate. He was thinking of himself when he was just a boy and in love with Lucy Webster, who he had thought was the most beautiful girl in the whole world.

"I'm going for ice cream," Betty Sue answered, immediately worried.

"No," Connor whispered, sitting down on the edge of a short block of wood. "No, please, no." He kept shaking his head.

"I'm going to buy me and Rufus ice cream," she stated. "The lady told me to buy ice cream."

Connor spotted the five dollars in Betty Sue's clutched fist and knew at once who had given her the money.

"Betty Sue," Connor asked next, softening his voice and speaking sweetly to the old woman. "Who killed those girls down at Buck's Landing?"

"The bald-headed boy," she answered, smug in her reply.

"How did he kill them?"

"He ate their pussies," Betty Sue said, skipping up the wooden stairs and running into Bonnie & Clyde's through the rear entrance.

Connor let her go.

13

LATER THAT MORNING, with Adam helping, Melissa cleaned out a section of the living-room space for Adam, making a studio for him in one corner of the schooner-house. He wasn't going back to the crafts school, to be exposed again to the likes of Gene Martin, she had resolved. But she did want Adam to keep painting.

She set up the easel she had bought at Bauer's store, and thumb-tacked several sheets of thick paper to the wall so if Adam needed more space, he could go onto the expanding white paper.

The child needed room to render his nightmarish paintings, she realized. And it would only be through his paintings, she knew, that she was going to learn about him. Melissa had taken enough art therapy courses to understand how a creative piece might be interpreted. Also, she realized, she could call up Carol Scott at the school and have her come see what Adam was painting. The woman was a professional, she remembered Martin telling her. Melissa felt a nudge of assurance, knowing she could turn to Carol Scott.

Yet even while she was logically making these decisions, she knew enough about herself to know she was blocking her own suspicions about Adam. The fact that he needed to draw such paintings, the fact that he had come home two nights before with blood smeared up both of his arms, were two incidents that she wasn't dealing with.

Her body shivered, recalling the sight of Adam. She had asked Connor to find out if anything had happened in town, or around the hills, but he had only shook his head when she questioned him, been vague, and said he hadn't heard anything in town. She wondered if Connor was lying to her for some reason. She wished she knew someone from town that she could turn to, someone besides the landlord. He was her only link to the isolated community.

Melissa let a bubble of fear escape, and took a deep breath, told herself not to become paranoid. Then she plunged herself into more work, hoping to keep from dwelling on Adam's odd behavior. She could not give up on him, she told herself once more. The system, she knew, had already discarded him, leaving him homeless in the tunnels. Well, she told herself once more, she wasn't going to give up on the boy. She was going to prove that she was better than New York City social agencies.

She sat down at Connor's kick wheel and grabbed a wedge of clay, banging it onto the smooth wet wheel. She had found the small portable wheel in a closet off the main downstairs space and set it up so that she might work in the living room and have a view of the woods and the creek, as well as be able to watch Adam paint. She needed to keep an eye on him at all times, she reminded herself. She had been too lax a parent, she knew. But, then, how does one learn how to handle a teenage boy?

She kicked at Connor's wheel, concentrating on her pottery, and also wanting to show Adam that the two of them could work together in silence, and in the same room. She wouldn't hover over his shoulder. The boy needed encouragement, she knew, not criticism.

She kept her attention away from his drawings while she made small cups, dozens of them, not to keep, but simply to learn how to pull up a simple attractive shape. When she did look up, it was to glance outside at the beautiful afternoon, to look at the tall trees that framed the house, watch for a moment the creek cascading down the rocky slope, shiny in spots where the sun broke through the branches and caught the rushing water.

She guessed there could not have been a prettier spot in the mountains, and with that her spirits brightened. Perhaps she was right after all. These mountains had to be better for Adam than living in the city. She thought of the urban crime, of how difficult it would be to supervise him. But here in the mountains, Adam could just walk out the front door and go play in the woods, and nothing but good, she told herself again, could happen to him in the hills. There were no drugs, no place where he might get into trouble. Still, she reminded herself, he had come home from the woods with both of his arms bloodied.

She glanced over him to see how his painting was going and saw that he had filled nearly a wall of paper with an oil landscape.

Unlike the paintings he had done before, this one was lovely, overwhelming in its detail, and, again, perfectly rendered. Yet the colors of this landscape were warm and inviting, and looking at it, Melissa beamed, excited by the painting itself, and the fact that Adam had done such a calm scene of a rushing river, surrounded by high mountain cliffs, all covered with evergreens, and a perfectly beautiful, cloudless day. He had caught, she saw, what a summer day in the mountains looked like. She could almost taste the freshness of the air, almost feel the warmth of the high noon sun.

"Adam, it's beautiful!" she told him, slipping off her potter's stool.

Adam didn't stop painting. He was crouched in the far left corner of the huge sheet of paper, momentarily blocking Melissa's view. She didn't approach the painting, wanting to give him space to work, and instead went into the kitchen and lit the gas under the water and reached for the coffee beans. She did, however, keep glancing over at Adam to see if he was finished.

She made her coffee, poured out a cup, and stayed where she was, sitting down on a high stool at the butcher-block kitchen counter, from which she had a view of the whole length of the far wall and what Adam was painting.

She watched him back away from his work, still searching the big painting, looking for places that might need work, where he had missed a patch. She did speak, telling Adam again how lovely his painting was.

"Isn't that the Toe River? Buck's Landing?" She sipped her coffee, not taking her eyes from the work, and then he moved slightly to the right, giving her a view of the far corner.

"Oh, no," she whispered, stunned by what she saw, and all her high hopes, her brief sense of security and well-being, dissolved. Again, in her heart was a rush of dark, cold dread. It swept over her, freezing her flesh. "Oh, God," she whispered, seeing what Adam had drawn, seeing, too, that he was smiling, watching her look at his painting. His gray silvery cat eyes bright in his head.

"What he had drawn," Melissa told Connor later, "were two naked women. They were on the shore of the river, you know, as if they had been washed up from the water. And they were embracing." She took a deep breath, and went on, "Or at least they had their arms together; that part wasn't too clear. But what was clear, and vividly drawn, was how they had been cut up, not dismembered exactly, but sliced and slashed, and poked full of holes."

She paused a moment in her telling, wanting to be sure that Connor got it all straight.

"The women's bodies were pale, like fine marble, and they were beautiful, too." She turned away, glancing over at the empty wall, then continued, "Looking at it, I mean, after my initial shock, I thought of Salvador Dali, one of his surrealist nightmare images." Melissa shrugged, and said apologetically, "If it weren't for his background, who Adam is or was, then seeing these extreme examples of violence, I wouldn't be so touchy. It's obvious the child is gifted. A genius maybe." She shrugged and looked at Connor, as if waiting for him to respond with a solution.

They were alone in his studio at the crafts school. It was just after six and the class of students had gone across the lawn to have dinner in the main dining room. They could hear voices and laughter, carrying to them on the still evening air.

Connor shook his head, shrugging, but he wasn't thinking of Adam's painting. He was remembering what Bobby Lee had said about the women at Buck's Landing, and what Crazy Sue had told him that morning outside Bonnie & Clyde's.

The kid could have done it, he thought next. The gay guys might have been telling the truth. They had said the women were dead inside the tent when they reached the landing. But Adam had drawn the embracing women outside, on the shore, as if they had been knifed and cut up there, out in the bright sun. He shook his head.

"Oh, there's one other aspect about the painting," Melissa said quickly, remembering. "Actually it's kinda important, really." She grimaced at her omission. "When I looked at the painting I was sitting in the kitchen drinking coffee and I knew he had just done a landscape, the Toe River. I saw the water was painted brilliantly red. I thought it was the reflection of the stained-glass windows, that the afternoon sun was shining through a red pane. Then I realized he had painted the river water another color, to show the blood of the two women had bled into the water, turning the river red."

Connor stood and paced the empty studio. He wasn't looking at Melissa, but she knew at once something else was wrong. Her heart leapt to her throat. She thought how she always froze up when things got too stressful. At that moment, she knew she couldn't stand, even if she wished.

"What is it?" she managed to say.

"Were you with Adam yesterday, after you left the crafts school?"

"Well, yes and no. Why?"

"Did he go running off at any time?"

"No, he just didn't disappear!" Melissa answered back, annoyed by Connor's tone. "He was around the place. You know how he likes to throw pebbles for hours."

"This was when?"

"Yesterday, after we went here, but before noon. I telephoned a friend in New York. I went into town."

Connor came back to where Melissa was sitting on her potter's wheel.

"You went to town alone?"

"No! Both of us! I don't leave him alone. Well, I did now, but I needed to speak to you, and I couldn't with him around. I left him at the house; he was painting again. I told him he couldn't leave the house." She stood talking, watching Connor. Then she asked, "What's this all about?" She knew her fear was registering in her voice.

"You took Adam with you to town yesterday afternoon?" Connor asked next, ignoring her question.

"Why are you being so prosecutorial?"

"I'm sorry." He gestured. "I'm just, I guess, trying to get a fix on where you were yesterday afternoon, that's all." He backed off, not wanting to tell her about the two women at Buck's Landing.

"When he came back from sitting out on the boulder, he had a small bouquet of wildflowers that he had picked for me." She smiled, as if taking some sort of credit for that.

"This was when?"

"Around noon. I went into town..."

"Alone?"

"No, not alone. I told you!" Melissa shouted. Connor had begun
to pace again, his boots sounding on the loose barn-board floor of
the pottery studio. Something was very wrong, she knew. She had
begun to see the way his face tensed when he was upset, and how his
jaw stiffened. He looked older when he was worried, like a man who
had once been a heavy drinker. He reminded her at that moment of
Roland Davis, her stepfather. Connor had the same hard-edged,
weatherbeaten face, raw and mean-spirited, a product of years of
mountain inbreeding. She looked away, angry at herself for thinking
of Connor that way. He had only been kind and helpful to her since
she arrived in Beaver Creek.

"So Adam was with you," he said, lightening up.

"Yes. We went to town, had lunch at Bonnie & Clyde's, did
some grocery shopping, came home." She watched Connor as she
recalled how she spent the afternoon. "I unpacked, and..."

"...And Adam?"

"Adam did what he usually does. He went off to play." She kept
watching Connor, her eyes widening. She felt as if she were taking
some kind of top-secret examination, where none of the answers
were quite right. It angered her, having to respond to his questioning.

"How long was Adam gone?"

"He wasn't gone! He was playing out back. I took a nap...Connor,
what's going on?"

He shrugged. "I'm curious, that's all."

"Bullshit! Something's happened and you wouldn't tell me what.
But you think Adam..." Her voice was level, without the rage she
kept trapped inside her. Only her eyes challenged Connor and kept
him in focus. Her own heart slammed against her chest.

"Something happened yesterday afternoon. Over on the Toe
River. At Buck's Landing."

She kept recalling Adam's painting as Connor, slowly and ellipti-
cally, told her about the two women, how they had been found
inside the tent, telling her the men with them were both gay, and
suggesting, implying, that they must have done it, in some strange
S&M sex ritual that had gotten out of hand.

Melissa listened without becoming hysterical. Trying desperately to be professional, to prove that she was a trained social worker. She kept nodding, overwhelmed by what Connor was telling her, and realizing how helpless she was, and knowing, too, that she must leave the mountains and take Adam back to New York, realizing, too, with a stab of pain, that she might be partially responsible for what had happened to the women at Buck's Landing.

Connor, watching Melissa, saw she was sinking into herself, shrinking and disappearing.

"Hey," he whispered, approaching her, "easy."

Melissa shook her head. Then, unable to control herself, she began to cry. She covered her face with both hands and pulled her knees up as she tried to hide her outburst, but she couldn't stop crying, and the tears came in a great wash, shaking her whole body.

Connor stepped around to where she was sitting at the potter's wheel and embraced her. She buried her face into his T-shirt. She had been trying so hard to be brave about Adam, trying to prove to herself, to Greg and everyone else back in New York, that she wasn't a damn fool to do this, to take the boy and raise him as her own.

She told Connor this, crying, and drying her tears on the sleeves of her blue cotton shirt, and then she found some tissues in her bag. It took several more minutes for her to calm herself, and by then some of the other pottery students were drifting back to the studio from their early dinner.

"Let's get a cup of coffee," Connor suggested. "I don't have a class 'til eight."

Melissa nodded, needing to keep talking to Connor, and she thought that was what she was missing, a community of people. If she had been back in New York City this would never have happened, she told Connor as they walked across the lawn. She wouldn't be losing it this way over Adam. She would have had her network of friends to give her support, to get her help. She would have had Greg to confide in and people at the agency. And thinking of all them only reminded her of how isolated she was and seemingly at the edge of the world.

"Who's Greg?" Connor asked first when they reached the dining room. "Your boyfriend?"

"Oh, no, not Greg. We work together, that's all. Actually, he is...was...my deputy. Greg's married and has a family." She felt better, just talking about Greg and mentioning his name.

"And he wasn't for this move of yours, for taking Adam?"

Melissa shook her head. She didn't tell Connor that she needed to get out of New York because of Greg, and that, when she was being totally honest with herself, she realized she was partially using Adam to escape her own romantic mess-up.

They took their coffee outside of the dining room and went to sit on the stone steps of the old building, which, at that hour after dinner, were deserted. They had a clear view of the valley and the setting sun, and were alone on the flagstone steps of the building.

"I don't think you should give up on Adam," Connor told her after she had finished explaining how she found Adam. "Nor do I think you should give up on yourself." He glanced over at her.

They were sitting side by side on the stone steps. Melissa was holding her mug in both hands, conscious of its warmth and weight, and looking over at Connor, letting her feelings show on her face.

She thought she could make love to this man, if he wanted, and knew her decision showed on her face. And she realized, too, that he knew what she thought. She didn't care. She was tired of masking emotions and being careful and coy. Why couldn't she have a little love and affection? she asked herself! All month she had been concentrating on Adam, giving him all her energy, and it had left her feeling wasted and worthless. If she couldn't have Greg, she thought next, then she needed someone else to love her. Besides, she told herself, he was being incredibly helpful to her.

"What should I do?" she asked Connor, wanting him to lift the burden of Adam from her shoulder.

"First, you got to keep trusting Adam. We don't know if he is involved in any of this."

"But you think he is...?" Melissa was watching Connor's blue eyes, the thin hawkishness of his face. He was struggling for an answer. She wondered if it was that he didn't want to tell her, or was he afraid of Adam too?

"I'm not sure," he said, trying to be honest, and knowing, too, that honesty was all that would work with this woman. She was someone who responded to trust. If she trusted him, she wouldn't leave, and he was certain if she did stay in the mountains, she would sleep with him. They could be lovers all summer long.

"It's possible, I guess. You never know what people, kids, too, might do. Do you want to go to the police, talk to the sheriff?" Before he finished talking, she was shaking her head.

"I agree. I don't think you should. What we need to do is find out about Adam, learn who he is." He tried to sound positive.

"I've been trying."

"The paintings," he said softly, staring off across the open meadow, watching how the coolness of the early evening was building into fog on the rise of land. "They're the answer! He's trying to tell us something. He's trying to talk to us."

It was only then, when he mentioned the kid's drawing, that he knew he was right. The child needed to talk. He hadn't killed those women. He had only seen the bodies at Buck's Landing, or maybe he had seen the two women get killed. Connor felt better at once.

"You're right, of course!" Melissa jumped up. Her dark face bright with excitement. She had been afraid of those paintings, and she shouldn't have. "I've been blocking on them," she told Connor, wanting to leave at once, to go home and make sure Adam was okay.

"I'll stop by later," Connor offered, standing with her.

"Yes, please do!" She was excited by the possibilities of what the paintings might tell her, and she also wanted Connor to know she wanted him to come see her, to help her, and also later, she fantasized, for him to make love to her.

The look and invitation was off her face in an instant, but it had registered with Connor, was as clear as a gesture, as if she had reached out and touched him.

"Good!" He smiled to mask his own lust and said at once, "Maybe you should start quizzing him on this painting. Give him a sketch pad or something. He could draw for you what he's seen."

Melissa nodded, having already thought of that answer. She had gone down the stone steps and was moving toward the parking lot, her van keys in her hand.

Connor leaned over and picked up her mug and threw what was left of her coffee in a long brown arch into the bushes, calling after her, "I'll see you 'bout ten." Then he snapped his fingers and gave her a thumbs-up.

She grinned like a girl going off to play.

Connor kept his eyes on her, watching her thighs under the cutoff jeans, and the shape of her small tight ass. He could already feel his hands on the slope of her back, feel the warmth of her skin after the day in the sun, feel the slippery sheen of her buttocks. His mouth went dry. When she had disappeared beyond the lilac bushes, he still had an erection, which he walked off, returning to the crafts house, now blazing with lights as dusk finally reached the mountain ridge.

Deacon MacCabe had found the bald-headed boy and brought him to evening services at the New Land Tabernacle Church. It had been easier than he would have thought, but he didn't tell the others, leading Adam up the center aisle in the hushed building, his big flesh arms wrapped protectively around the thin shoulders of the little boy.

He had driven down to Connaghan's house after closing up the shop and found the boy. He had been planning on inviting the boy and his mommy up to the church, as a way of welcoming them into the community, but the bald-headed boy was alone, sitting on a boulder out back, tossing pebbles into the mountain stream.

MacCabe had gotten some candy to bribe the kid, as a way of luring him into his Chevy, but the kid came readily enough, with a bright smile, and not a word of objection. MacCabe had just told Adam they were going to meet some "real nice folks" up at the church, and when he asked Adam his name, the boy had printed the letters A D A M in the dirty dashboard of the old car.

MacCabe had grinned, seeing it, then said out loud, "Ain't that the truth, boy! Ain't that the truth! Hallelujah!" The boy had grinned back, showing a perfect set of teeth. MacCabe had marveled at those teeth, wondering if they were human teeth or not, and then decided they weren't. Only the chosen one would have such fine, wonderful, shiny teeth. Driving to the church, he gave the child a bag of gummi bears.

When MacCabe and Adam reached the platform, Janna Tewell pumped up her organ and began to play "Angels of Heaven," leading the others in the chorus. Even MacCabe joined in on the final verse.

"God's holy arms we meet
Lord, save us who seek."

MacCabe raised his left hand, keeping his embrace on the boy, then slowly lowered his outstretched arm, bringing the spiritual to a close and gathering the attention of the congregation. They were all watching the bald-headed boy, smiling up at him and MacCabe. The deacon took his time, enjoying his moment.

"God loves us all," he shouted out in the silent church, his voice ringing to the steeple, "for He has brought us our salvation. Amen I say to you!"

"Amen!" a chorus of voices sang back.

"We have believed in Our Lord Jesus Christ. We have waited for our salvation as we have been told. And the good Almighty God, he has believed in us."

He moved his arm off Adam and nudged the boy forward. For a moment, Adam stood alone in the beacon of light, the spotlight focused on the altar platform.

MacCabe circled around, still talking. The congregation's attention was riveted to the child, who stood perfectly still, returning a sweet smile, watching them with his big, silvery eyes.

"And our Holy Book tells us, 'A child will come into our midst and lead us to the promised land,'" MacCabe intoned. "I say, behold the boychild."

"Amen," came a single word of acceptance from the hushed gathering.

"We are the chosen people," MacCabe told them.

"Amen."

"Hallelujah," Sam MacCabe told them, "Hallelujah!"

He had reached the corner of the small platform where Hilda-Jo Crawford stood, holding the large, brown, vinyl-covered guest book and a folded blue velvet cape she had made for the bald-headed boy.

MacCabe smiled down at Hilda-Jo, taking it from her. They had made love that afternoon at her place, after her husband Treat had driven his rig out of Beaver Creek. He hadn't washed after leaving her house and could still smell the woman on his fingertips.

He took the velvet cape she had trimmed with lace for the evening service and flung it open, then swept it through the air as if it were a swooping bird. It landed on the bald-headed boy's thin shoulders, floated down around his frail body.

The boy looked up at MacCabe. There was a new cold look in his icy eyes, and beneath the thin warmth of his smile. Sam glanced away, thinking to himself, Dear God it was true. The boy had come to claim the souls of Beaver Creek. He turned to Hilda-Jo, who, as they had rehearsed, stepped toward the congregation with the open book, saying, "Come on up here, folks. Sign up now for the chariot of fire. If you're going to see God, well, bless you, and sign the book. Sign the Book of Righteousness!"

He stopped talking, not knowing when the Lord would call them. But he knew, from watching all the preachers who had come to Beaver Creek, that they would need money, regardless. He held up a straw basket, already seeded by himself with a few dozen bills, fives and tens, so everyone would know what was expected, and told the congregation. "Provisions are needed. We go on a heavenly journey and need food and drink to carry up to the stars."

He looked out over the congregation crowding into the tight aisles, coming toward the altar, already reaching for wallets, opening their small purses. There were a few people who had remained seated. People he didn't know. They were glancing at each other, grinning.

Then he spotted Betty Sue Yates. She was coming up the aisle squeezed in behind thick rows of others, trying to hide, but she was too tall, too gamely. He saw she, too, was grinning, talking to herself. He wondered why Mary Lee wasn't in the church to handle her. Jesus H. Christ, he swore, that was all he needed, having her in the church.

He tried to catch Ralph Yates's eyes, but the old farmer was walking in front of Betty Sue, inching forward, looking down. All that Sam MacCabe could see was the pale moon of the big man's bowed head.

The line had jammed up with people signing the brown vinyl book.

"Now is the time to sign up in God's name," MacCabe went on. "And when the time comes, sisters and brothers, let us all be here together in the Tabernacle Church."

"Amen," a chorus answered him.

Sam MacCabe kept his eye on Betty Sue, thinking how he might handle her. He didn't want the woman signing the book. But he wasn't sure she could write. He remembered in grammar school the teachers had given her dolls to play with, put her off in the corner of the one-room schoolhouse, or let her go play in the fields, chase after the squirrels.

Goddamn her simple mind, he swore. He didn't like having the crazy bitch around. Looking at her, watching her, he hadn't paid attention to his collection basket and when he glanced down he saw the loose money, all the fives and tens and twenties. His pulse picked up, excited by the sight of the fresh money.

The bald-headed boy looked up at him, his eyes still glassy cold. MacCabe turned away. He spotted Betty Sue again. The old woman had reached front. She was grinning, talking out loud. She was talking to her little brother, Rufus, the brother she had killed at the age of six, tossing the child down the farmhouse well.

"Goddamn," MacCabe swore under his breath. He let go of the boy, stepping forward to intercept Betty Sue Yates, to block her from approaching the brown vinyl Book of Righteousness.

The boy caught his arm, hurting him. MacCabe's knees buckled from the pain. Adam had simply seized his elbow, snaplocked his arm in the tight grip of his fingers.

"Jesus Almighty," MacCabe whispered, gasping for breath and stunned by the boy's strength.

Adam stepped around the Deacon, moved the fat man aside, and stepped up next to Hilda-Jo as Crazy Sue reached the platform.

Hilda-Jo looked down, spotted the bald-headed boy, and was puzzled by his action. She glanced back and saw Sam MacCabe grab hold of the pulpit. He was spinning around, dropping in slow motion like a giant top. She thought the bald-headed boy was alerting her, that the man was suddenly sick, suffering a heart attack.

"Sam!" Hilda-Jo shoved the brown vinyl book into Adam's arms and ran for her lover.

Adam looked up, caught Betty Sue's eyes, and smiled.

The tide of people coming forward to be saved were momentarily baffled by the commotion. Several men pushed forward and jumped onto the wooden platform, rushed for Sam MacCabe, who had slumped to the floor, grabbing on at last to the pulpit, trying to save himself. Then he tumbled over, so the only noise in the crowded church was the crash of the pulpit as it toppled.

A cry went up from the congregation, a soaring of voices, all startled by the sight of yet another of their brethren, dying in the last moments before their salvation.

When Melissa came back to the schooner-house and found Adam gone, she telephoned Connor at the school and told him. She had thought she had conquered her own fear about the boy, but his absence made her frantic. She kept pacing in the kitchen, stretching the long cord, as Connor tried to reason with her.

"He's gone off before," he reminded her.

"I know, but I told him I was only going to the school for a half hour. I told him not to leave the house."

"He'll come back."

"But I don't know that!" Melissa shouted.

"Yes you do."

"How!"

"Is anything gone from his room?"

Stretching the cord, Melissa rushed to his bedroom and scanned it.

"No, I don't think so," she told Connor, standing in the bedroom doorway.

"Okay, that's a good sign."

"Where's he gone?" she asked immediately.

"In the woods most likely," Connor told her.

"How do we know that!"

"Melissa, we don't know that," Connor said sternly. "Let's cool it, okay. It doesn't do you any good to get hysterical."

"I'm not hysterical!"

"Okay, I'm sorry, but I just mean..."

"He's with that Crazy Sue, I bet," Melissa said next, her mind jumping from thought to thought.

"I don't know. I told her to keep away from him." He was silent a moment, and then he added, "Try to keep cool. I'll be there in less than an hour. I'll cut this class short."

"Thank you," she whispered, feeling overwhelmed and desperate.

"Get a drink or something. Try to keep cool. There's nothing you can do, right?"

Melissa nodded into the receiver.

"Are you okay?" he asked, letting the question register in his voice.

"I think so."

"See you in forty-five minutes."

"Connor, he's driving me crazy."

"I know." He sighed, and then said encouragingly, "But it's going to get better."

"I don't know," Melissa told him. "I don't know." And she meant it.

Melissa hung up the phone and turned away from the tree-post and was startled by the sight of Adam. He had come into the house as always without making a sound.

"Where were you?" she demanded, trembling from her shock and also thrilled that he was there, safely home again.

He looked away and shrugged.

"Adam, you know I don't like it, your going off like that, running into the woods. Especially when it is dark out."

He did not move away from her, nor nod, showing he understood, but she knew he did understand her.

"I don't want to be afraid for you, or that something might happen out there, and I'm not going to follow you, but you just can't run off, leaving me without a word. I told you where I was going, didn't I?"

She waited for him to reply, and he did, shaking his head.

"All right," she told him, taking a deep breath and knowing she had to stop lecturing the boy. "We understand each other. How 'bout some dinner?" Her voice lightened up. "What about a hamburger and some home fries?"

They were both standing in the kitchen space, and he smiled back.

She stared down at him, still smiling, and thought how much a boy he had become in the hills. When she looked at him in his new jeans, which he had already worn down and dirtied, and saw the way his crafts school T-shirt hung loose on his slight body, she felt immensely happy.

Connor made them both a drink after dinner and they sat together on the sofa talking about the great ceramic teachers Connor knew. He was telling her stories about M. C. Richards, Bob Turner, and Bernard Leach of England, who first taught him how to center and throw a pot.

It was not true, of course. Connor had never been to England, never knew Leach, but he described what he once read in a book, told Melissa how Leach had made him make a thousand mugs before he accepted one.

"And even that one," he whispered, leaning close, smiling wryly at Melissa, so she was only aware of his eyes, "wasn't any good. Leach, I think, just got tired of saying no to me."

Melissa kept smiling, unable to move, and not wanting to move. She was curled up, feeling safe and warm, and she thought she could listen to Connor forever, that every time he told her another story, she learned more about him, where he had traveled, what he had done.

"You have had such a wonderful life," she said. "I'm jealous of all your adventures. I feel deprived. I'm ashamed of myself for not, you know, having done more with my life."

"You have time," Connor said. "But you have to realize that your genius is now smothered by your ambitions and egotism, even your ignorance and fear. All of this you have to overcome first. You mustn't be envious of me, nor feel cheated by life. If you wish to make that perfect pot, then you must become the perfect person. You will never be satisfied or happy until you do. Great pottery comes from a great heart."

Melissa had lost track of what Connor was saying. She could not focus her mind. She was aware only of his voice, and her own smooth happiness. They had someway found themselves stretched out with their legs scissored together. Connor moved his stockinged foot and nestled it between her thighs.

She remembered Adam and looked up. He was across the long room, painting again and not concerned with them.

"Adam," she said nicely, "I think it's time to think about bed."

He glanced at her over the top edge of the easel. She could just see the round bullet of his bald head, the smooth shape of his forehead, all shiny and soft white in the glow of the lamp.

He didn't nod, nor recognize her instruction, but he did begin to clean off his brushes, to reach out and turn off the lamp beside his painting. The living-room space of the schooner-house was instantly shadowy, lit by the moonlight filtered through the stained-glass windows, the high overhead skylight.

Adam moved through the house, doing all of his nightly routines, going first to the kitchen and pouring himself a glass of water to take to bed, then to stop at the bathroom. Sitting on the couch, they could hear him pee. Melissa smiled at Connor. "Boys," she mouthed to him. Adam flushed the toilet and without a wave headed for his own first-floor bedroom.

"Good night, Adam," she called after him.

He shut the door to his room, leaving them in the shadowy darkness of the living-room space.

They sat together in silence. Melissa had leaned her head against the back of the sofa, watching Connor down the length of the couch. She was aware of his every move, of his physical presence. There was nothing like a man, she thought, thinking about his body, how his muscles moved, remembering him throwing a huge pot on the wheel, remembering how he'd leaned forward with his whole body, and pulled the wet clay up with the strength of his hands and arms.

She thought again of his forearm muscles bulging against his tight T-shirt. She felt her own body getting excited, felt her blood pump to the center of the vagina. Jesus, she thought, closing her eyes. She should get up, she thought, and get a cold glass of mountain water to cool herself down. Her whole body was sweetly swept up with pumping blood. Connor moved his foot, pressed it gently against her again, moving his toes lower, seeking her opening. She shifted her position, spread her legs, gave him room.

Then Connor reached for her.

It was done with such effortlessness. He stretched across the sofa and took hold of her shoulders with both his hands and pulled her toward him. Her legs slipped out of the way. She glided into his embrace and slid down on top of him as he settled back on the long couch.

She felt the ridge of his erection against her crotch and she smiled dreamily down into his close face, and then she kissed him on his lips, let his tongue dart into her mouth. She held his face with her hands and fingered the soft hollows behind his ears. He clutched her closer, reached with both of his hands to seize her buttocks, then slipped his hand under the waist of her skirt, under the silk of her panties, running his forefinger quickly down between her cheeks and slipping it inside her.

She gasped when he entered her anus and frantically she moved her free hand down his body, pushed her fingers between the buckle of his belt, flipped open the top button of his jeans, and dove her hand down under his shorts and captured his erection in her tight fist.

Connor was frantic trying to get her. She sat up, pulled her hand from his penis, and began to strip off her clothes. He grabbed her white cotton blouse and pulled it up over her head. She wasn't wearing a bra and when he moved forward to kiss her breasts, a wave of her perfume filled his nostrils. He took a deep breath and filled his mouth with her left breast.

Melissa was straddling him, had him pinned between her legs, and was naked from her waist up. There were no longer any lights on in the open living-room space, and what they could see of each other was from the moonlight, flooding the high windows and casting the whole house in ghostly white. Even she was aware that her body looked strange. It upset her, reminding her of the one time she had seen a naked corpse on an autopsy slab. She thought next of Adam's painting of the two women, embracing on the bank.

She wanted to get away from the moonlight, and she wanted to get off the couch. Adam might wake and come into the living room and find them making love.

"Wait," she whispered, "let's go there." She nodded toward the small loft, tucked under the cathedral ceiling.

Connor nodded, agreeing, and moved.

Melissa slipped off the sofa, picking up her white blouse. In the moonlight, the white cotton blouse looked eerie.

She held the blouse in her hands, clutching it to her breasts and not knowing what to do. And then she thought, This is ridiculous. She was going to make love to this man. She wanted him to make love to her.

She dropped the blouse on the back of a rocker, then pulled down the zipper of her skirt and stepped out of it. She was wearing black panties, which she hoped in the moonlight looked erotic. She glanced over at Connor, wanting him to watch her strip, and then turned slowly, so that he could see her in profile. He had taken off his shirt and she noticed the way his shoulders squared off his body. Seeing him partly naked took her breath away. All she wanted to do was give herself to him, to let him do with her what he wanted.

She stripped off her panties and walked away from him so he saw her back and bottom, knowing she had a perfectly pear-shaped behind, her only truly sensuous physical asset. She stepped to the kitchen sink and poured herself a glass of water. The red wine had dried her mouth, and drinking one full glass to quench her thirst, she poured another and took it with her, back to where Connor stood watching as she soundlessly walked toward him through the misty moonlight.

It was only when she was returning naked to Connor, thinking that she must look lovely and inviting to him, for he was watching her with the same look of wonderment, that she glanced at Adam's newest oil, still up on the tripod easel.

She saw Adam had depicted the two of them, her and Connor, in the act of sex. Painting them not with a brush, but a palette knife and thick paint. It was an impressionistic painting, but clearly Adam had wanted to show them coupling on the sofa. She was naked and on top of Connor and both of them were pawing at each other with hands shaped like jackasses' hooves.

"What is it?" Connor asked, seeing her startled face. He came quickly around to look at Adam's art.

"But we weren't making love!" Melissa exclaimed. "Goddamn him!"

She spun around at his closed door, then remembered she was naked, and rushed to the rocker and seized her underwear, crying in her rage and from her humiliation. "I'm going to get him up," she told Connor, slipping on her blouse, buttoning it as she headed for his bedroom. "Who does he think he is? I saved that child..."

"Easy, easy," Connor whispered, seizing her arm. He kept talking as he calmed her. "This isn't personal, Melissa."

That stopped her.

"What are you talking about?" She did not lower her voice. She did not care if Adam was behind the bedroom door with his ear pressed against the keyhole.

"The child is a genius!" Connor said. "That painting! All of his art! They are works of a genius. You're not dealing here with an ordinary kid."

"You're goddamn right I'm not! I can't take it! This was a mistake. My mistake. Okay, I accept responsibility, but he's going home—we're going home—to New York and I'm turning him over to the agency, let them find him a foster home, let them turn him loose on the streets, or return him to the institution where he came from. I've had it!"

"Melissa, Melissa," Connor begged, still whispering.

"Dammit, stop whispering! You think he's not listening?" She pulled from Connor's grasp to button her blouse, and reaching for her skirt, she turned away from him and slipped it on. She was crying again, but now it was from her own humiliation.

Connor waited a moment, letting her dress. Women, he had come to learn, were always less hysterical once they were dressed.

He wouldn't let her leave Beaver Creek, leave before he had even made love to her. He was furious at the kid for screwing it up. If she hadn't gone to get a glass of water, he would be fucking her at this moment.

And then there were the paintings. He stared at the one of them making love. He wasn't wrong about Adam's talent. He had enough art courses to realize the boy was gifted. What he had to do was get hold of all Adam's drawings. He had a contact in Washington. He'd call her, have the woman fly down to see what the boy had done.

Melissa finished dressing and turned to him. The tears were gone. She was too angry to keep crying.

He said quickly, taking another tack, "Melissa, you have a responsibility to the boy."

"Not any longer. The child is crazy," she said, accepting that fact. "And I'm crazy for trying to take care of him." She pointed toward the closed bedroom door. "My life is in danger." This time, she did lower her voice.

"I told you we could learn about him through his painting. The child is trying to communicate with us."

"Connor, I don't care." She stepped away, walked to the wall, and flipped the switch, turning on the high lights in the center room. Immediately the shadowy mist of the moonlight vanished. "Do you want a drink?" she asked, and not waiting for a reply, she went to where the bottle of red wine had been left open on the counter. She would have a headache in the morning, she knew, but she needed something to drink.

She reached for a glass in the open shelf and saw her hand was trembling. She would not be able to pour her drink.

"Connor, would you please get me a glass of wine?"

She began to pace the open space, walking past Adam's bedroom door, debating with herself whether she wanted to confront him, and then circling the butcher-block counter, walking by the long panel windows that faced the creek, walking fast, and feeling her stomach muscles tightening.

She was never any good in times of stress. It always paralyzed her. She just couldn't handle stress, and she knew why, too. It was her childhood; all those years of being carted around by her mother, never knowing where she would be living next, or who might her next stepsister or stepbrother be. Even now, thinking about her childhood, she started to tremble. She felt a square of headache building and she reached up with her right hand and squeezed her forehead, trying to force out her pain.

"Here," Connor said, cutting her off in front of the fireplace and stopping her pacing. "Look!" he said. "Listen to me."

Melissa took a glass of wine from him and widened her eyes, indicating she would listen.

"Let's separate your feelings about him for a moment, okay?" he asked, talking on his feet. "You've been bruised, and you're feeling hurt, betrayed even by his painting. But what's amazing, right, is that you and I were just sitting together on the sofa when he was painting, right? I mean, he imagined it, the two of us, you know."

"It doesn't take a genius to know what was about to happen. Adam could feel it in the air. Look, street people, street kids especially, they are damn good at reading a situation. That's how they keep alive in city shelters, where life can be real dangerous. I'm not talking about what he understands. I'm reacting to how he was depicting me, us, in his painting. He has no right...!"

"So what?"

"I'm a jackass, that's what."

"You know what surrealism is. Give this kid some artistic license."

Melissa kept shaking her head. She had set the glass of red wine down on the wooden mantelpiece behind her and folded her arms across her chest. She wasn't looking for Connor, but staring off, watching Adam's closed door. Her lips were pressed tight, and she kept working her mouth back and forth, as if chewing up the insides.

Connor started talking, telling her how he was convinced of two things: that Adam was an artistic genius and that he had to be encouraged and helped to develop his creativity. This was his only way to find his place in the world, Connor told her, saying Adam's painting would tell her about the boy's hidden life, and also it would be through his work that Adam would reveal his identity.

"You're on the verge of a real breakthrough," Connor told her, whispering again, leaning up against the fireplace mantel. "You're not only saving the kid's life, but you're also giving him a future. I'll help you. I have some contacts in the art world. Dealers, you know. I'll have a woman I know fly down and look at his stuff. We'll see if I'm right, but I know I am." He smiled nicely at Melissa.

"I won't have him making a fool of me."

"He wasn't making a fool of you, Melissa. Look, you said yourself that there was sexual tension between us. Okay, he picked up on it, just like he knew about the murders down at Buck's Landing. He's sensitive."

Melissa nodded, but did not respond. Connor might be right. The child could be telepathic. She had read about such people. That made her edgy again. She moved away from the mantel, as if by pacing she might shake her anxiety. She kept glancing at the closed bedroom door, wondering about him. She couldn't live like this, she thought, having him always on her mind, wondering what he was thinking. She'd drive herself nuts.

Behind her Connor was saying something more about his friend in the art world, someone he could telephone about Adam's paintings. She then decided to call Greg first thing in the morning and ask him what he thought.

"Okay," she said, turning to Connor, surprising herself with her quick decision, "let's talk about it tomorrow." She immediately felt better, knowing she could talk to Greg about her problem.

Then she stepped over to the easel and looked closely at Adam's painting, seeing it in bright light and realizing that she had been wrong.

It wasn't her and Connor making love on the sofa. Adam had painted her, she realized, but when she was just thirteen years old and when Roland Davis made her fuck him.

She spun away from the easel and ran to Adam's bedroom, pushed open the door and flipped on the lights. The room was empty, the bed was made. Adam, she saw, had slipped out of the house through the side window, disappearing into the mountain night.

What she did not know was how he knew she had been forced to make love to her mother's husband, there in Kansas, long ago, when she was just a child and terrified by the man who said he would cut out her throat if she ever told her mother what he did to her when her mother was off working at Sears and the two of them were alone in the rented house on Jefferson Avenue.

14

GERRY LEE WALKINS PULLED his state trooper vehicle off the Blue Ridge Parkway and into the overlook parking lot southwest of Beaver Creek. He needed to piss and was also halfway looking for a shady spot where he might park his car and sleep for a half hour.

The overlook was empty. There weren't even northern tourists with carloads of kids having lunch, or sitting up on the stone fence having their picture taken facing the Great Smoky Mountains.

He glanced west and caught a glimpse of Asheville in the far distance, at the opposite end of the long valley. The bright midday sun reflected off glass and steel, and far beyond the city, crossing the horizon, was the long stretch of mountains, capped with clouds.

It was a pretty sight, but he was sick of it. He was fifty-six years old and tired of mountains. All the hills bored him. He couldn't fathom why people drove up to gape and gawk. He thought next of the two women who had been found down by Buck's Landing. Well, the two gay guys won't be coming north again, that's for sure. He slammed the car door, locking it. He tightened his thick belt that carried his revolver, stick, and flashlight, and walked along the low stone fence to a small opening, a way for people to reach a few picnic tables set out on the grassy slope.

The highway crew had mowed the slope earlier that day, and he could smell the freshly cut grass. He liked the smell of mowed grass. It was about the only thing he liked about outdoors, that and the smell of pine cones.

But he didn't think he was ever going to like the sight of pine cones again.

"No, sir," he said, talking out loud and surprising himself with his own voice. He couldn't stop thinking of pine cones, thinking of how they had looked shoved up inside the two women down at Buck's Landing.

"Goddamn!" he said out loud, raising his voice and startling a few birds from the thick underbrush. He zipped down his fly and tugged out his penis, facing downhill so he wouldn't be splashed with his own urine.

He took a deep breath, blew a fart, and let go, closing his eyes and enjoying his pee. When he opened them again, he saw the old woman grinning at him. "Jesus Christ," he swore, trying to cut off his stream. She was downhill from him, less than twenty feet away, standing straight up, with her hands on her hips. She had grass in her gray hair, and there was more grass stains on her thin yellow dress and her bony knees. She kept grinning, her head cocked to one side.

"Where the fuck did you come from?" he mumbled, angry at the sight of her, angry that she had been there watching and he hadn't seen her.

She picked up her dress, still grinning at him, and exposed herself.

"Hey, you! Goddamn, put down ya dress!" he shouted at her, and turned around to hide his limp penis, which he couldn't get into his tight pants, and then he saw he had sprayed himself with his own urine, and a wet stain spread across his crotch, down the inside of his left leg. "Oh, Jesus H. Horseshit!" he swore, and moved again to walk up the hill, and his right foot caught on a buried branch, and stumbling on the uneven growth. He tried to regain his feet, but slipped on the soft damp earth, the thick bed of newly cut grass.

He tried to grab hold of something on the slippery slope, but couldn't find a hold and went rolling over, gaining speed on the slope. Fifteen yards farther down he hit a tree and that stopped him, knocking the wind out of him.

"Oh, shit," he exclaimed, grabbing his stomach. Pain was already shooting up his back. He was hurt, seriously hurt, and he knew that he wouldn't be able to get back to his car to call for help.

He opened his eyes and looked up into the bright sunlight, tried to shield his face but couldn't and didn't see who it was approaching him, standing over his prone body, though he knew it wasn't the old woman.

He spotted her out of the corner of his eye. She was standing below him still, so that they were almost at eye level, and a dozen yards apart. He saw her drop her dress and stop smiling. She was frowning, puzzled by something.

He turned his face away from her and was briefly blinded by the sunlight, and then saw who it was kneeling beside him, who had come to comfort him, there in the long grass with his back hurt and unable to move.

"Help me," he begged.

Mimi Segal was crying. She kept crying, kept telling her daddy to stop.

"My bottom hurts," she told her mother, doubling over.

"Alan, will you stop this damn car!"

"Where?" he shouted at both of them, throwing up his hands, and then he spotted the overlook sign, and raced the big station wagon to the inside lane, cutting off a semi, which braked and blasted him with an air horn.

"Ah, shut up," Alan yelled out, mad at everyone, especially his four-year-old daughter. They had stopped at a restaurant in Bristol less than an hour before, and Mimi wouldn't go to the bathroom.

He hit the entrance ramp to the overlook at fifty-five. He was still traveling too fast when the station wagon shot into the parking area and he saw the white highway patrol car.

"Goddamnit," he swore under his breath, spotting the cop car. Behind him, his child was crying hysterically.

"Stop the damn car!" his wife shouted at him. He slammed the brakes and all three of them tossed forward, held in check only by their safety belts.

"Okay! Okay!" And then to his daughter who was already fumbling with the back door, "Next time, dammit, you go to the bathroom when I tell you!"

"Don't speak to her that way!" his wife ordered, opening the passenger door.

Alan felt a rush of hot air push against the cool interior. He tried to reach over and pull the door shut, but it was too far of a reach.

When he looked up his wife and daughter had disappeared, and again, as he often daydreamed on such family trips, he thought of just leaving them, driving off onto the highway, to be gone before they finished peeing in the woods.

The brief fantasy made him feel better at once. He kept staring at the parked highway patrol car and finally the reality of the car registered on him. No, it won't work. She'd be after him with cops, having this cop radio ahead to set up roadblocks.

Where was the cop, he wondered next, realizing the vehicle was empty. He reached down and touched the electric button and lowered his window. The day was silent.

He looked at the rock wall, wondering about Crystal and Mimi, and feeling a tinge of apprehension. The two of them were taking too long, he thought, and debated a moment about getting out of the wagon and going after them. But the thought of getting up, going into the hot day, delayed him, and he thought how pissed off Crystal always got when he rushed her.

"Shit!" he shouted, needing to express his frustration about his life, his day, and having to stop in the middle of nowhere forty minutes after lunch.

"Shit! Shit! Shit!" he said quickly. The words disappeared in the heat of the day, the smell of the soft tar, the distant sound of traffic, a steady hum and then a swish of a speeding car on the expressway.

"Shit," he whispered a final time, and decided to get out of the tight seat. He opened the door, felt another wave of summer heat, and looked toward where the girls had disappeared, and saw something. A brief glimpse of someone. They were coming back, he realized, and waited for Crystal's red hair to pop into sight.

Then, farther to the right, he caught a glimpse of something else.

"What the...!" He kept his eye on the low wall, scanned its length. Someone was playing a game with him. It was Mimi, he realized, grinning.

But it wasn't his daughter.

"Oh, shit," he said, struggling to get out of the car, but realized his seat belt was still buckled. He fumbled with the belt, thinking: Why is that old woman wearing a cop's hat?

He kicked wide open the driver's door and grabbed the wheel, pulling up from the deep leather seat, but that was as far as he got.

Crystal Segal did not have to pee with her daughter, but she did have to take Mimi down the freshly cut grassy slope of the overlook and into the midst of the evergreens because Mimi was afraid someone might see her, someone in a passing car.

Crystal sympathized with her daughter. She was just as nervous when it came to public bathrooms.

Still, she didn't like tramping through all the weeds and wildflowers to find a hidden spot. Crystal kept searching for poison ivy, having no idea really what to look for, fearful, too, that Mimi might get bitten by a deer tick, though she wasn't sure Lyme Disease had come that far south.

That's all she needed, she thought.

"Okay," Mimi announced, pulling up her panties. She was grinning.

"Your father is right," Crystal said at once, "next time I want you to use the bathroom before we leave a restaurant. No more of this behavior, understand?"

Mimi, feeling better and wanting to escape her mother's voice, ran ahead, easily climbing the steep hill.

"Honey, be careful. Don't go running off!" Crystal shouted after her daughter, who had reached the low wall and slipped through the opening, disappearing from sight.

Crystal stopped to catch her breath. Her head hurt from the exercise.

"Dammit, Mimi!" she shouted after her daughter, but concentrated on the climb, forced herself to keep moving. She would stop at the top of the slope, she told herself, sit down and catch her breath.

She made it without stopping, and grabbed hold of the low rock walk. Mimi was already running across the empty parking lot, running toward the station wagon.

Crystal saw Alan had opened the door. She thought next, Why would he do such a thing on such a hot afternoon. Then Mimi began to scream. She screamed and held her face and fled backward, never taking her eyes away from something Crystal could not see.

"Oh, God," she whispered, running for the car. Alan was dead. He had a heart attack. And she thought next: Where could she get help? She spotted the lone white police car and immediately felt secure.

Mimi kept screaming. Her screams filled the day, were louder than the speeding parkway traffic. The screams had a life of their own. They kept building and building, becoming shriller and shriller. And then just as suddenly Mimi stopped screaming and Crystal, running across the hot tarmac, saw her daughter vomiting onto the black tar.

Crystal fell forward, reaching the station wagon. She hit the hood with her hands and singed both palms on the hot metal.

"Ouch," she cried, pulling away, stumbling around the front of the big car, trembling with exhaustion and fear, and grabbing the driver's door to see what had happened to her husband.

Alan was slumped down in the front seat. His short fat body wedged between the wheel and the floor with his left foot stuck out the door. His pants leg was pulled up and exposed his white leg, his thin yellow silk sock.

She looked from his brown tasseled loafers to his new summer plaid slacks, then to his enormous belt buckle wedged against the steering wheel and saw the stain down the front of his clothes. It had darkened his pink Lacoste shirt and drawn flies. She never saw his face, nor his milky cheeks.

She saw his neck, saw that the thickness of his throat had been sliced as if it were just the wet belly of salmon, cut open with the entrails gutted, leaving a fat puffiness of chalky flesh, soaked with the blood that pumped steadily from deep within him, bubbling up like dirty sewage water out of a busted pipe.

15

"TELL ME, WHAT WAS it that frightened me when I was small?" Melissa asked. They were alone in the house. It was late afternoon and the house was hot. Melissa had opened all the windows and turned on the only fan Connor had, but the heat of the day was trapped in the high ceiling. He had made dozens of mistakes in the building, Melissa realized, and this was another. He had forgotten to ventilate the schooner-house eaves and on hot afternoons the house baked.

Adam picked up a black magic marker and drew a few lines on the paper, then he reached for another color and uncapped the marker. He was sitting across from her, sitting sideways on the couch. He was using the large pad of white paper she had given him, and had it propped up against his bare knees. He was wearing shorts she had bought for him at the Banana Republic, and a loose T-shirt from the crafts school. And he was barefoot. As the weather warmed, she noticed he never wore shoes, not in the house, nor outside. Adam was a child of nature, she thought, with satisfaction. Having him outside, gaining a tan, running barefoot through the trees, playing in the grassy lawn, all of that made her feel immensely better. She was responding like a mother, she realized.

Melissa did want to see what he was sketching, but the unspoken agreement between them was that Adam would finish his drawing before showing it. For the last few days, since he had drawn her secret thoughts, they had been playing this game of him sketching scenes and incidents from her childhood, though now, she knew, it was no longer a game.

Somehow he knew the secrets of her heart and could vividly sketch her hidden life, all her dreams and passions. It was as if she were looking at pages from her lost diary. He remembered her childhood, all the nightmares that she had trapped deep in her subconscious.

It was both frightening and thrilling. She was too afraid to question why she was probing the mute child, needing him to tell her the secrets of her life.

Adam held up the drawing, turning the pad so she could see it from where she was sitting on the other side of the piece of driftwood Connor had polished and finished and turned into a coffee table. Her own bare feet were propped against the table and she was holding a glass of iced tea in her hand.

Melissa stared at the drawing. It was a simple line sketch: an open window with white flimsy curtains blowing in a summer's breeze. Beyond the window, he had drawn a moon, several small stars, and the suggestion of an open field. She wasn't sure what it was. She was thinking how much the sketch reminded her of early Picasso, something the artist might have done as a young child.

Melissa glanced from the drawing to Adam. He was watching her with his same large silver eyes. He grinned, surprising her and showing his perfect teeth. He took back the drawing, started to sketch again. Melissa sipped the iced tea.

She was anxious. She sipped the drink, camouflaging her nervousness. She wondered if this was deliberate. Was he toying with her, making her sweat this deliberate routine of guessing to see if she could remember the secrets of her young life?

She tried to recall such a window, some incident from her childhood, but she had lived in so many places. Her mother was always picking up and moving on whenever she met a new guy who came into their lives for a brief moment in time, and then disappeared. She got very good at knowing when her mother was breaking up with some guy. She learned to recognize the signs in the sounds of their voices, how they became bitchy and mean to each other, to her, and then she always knew, even before her mother, when the boyfriend was spending less and less time with them. It hurt her, too, just as it did her mother, but unlike her mother she never let herself become too friendly, too nice, to the next man, knowing even as she met him that he wouldn't be in her life for long. None of them ever were.

Sitting in the rocker, her bare feet up against the smooth driftwood, Melissa felt her stomach tense, remembering herself as a child, knowing what was going to happen, how she'd have to leave school, leave new friends, and pack up hurriedly, with her mother in tears and shouting at her, cursing and smoking, and then go storming off in the middle of the night sometimes, just the two of them, racing out of town in the old Ford.

She remembered sitting silent in the front seat and staring ahead, out into the dark night with summer bugs hitting the windowshield of the speeding car. They were in Oklahoma or somewhere, one of those miserable flat Midwestern states, racing away. Her mother crying beside her, sobbing while she leaned forward and clung to the steering wheel, wiping away her tears as she concentrated on the black road, the quick, milky center strip. She knew her mother hated to drive at night. She wanted to ask, Why hadn't they waited 'til morning? But her mother was never nice when she busted up with a boyfriend. So Melissa sat silently, clutching the one toy she had that was most dear to her, the small brown teddy bear given to her, she was told, by her real father.

She curled down in the seat and slept, and when she woke it was bright and sunny and hot in the car. Her mother reached over to caress her cheek and told her they were in Texas and they had to find a motel and get something to eat. She knew she'd be left alone, locked inside the small room to watch daytime television while her mother went off to find work, to start a new life in another town.

Adam stopped drawing and turned the large pad so Melissa could see. He had completed the sketch. He had used the other magic markers, the green and red and blue ones, adding color to the first line drawing, adding shade and depth of field. Melissa marveled again at the child's talent, then she concentrated on the work, searched for the meaning of this innocent view of an open window, a warm spring breeze blowing the white curtains. She leaned closer, saw how he had shaped a green lawn beyond the window. She was looking out, as if she were a child perhaps, waking early to run to the window and see what kind of day it might be.

She realized next it wasn't a green lawn, there beyond the window, but a swimming pool at night, lit by the ghostly green lights floating up from the depths. It was a motel pool, she saw, and there was a dark shadow deep in the still water.

Melissa searched for the one detail that would trigger her memory. She had so many memories that were locked deep in her subconscious, sealed away and forgotten.

"What is it?"

He kept staring at her. It was as if he was only meant to reconstruct the memory. This bizarre link between them—his memory of her past life was all that he had. She had to remember and understand her own life.

Melissa stared at the puzzle, concentrating on the dark shadowy depths of the pool. The line appeared to shiver in the turquoise water. She was a swimmer, she gradually began to see, alone and late at night. She had slipped out of her room, she remembered, she had gone out to take a midnight swim in the deserted pool.

It had been hot all day, the dry heat of the Southwest. Where were they living? Was it still Texas? If so, she would have been nine, almost ten. She had learned once to keep track of her circus life by matching states with her birthdays.

It had been so hard to remember when she was this young. Her mother kept moving. One year she had been in six schools, six towns. Nothing was ever right for her mother. It got so that Melissa refused to unpack. She kept her clothes in one suitcase, and when she grew out of a dress or wore through jeans, she threw them away. There was no thought of saving anything. No place to store anything old or treasured. They lived out of the suitcases that they kept in the trunk of the Ford.

Yes, she remembered, this was Texas. Amarillo, Texas. Her mother had found work in the office of a wildcat oil company and started to date Ralph. She remembered the smell of the man when he came around the motel to pick up her mother. The man was clean-shaved, and wore shiny boots and jeans, and he smelled of oil.

All of Amarillo, Texas, smelled of oil. She hated the smell. It was only when she was deep beneath the surface of the pool, down near the green bottom lights, that she felt she could breathe fresh air.

She was nine years old and they were staying in two rooms of the Bushland Motel. It had a swimming pool and two color televisions, and a small diner where she went after school and charged Cokes and hamburgers.

Melissa smiled. All of it came back to her in a flood of memory. Why had Adam drawn this sketch, she wondered, not feeling any anticipation of dread.

She concentrated on herself swimming in the pool. She had loved to swim. It was the only way she found of escaping the heat of West Texas. Day and night, she was in the pool. There was no lifeguard, no one to watch her, not when her mother was at work, nor when she went off "searching for a beau," as she put it, smiling at Melissa, winking with her long false eyelashes, asking, "Ain't I lookin' pretty, honey?" She'd stand at the open doorway of the motel room and blow a kiss, then disappear, locking Melissa into the small rooms with the plastic flowers, the two prints of sailing ships, the color TVs.

Melissa learned to listen to her mother's heels on the sidewalk, to hear her feet crunch against the gravel of the parking lot, and then the roar of the Ford's engine as she pumped the gas, tooted the horn good-bye, and sped away into the Texas twilight, going off in the distant, dark night.

Even before her mother had sped away to seek a boyfriend, maybe a new husband, Melissa had pulled off her cotton dress and, wearing her swimsuit, slipped out through the bathroom window at the rear of the run-down motel, dropping onto the hard ground and running barefoot to the pool. After nine there was never anyone in the pool, and swimming alone, she'd pretend she was a dolphin, diving deep to the green bottom, where the paint was peeling, and where, when she turned over and looked up through her own bubbles, she saw the faraway, glassy surface, the turquoise light, and the West Texas night.

She tried to kill herself once in the depth of the small pool. She fought with herself to open her mouth, to gulp, to let her lungs fill up with the smelly chlorinated water, and then, terrified, she had fought her way to the surface, burst up into the hot night, coughing and clinging to the pool ladder. She couldn't kill herself. She couldn't escape the loneliness of her life, and she clung to the side of the pool, crying in despair, not understanding why she was so unhappy, thinking only that no one in the world loved her.

It was the beginning of her new life. She pulled herself up onto the cement, still hot from the day's heat, and sat in the dark, letting the water drip from her slim body. She was alone in the world. The thought clicked in her mind and made perfect sense, like solving a math problem at school. At once, she felt better.

At that moment, she now realized, her childhood had ended. She got out of the pool and walked back to the room, back to watching television, back to bed, back to reading *The Little Prince*. Knowing she had no one made her life suddenly seem easier. It gave her focus. She no longer was waiting for someone—her daddy she guessed—to come save her.

She wouldn't waste her time seeking help. Her mother couldn't help. Melissa was alone and that was just the way her life was. No need crying over another lousy lover, as her mother always said when she packed them up and took off, leaving another man, another job, and taking, as she always said through her tears, "the fastest road out of this asshole town."

Melissa had forgotten Adam. She pulled her attention away from the swimming pool, the open window. Her memory felt as if it were zooming away, as a camera does, pulling back.

Melissa was again aware of the living room of the schooner-house, of where she was sitting with the cup of tea. She felt the heat of the day, and the mucky dampness of the creek. She saw Adam. He had gone back to his sketching and she spoke up, telling him to stop. He glanced at her over the top of his drawing. She shook her head, saying, "Adam, please, don't draw anything, okay?"

She forced a smile and sat up, needing to move, to get away from her memories. "Oh, God," she sighed, standing. "Why don't you go out and play?" she suggested, moving away from him, and seeing he did heed, as always, her instructions.

"I think I'll get dinner started." She tried to sound enthusiastic, though all she wanted was to go up into her small bedroom loft, to curl down into her pillows and wallow away the late afternoon in self-pity.

But she didn't. She was thirty-three years old, not a teenager. And she had a child to care for. She opened the refrigerator door and stood a moment in the icy coolness, staring at the leftover foods.

She wished again that there was a Chinese restaurant somewhere in the mountains. What kind of a place were these hills without a Chinese restaurant? She would buy a wok; she'd cook Chinese at home.

"How 'bout meat loaf?" she asked Adam, reaching for the ground meat, then glancing back through the open space she saw he was gone. The long, open space was empty.

"Adam?"

The child was like a ghost, she thought.

The phone rang, startling her, and she rushed for it, angry that the silent pace of the schooner-house was interrupted by a ringing phone.

"Hello?" she said, letting her annoyance show.

"Melissa? It's me...Connor...Sorry. Did I wake you?"

"No, I'm sorry. I'm a...little jumpy." She glanced around, as if half expecting Adam to be sneaking up on her.

"What's the matter?"

"Nothing's the matter! I'm...a little jumpy, that's all." She stopped speaking. How could she explain it all to Connor? Adam's drawings, her memories. Besides, she wasn't sure she wanted Connor to know. "What's up?" she asked, shifting the conversation.

"Where's Adam?"

"I don't know."

"Oh, shit!"

"I mean, I don't know where he is right this minute." She glanced around the room, feeling guilty, as if she were a bad parent. "He was here a minute ago. I told him to go out and play while I made dinner." She kept explaining herself.

"He's been with you?"

"Yes, he has. When I got back from school this afternoon he was here or, rather, outside. Why? What's the matter?" She felt her insides clutching up.

"I just heard on the CB coming back to my place that there were people killed up at the overlook on the parkway. They're not saying much. One was a cop."

"Oh, God." She leaned against the wooden beam that divided the kitchen from the living-room space. It could have been him, she thought. He was all alone, all afternoon. "You think it was him?" she whispered. All of her memories of the Texas swimming pool vanished with the thought that Adam was indeed a murderer.

"I don't know..."

"That's what you're implying." She was furious at him, angry that she was led to doubt the boy.

"Come on, Melissa, we know about Adam. His drawings. What are you getting off about?"

She thought of his drawing, of herself as a child swimming in the Texas pool. She turned around again in the kitchen, stretching the cord to see where the boy had gone.

"See if you find out anything," she asked.

"Okay, I'll call."

"Connor, wait! What are you doing later, tonight I mean. Would you like to come over for dinner; we're having meat loaf." She tried to sound up herself, but realized she was inviting Connor because she was afraid of being alone with Adam.

"Sure, when?"

"Oh, I don't know. After your class, I guess. Eight o'clock?" She glanced up at the wall clock and saw it was already five. Daylight in midsummer misguided her. She couldn't get a fix on the time.

"Eight o'clock, then."

Connor hung up the telephone and reached over to turn up the volume of the CB he kept on his kitchen counter. He watched a moment as the light scanned the channels, searching for a voice. The radio, however, was strangely quiet, and that interested him. Something was going down, he knew, and he wondered if he should take the long way over to the crafts school and check out the overlook, then the girl called from the bedroom, wondering if he was coming back, and he remembered the woman, and opened the frig, and from the freezer section took out a small jar and walked back to the bedroom, picking up a teaspoon as he left the kitchen.

"What took so long?" she asked, sitting up. The waterbed was on the floor, in a bedroom full of secondhand furniture and building tools. There were two horses and an unfinished door being used as a desk, on which sat a new IBM computer. The computer and a Black and Decker electric saw were the most expensive pieces of equipment in the room.

The woman's breasts were exposed and Connor looked at them without interest, thinking that less than an hour ago he couldn't take his mouth from them.

He sat down on the bed, but away from the woman.

"I was listening to the CB," he said, unscrewing the top of the small jar.

The eyes of the woman widened, seeing the jar. "My friend," she said, grinning.

"There's been another murder," he told her, matter-of-factly.

Her eyes never left the cocaine.

He knew the students at the crafts school had heard about the women down at Buck's Landing, and what had happened to Glen Batts, and Royce Brother's sheep.

He told her more about Glen Batts as he spread two lines. He told her how Glen had butchered his family, and watched her eyes. He saw the fear seep through her. He enjoyed it, getting her scared. Then he told her more about the women at Buck's Landing. He didn't tell her how the women had been mutilated, or how Royce Brother's sheep were cut up, but still, when he finished his story, she was clutching the top sheet.

"You just said someone else was killed?"

Connor nodded toward the kitchen. "I heard it on the CB. A cop was killed and some tourist. He had stopped with his family, you know, to look at the scenery." He took a drag on the line of cocaine and jerked his head back, waiting for the rush.

"Oh, my God!" she whispered, her eyes bright.

"It's okay," he said quickly. By that night, he knew, it would be all over the school about the murders. He wondered why he had told her.

"Are we safe?"

"Sure." He grinned, feeling the joy of the cocaine flood his mind. He touched her under the sheet. He wanted to have sex again, and he handed her the second line, saying, "Hurry."

"A maniac is killing these people!" she said, staring out the windows. There was nothing to see but trees. He had built the house into a grove of white birch, saving all the trees he could, and positioned the building so it appeared as if a giant boulder had come to rest among the grove.

"No, they're unrelated. Coincidence, that's all." He crawled up beside her and thinking he might have made a mistake by telling her.

He told her another story, this time of when he was living in Japan, studying pottery from an old master. It was not a true story, but something he was making up, of how a whole village was going to be killed by a rival town because his pottery master had stolen the formula of an ancient pottery glaze. The woman was a potter and she appreciated the value of a rare glaze recipe.

Telling the story, Connor did not know how it would turn out. He lay back on the mattress, staring at the unfinished beams of the bedroom ceiling, watching the late afternoon light create patterns of light on the high, exposed plasterboard, and weaved the tale as he talked. The coke made him expansive, creative, and he remembered he was getting another shipment that week and he'd be sending the "ice cream" north in his next pottery shipment. He thought of all the cops prowling the hills, looking for the killer, and that made him nervous. To keep from becoming paranoid, he plunged back into his story.

The girl had settled down beside him, watching him intensely with her chocolate brown eyes. He moved the story along, filling it with small details, the background information on Japan, so that it seemed possible and not a lie itself.

He told her how the old man had been publicly accused and that he had gone back to his pottery shed and killed himself, for the shame that he had brought the village.

"Some say, you know, that I should kill myself, as I was his student," Connor whispered. They were facing each other on the pillow. He was concentrating on her small mouth, how it opened like a perfectly round dark hole, and then he touched her, just letting his fingers graze her cheek. He moved his hand lower, pushing away the sheet, finding her breasts.

"Did he do it?" she asked, her eyes widened by the drug, by the way he was touching her.

"What?"

"Did he steal the glaze recipe."

Connor shook his head.

"And he killed himself anyway!"

"It's the tradition."

"Oh, darling," she whispered. She closed her eyes, feeling his fingers.

He often wondered if it were his stories or just his voice that so overwhelmed women. How did he make them comfortable and submissive? Was it his only craft? He found he could have any woman he wanted as easily as centering a mound of wet clay on a pottery wheel. The effortlessness in which he seduced women had begun to bore him.

He reached over and slid her beneath him with one hand, tossing away the sheet with the other.

"Oh," she asked.

Connor already had his hands on her hips, positioning her under him.

"Please," she whispered.

He looked away so he would not laugh in her face, and thought at once of Melissa and what he would do to her that night, and that aroused him, heightened his interest in the woman beneath him, and now he wanted her.

Tyler Donaldson had brought his electric guitar and, plugging it in, began to play, though the small white clapboard church wasn't half filled, and there was still a good hour before sunset.

Reverend Littleton never started services before dusk, but Reverent Littleton was gone from them, as was Sam MacCabe, Tyler thought, and no one was there to direct him, or the congregation. He took it upon himself, knowing that night when he pulled into the churchyard that the Lord was with him.

The doctors in Asheville had said it was his heart that had killed Sam MacCabe, talked about him having a busted artery, but Tyler knew better. Every one of them in the New Land Tabernacle Church knew better.

Tyler kept playing softly, looking out at the congregation as they filled the pews, nodding hello to friends and neighbors. Tyler was a happy man. Tonight, God willing, they'd all be going off to meet their Maker. He looked down at his old guitar and sang out:

"Folks, get ready, for He's callin' you
Children, get ready, for He's callin' you
Women, get ready, for He's callin' you
To sit on the throne of JE-sus!"

From out in the congregation, a chorus of soft voices picked up the old hymn, and sang:

"Away in Sweet Heaven,
Away in Sweet Heaven,
Sisters and brothers, get ready when He calls you
To sit on the throne with JE-sus!"

Tyler quickened the beat of the mountain tune. He saw his cousin Ralph come in with the wooden box and set it down before the small pulpit. He saw the congregation stare at the old box, and he sang louder to hold their attention.

"This world is nothin' but troubles,
This world is nothin' but sorrow,
This world is nothin' but sorrow and troubles,
But tomorrow we're in heaven with JE-sus!"

Tyler stood, left his place at the back of the small platform, and approached the crowd. He felt the heat of the congregation, felt the pulse of his people. It was like singing at Bayler's, down in Asheville, he thought, though here there was no odor of stale beer. Here the evening air was clean and cool, a breeze off the mountains.

The others had joined in singing, and he kept playing faster, harder on his guitar.

"We'll be singing in the morning, sisters
We'll be singing in the morning, brothers
We'll be singing in the morning, all together
A-sitting on the throne with JE-sus."

Jeannie McCallister swung out of the pew onto the smooth,

polished floor in front of the platform altar and began to dance. She was alone for a moment, swaying gently to the sweet church song. She had hold of her dress hem, and as she stepped closer to the wooden box, she dipped and curtsied, then danced off.

In a moment she was joined by Sara Henning, and the two women danced in each other's arms, danced like girls in the high school lunch hall. Jeannie was taller and younger than Sara, but she didn't slow her quick step, nor open her eyes.

Tyler moved closer to the microphone attached to the pulpit, using it as he sang one last verse:

"Mother, get ready when He calls you
Mother, get ready when He calls you
Mother, get ready when He calls you
To sit on the throne of JE-sus."

Tyler glanced over at his cousin Ralph and signaled the small man to pass the jug of water and strychnine, to get on with the service, now that Jeannie McCallister was committing herself to God.

He reached into his back trouser pocket and pulled out his Bible, slipping it open to the Gospel of Mark, and read into the microphone, "In my name they shall cast out devils; they shall speak with new tongues; they shall take up serpents; and if they drink any deadly thing, it shall not hurt them."

The jug of strychnine was passed into the midst of the congregation, going swiftly from hand to hand, each one of the faithful taking a small swallow, committing themselves to the Bible's word.

"We are here without our brother Littleton, without our brother MacCabe," Tyler told the crowded church, "but God is with us all."

"Lord have mercy!" shouted the faithful.

Tyler kept strumming as he spoke, kept one eye on the two dancing ladies, and shouted next into the microphone, "We are ready to go to heaven, dear Jesus, come take us from this evil world."

"Praise JE-sus!" shouted back the congregation.

"The Spirit is with us!" Tyler told the people.

"Amen!"

"And we are with the Spirit! Sister Jeannie is with the Spirit!"

"Amen!" shouted the faithful.

Tyler nodded to his cousin, motioned for him to push out the wooden box. The small man shoved the small box and it went spinning across the polished floor, spun around in the center of the church.

Jeannie McCallister was on it at once, dizzy from her twirling, and feeling the Lord's power. She let go of Sara's hand and knelt behind the box, reached down and lifted the wooden top, smiling up, for this was the first time she had been the handmaid of the Lord.

Behind her on the platform, Tyler started another quick dance tune, livelier now, and as he played, he called out, "Do you see that the Lord God Almighty is amongst us!"

"Yes-s-s," the answer came back to him.

"Can you feel the Lord God Almighty?" Tyler asked, answering them with a roar into the small microphone, making it crackle with his voice.

"Yes-s-s!"

"I see 'm!" Sara Henning shouted, dancing in a tight circle around the wooden box. Her eyes were closed; her arms were stretched high over her head.

"Are we saved and ready to go?" Tyler asked the church members, all of whom were on their feet, stomping to the steady hard beat of his electric guitar.

"Yes-s-s-s," came the answer.

"Jesus Christ is our God and has prepared a place for all of us," Tyler told them. "Look toward the sun. Our Lord is coming in a rage of fire."

The evening sun did flood the side windows of the hilltop church. It was brilliantly orange and red, and burst through the windows, touching the congregation.

"We are all sinners," Tyler shouted, "and if you think you ain't, then you ain't comin' to heaven with us."

"Amen! Amen!"

"All of you who ain't sinned are liars and fools and you better get right with God," Tyler told them. He had stopped playing the guitar, but his voice caught the rhythm of his music, and it seemed as if he were still singing to the congregation.

"Some of you say you don't got good clothes. Some of you say you ain't got enough to eat. But all of you who have confessed and drank the bitter water, you are ready to meet your God. Evil all around us," Tyler shouted, "in the hills. On the street. Right beside you on your seat."

"Yes-s-s, amen, amen."

"Sister Jeannie!" Tyler instructed. "Take up the serpents and cast out the devils in our lives."

Tyler Donaldson struck a deep chord on his guitar and the sound screeched through the little church, cut into everyone's eardrums. He reached over and spun the volume knob. The amp, he realized, was getting feedback.

Jeannie McCallister lifted the heavy gum-tree lid of the old box and exposed to the bright lights of the church a nest of timber rattlers. There were over two dozen, curled together like a tightly knit ball of pretty thick thread.

"Praise JE-sus!" Tyler shouted.

"Lord have mercy," came the chorus reply.

"Come and be saved," Tyler demanded, picking up his strumming as the snakes moved, lifted their delicate heads, and one after another, in slow and graceful moves, slithered their four- and five-foot lengths from the deep warm box, dropping soundly to the waxed floor.

A woman screamed in the midst of the congregation. It was a scream of ecstasy that thrilled the faithful. Others began to shout, to pound their feet in clogging step on the hardwood floor.

More voices rose in a collective hum, as if they were calling up the timber rattlers. No one was watching the snakes. The congregation had their arms raised, their eyes closed, and swayed to Tyler's music, which now was coming fast, hard, and shaking the clapboard church as he sang:

> *"We'll be singing in the morning, sisters*
> *We'll be singing in the morning, brothers*
> *We'll be singing in the morning, all together*
> *A-sitting on the throne with JE-sus."*

The timber rattlers swept across the waxed floor. They moved swiftly, slipping between the legs of the faithful, curling up against the walls, rattlers clicking. Some raced the length of the center aisle seeking the cold softness of the damp earth outside. More moved into the pews as if seeking someone to strike, slithering over shoes, rubbing on trousers and overalls, slipping over the bare feet of children, the bare legs of mountain women.

Jeannie McCallister reached into the box and seized the last snake. Its weight surprised her, as did the thickness of its body. She was surprised, too, by the coolness of its smooth V-band–marked skin. She had never held a snake before, not even as a child.

The snake curled and arched, gripped its lengthy body around her wrist and arm, and arched itself. The small diamond head turned, swaying in the attempt to stay aloft, and the rattler opened its pink mouth. The lower jaw unhinged as the rattler bared its white puffy gums. The red tongue hissed and the snake struck, digging its fangs into her pretty cheek.

Jeannie McCallister dropped to her knees, still with the long rattler wrapped about her right arm. The snake struck again, catching her in the mouth, its teeth clamping like staplers onto her lower lip.

She fell over onto the floor without a sound, as if a spike had been driven into her face, letting go of the rattler. The snake curled up her arm, across the smooth arch of her neck and through her hair, slipping away as swiftly as a bird in flight, its silky skin brilliant as it slipped through her long, loose blond hair.

Adam seized the snake when it touched the floor and the congregation saw the bald-headed boy for the first time.

He held the snake behind its head and pinched the flesh with his thumb and forefinger, as if to squeeze the life from the reptile. The pressure exposed the rattler's throat, the pink mouth. The snake hissed and a spray of venom arched from the open jaw and shot harmlessly across the floor.

He dropped the long rattler into the deep wooden box where it curled defensively into a tight ball. Then, kneeling, he softly tapped the wooden floor of the church and from across the room, from out of the cool dark edges of the clapboard building, and from among the crowded pews, the timber rattlers returned, summoned by the mysterious signal. They curled around the high wooden box, then one after another, the serpents returned to the wooden box, sliding over the edge, dropping inside and twisting themselves into a nest of vipers.

Adam slammed the box shut and fixed the crude latch.

The music had stopped. Tyler Donaldson stood behind him, his guitar loose, his left hand clutching the shaky pulpit. The faithful had stopped humming. They had lowered their arms and opened their eyes. They stared in wonder at the boy.

And then came one last timber snake from a dark corner of the church. It moved fast across the gleaming polished floor, its rattles singing as it sped from the wooden box. It was shorter than the others, and slim, as thin as a pencil.

Adam reached down when it touched the wooden box, lifting its finely shaped head a few inches off the floor, searching for the opening. Adam seized the snake with his thumb and forefinger, but instead of dropping the last rattler into the box, he took it in his mouth. Then with his perfect teeth, he bit into the slick flesh, bit the head off in one sudden bite, tossed the bleeding and curling snake away, and spit out the venomous mouth. The tiny exposed mouth lay beside Jeannie McCallister, who was already stiffening from the fatal venom.

16

GREG SCHNILLING FOUND THE phone message when he came back from lunch. There was a number and a name, Detective Nick Kardatzke. The word *important* in the message was underlined and his secretary had added that Greg was to call back ASAP.

"Shit!" Greg said, staring at the note. Then he picked up the phone receiver and dialed the cop, who wasn't there. He left his name and hung up.

Greg opened up his lunch from the deli and started on that, as he read Katz's column in the *News* about the game with Philly the night before. A game that he had seen with his young son. Thinking of his son, and the game, and how excited his boy had been, about being out alone with his dad late at night, made Greg smile. He bit into his sandwich as the phone rang.

It was Nick Kardatzke calling, shouting over the blare of subway traffic.

"I'm sorry I can't hear you," Greg said after a few minutes of trying, "I think we've got a bad connection."

"No, we don't. Hold on, willya."

Greg heard Nick shouting to someone, telling them to shut the "goddamn fuckin' door."

Greg went back to his sandwich, and was finishing a sweet pickle when Nick returned to the phone. The subway noise was gone.

"Look! We got a problem here," Kardatzke told Greg.

"Who's we? And whom am I speaking with?" Greg asked, angry at the man's attitude. He would never get used to New Yorkers, he knew.

"Is this the Child's Care Center?" Kardatzke asked, sounding put out and bored at the same time.

"You're speaking to Greg Schnilling. I'm the Acting Deputy here, yes," he replied.

"You took a kid in there a month ago. A John Doe, couldn't talk, right?" Greg heard the man shuffling through papers, and then he asked over the phone, "I spoke to someone named Vaughn. Melissa Vaughn?"

"That's right," Greg said calmly. He leaned back in the chair and propped his legs up on the desk. He was looking away from the office, looking out the window, where he saw a slice of the sky and the bright windows of a high rise across the street. It was all going to come crashing down around her, he thought.

"She's no longer with the agency, right?"

"She's on personal leave," Greg answered carefully.

"What about that kid . . . the John Doe?"

"Pardon me?" Greg swallowed.

"What happened to that kid? The city doesn't have the paperwork on him. I called welfare myself. There's no file, nothing in the files, except from Metro-North."

Greg knew what he should say, knew he should be able to pull up a file number on the computer and tell the cop that the feral child had been assigned to a temporary foster home, then was moved to a state facility. He should have been able to give the cop a file number and a paper trail and send the man on his way, if they had done it all by the book, if Melissa hadn't gone crazy about the boy.

"Well, he did have a name," Greg answered truthfully. "We found a name 'Adam.' Someone, his mother I presume, had sewed a name tag into the boy's underwear. We put a photo out on the computer and nothing turned up. So, what is it? Have you found another boy?" Greg leaned back in the office chair and ran his hand through his hair, feeling his own perspiration dripping down his underarms.

"No, I don't think we have," the detective said slowly.

Greg felt his insides tensing, trying to guess if the man's slow deliberation was some sort of cop ploy.

"We got the remains of a naked body over at the morgue. We found him a while back in the tunnels, under Grand Central."

"Yes?"

"A kid about fifteen maybe, maybe older."

"I'm not sure I follow you, Lieutenant," Greg said, frowning, baffled by the cop's question.

"The kid we found. We did a computer search...using his teeth. A file turned up." The man spoke slowly, carefully, as if verbally closing in on Greg. "Seems he's got a long rap sheet. Male prostitution, drugs. We found maybe twenty-five grams of crack shoved up his ass. He's one of maybe a couple kids we found this way. Some dead. Some crazy. All of them nameless.

"Except this kid," he added then. "I guess a few years back when he was in school, he got fingerprinted. We've got a match on him." The cop paused, as if he wanted to make his story dramatic, then he said, "His name is Adam Chandler and he's from Tom's River, New Jersey. The father came in 'bout an hour ago and claimed the body."

"Jesus Christ," Greg whispered.

"That's right," the detective went on in the same level voice, "so who's this 'Adam' that you have. And where is he? I'd like to try and have a chat with him."

"I don't know," Greg whispered. He thought immediately of Melissa, of listening to her crying on the telephone. "Jesus Christ," he whispered. He had to get off the phone and call Melissa.

"I'd like to talk to that boy," the cop said again.

"Wait a sec!" Greg sat straight up in his chair. "Do you think our 'Adam' killed this boy for his underwear?"

"I've seen it done for less."

"The kid can't talk."

"We'll give it a try. Where is he?" the cop asked.

"Well, you caught us at a bad time. A couple people off on vacation," Greg said quickly. "Our computers are down. I mean, I'll have to do a paper chase on him. I'll give you a call later."

"I'll come over. Maybe we can jack that system of yours."

"Who are you anyway?" Greg asked next, realizing then that this cop wasn't responding the way New York cops did.

"Narcotics," Kardatzke answered bluntly. "We've got a special team dealing with this interstate shit. Pull up what you got on this 'Adam.' I'll send over a uniform."

"Wait . . . !" Greg started to say, then realized the cop had hung up. He sat for a moment with the disconnect sound ringing in his ear. He hung up and sat back in his chair. Staring out the window, stunned by what the cop had told him. He knew he had to telephone Melissa to warn her. But what was he warning her about? That the New York police wanted to question her about Adam, or that she might have with her a boy who had been killing kids under Grand Central?

Melissa reached for the telephone and dialed New York. She was calling Greg on his direct line. His phone was busy and she hung up, telling herself she was a fool, calling him this late on Friday. It was already after six.

She missed having him around, of being able to tell him what was bothering her. She knew she would never take Greg away from his wife—she would never wreck a family, not after what her life had been—but it made her angry at times, especially on long weekends in the city, to know he lived only ten blocks from her, and that he was married. Happily married with a family.

"No!" she said out loud. She would not bother Greg. She couldn't just go calling New York every time she felt tense or upset about Adam and her life in the mountains. It was her decision, she reminded herself for the thousandth time, to leave the city and go off with Adam.

Thinking of Adam, she glanced at the sketch he had done that afternoon, the one of her in the pool in Texas. She had thumb-tacked it to the living-room wall, adding the magic-marker drawing to his bizarre collection. She remembered he had taken his sketch pad with him to go sit on the backyard rock after Connor had called. She stepped over to his room and glanced inside, looking for the large pad, and saw he had left it out, tossed it onto his bed. She stood in the doorway staring at the pad, deciding whether she had the courage to open it, to see what else the boy had drawn.

She was afraid of being caught by Adam, of having him know that she, like any mother, went through his private things just to learn about his secret life. It made her feel lousy, but she couldn't help herself. She rationalized it by saying she needed to understand him, that the boy was disturbed.

She walked into the shadowy front bedroom and, without disturbing the position of the sketchbook, lifted the cardboard cover. The inside page was blank. She smiled to herself, amused by her own nervous reaction, and the fact that her fingers were trembling. He hadn't drawn anything while outside on the rock, she thought, but to make sure she thumbed through the thick pad until she did spot another drawing.

Melissa slid her forefinger between the heavy white sheets and flipped open the pad. The sketch was upside down and she didn't want to move its position on the bed, so she stepped around the bed, going farther into his room to see what he had drawn while sitting behind the house.

He had used charcoal sticks on this hasty sketch, and she guessed he had planned to finish it later, after he came back inside. When he had left the house, he had only signaled, in the crude sign language that they had developed between them, that he was going off into the woods.

It made her nervous, as always, his disappearing from the house. She didn't know how to handle a growing boy, especially this one. Connor told her it was perfectly natural that Adam wanted only to explore the woods, but since the night he had come home with bloody hands, and with no explanation possible, she didn't know what to do with him.

If she had been a real mother, she though guiltily, this wouldn't be a problem. She'd know how to discipline him. It would have come with her through pregnancy.

She looked down at the drawing and saw it was a sketch of Crazy Sue, though the lines were minimal and only suggested the portrait of an old woman. Melissa reached over and switched on the bedroom lamp, and with that soft glow, she saw he had also drawn a country church behind the woman, and she realized the female figure, the Crazy Sue figure, was standing in a church graveyard.

She sighed, thankful that the drawing wasn't another of his lewd sketches. She closed the book, shut off the bedroom lamp, and went back into the living room of the schooner-house, where she heard Connor's pickup and then his friendly beep as he parked.

Melissa smiled, feeling immediately warm and special, and spontaneously, surprising even herself, she threw up her hands and danced lightly across the polished, smooth barn-board floors, spinning on her bare feet, just before Connor knocked on the side door and shouted hello.

"Adam has been drawing sketches of me," she said when she saw him looking at the drawings that she had pinned to the wall. She had planned on telling Connor about the drawing, and also to tell him about herself, when she was a child living in two rooms of a motel in West Texas.

"It's another one of his phenomenal leaps into my mind," she explained, smiling, amused even at herself for accepting what Adam was able to do, how he knew her mind, read her thoughts.

She told Connor what the painting meant, showed him the dark wavy line deep in the blue-green water. And then she told him about herself, how her mother would leave her at night, and how she swam deep down in the cool water, escaping the heat of West Texas, escaping as well her own terrible childhood.

"I grew up that summer," she told Connor, "in ways that a child doesn't when she's in the middle of a big loving family. I became real tough, and for a while I was in lots of trouble. I was picked up once in Bushland. That's the town we lived in. I was caught stealing magazines from Snyder's." She frowned, suddenly depressed, and she blinked to keep from crying.

"You haven't told Adam any of this?" Connor asked. "I mean, are you sure this is you, these little squiggly lines?" He looked from the drawing to Melissa, frowning at her conclusions. Connor wasn't sure he was even seeing a Texas swimming pool, let alone a young Melissa Vaughn swimming alone late at night.

"This was the color of the pool after dark that summer," Melissa answered, remembering the way the water looked from the motel window.

"And you accept it all?" Connor asked, letting his puzzlement sound in his voice. "I mean, that Adam is able to recall your life?"

Two days before, when Adam had done an oil of people making love, she had been in hysterics, crying at a memory of being raped by her stepfather. Now he had the sudden insight that she had fabricated such a recollection, that she was involved in some elaborate psycho-drama with the boy.

"He's done others," she answered quietly, not responding to Connor's disbelief. "He has recalled other events of my life. I can't explain it." She gestured to the oil-color painting he had done of Buck's Landing. "And, of course, he somehow knew about how these women were killed by their boyfriends."

"That's not a great painting to leave hanging around."

"Why?" Melissa looked at him.

"I mean, there was a double murder over there, and this kid's got an oil painting of it"—he jabbed his finger at the oil, raising his voice—"and he's painted the river running red with blood."

"There's no need to shout."

"I'm just..." He gestured, implying that it was all beyond him, that none of it made any sense. Already he had the feeling the evening wasn't going to end up as planned. He wasn't going to get Melissa Vaughn into bed, and he wasn't sure he wanted to. He had been involved with a crazy lady once before and had nearly gotten himself killed.

"Connor, I'm not crazy," she told him, reading the expression of his face, and upset by his assumption.

"I never said you were."

"I can see it on your face. Look! I admit Adam is strange. He looks strange. He might even act strange. I know all of that. But I also knew when I first saw him back in New York that he was a wonderful child who had been fucked over in life, and he deserved a chance. But I also know—and if I didn't believe it, I'd be out of here—that Adam isn't a killer."

She kept talking, needing to defend Adam, needing to defend herself, forcing Connor to realize that Adam wasn't involved in the death of the two women at Buck's Landing. "He's extraordinary," she told Conner. "He's telepathic."

Connor went to her and put his arms around her as she continued to defend Adam, her voice rising. He pulled her into a tight embrace. He was aware of her body, the softness of her body. But beneath her flesh, he could feel the strength of the woman. She seemed small and slight from a distance, but holding her, he knew how tough she really was. He also realized he was comparing her to the young pottery student that he had slept with that afternoon. She had been eighteen or nineteen and had the body of a child.

"Melissa, I didn't mean to suggest anything," he told her. "I only wanted to make sure a lot of unnecessary attention isn't drawn to you and Adam because of his painting, that's all." He smiled, knowing his smile always worked with women.

Melissa nodded. "I guess you're right. Perhaps I should put it away...But I don't know why."

"Because you want to take care of Adam, that's why." And then he thought how bad matters might get if the cops and highway patrol were to swoop down onto his property looking for the kid and found the marijuana he was growing out back, between the rows of vegetables.

"Okay, I'll put them away," she agreed. "But no one comes to this house anyway."

"You never know. Someone might stop by looking for me." He tried to make it all sound rational.

"There's nothing wrong with Adam."

"I didn't say there was."

"You think there is." She pulled out of his arms, measuring him with her eyes, watching his face.

"You said yourself he looks a little weird."

"There's a waitress up at Bonnie & Clyde's who can't do enough for him. She thinks Adam is wonderful!"

"You mean Lucy?"

"The thin one with the dyed-blond bouffant."

"They just arrested her for trying to kill Clyde. Didn't you hear?"

"How would I hear?" She was stunned by the information. "What happened?"

Connor shrugged, looking off. "Well, the cops were there yesterday morning and Clyde told them about Adam, 'this bald-headed boy' sort of shit, and Lucy got all over him for picking on her church and everything, and she just jumped up in a frenzy and jabbed Clyde with a kitchen knife."

"My God," Melissa whispered, thinking how the mountains were full of violence.

"Clyde was telling the cops about the Tabernacle Church,"

Connor went on, "and how they were waiting for this 'chosen one' to come to take them to Kingdom Come."

The breath went out of Melissa. She had a clear image of the half-drawn charcoal sketch of the church that Adam had done.

"Connor, come here," she instructed.

"What?"

"He might be with those church people you're talking about. I found this sketch. It shows Crazy Sue, or whatever her name is, standing in a cemetery, and there's a church behind her, and..."

In midsentence, she veered away from the kitchen counter and walked into Adam's room and grabbed the big sketch pad off the bed and brought it back to the kitchen, opening it on the butcher-block table.

"That's it," Connor said matter-of-factly, "the New Land Tabernacle."

"Dammit!" Melissa felt the pain of a headache press against her eyes. "What do you think?" she asked, and for the first time since coming to the mountains, she felt an enormous sense of helplessness.

"We go find him."

"Where?" She glanced at once toward the kitchen windows that faced the hillside behind the house and realized with surprise that darkness had settled over the valley.

Connor tapped the charcoal sketch. "Here. That church has services at night."

Connor raced his pickup to Simon's Ridge. The old truck roared up the last of the ridge and raced onto the top of the hill where cars and trucks were parked at random in the dirt yard of the white clapboard church.

They could hear music as soon as Connor shut off the engine. They sat a moment looking across the yard at the small white church, all lit up, a bright spot against a hillside of trees. Melissa said in a note of surprise, "It's pretty."

"This is a serpent-handling church," Connor told her.

"You're kidding!"

"Nope, I'm not kidding." He pushed down on the door handle to get out and Melissa reached over and grabbed his arm, telling him she was afraid of snakes. "Well, don't be. We won't see any."

"What do you mean, we won't see them?" She was more alarmed than curious.

"They keep the copperheads and rattlers in a box, as I remember. I've only been a couple of times. Years back I had an aunt and uncle who were members of this place. The Bible says that you are saved when you take up serpents and drink poison, or whatever."

"I thought you said they believed in chosen people come to save them?"

"Well, yes, that's the local story. I don't know if they found that in the Bible, too, but it's something they believe. Look, they're all nuts. Let's go." She slammed his truck door.

"Is he here?" Melissa asked, raising her voice to be heard over the electric guitar. They had crossed the parking lot and were standing on the steps of the church, looking in at the crowded room.

"Yeah, there!" Connor pointed, then took her arm, moving her forward.

Melissa shook her head.

"It's okay." he said. "I'm related to half of this crowd, remember."

She leaned closer and told him, "Don't take me near any snakes."

"I won't. I'm afraid of snakes, too. I ain't saved either."

The pews were empty. The congregation was crowding the front platform, dancing in the aisles. Melissa wouldn't sit down. She felt nervous in the church. She was an outsider and didn't want to interfere with their religion.

She searched for Adam, tried to spot his bald head among the dancers, but more than two dozen people—men, women, and children—were dancing to the fast country church music. In one corner she saw a woman slumped down, being cared for by several other women.

"They're getting out the snakes!" Melissa grabbed Connor's arm as she saw a man bend down to open a box. He calmly lifted out a brightly patterned snake.

She pulled back and Connor wrapped his arm protectively around her shoulders. The man grabbed four more snakes from the box. They dangled from his hands as he stepped into the center of the dancing congregation.

Then Melissa saw Adam.

The crowd had separated to let the man reach Adam, and she saw Adam accept the snakes, let them be draped around his bare neck.

"Connor!" Melissa tried to pull loose.

"Easy, he's okay."

"He'll be bitten. He'll die." She tried to break free of Connor's hands and go for Adam.

"No he won't. Nothing will happen." He had hold of both her shoulders.

It was already too late, Melissa saw. Adam had accepted the snakes and had begun to dance to the electric guitar. He stood in one place, quickly clogging to the country music. The snakes had slithered down his arms, twisted in a tight, thick snake collar around his neck, clung to his body as they raised their small diamond heads, hissing at the dancers who circled around Adam, now all ordained with the cottonmouths and timber rattlers.

Melissa backed away from the circle of dancers and, without explaining herself, turned from the music and the dancing and ran out of the small white clapboard church, leaving Adam with his new family of snake-handlers.

Crazy Sue had started to dance in the aisle when the bald-headed boy picked up the snakes. She stood at the back of the church, stomping her feet to Tyler Donaldson's music. She had wet herself earlier in her excitement and the pee had run down the inside of her thigh, but she didn't stop dancing.

She loved clogging music, loved the steady beat of heavy shoes pounding on the old floor, shaking the clapboard. There were others dancing in the aisle, and more dancing on the raised platform.

Tyler had picked up the beat of his electric guitar, and Mrs. Conley started with her tambourines. Betty Sue wished she could play the tambourines, but she knew they wouldn't let her, and she knew, too, she was lucky just being inside the church, dancing at the rear.

And then thinking of that, she glanced behind her to see if Rufus, too, had crept in from outside, from where he always sat during church meetings.

He was there, grinning at her through the open window, and

she stuck out her tongue, then looked up front again, where, in the middle of the floor and surrounded by dozens of people, the bald-headed boy stood.

He was dancing with the snakes. A timber rattler in one hand, a copperhead in the other. The snakes' heads were raised, their mouths open. Betty Sue grinned at the bald-headed boy, and holding the hems of her dress, she skipped up to join the circle.

Betty Sue couldn't stop dancing. Nor could the others. She reached the inner circle around the bald-headed boy, who was dancing, too, and grinning at everyone. He held up his hands, letting the snakes curl down the length of his white arms.

Betty Sue hated snakes. She had hated snakes all her life. When she was in school, the boys would come after her with rattlers they found curled under rocks.

They would stick the snakes down her dress, or put a fat milk snake up between her legs, until the one day she had gone after them, hitting Davy Berlew and Jim Thompson on the head with a shovel she had found leaning against the shithouse.

Blood had flooded from both their mouths and noses and that had frightened her more, and she had to run with Rufus into the woods and lived there three days until old man Armstrong caught her stealing vegetables from his garden.

After that, her aunt Mary Lee said she didn't have to go to school, and she didn't, though she missed singing with the kids. When she cried and told her aunt how the boys chased her with snakes, Mary Lee had scolded her, saying she was too old to be running around with children.

Now, dancing with the bald-headed boy, she wasn't scared of the snakes. She kept grinning at him, hoping he'd see her, smile at her, or something. No one ever smiled at her, she knew, and Rufus told her it was because she was too ugly. That wasn't right. Her aunt Mary Lee had told her God loved her, and didn't care if she had a brain or not.

Betty Sue had a brain, she knew, and when people made fun of her, laughing at her sometimes in church or when she went down into the valley to shop with her aunt, she'd just shake her head and let everyone hear her brain rattle, just the way a timber rattler sounded before it raised its ugly head and struck.

The snakes that the bald-headed boy had wrapped like thick twine around his skinny white arms were holy ones, she knew, and they wouldn't hurt her. She closed her eyes and listened to the music, to the sound of all the heavy clog shoes stamping the wood floor.

She wasn't allowed to dance at home, even if really happy music came up on the radio. Her aunt hit her when she caught her dancing. Sometimes she danced anyway when she was out in the woods, when she'd crept up behind the boat-house Connor Connaghan had made.

She'd dance there in the dark and watch him and his women fucking on the barn-board floor. Betty Sue grinned, thinking about it, how she'd dance away in the dark while watching them all buck naked on the wooden floor.

She opened her eyes. The bald-headed boy was coming at her, grinning, peeling off one of the timber rattlers from his white arms.

Behind her, in the doorway of the small building, over the happy sound of all the music, she heard Rufus screaming, telling her she had to touch those slimy snakes if she wanted to fly away to heaven in the bald-headed boy's chariot of fire.

The bald-headed boy held out the snake. She did not look at its raised diamond-shaped head, but kept her eyes fixed on the milky underbelly.

No one stopped dancing or singing. She listened hard to the music, wanting to escape into the sound, to disappear down its lovely noise, but the bald-headed boy wouldn't go away, and when she looked again, he had stopped grinning.

She saw he was looking real mean to her, as if she had done something wrong, and she knew that next he'd hit her, as people always did. She didn't want to get hit or sent out of church. She was having fun, dancing, singing, feeling the excitement of everyone around her, being with all the people and not having to sit outside in the dark with Rufus and only watch the praying and singing from the cold outdoors.

She closed her eyes and reached for the slimy snake, feeling the puffy underbelly. The long snake grabbed her hand and wrist, curled its scaly body up her arm.

She screamed.

Aunt Mary Lee screamed.

She thought of how once she had kicked over a rock in the woods and a diamondhead had raised its head and spit at her.

She tried to shake the coiled snake from her arm. She opened her eyes and the timber rattler leapt at her again. She saw the wide mouth and flashing bright red tongue, felt burning pain in her face. She screamed and swung at the soft fat body with her free hand, grabbing at it. The snake bit her hand, dug its fangs deep into her flashy palm.

Adam grabbed the old woman by the hair, pulled her off her feet, and with his other hand seized her arm and stopped her from thrashing the rattler. He squeezed the snake beneath its open jaw and the rattler's jaw popped open, its long fine fangs retracted like needles from the old woman's flesh. Two small streams of blood jetted from the teeth wounds, and the blood flowed into Betty Sue's open hand.

Adam let go of her long, tangled hair and the old lady slumped down. He stood, took the rattler into his arms. The long snake curled down next to the warmth of the boy. It found a nest in his folded arms.

With his eyes, Adam motioned that someone tend to Crazy Sue. The congregation stopped dancing and Aunt Mary Lee pushed through the crowd.

Spike Harlem announced, crouching beside her, "She's a goner."

"No, she ain't," cried Mary Lee, and she slapped her niece across the face. "Get you up, girl!" the thin woman demanded.

Adam placed the rattler in the box and closed the lid, then he went back to Betty Sue, kneeling close to her face. He put his lips to the old woman's mouth and blew breath into her lungs. He did it twice in quick succession, and the woman's legs jerked. She kicked out and thrashed her arms, still trying to rid herself of snakes.

"Jesus Almighty," Tyler Donaldson called from the platform, "Jesus Almighty, the Lord is with us!" He began to play, frantic to fill the small clapboard with music to honor God's spirit.

"Oh, dear Jesus Lord, be my staff,
Oh, dear God Almighty, be my staff."

Around the church, the faithful joined in, dancing to the steady rhythmic beat of Tyler's music. They formed a circle around Betty Sue and Adam, holding hands as they kept clogging, moving swiftly in the tight space in front of the pews.

Adam held Betty Sue's face in his hands. He pulled her off the floor, pressing his thumbs against her high cheekbones. The woman's eyes popped open and she stuck out her tongue, grinning.

"Amen!" Tyler shouted into the microphone. "Amen, and God love ya."

Betty Sue kept grinning, kept her eyes on the bald-headed boy. The pain was gone from her face, and she was thinking that now she would go to heaven with the boychild in his chariot of fire. She kicked out her heels, and just for a moment, she turned her head toward Rufus, who was still looking in through the open window, but he had gotten hold of the snakes, the timber rattlers and the cottonmouths, and had twisted them together into a thick round nest.

She screamed at her brother. Her voice rose over the electric music, and she pulled loose from the bald-headed boy and pushed through the circle of dancers, running after her baby brother, who had disappeared through the open window and was running off into the woods, carrying under his arm like a live football the thick nest of mountain snakes.

"When I was thirteen, I had one of those religious experiences," Melissa told Connor, "you know, like Jimmy Carter. I was born again."

They were back at the schooner-house, sitting together in the dark living room. Connor had the lights off inside the house, but turned on the outside floodlights, so they could see the woods behind the house, see the small creek and the huge boulder where Adam liked to sit.

"I was saved," Melissa went on, "or whatever it is that Baptists say. I was even baptized in a lake. The whole ball of wax. For two or three months, I felt just great! I had this new, extended family, all the faithful of the Second Baptist Church of South Kansas City. They were my people. My folks.

"Then I began to go a little nuts. I had scruples about everything. I would stand up in church on Sundays and confess my sins and all my secret desires. The more I confessed, the more sins I had. I was driving myself crazy.

"I remember the minister, a Reverend Jim McCaffery, trying to console me. And there were church women, too. They came out to see my mother at the trailer camp. We were living in Kansas City again, this was after Texas, after the period of the drawing of me in the pool that Adam did.

"Mom was living with, and planning to marry, Roland Davis. That's why she never believed that he came on to me. I mean, she couldn't believe it, otherwise, how could she marry the asshole, and, you know, she was getting on in years, she hadn't been dating anyone when he came along. She was a pretty desperate woman, when I think about it."

"So don't think about it," Connor suggested.

Melissa stared at him a moment, then said calmly, "I think about it all the time. It's my life. How can I not think about it?"

"You can think about your future, for christsake." He sighed, weary of her histrionics.

"I'm sorry I'm boring you." She stood up.

"Melissa, look! I'm sorry. I didn't mean that. I just don't think you should get yourself depressed about events that you've lived through long ago, that you've triumphed over, really." He tried to smile, to entice her again with his looks.

"The point I'm trying to make is that I understand this need of Adam's," she told Connor, continuing into the kitchen. "His need for some sort of religion, however strange. He wants to belong, you know, to a family of some sort. It was the same with me. I'd get up in church and confess about my mother's boyfriend coming on to me. 'Course I thought it was my fault. That I was leading the poor son of a bitch into sin or whatever."

She stopped at the counter to fill her mug with more red wine, and walked across to stand in front of the unlit fireplace. She leaned against the wooden mantelpiece, holding the cup of wine in both hands, and looking out the windows. From where she stood she could see the thin mountain creek.

Connor had focused a spotlight where the water came out of the trees, and in the darkness, the bubbling water was silvery, like thousands of small fish cascading down the slope and disappearing into a dark pool at the base of the hill.

"I was simply looking for help," Melissa continued. "I wanted these people in the Baptist church to be my family, to take me away from the trailer park, take me away from Roland Davis. But they wouldn't believe me, about what Davis was doing to me." Melissa looked over at Connor. Her eyes were shiny.

"I grew up. I learned in Texas that I was alone, all alone. Understanding that was a comfort to me. At least I didn't have to pretend or dream I was living a normal life. In Kansas City, I also learned I didn't have a family. Not in the trailer park, not with my mother, nor at the Baptist church. You understand, don't you?"

Connor couldn't take his eyes off her body. He was thinking about her body all the time she was leaning against the mantel, watching the way her breasts moved under her thin fabric top. His mouth was dry, thinking of making love to her.

"Connor, are you listening?"

"I'm listening! I'm listening!" He pulled himself up, as if to attention, and said at once, "I'm trying to understand why you're still upset by all of this. Look, we all have shit lives."

"Are you that insensitive?" she asked from the mantel, then walked toward him, continuing, "How would you like it if someone you're responsible for, your son or daughter, were handling snakes, jumping around like a goddamn crazy person?" She splashed red wine on her hands and realized her whole body was trembling.

"Melissa, hey, these people may look crazy to you, but they're serious, believe me."

She leaned into his face and told him, "They'll kill Adam!"

"They've been handling snakes for centuries. It's not some fad, you know. It's their way of proving that God loves them and will protect them. It's an act of faith."

"Adam doesn't believe that bullshit."

"How do you know?" Connor challenged her. "You think they're all hicks and hillbillies, poor white trash, all 'no'counts,' right? Well, let me tell you something, sister. They know what they're called in sociology books. The 'undesirable poor.' That's it! And they know they're uneducated, live in poverty, and pick their noses and whatever in the most beautiful part of the country that ain't worth shit to them.

"But they also have this one trick up their sleeves. They believe in the Holy Spirit. They believe they can be saved and go to heaven, just like the next guy. Heaven is waiting for the undesirable poor, too."

"Yeah, I know." Melissa picked up her mug of wine. "They're all going to heaven in a fiery chariot." She wouldn't back off.

"Give me a break! Give me a goddamn fuckin' break! What harm does it do, handling snakes, believing that someday a goddamn 'chosen one' is going to come down to Beaver Creek and take them off this hellhole of a mountain?"

"Because they're doing it with my Adam. They think he's the driver of the goddamn fiery chariot, that's why."

"Hey, we're talking about something else here!" He jumped to his feet.

Melissa pulled away, frightened at once by Connor's sudden anger.

"First off, he's not your son!" he told her, pointing his finger. "Second, you're angry for another reason. You're upset because Adam has gone off and found some friends who have taken him in. You're jealous of these people, Melissa."

"Bullshit!" She turned from him and walked deliberately to the windows. Connor continued to lecture.

"You see this situation as parallel with your life, how you went into a goddamn Baptist church in Kansas City to find a family and they wouldn't help you with this Roland Davis. You're mad because Adam is doing the same thing, only he's got a faithful family. Not you!"

"That's unfair and untrue."

Connor thought of something more to say, how it was only natural for a teenager to want something else beside her, that the boy might simply be curious about this world around him in the hills, but he kept quiet.

Melissa turned from the windows.

"Of course I think they're all strange up at that church," she told Connor, her voice lowered, "holding rattlers, drinking strychnine or whatever it is, and believing a 'chosen' boy has come to whisk them off to heaven. Who wouldn't think so? But Adam, I know, has lived through worse than these people. I can only imagine what he's been through down in those New York City train tunnels."

She pressed her lips together, nodding, and came back to where Connor was sitting on the sofa. She sat down beside him, weary from arguing. "I'm worried about something else, and that's what has gotten me over the edge."

Connor shifted around and set his drink down on the driftwood coffee table. He was curious again.

"He knows things, Adam does. He knows about me. I don't know how or why. And he knows about these people getting killed down by the river." She shook her head. "He's so strange. He frightens me." She was whispering and the fear registered in her voice. "Watching him up there at the church, I realized how much I didn't know about him, but at the same time, he knows so much about me. He knows everything that he shouldn't know."

Melissa shook her head and pressed her lips together. "Maybe he is the 'chosen' one. What do I know!" She laughed, sounding helpless.

The telephone rang, startling them both.

"Should I get it?" Connor asked.

"I'll get it," Melissa said, needing to show Connor she was capable of taking care of herself. When she picked up the receiver and said hello, she realized she was holding her breath and expecting the worst: that someone was calling to tell her Adam had been bitten by one of the snakes and was dying. But it wasn't more trouble. It was just Greg, calling her late at night from New York.

She smiled at Connor, signaling that there wasn't a problem, and kept grinning.

But Connor, watching her, saw the smile fade on Melissa's face. He thought how different she was when she smiled. He wondered if she was just sullen by nature, or if taking care of Adam had put her on an emotional roller coaster.

She fell silent on the phone. She was staring off, intently listening to whatever he had to tell her, not speaking, not moving. She held the phone with one hand, and had twisted the cord around the fingers of her other. But she didn't move. It was as if the information she was hearing had paralyzed her.

Connor debated getting up and going over to the counter, to stand near her at least, but he couldn't move. He sat watching as she sank into herself. She looked beaten and defeated by whatever she was hearing.

Unable to keep quiet, he asked, "What is it?"

She didn't respond. She stared off into the woods, running her free hand through her short black hair. She leaned her elbow against the tree post and wedged the palm of her hand against her forehead.

"I understand," she finally said in words loud enough for Connor to hear. "I'll meet you, yes." She stirred herself enough to reach for a pencil and jot down a few numbers. Saying good-bye, she hung up the phone and finished writing.

"What is it?" Connor asked again.

Melissa did not look up from her writing.

"That was Greg Schnilling. My friend from work. The police called him earlier today, asking about Adam."

"And?"

"A body was found in the subway."

Connor kept frowning, waiting for her explanation.

"When Adam was found in the subway all we knew about him was his name. Adam. We only knew that because 'Adam' was stenciled into his underwear. We weren't able to find any evidence of a family. Not in the city shelters or the subways."

Melissa nodded toward the phone.

"Greg just told me the police found the remains of another body. A young boy Adam's age. The body was found in the subway, too. A naked body. And there were drugs on the kid. A device of some sort full of crack was shoved up his ass."

Connor broke into a sweat. "Oh, shit," he whispered, stunned by Melissa's matter-of-fact way of telling him.

"They were able to identify that kid," Melissa continued calmly, "because when they did a computer search of the boy's fingerprints, they turned up a name. He's Adam Chandler, and he's from some-place called Tom's River, New Jersey."

"Then who's this Adam? Your Adam?" he asked, feeling his skin tighten.

Melissa shook her head. "He's not Adam Chandler, that's for sure. We were wrong about him." She moved back into the middle of the big room and paused, as if not knowing which way to turn, what to do next, and then said softly, with resignation, as if speaking to herself, "No, I was wrong about him."

"What's this friend of yours going to do, this Greg?"

"He's flying down here in the morning. I have to go to Asheville and pick him up."

"And?" A thought had swept across his mind: It was all a trick, a way of getting at him. Adam, her, all of this bullshit about the paintings. They were setting him up!

"Greg is coming here to help me," Melissa answered calmly, feeling enormously relieved. "He's going to take me home."

And then she smiled, and began to sob.

17

THE BYOB PARTY THAT started every Friday afternoon after the last class of the two-week session had been going on for six hours, beginning with the volleyball game before dinner, then picking up again with the firing of the pottery kiln, and moving into Gene Martin's house, down the road from the main crafts buildings, where records and tapes were played, and everyone drank, got stoned, and danced.

Now at two A.M. the party was petering out. Only a half-dozen people were left on Martin's front porch. They sat in the dark, drinking what remained of the hard liquor, sharing joints, and telling stories of past summers in the mountains.

Trent Rhodes didn't want to be there. Trent wanted to go home to bed, but he wanted to go home with Lesley Moyers, and as yet she hadn't shown any interest in leaving.

Earlier, he had tossed off a suggestion while they were dancing, saying he'd walk her back to the dorm. She only smiled and said something vague about wanting to stay and enjoy herself.

The next morning Lesley was going home to Ohio. She'd pack up after breakfast and drive off the mountain and head west. A whole caravan of cars would pull out of the crafts school early, and he'd be back at work, cleaning the dormitories for the next group of summer students.

This was Trent's first year in the mountains. He couldn't afford to take classes at the school, but as a work/study student, he was able to pay his way by keeping the dormitory clean.

It was also the best summer of his life, for he had met and fallen in love with Lesley Moyers. At sixteen, he had never known anyone like her. She was a half-dozen years older, and she had a boyfriend, she said, back in Ohio. She had told him that when he confessed he was in love with her.

She hadn't laughed, as he realized she might when he blurted it out. They were sitting together beside the makeshift volleyball court, waiting for a game to start up. She was sitting with her bare knees pulled up, her head cradled in her folded arms, and she had said softly, "Thank you, Trent, I believe you really are." She had reached over and touched his face with the palm of her hand. Her touch had pierced his heart.

Now he sat in the dark of the front porch thinking of making love to Lesley Moyers. There were no stars, he saw, glancing up, but having sat outside all evening, his eyes had adjusted to the dark. He could see clearly across the porch. He could see Lesley. She was sitting sideways on the wooden bench with her legs curled up, the way she always liked to sit, and her head was turned sideways watching him. She had a very small, thin face, with perfectly formed lips and very small teeth. Her hair was brown and straight and she always let it hang loose, except when she was working at the wheel, or when it needed to be washed. He thought he knew just about everything about her.

She raised her head off her knees and focused on him. And so slightly, she nodded, indicating that she wanted to leave, and she wanted him to come with her.

In his excitement, he jumped up and toppled a bottle of beer.

"Easy, Trent, you're spilling the booze," someone warned.

"I'm off!" he announced, not looking at Lesley.

There was a chorus of good-byes and then Lesley asked, "Let me go with you, Trent." She slowly stirred herself from the bench, saying her good-byes.

"See you at the dining hall at eight sharp, Trent," Martin called after him. "It's changeover, remember."

"I know! I know!" On the dark path, Trent was already grinning.

"Night, everyone," Lesley called out as she skipped after Trent, hurrying, as if she, too, was in a rush to be alone with him. "Do you know the way?" she asked innocently, approaching him.

"No problem!" he told her, and his voice rose.

She came up beside him and without a word slipped her arm into his, leaning closer, smiling into his face.

"All right," she said softly, "show me." And ever so gently she pulled him after her, down the path and into the trees that stretched for half a mile between the director's house and the school.

He was aware only of the press of her body against his arm, the way her thigh brushed his leg. He could smell the dampness of the forest mixed with the scent of her perfume. His nostrils were filled with the sweetness of the woman. He found he couldn't breathe.

"Are you okay?" she asked.

"Sure! I'm fine. I'm great!" And he laughed.

Lesley had dropped her hand from his arm to take hold of his hand, to lace her fingers through his.

"How are you doing this?" she asked, sounding impressed. "I can't see a thing."

"I know," he told her, pumped up with pride. "See the crafts house," he said, pointing, and realizing he could not see his hand in front of his face. "Shit, it's dark out here!"

She giggled like another kid might and ducked her head toward him so his face was filled with the softness of her hair. He took a deep breath, his nostrils swimming in the scent of her shampoo.

He slipped both his arms around her waist and pulled her into an embrace, ducked his head so he could find her face with his lips. She responded in a rush, seizing his face with both her palms and diving her tongue between his teeth.

"Oh, God," she whispered, pulling away from him. "I shouldn't be doing this. Trent, you're just a . . ."

He pulled her back into an embrace, stopping her from talking, kissing her again, and holding her.

He was taller by two inches, and stronger, and his size and strength overwhelmed and surprised her. She gasped in his arms, weakened by his strength and from the force of his kiss.

She pulled her lips from his and dropped her head against his chest, asking softly, "Who taught you to kiss?"

"Come on," he told her, gaining confidence.

She followed him in silence as they walked ahead another hundred yards, and then stepped off the path, pushed back bushes, and stepped into a natural clearing of smooth grass.

"You're wonderful!" she told him, sinking with him to the matty carpet of grass. "How did you find this place?" With their faces inches apart, she grinned, asking, "Is this where you take all your girls, Rhodes?"

He couldn't talk. He was afraid to talk. He wanted only to take off all her clothes. He wanted to touch her body. To look at her. He was sorry there wasn't more light, a partial moon to let him see how lovely she'd look naked.

He pulled her into an embrace but she stopped him from kissing her.

"Is it safe here?" she asked, pausing to glance around, to look at the dark, deep wood.

"Sure, we're off the path. No one will see us."

"I mean, you heard about those two women..." The thought of what had happened to the women at Buck's Landing made her nervous at once, and she pushed her mind off them, afraid she would terrify herself.

Then, farther off, deeper in the darkness, she heard water. Over the sound of water, she heard a shuffle of dry leaves and she grabbed Trent's shirt, cutting her nails into his skin.

"It's a squirrel," he told her, "or maybe a rabbit. It's nothing. I'm from these mountains, Les. I know." He spoke calmly. "Listen!"

They were both silent and just as suddenly there was another rustle of leaves.

"See!" he said. "'You don't hear the woods when you're walking or talking, but squirrels and rabbits are out there, nothing serious. No bears." He turned her face back to him and kissed her lips.

She relaxed with his second kiss, let her body sway against him, let him hold her, and when he kissed her next, with more force and hunger, she broke away from his lips and asked, "You've never made love to anyone, have you, Trent?"

The look on his face told her he hadn't and she shook her head, saying, "I wouldn't be doing this if I had half a brain. I don't want to get arrested for corrupting kids."

"I'm not a kid!'

"Shhh," she pressed her finger against his lips. "I know you're not. I'm sorry. But you know what I mean. I'm six years older."

"I love you, Lesley," he confessed.

"I know you do, Trent. You're such a sweet, sweet boy." She kissed him very softly, and then pulled away and stared into his face.

She did not speak. She simply unbuttoned her blue shirt, holding her eyes on him while she pulled the shirttails from the waist of her jeans shorts. She wasn't wearing a bra and her small breasts were suddenly exposed, appearing like magic, a wonderful gift from her.

She watched the way his dark eyes widened and focused on her breasts. She stopped undressing and said, "Here."

She lifted his left hand and brought it to her breast, closed her eyes and caught her breath as his cool fingers touched her hot flesh. Her nipple hardened against his palm.

She wanted him, she realized. She wanted Trent not to want her. It made her feel guilty, knowing how easy it would be to love this boy, knowing, too, that she'd be off the mountains and gone from his life.

Now she was determined to make this moment perfect for him. She would give him something she had been cheated from having, a loving and tender first experience. She reached out and pulled the boy to her, buried his head in the shallow valley of her chest, shifted her breasts so he could suck both of her nipples. She closed her eyes, letting her desire for his young body take control of her good senses. It was not really wrong, she told herself. She was not taking advantage of him. She was giving him a gift, one he could look back on and remember after he had grown up and had other women. This was actually an act of charity, she thought, amused by her own rationalization. She reached to help him unzip her tight cutoffs and pull them down off her thighs.

"Wait," she asked, jumping to her feet.

Trent let go of her. He was on his knees, and when she stood, her panties were at eye level. She pulled off her cutoffs, tossing them away, and then paused, looking down at him, as she reached up and deftly unfastened her hair, letting it fall across her face. She stepped even closer and asked him softly, her breath catching, if he would finish undressing her.

Her panties curled down with his fingers, twisting into a tiny ball of cloth. She plucked them off, leaving herself naked.

Trent had never seen a woman's web of pubic hair and he was surprised by the width and breadth of the dark spot.

"You may kiss me," she instructed, moving her pelvis, and when he did kiss her, it was quick and abrupt, and she thought with a tug of disappointment that the next woman he slept with would benefit from what she was teaching him.

"Again," she instructed, stepping closer, filling his face with the triangle of her sex. He kissed her a second time, and this time his tongue reached out to lick her.

She dropped to her knees, and swept up with her desire, she grabbed his T-shirt and pulled it from his slight body. Caressing his flesh, her hands slipping across his shoulders, down his chest. He had a thin, sleek body, with no waist at all. She grabbed the buckle of his belt, and ran her small fingers down the front of his jeans, finding his erection.

"There!" she whispered, grinning in his face. She kissed him, licked his teeth with her tongue. "Now, how do you like this?" she asked, gently cupping his testicles.

"I love it."

"Okay, and now I'm going to show you the best part. A real treat!"

She used both hands to pull down his jeans. He would remember her, she thought, as she bent over him. Whomever he slept with for the rest of his life would have to match her, and the first time he had sex on the forest floor in a southern mountain. She bent over and took hold of his penis with her teeth, ran them gently down his erection. He came in her mouth.

They made love three times, quickly, and with few words between them. She did not need to show him what to do. He took command of their lovemaking after her fellatio. He was like a young colt, she thought. He could not stop, but her back hurt from lying on the damp earth, and she was growing cold. His endurance astonished and amused her. She wished they were in a warm bed where they could sleep in each other's arms and wake in the morning and make love again.

"I have to go," she told him. She kissed his face and slipped from his arms.

"No," he said, sounding hurt.

"Trent, darling."

"When will I see you?" He was on his feet, reaching for his clothes.

"You'll see me at breakfast."

"No, you know what I mean. When will I see you?"

"Oh, Trent, please! You know—I know—this was lovely and everything, but I'm leaving." She put on her blouse but did step back into his arms, briefly burying her breasts against his chest. She reached up and kissed him. "Don't spoil this, okay?"

He nodded, but he wanted to go back to the dormitory with her, to sleep with her in the small second-floor room. He knew where her room was, knew her roommate, Allison, too, and he guessed Allison was down at the swimming hole, on the late-night swim that always happened on the last day of a session.

"Good-bye," Lesley whispered. "I want to go back to the school alone."

"You'll get lost."

"Don't be silly." She buttoned her shirt and tucked the tails into her cutoffs. "Besides, I look a mess and I don't want everyone gossiping how we were in the woods together." She kissed him quickly and, looking into his eyes, told him, "This was very lovely, Trent, and I mean it. Thank you for saving my summer. You're the best thing that has happened to me up here."

"I love you."

She smiled, but her same sadness filled her face and Trent wanted to kiss her at once, to make her happy again. She held him back with the palm of her hand flat against her chest.

"I'm very fond of you, Trent. I won't forget you." And she turned and left him in the small clearing, finding her way quickly through the bushes and onto the path, and then in the dark, alone, she was frightened, and she broke into a run, running toward the brightly lit crafts house higher on the ridge.

Trent stood very still and listened to her footsteps. He could even hear her pushing through the bushes, then breaking into a run. He stood naked in the dark woods and wanted to cry. This was worse than never having made love to her. He could tell by the way she kissed him that she knew it, too. He felt shitty. He loved her. And he hated her for not loving him.

He reached down, felt on the forest floor for his white jockey shorts. He could not find them in the darkness, and he reached out with his toe, felt around.

"Shit." He was mad for not remembering to bring a flashlight.

Farther away, in the direction of the path, he heard something. He stood perfectly still. It was not a squirrel. The sound was too loud, too much breaking of branches. It was Lesley, he realized, coming back to him.

"Les?" he called and when she didn't respond, he thought, No, it wasn't Lesley. It was someone else, someone from the crafts house spying on them. That frightened him.

He dropped to his knees and swept out his hand frantically in the dark, feeling for his clothes.

"Goddamnit." He was angry about everything, about being naked on the grass, about hunting for his underwear. His left hand felt the coarse material of his jeans and he relaxed at once and pulled them toward him, but the jeans were caught and wouldn't budge. "Shit!"

He crept forward, holding the leg of the jeans and trying to guess if the pants had caught on a branch or a prickly bush. He felt the edge of the gully, where the ground slipped away, hidden by the underbrush, and slid straight down to the mountain creek. How could his jeans get there? Someone must have grabbed them away while they were making love.

He remembered Connor, and how the potter had watched them as they left the porch together.

He was going to kill that son of a bitch he promised himself, and then he felt a hand seize his right ankle. He kicked out, trying to pull free. His leg was jerked and he lost his balance on the slippery, wet grass.

He swore again, reaching down, feeling for the arm. He knew by the feel of the hand that it was someone small, a kid maybe, maybe a woman. And he knew, too, he could handle this son of a bitch, whoever it was, as he was jerked forward and dragged naked through the prickly bushes, and down the slope of the gully, and into the creek water at the bottom of the small ravine.

Lesley was thankful her roommate wasn't in the room. She stripped out of her clothes, pulled a clean short cotton nightie from her suitcase and laid it on her bed, then wrapped herself in a towel and walked down the hall of the old building, into the bathroom, which was barely lit and empty at three o'clock in the morning. She could smell Trent on her, and Allison would, too, once she got back from the swimming hole party. She needed to wash. She turned on the shower and stepped into the cold water. She thought of Trent Rhodes, of making love to him, and she was surprised she was excited again. She wished she'd let him come back to the dorm. Allison wouldn't be home, and they could have spent the night together. She felt a wave of regret. She deserved more than a one-night stand. And so did Trent.

She shut off the water and dried herself off before stepping from the small metal shower and going back to the bathroom, which was still empty. She walked out into the quiet hallway and to her room. She could hear music coming from downstairs, and voices and a few bursts of laughter. Students were sitting on the open front porch of the old building, she knew. Perhaps she should make an appearance.

She guessed everyone at the director's house would have noticed her leaving with Trent. If she made an appearance alone it would squash the gossip. But she didn't care what they said. In the morning all of them would be leaving, going off the mountain. She'd never see any of them again, unless she came back for another summer course, and at that moment she had no desire to return. She'd miss Trent, but not this place.

She walked in through the open doorway of her dorm room still thinking of Trent and found the boy there, the small bald-headed boy artist, sitting on her bed.

"What are you doing?" she demanded, clutching the towel to her body.

He looked up and smiled.

"Get out!" she told him, grabbing for her nightie.

The child did not respond, but she wasn't frightened. She knew she could handle the strange boy.

"Out!" she told him.

He stood very slowly, as if to follow her direction. He was barefooted and wearing cutoffs that she suddenly saw were hers. And he had taken the T-shirt she had purchased from the crafts store that day and was wearing it. It was a silk screen of Dick Rickler blowing glass, and had cost her fifteen dollars.

"My clothes!" she demanded, but the boy darted past her, out of the room, disappearing down the long dark hallway of the second floor.

"Damn you!" she shouted after him, throwing down her bath towel. She though of giving chase, but she knew the boy would outrun her. She could never catch him. And she was left, swearing after the boy. She would tell Trent about him in the morning. Trent would get back her clothes.

Betty Sue, hiding behind the dormitory door, had followed the boy out of the woods and up to the crafts school. He had been like a hound dog, she saw, crouching down in the dirt and sniffing the ground. He could smell her sex, the old woman thought.

She had followed him upstairs in the big house and waited while he stripped and put on the woman's clothes, first holding up the girl's short jeans and smelling them to make sure she was the one. Betty Sue grinned and wet her lips with a wipe of her tongue, watching him watch the young girl.

Betty Sue was perfectly quiet hiding behind the door, holding her breath, and keeping her hands on Rufus. She was afraid of what Rufus might do. He was acting real strange, now that he was running with the bald-headed boy.

Betty Sue closed one eye and peeped through the doorjamb. She saw the girl throw down the towel and pace back and forth in the tiny room, slamming dresser doors, talking to herself. Her hair was wet and loose and she kept stopping to rub the lengths of it between the folds of the towel. She tossed down the towel and reached under the narrow bed, pulling out a suitcase. Turning to the dresser, she grabbed a pile of folded clothes from the top drawer and dumped them into the open brown case.

The girl was mad, Betty Sue knew, and that made her nervous.

She was always afraid around people when they got mad. That's when they hit her.

The girl was naked besides. Betty Sue couldn't decide what to look at first, her breasts, the black patch between her legs. She had never seen a young girl like this, up so close. She always watched the crafts school kids from the dark woods. This was the first time she had come inside the building and gone to where they slept. It was the bald-headed boy's idea; she had just followed along with Rufus.

She looked down at her little brother. He had his good eye shoved against the crack, and was breathing hard. He wanted to do something to the girl, Betty Sue knew, and that made her excited. Her left leg pumped hard against the wooden floor. She bit her lower lip to keep from making more noise.

"Who's there?" Lesley demanded, grabbing her white terry-cloth bathrobe. She slipped it on without taking her eyes from the dark entrance to the hallway. Lesley had purposely left the bedroom door open, hoping one of the women would come back from swimming, or wherever, but now she realized the bald-headed boy was still out there in the dark watching her.

"Get out of here!" she told him.

She realized then that the sound was coming not from the hallway, but from behind her bedroom door.

"Who's there?" she asked, losing her courage. "Trent? Don't do this to me. Don't play games, please." Her legs and arms went weak and she braced herself momentarily on the wooden dresser, then grabbed a vase off the top. Allison had put water and wildflowers in the vase, and the flowers spilled out as she raised it over her head.

"Get!"

Betty Sue couldn't stop her leg. It thumped hard against the floorboard. Her bony knee banged the back of the bedroom door. She couldn't move, and Rufus had her pinned against the wall. He grinned at her, then peeped through the wide crack, watched the girl approach, come around the narrow iron bed, holding the vase high in her right hand, as her other hand reached for the doorknob of the thin pine door.

She had to run, Betty Sue knew. She had to get off into the woods with the bald-headed boy. She pulled loose from Rufus and shoved the door, hitting the girl and driving her back, out of the way.

Lesley broke the impact of the door with her raised right arm. The door, swinging into her face, smashed the pottery vase and hit her, sending her tumbling over the narrow bed.

It wasn't the bald-headed boy, Lesley saw, surprised by the sight of the gaunt old woman. Lesley realized the old woman was crazy, and at the same time, she saw the woman raise her arms, heard her screech, and saw her come tumbling over the bed after her.

She seized Lesley's wet black hair, pulled it between her bony fingers, and then with a strength and speed that surprised Lesley, the woman bared her broken and brown teeth and bit her neck as if it were nothing more than meat. Her rotten teeth broke Lesley's skin and popped open the left artery.

Betty Sue turned her loose. Lesley seized her throat, startled by the flow of warm blood running between her fingers. She spun away from the grinning woman.

Her head was dizzy from the shock. She gasped for breath and the blood flooded her mouth. She was worried she was making a mess, seeing how the blood sprayed the small room, splashed against the close wall as she spun around. She tripped and fell, aware the crazy woman was still there, dancing out of her way, hopping over the bed and keeping clear of the spraying blood.

Lesley tried to speak, to ask for the woman's help, and knowing, too, the crazy person wasn't able to help anyone, least of all her.

She wished she hadn't sent the bald-headed boy away, and finding the doorway in her blurry sight she fell forward, knowing there must be help somewhere downstairs, and aware, too, that she was naked and embarrassed by that. She reached the landing, tried to grab for the railing, but the old woman rushed her from behind, hit her squarely in the shoulders, and Lesley stumbled forward, tripped over her weak legs, and fell the long length of stairs, landing in a bloody crumple on the first floor of the old dormitory building.

18

MELISSA WAS WAITING IN Asheville, standing just outside the crowded Piedmont Airlines gate. Seeing her, Greg realized something else had happened since they had talked the night before. He could tell she had gotten very little sleep. The exhausted look in her brown eyes made her look at once younger and older, like a child who has been sick for a long time.

He went straight to Melissa and kissed her lightly on the lips, realizing that she had attempted to look pretty for him. She had put on lipstick and eye shadow, and she was wearing a bright summer dress. Kissing her, he thought: This was something he would never have done in New York, and also it was something he had wanted to do since he had first walked into her office at the agency.

"He didn't come home last night," she said at once.

"Okay, well, maybe he senses trouble. Street kids are like that. Let's get my bag, and we'll get out of here." He glanced up to see the sign for Baggage, and then casually, as if he had been doing it all his life, he slipped his hand over her shoulder and turned her toward the claim area.

He admitted to himself, feeling the slight pressure against his side, her suggestive surrender to his direction, that he was in love with Melissa Vaughn, and that he was going to leave his wife and children and marry her.

"How is Helen?" Melissa asked.

"Fine. I mean, she's upset that I had to leave town, of course."

"I don't blame her. We'll buy her something at the crafts school. They have lovely things in the shop." She squeezed his arm. "Thanks for coming down to help. I have no right, asking." She looked up at him. Her eyes were glassy with tears.

"It's okay," he whispered. "Everything is going to be all right." He kissed her a second time as they walked the length of the corridor, and this time his lips lingered. She turned slightly as they walked and pressed her hand against his chest to balance herself. She felt his heart pounding her palm.

Greg thought they were on another planet. He and she could do anything they wanted, behave as they always wished. No one there. No one was watching. No one cared.

They held hands waiting for Greg's bag, and did not talk. Melissa stared at the revolving rubber baggage track and mentally composed what she might tell Helen once they were in New York. How she would explain to this woman that it was all right for her to take away Greg. It all sounded so easy and logical, here in the mountains and far from home.

"You want to tell me about Adam?" Greg finally asked.

"Oh, God, I guess, I should, but..." She shook her head. "I don't know where to begin...and now he is missing."

She thought how much easier it was to think about Helen Schnilling, about how she was taking away this woman's husband, the father of her children, than it was to think or talk about Adam.

"Did you report that he was missing?" Greg spotted his single piece of Land's End luggage pop through the rubber curtain and come onto the moving track. He stepped closer to the belt.

"I didn't, but Connor...He's a friend. I rent his place. I told you about Connor. He teaches at the school. He said he'd stop by the sheriff's office this morning. The mountains are going crazy. There have been all these killings."

Greg glanced over, catching Melissa's eyes, but did not say anything. Melissa looked away, and immediately began to talk about Adam.

As they walked to the parking lot, she told Greg everything. She retold him about the Church of the New Land Tabernacle, and added the story of the snakes; seeing Adam holding a nest of them in his arms.

"Everything is so strange up here, I guess. I can't get a fix on what's normal. So when he didn't come home after church, I didn't do anything but wait. Connor was with me at the schooner-house."

"Schooner-house?"

"Yes, that's Connor's hand-built house. I rent it. It looks like a schooner. You'll see. Well, we started to wait for him, you know, to come home. He's always off in the woods. Connor says that is perfectly normal for a teenage boy. I don't know. But, Goddamnit, that's why I came down here in the first place, so Adam might have a normal life!"

She reached out and leaned against her van, sobbing suddenly, and Greg dropped his bag and took her into his arms and let her cry. She was so small against him that she felt as if she might disappear into his body.

She pulled away finally, and he handed her a tissue. As she dried her eyes she told him, "Last night was just the worst. We waited and waited. I couldn't sleep. And I had to leave at the crack of dawn and drive here."

"Where's this town?"

"About an hour northeast."

"How many miles?"

"Miles don't count up here. All the roads are narrow and twisting. You can't make any time. Come on, let's get started."

She was in a rush to get out of the hot airport parking lot and into the mountains. At least, she thought, it was cooler higher in the hills. She had spent less than a month in the remote town and already she had developed a dislike for the rush and crowd of the lowlands.

Greg drove to Beaver Creek. He did not talk about Adam, or what the cops had said. Instead, he did a quick survey of everyone at the office, while Melissa gave him hand signals, told him which way to go. She did not say anything until they were out of Asheville, and climbing the Blue Ridge.

"It seems so far way," Melissa said, thinking of New York, "and I've been here less than a month."

"A lot has happened to you here. Besides, this world is so different." He waved out the windows at the landscape. "It looks like the middle of the Depression," he added, spotting a clearing where two trailers were parked together and raised up on cinder blocks to make a house.

"Welcome to rural poverty."

"You can't hide it, can you? Even with all these green hills and mountaintops, you still have the mobile homes, broken-down houses."

"You can't hide it in New York, either." Melissa watched the narrow road twisting up, climbing into the green hills, which even now, at nine in the morning, were still shrouded in mist. She thought of walking the streets of New York, of coming home on a rainy night to Brooklyn and passing the homeless trying to sleep under corrugated boxes, wrapped in tattered clothes and old sleeping bags.

It was the same all over America, she thought next, the whole country was homeless in one way or the other. She was homeless, too, without parents, without a family.

She had only this temporary adopted son, and now he was missing. She began to cry. Her tears washed silently down her cheeks.

Glancing over, Greg saw her and slowed the van, ready to pull off the road. Melissa motioned that he should keep driving, that she was okay.

She curled into the bucket seat and watched him through her teary eyes. She asked him about his boys. She loved to hear stories about Timmy, his oldest, what he was doing, what funny things he had said to his father. It was all so innocent and good. It made her feel better, knowing Timmy was in Brooklyn, growing up healthy and normal.

Melissa didn't ask about Helen. She existed there in Brooklyn, too, always there. Melissa knew it, and knew how she stood between her and Greg and all her secret dreams.

"What's this guy Connor?" Greg asked when they were well into the mountains. He had spotted a local sign saying Beaver Creek was six miles ahead.

"He's been just great," Melissa said, meaning it, and very glad she hadn't gone to bed with him, which would have made her feel awkward when she introduced them. She thought wryly, amused by this herself, that she hadn't slept with Greg either, nor could she, though this was really the only man she did want. He wanted to sleep with her, too, she was certain, but it was something that wouldn't happen. She wouldn't let it happen.

"He's been a good friend, especially about Adam." And she started to talk, telling Greg again about the schooner-house, and the crafts school, and how they had gone the night before up to the church. She told him about seeing Adam with the snakes curled along his arms, and how the people believed a chosen child would come to take them up to heaven.

Then she listed all the recent deaths and murders, telling him everything she had heard from Connor. She talked about Crazy Sue, and told Greg how the old woman and Adam had teamed up together.

"Connor says the woman is harmless, but Adam is with her, and he's drawing these paintings of what's happening, trying to tell me, you know. But what am I doing? Going to the police? No! And why not? Because I'm terrified, I guess, that Adam is more than, you know, just an innocent bystander."

"The cops have questioned you?"

Melissa shook her head. "Connor tells me to keep a low profile."

"What about reporters?"

"There's none, as far as I can see. Everyone seems to get the news off their truck's CB."

"Nothing on TV."

"No, nothing. The local paper comes out this Wednesday. They'll have to have something." She shook her head, smiling wryly at Greg. "We might as well be in Outer Mongolia."

"In Outer Mongolia, there'd be a television crew and Dan Rather in his safari jacket."

"True." Ahead of them on the narrow road they both spotted a television van racing down the mountainside.

"There goes Dan," Greg quipped.

In the side mirror, Melissa watched the van disappear, sinking out of sight, then finally disappearing as the van turned a sharp corner of the mountain road.

"It's scary," she said out loud.

"What's scary?" Greg used the question to reach over and touch her thigh. He could feel the warmth of her body under the thin fabric.

"Everything," she admitted. She did not try to remove his hand, nor did Greg pull away. He drove with one hand on the tight, twisting road, and kept the fingers of his other hand resting lightly high up her thigh. "This is scary," she said, meaning the way he was touching her.

Greg kept watching the road.

"Greg, what are you doing?"

He shook his head, and then grinned at the foolishness of their coded exchanges.

"Do you?"

"You're afraid to look at me, aren't you?" she said, laughing at their situation. She had learned from working with him how he liked to hide out when there was trouble brewing. His disappearing act, as she called it.

"I'm afraid of you," he told her, squeezing her thigh.

"Ouch!" She slapped his hand, hitting him harder than she wanted and stinging her fingers.

"See!" Now he glanced over and held her gaze for an instant.

It was Melissa who turned her eyes away. She took a deep breath. She remembered being a child in Texas, hiding deep in the turquoise water and feeling the pressure for air building within her chest. She felt that way now, high up in the Blue Ridge Mountains.

"I don't want to harm your family," she told him, still watching the road. They had almost reached Beaver Creek, one last turn and the little town would be ahead of them, nestled in the hollow, and slightly below the parkway. Seeing it, she knew Greg would be impressed. It looked so pretty, from a distance.

"You're not harming anyone," he told her.

"I'm harming Helen, and the boys, and I'm very sorry. It makes me feel rotten, being such a terrible, selfish person."

"Mel, please." He had slowed the van almost to a stop and he reached across and found her clasped hands and smothered them with his fingers.

Immediately behind them there was a sharp blast from an air horn and a red pickup truck shot around the van with the horn blaring. A young, blond-bearded face leaned out the passenger window and gave them the finger as the driver fishtailed the pickup back into their lane and sped away, wheels screeching.

"Up yours!" Greg shouted.

"Welcome to the south," Melissa added, and then said, "we're almost in town."

They reached the turn and Beaver Creek came into sight below and to their left, tucked into the hollow and shadowed with trees. From this entrance, Melissa thought, it was picture-perfect.

"Nice," Greg said.

"More than nice, Schnilling! Give me a break! Don't be such a snooty New Yorker." She was grinning at him, loving the way he always understated everything, trying to keep his cool, always being sure that he couldn't be caught off base.

They were so alike, she thought, and thinking of that brought more tears to her eyes and she quickly blinked them away, speaking up at once, telling Greg where to turn, and telling him that they should go to the house first, see if Adam had returned, and then call Connor at the crafts school and find out what he had learned from the sheriff's office.

Connor found the sheriff at the crafts school. A half-dozen highway and town cop cars were parked around the main buildings when he came up the dirt road from his place and drove into the parking space behind the pottery studio.

"Shit!" he swore. "Goddamn shit." He jumped out of the truck and crossed the gravel lot to where Gene Martin was standing with a cluster of students.

The director saw him approach and came to him, speaking before Connor could even ask what had happened.

"A girl got killed last night."

Connor stopped walking. He was staring at the front porch of the big dormitory building where several cops had just appeared. He spotted Bobby Lee coming out the front door. The small man was holding the front end of a stretcher. He heard Gene say something else, tell him the name of the dead woman, the corpse was wrapped in the body bag, but the name didn't register, and Martin kept going on about how they had found the body.

Connor grabbed the fat man's wrist and interrupted, "What?"

He did not take his eyes off the small black body bag, watched Bobby Lee and two cops carry it swiftly, as if it were no weight at all, down the stone steps and to the open back door of the Marian County Hospital ambulance.

"Lesley Moyers," the director whispered, watching Connor with his soft wet eyes, "she's one of yours."

Connor closed his eyes and swayed back, as if the whispered name had physically hurt him.

"I'm telling you, Connor," the director warned, "wait until this fuckin' murder hits the out-of-state papers. We ain't going to fill a bed come August." There was a wide band of sweat across the man's forehead. He had a toothpick pressed between his lips and Connor resisted the urge to reach out and shove it up into the roof of Martin's mouth.

"Students get killed on college campuses every day," Connor said slowly. "Why would this be any different?" As he spoke, he was thinking of Lesley Moyers naked in his bed, remembering how cold her flesh was under his body. She had not wanted to have sex with him, he knew, but had done it anyway, passively, as if she had nothing better to do with her time. He remembered being furious at her for ruining his good time. Now he was upset at himself for remembering his attitude.

"Yeah, college kids kill themselves all the time," Martin whispered, leaning close to Connor's ear, "but they don't get killed! I've got to telephone her family and tell them she's been murdered at my school."

"Goddamnit, Martin, quit your bitchin'," Connor told him, walking off.

"Fuck yourself, Connor. I wasn't screwing the girl."

Connor turned back to Martin and pushed up against the fat man, jamming his forefinger into the director's flabby chest.

"You keep your fuckin' mouth shut, hear me?" he said slowly and carefully, without taking his eyes off the bigger man. "What I do when I'm off these grounds is none of your asshole business, understand, boy?"

He turned away at once and strode off as Martin called after, "I told you before, Connaghan. This place goes down, then you're back to pumping gas at the Mobil Station."

Connor kept walking, in a rage at Martin, in a rage at Lesley Moyers for getting killed, and in a rage at himself for having slept with the woman. "Goddamnit," he swore out loud, thinking how women were always getting him into trouble.

He banged open the door of the pottery studio and stopped at once, remembering he hadn't called the sheriff's office. He should go back outside and see them, but that made him edgy. He didn't want to be needing any cops. He glanced at his watch, trying to remember the flight time of the New York plane.

He could telephone the cops later, he thought, after they had left the crafts school and were done with Lesley Moyers. He doubted if the cops knew where Adam was. They had more to worry about than a strange little bald-headed boy who kept running off into the woods at night.

Melissa stepped into the schooner-house, calling Adam's name. She went to the doorway of his room hoping she'd find him there, sprawled out asleep on the small bed. The bed had not been slept in. He had not returned to the house. Her hopes sank. She dropped her bag on the kitchen counter, feeling her fatigue.

"Not here?" Greg asked, following her into the house.

Melissa shook her head.

"Okay, let's go find him," he said, sounding upbeat and confident.

"How?"

"Well, we go looking."

"Greg, go look out the windows and tell me where we should start, okay?" She shot him a glance, and realized how she must sound to him, and knowing also that it wasn't his fault, none of this was his fault. She had brought it all on herself, and she said quickly, "I'm sorry. I'm tired. I'm blaming you. I'm blaming everyone, and I'm the one who's at fault." She kept shaking her head, fighting back her tears. "How 'bout some coffee?" she asked, needing to keep busy.

"You need to go lie down, that's what you need." He followed her into the kitchen space and put his hands on her shoulders, holding her still. She leaned back against him. He let go of her shoulders and shifted his arms, wrapped them around her into a gentle bear hug, his chin resting on the top of her head. It surprised him that he was that much taller than she. In the office she seemed taller, and more imposing. He had always been slightly intimidated by her sureness.

From across the room, he could see their reflections in the bathroom mirror. He liked looking at himself, holding her. It seemed real, not just one of his daydreams. Looking at them, he noticed he was a good foot taller. She seemed almost like his child, smaller and slight and needing the protection of his strong arms.

"Everything is going to be okay, isn't it?" she asked.

"Yes, everything. You're going to be okay. Promise."

"I mean Adam."

"Yes, Adam, too."

"But why do the cops want him in New York?" She had found their reflection in the distant mirror and was watching Greg as she asked her questions.

"This guy Kardatzke has got some questions, that's all."

"Doesn't he know Adam wouldn't talk. Can't talk!"

"I told him."

"Adam didn't hurt that other boy, did he?"

Greg pulled back and turned Melissa in his arms. She didn't look up. She was staring at his chest, waiting. He touched her cheek and she looked up, managing to bring a smile to her face.

"I don't know, Mel. My guess is that he stole the kid's clothes, or maybe he found them. Whatever. Melissa, we've talked about this before. Neither one of us knows what it's like in those tunnels. It's another world. A life-and-death struggle for everyone."

"I know it, sort of." Melissa had a flash of the forty-eight hours she had lived on the streets when she was doing her masters research. She had never been so frightened in her life, not even when she was living with Roland Davis.

"We go back to New York. We take Adam to see Kardatzke. We let the cop question him, however he thinks he can, and then we start over with Adam, okay?"

Melissa nodded. She knew what Greg meant. She had to give up her notion of being the child's foster parent.

"I thought I could take care of him," she whispered.

"It's okay, Melissa."

Melissa shook her head. "No, it's not okay. I got the boy into trouble. I wanted..." She stared off, looking outside, letting the view of trees comfort and calm her as she tried to evaluate her action. "I was telling Connor about this need of mine. My need to help others.

It's pathological, I think. Because I had been abandoned as a child, I have to care for others. I can't let children suffer the way I suffered."

She shook her head. There were no more tears.

"Okay," she announced, "you're right. I was wrong."

"It's not a question of right or wrong. We all do things out of the craziest of reasons."

"You never did, Greg." She looked up at him. "I always turned to you at the office because I knew if there was anyone around me who had their head screwed on straight, it was you."

"Thank you, but it's not true. I've done plenty of dumb things."

"What?" She smiled, wanting him to say that falling in love with her was one dumb thing, but instead he said:

"I married Helen when we were too young—both of us—to know that it wouldn't work. We aren't the same kind of people. We don't want the same things out of life."

Melissa pulled out of Greg's arms. She wouldn't let herself think of Helen and the boys, of Greg's family, back in Brooklyn. She walked to the kitchen windows. She could see the boulder and the creek from there, as well as the solid wall of trees.

Greg had fallen silent, watching Melissa. He followed her to the windows and, putting his hands on her shoulders, drew her against him.

"We all make dumb mistakes, Mel. What we do next, how we solve those dumb mistakes, that's what counts. Right?"

She nodded.

"It's what I have to do in my life. It is what you have to do with yours."

Still staring at the peaceful mountain scene, Melissa said, "I was sexually abused when I was a little girl. It was a man who lived with my mother for a while. One of the men, I should say. Alice had lots of lovers. She was always bringing home these guys, you know, she was hoping to marry.

"My mother wouldn't believe me when I said her boyfriend, Roland Davis, came on to me." There were tears on Melissa's cheeks again. "I was thirteen years old and it frightened me when my own mom wouldn't believe me. It was worse than what Roland Davis tried to do. I couldn't tell anyone. I was afraid of telling anyone. I thought it was my fault because that son of a bitch wanted to screw me."

She started sobbing and, holding on to the counter, retched into the sink, vomiting what little she had in her stomach onto the stack of dirty dishes.

Greg reached and turned on the cold water. She kept vomiting, though there was nothing in her stomach. With his free hand, he grabbed a dish towel, wet it in the cold water, and pressed the towel against her forehead. Then he wiped her face and mouth, handling her like a child.

She was trembling in his arms, clinging to him. Greg kept whispering that she was all right, that she was just upset because of Adam and everything else that had happened to her. She stopped retching and gasped for breath.

Greg pulled a kitchen chair over and made her sit down.

"Bend over," he ordered. "Put your head between your legs."

He held her that way until she had regained her breath and calmed, and then he let her sit up and gave her a glass of water while he went into the bathroom, got a washcloth, and came back to the kitchen and pressed the cold damp cloth against her forehead.

"How come you're so good at this?" she asked when she had recovered.

"I've got two boys, and a wife who was sick constantly when she was pregnant. You become a pro, real fast, let me tell you." He knelt beside her, smiling, trying to cheer her up just with the force of his good humor.

Melissa smiled dolefully, then she reached out and touched his cheek, let her fingers linger on his face.

"Why is my life so fucked up, Greg?"

"It isn't, Melissa."

"Oh, yes it is."

Greg stood and pulled her into his arms, nestling her head against his shoulder.

She did not cry. She was too tired to cry, and her wave of helplessness and self-pity was slipping away. She knew deep in her soul that she was as strong as anyone else, and that if she hadn't been destroyed as a child, she wouldn't now be overwhelmed by what was happening in her life. She was too proud, too self-assured. She was a survivor.

Still, she didn't pull herself out of Greg's arms. This was her weakness. Greg was her weakness. She needed someone to love. She had thought all those long years ago swimming deep in the cool Texas pool that she didn't need anyone, not even her mother. But she was wrong. She was wrong about Greg.

She pulled back slightly, not to leave his embrace, but to reach up on her tiptoes and kiss him on his lips. She thought how dry his face felt. But then, she had been the one crying all morning, not him.

"This isn't fair to Helen," she said at once.

"This isn't about Helen," he said, "this is about you and me."

"Greg, please..."

He silenced her with a kiss and she struggled in his arms, but he wouldn't let go of her, and she kept fighting him off, and he kept her captive. He picked her up and looked around. He saw her bedroom was just a tiny loft space cut into the high cathedral ceiling, and he turned instead to Adam's bedroom off the kitchen and carried her to that bed.

She stood at once, as if to escape, and he seized her around the waist. Already her white dress was pulled off her shoulders and he plunged his hands into her neckline, into the coolness of the valley between her breasts. She beat her fists against his chest, and reached up, seized his head, and curled her fingers into his hair. Pulling him down, she bit his shoulder.

Greg swore at her, pushed her away, and slapped her bottom.

"Ouch," she yelled, jumping from the hard slap, and hit him again, pounded her clenched fists into the hardness of his stomach. Then, realizing he had loosened his belt, she stuck her hand down the front of his jeans, slipped it under the elastic of his shorts, and grabbed his testicles.

"There!" she answered, grinning up into his face.

Greg cupped his hands under her buttocks and lifted her off her feet and onto the narrow bed.

"There, yourself!" he answered, lying on top of her.

She was out of breath, panting from her attack, and she whispered, "Do it again."

Greg frowned.

"Hit me a little bit, please. But not too hard." She lowered her eyes, embarrassed by her request.

"I'll tie you up," he told her.

She closed her eyes and nodded, feeling a surge of warmth pump through her body.

Greg stood and stripped her naked, pulling off her dress and panties, than let Melissa lie down again on the narrow bed. Lying on her bed, she raised her right knee to cover the dark patch of her vagina and looked up at Greg. Her eyes were dilated in her desire.

Greg pulled his shirt over his head without unbuttoning it, stripped off his jeans. He spotted a bath towel hanging from a wall peg and, grabbing it, twisted the towel into a thick whip, and came back to her.

Melissa, seeing what he was doing, had turned over on the bed, shoved the pillow up, and reached to hold the bedposts with her outstretched arms.

Greg came back to the bed and, kneeling beside her, leaned over and kissed her lightly on the shoulder.

"Okay?" he whispered.

She opened her eyes and smiled dreamily at him.

He ran his hand down the length of her back, through the hollow of her spine, and across her taut buttocks. He kissed her bottom and softly slapped her with the twisted towel. She moaned, encouraging him. He hit her again.

Melissa had never been beaten when she made love with a man. It had been what she secretly wanted, and she wondered if there was something wrong with her. Did it all go back to her childhood, to having been abused as a little girl?

She felt the sting and slight pain and concentrated on the towel swatting her buttocks, letting her mind wander, fantasizing that Greg had kidnapped her, had taken her off into the mountains, where no one knew them, where she would be his love slave for the rest of her life.

Her hands tightened around the wooden posts as she braced for the next blow. He hit her harder and she cried, realizing as she sobbed that she was having an orgasm.

"Don't stop," she told him, biting into the thickness of the pillow.

Greg did stop.

"Someone's here," he said, turning toward the open door.

Melissa grabbed her clothes. "It must be Adam."

Greg stepped to the doorway of the bedroom. His heart was pounding and he was having difficulty breathing. The sudden noise had terrified him. He held the towel in front of him, concealing his half erection.

"Who is it?" Melissa whispered, scrambling to dress.

"No one's here," he said, stepping into the living room, scanning the house. He wrapped the towel around his waist and stepped farther out into the open living area, and there she was, behind him, crouched against the wall.

"Goddamnit!" he shouted, jumping back, startled by her, and aware immediately that his life wasn't in danger. He could handle the old woman. "Melissa!" he shouted.

She kept grinning, wagging her head.

Jesus Christ, he thought next, the old lady had seen him beating Melissa.

"It's Betty Sue," Melissa told him, coming to the doorway, still straightening her dress. "What is it, Betty Sue?" she asked calmly.

"It's the bald-headed boy," Betty Sue said. She had hooked her tongue inside her lips and was making circles with the tips of her tongue, distorting her mouth.

"Adam? Where's Adam?" Melissa's voice rose slightly and she moved toward the old lady who skipped back, keeping her distance. Melissa stopped.

"Betty Sue, where is Adam?" Melissa asked nicely.

The old woman slowly shook her head, taking delight in her secret.

"Oh, dear God, no," Melissa sighed. She reached out and braced herself against Greg.

"Where's Adam?" Greg asked.

"In the trees. There!" She pointed a long, crooked arm toward the back of the house.

The woman was a witch, Greg thought.

"Would you show us Adam, Betty Sue?" He smiled at the woman.

She nodded with delight, skipped toward the open sliding doors.

"Wait!" Greg asked, going back into the bedroom to dress.

"He's not dead," Melissa called after him.

"You stay here," Greg told her.

"No, I will not stay here." She slipped into her sneakers, and said again, "He's not dead!"

Greg returned to the living-room space and said quietly to Melissa, "It would be better if you stayed here, just in case."

"No, he's my responsibility." She turned and went toward Betty Sue, who was standing on one leg at the glass doors, hopping back and forth, from one wide floorboard to the next.

They couldn't keep up with the old woman. She ran up the ridge behind the schooner-house, up to the top of the hill and above the tree line. The climb was almost perpendicular and within fifty yards, Melissa stopped and gasped for breath.

Greg paused to help, and she shook her head, gestured for him to keep going. Already the old woman was out of sight, climbing easily through the dense underbrush.

"No," he told Melissa, "she'll see we're not following and wait. I'm not going to leave you. Besides, I'm exhausted." He massaged the backs of his thighs.

"Okay," she told him, reaching out for him to pull her up. "Let's just walk."

He went on ahead so he could push back the branches and make it easier for her, but within twenty yards, they were both again out of breath and soaked with perspiration.

"How does she do it?" Melissa managed to ask. "The woman must be sixty-five!"

"She's been climbing through these hills all her life, that's how she does it."

"I'll never make it, if it's much farther," Melissa announced, pausing to stand up. Her back and legs both hurt, and there was a pain in the depths of her stomach. This was a mistake, she realized. She should have telephoned Connor at the school, and then she remembered she had forgotten to call him, as she had promised.

"Okay?" Greg sounded concerned. He had halted a dozen yards higher on the slope.

Melissa looked up but could not see him clearly in the thickness of the trees and growth of underbrush. Yes, she told him, gathering her strength and following the sound of his voice.

In another fifty yards, they reached the summit and came out into an open field. Betty Sue was running long-legged through the high wild weeds of the open pastureland that sloped gently down, toward more trees, a forest of them, a half mile away.

"Where is this?" Greg asked, then spotted the fleeting figure of the old woman, thinking that if they lost sight of her, they might be lost.

"I have no idea," Melissa told him, but then in the distance she spotted the top roof of the crafts house, saw the sun flash off the metal pieces of art on the lawn, and she remembered having see this field from the volleyball court. From the court, the field looked postage-stamp small. "Yes, I do know!" she announced, pleased with herself. "Sort of, I know."

"She's disappearing!" Greg exclaimed. He had been watching the old woman, saw she had run straight into a patch of white birch without looking back.

"Is this some kind of game she's playing?" he asked.

"I have no idea." Melissa shielded her eyes against the bright midday sun.

"Well, come on!" He took her hand, as if they were kids together cutting classes, and went running after the old lady.

It was easier going down the slope, but still Melissa's legs gave out when she reached the other side, and the shade of the white birch. She fell to the ground, too exhausted to go farther.

"Melissa, come on," Greg said encouragingly. "We've got to find Adam."

Melissa shook her head, momentarily unable to talk.

Greg knelt beside her, saying, "Okay. You stay here and let me find out which way she's going."

It seemed to Melissa that Greg was speaking to her from a great way off. A hot flash swept through her body, exploding in her head. Briefly her vision blurred and she thought that if she didn't rest, she would be sick.

"I don't think," she whispered, trying to stand.

"Easy," Greg told her, and lifted her up. "Sit here." He shifted her around so her back was up against a tree stump. He was full of words of consolation, telling her to take a rest, then go back to the house. He would find the old woman, and "make sure about Adam."

Melissa nodded, wanting him to leave. She didn't want him there if she was going to be sick again.

He kissed her quickly on top of her head and was gone. Melissa didn't hear him sprint away. His footsteps were muffled in the soft dampness of the earth.

She lowered her head, hoping she'd throw up. She'd feel better, she knew, if she did. But hanging her head between her knees only made her dizzy. She sat up, wiped away her tears, and wished she had something cool to drink. Greg was right, she thought. She should go back to the schooner-house and get something to drink.

Still, she didn't move from the rough tree stump, and in a few minutes she was aware of the trees around her, the cool dampness of the shadowy slope, and heard in the distance the sound of water running, much as it did behind the schooner-house. She listened hard, trying to guess what direction the water might be, and feeling already the coolness of the mountain stream as she scooped up a handful and splashed it against her hot face.

Melissa stood, determined to find the stream, to get a drink of water. She continued down the smooth path for another few yards, until she guessed by the low, steady rush of water that the stream was to her right, deeper in the trees, and she left the deer path and walked into the underbrush, going downhill as she went deeper and deeper into the woods.

The only sound around her was that of the forest, and it frightened her, the sudden rustle of fallen leaves as a small animal scurried away, and then a deer burst through the underbrush. She screamed at the sudden sight of a big spotted tan animal as it crossed her path. She fell backward into the thick bed of dead leaves, bruising her hands as she went to brace herself.

"Dammit!" she shouted, and then laughed. She felt better at once and shook her head, amused by her silly fright.

In another dozen yards she found the stream.

Pushing through the trees and bushes, she realized at once where she was on the crafts school property. She spotted the red roof of the school director's house to her left, and heard the sound of a car passing on the school's road below her. She grabbed the branches of the overhanging trees and eased her way down the slippery bank of the gorged-out creek bed, feeling better already.

Melissa took a deep breath, knowing she was safe, and stepped over to the rushing water, which narrowed at that point and tumbled over the makeshift rock dam. She faced upstream and for a moment enjoyed watching the way the water came down the hillside, sparkling in the sunlight. Then she reached down into the stream to palm a cup of water onto her face and her fingers touched soft, cold flesh.

She jerked her hand away but lost her balance on the slippery rock perch. She fell face forward, trying to grab onto an overhanging tree branch, but tumbled into the watery pool instead, where, a foot below the surface, as if submerged in a natural water sarcophagus, was the naked body of a young man.

19

MELISSA HAD TO RETURN with the police to where she found the young man's body, but both Connor and Greg were with her, each holding an arm and helping her climb up through the woods to the mountain creek. She stopped a half-dozen yards from the rocky dam and pointed to where the body was, but wouldn't go closer. Her fingertips still felt the cold, meaty touch of his skin.

The body had been "buried" in the river with rocks over him to keep it submerged, but his left hand had broken loose and floated to the water's surface like a pale lily pad.

Melissa sat on the bank downriver from the spot. She had a blanket from the director's house wrapped around her. Melissa had refused to change her wet clothes, and in the shadowy grove there was no sunlight to warm her body. She sat shivering, while Greg rubbed her back through the thick blanket, and held her in a tender embrace every time she broke down into tears, remembering the sight of the boy's glassy eyes staring at her through the clear, cold creek water.

Connor walked back from where the body had been found and found Melissa in Greg's arms. He was furious, realizing then that he would never sleep with the woman. He guessed they must be lovers, and that pissed him off more. The man was married. What was she doing fucking married men? She seemed so pure and nice when he had first seen her, driving into the schooner-house yard with the bald-headed kid. It was another example, he told himself, that he couldn't trust women. He thought about Lesley Moyers, and how she had gone off and killed herself, or had this kid done it, this nose-pickin' Trent Rhodes, who spent all session mooning after her?

Well, he was another goner. The goddamn woods were filling up with death people, he told himself, trying to make it sound like a joke, but he knew there was nothing funny about the killings. Not anymore. There was someone real crazy in the mountains. And he knew exactly who it was, he thought, reaching the New Yorkers.

"Greg thinks I should leave this afternoon," Melissa said at once. "He'll drive back with me. The police in New York want to see me about Adam. Greg says they're looking for him, but I don't know where he is."

"Neither do they." Connor nodded to where the cops were huddled around the dead boy. "The kid you found buried in the water is Trent Rhodes. He worked at the school." Connor had a small twig in his hands, and breaking it in two, he tossed the pieces into the swift water, saying to Melissa, "Those cops aren't going to let you leave this afternoon."

"We're leaving," Greg said, standing and hitching up his jeans. He was tall and underweight and had no hips. His clothes hung on his body.

"Greg," Melissa said softly.

"You've talked to them!" Greg protested. "What else do they want?" He waved toward where the cops were gathered at the rocky dam. "That kid's death has nothing to do with you." He took quick steps along the bank, then lost his footing on the steep slope and had to jog downhill a few yards to the edge of the water to keep his balance.

"We've had a half-dozen killings in the last few weeks, buddy," Connor called after him. "The sheriff doesn't give a shit what you think. You drive off the mountains with her and there'll be smokies from here to Richmond covering your ass." Connor thought again how much he hated New Yorkers. They all thought they owned the world.

Standing beside him at the edge of the creek, the men were at eye level. Connor watched the younger man, gauging him by the gaze in his eyes. If they were to fight, he would win, and that gave him a boost of confidence. He grinned at Greg, saying, "You're in the mountains, boy. You do it our way here."

"Fuck you!"

"Greg!" Melissa jumped up. "Let's go. I'll stay and answer these damn questions!" She was terrified the two men would start to fight. Even the thought of them fighting frightened her. She remembered as a child hiding under the bed whenever men fought with her mother.

Greg was young and foolish, and he'd get himself hurt standing up to Connor. She knew, too, watching the men, that Connor was jealous of Greg. This was all her fault.

"What do you think I should do?" she asked Connor, giving him her full attention.

"Go back to the schooner-house and hang loose." He pulled a long blade of grass from the weeds and slipped it between his teeth.

"And?" Greg demanded, sensing he was losing face with Melissa.

Connor raised his eyebrows, looking down at Greg, then said, "I'll tell the sheriff where she is."

"We'll wait," Greg answered, as if it were his idea. "Let's go, Melissa."

Melissa nodded. "How?"

Connor pointed across the narrow creek to where there was an opening in the trees and the hint of a path.

"Up there. The way you came. It's a short way. You'll see where you are, once you reach the ridge." He didn't bother to watch them leave. He watched the cluster of cops, who in their bright green uniforms all looked like Robin Hood and his men. He thought of the New Land Tabernacle Church, and said over his shoulder to Melissa, "Let me know if Adam turns up."

Melissa nodded, and then she remembered Crazy Sue, of how the old woman had come to tell them where the boy was, and asked Greg why Betty Sue Yates had taken him back to the crafts school and not to the creek.

"I have no idea. I followed her. She ran this way." He pointed to the path. "Across the creek bed, down to the road, and to the school. Then I heard you screaming."

He had both of their attention, and looking from Melissa to Connor, he shook his head.

"So where was Adam?" Connor asked.

"I never found out. I came back to Melissa."

"He's around," Connor commented. "Those two are running together like hound dogs."

"What do you mean?" Melissa asked, alerted.

"She's crazy. Anything could happen. Has happened." He shrugged, being vague.

"What do you mean by that?"

"I said I don't know! And I don't know." He stared back at Melissa, challenging her. Then he said, "They could be in this together."

"In what together?" she asked him, but she knew what he meant. She had tried desperately to keep herself from thinking of that possibility, of Adam somehow...with the crazy woman. In defiance and to keep her claim of innocence, she said, "You said yourself you saw the waitress at Bonnie & Clyde's try to kill the owner. That didn't have anything to do with Betty Sue Yates, and certainly not Adam! And that guy Batts killed his whole family, and himself. Right? Those deaths have nothing to do with Adam."

"I didn't say he did." Connor lowered his voice, knowing how voices carried along the creek water and not wanting to alert the cops. And then he said, to silence her, "A woman was killed at the school last night. They found her body sometime after midnight. She had been bitten in the throat, or something. Like it was a goddamn vampire."

"Oh, God." Melissa spun away, as if the weight of the news was tossing her aside. Her gaze caught the sheriff's men higher on the creek. They had pulled up the body. It was already wrapped in a wet black bag. The sun glittered off the thick plastic. "Greg, I've got to get out of here." She bolted across the narrow bed of rocks, splashing through the water, and ran up the path, disappearing immediately into the thick underbrush.

Greg glanced at Connor and then without a word ran after Melissa, along the worn path and up into the woods.

Connor didn't move. The police were coming down the creek bed. He could hear exchanges of conversation. The cops were laughing, talking among themselves about someone named Willy

Seemer, and how his wife caught him the night before with another woman and cut off his balls over in Catawba County.

The men had Trent's body between them, wrapped up like a tight black air express package. He thought next how he hadn't made a shipment north in two months. That already he had threatening calls from Philly, asking about his new glaze. Warning him to produce, or else. He wasn't tending to business, and it could cost him more than money. Those gangs were as crazy as Betty Sue and the bald-headed boy, Connor knew.

A half-dozen men went by him but he stayed in the shady spot by the mountain creek. A few nodded, leaving the hillside. Some of them he knew from town, others he had spotted through the years on county road, cops flashing by in white trooper cars. He never saw one without feeling a tinge of anxiety.

None of them spoke to him, not even to say, "Hi, ya," or "Good-bye."

He stared at the body bag and speculated about the boy, wondered if Trent Rhodes had somehow, for some reason, killed Lesley Moyers.

Possible, he thought, anything was possible in the mountains. He knew that well enough himself. But then who had killed Trent Rhodes?

He followed the cops down the hill to the school road. He thought about mentioning how Rhodes had a hard-on for Moyers, and at once realized he wasn't going to say anything. He didn't need the sheriff asking questions about his involvement with the dead girl. He didn't know the girl, he told himself. He had slept with her once, smoked a little dope, that was all. But he certainly didn't know her.

He jumped the creek and walked away from the cops, walked back up toward the buildings of the crafts school, hearing in the distance the sound of the dinner bell. It was time for lunch.

Greg got ice out of the refrigerator and made them both gin and tonics. They went outside to sit in the shade, near the boulder where Adam liked to perch and throw small pebbles into the swift water.

Melissa told Greg about that, and kept talking about Adam,

telling stories that had happened between them on the drive south, and since they arrived in the mountain.

She needed to talk and Greg kept quiet and listened attentively, though he was thinking he should phone New York and tell Nick Kardatzke how Adam had disappeared. He thought, too, how his involvement with Melissa might cost him his job. He had, as she had, misused the social agency, and he should also call his wife, he thought, and tell her he had arrived safely in Asheville.

He took a long sip of his drink, thinking that he would like to get drunk and go back into the house and make love all afternoon to Melissa Vaughn. It might be the only time he could. The cops would be arriving soon. He could count on that, thanks to Connor.

He wondered if Melissa had slept with him, remembering how Connor had watched the two of them. Greg had seen the hard edge of rage in the potter's eyes. There was one crazy guy, Greg realized, thinking how he had learned to spot the psychos in the homeless shelters of New York.

Connor was Melissa's type, he knew. She liked off-beat men. Men with long hair and no real jobs. Artists. Writers. It was what she always wanted to be. It was everything he wasn't. But she loved him, he now knew, and that gave him a great sense of comfort.

"I'm going to take a shower," she told him, finishing her story.

He nodded, pushing the bridge of his glasses up the ridge of his nose. He raised his glass, indicating that he would stay and finish his drink.

"I'm okay," she told him next, leaning forward and smiling.

"I know you are." He touched her bare leg. Her flesh was burning. He knew she wasn't okay, and she knew he knew.

She could leave him there for a while, and go take a long shower; let herself sob under the steady pounding of cold water. After that, she would feel better; she always did.

"Why don't you take a rest?" she suggested.

"Where?"

"Upstairs." She pointed to the ladder as they walked inside.

"How do you lock this?" He pulled the sliding door closed behind him.

"I don't know. I never have." She stopped on her way to the bathroom. "This isn't Brooklyn, darling." She smiled wryly, pleased with herself for calling him darling. Her sudden boldness made her feel a bit more in control of her life.

"Brooklyn seems pretty safe compared to what's been happening down here." He slid the glass door closed and spotted a small latch, which he flipped, locking them inside.

"I'll lock the other one," Melissa told him. She thought of Adam returning and being locked out. Still she didn't want him barging in on them. She knew that this afternoon she was going to make love to Greg Schnilling. She headed for the bathroom. "You better call home."

He paused at the ladder.

"Call home, Greg. Helen will be worried." And she shut the bathroom door so she wouldn't hear him talking to his wife.

Greg had fallen asleep, exhausted from his trip and the hot trek through the woods. Exhausted, too, by his guilt. He fell asleep and had a brief and intense dream about Brooklyn. He was trying to find his family in his apartment, and kept opening doors into empty rooms. He began to run through the huge house, panting for breath, and woke up, crying out in agony.

Melissa had her hand on his arm, sitting up on her elbow. She had a sheet over her, but he realized she was naked, that she had come up into the loft after her shower and lay down beside him while he slept.

"What time is it?"

Melissa shook her head, indicated that it didn't matter. Through the small porthole window, Greg saw the day was still bright with sunshine.

"You had a bad dream," she whispered, as if to a small boy.

"I know." He sank back onto the wet pillow. He hated to fall asleep during the day. He needed to take a shower, but he lacked the strength to get up and go downstairs. Also, he wouldn't leave Melissa. He loved having her stretched out beside him in the tight loft space.

"Would you like to go back to sleep?" she asked, feeling slightly foolish, saying that. She could smell his body and she couldn't remember the last time she was so excited about the smell of a man. It was simple lust. She had to keep hold of the sheet so she wouldn't just grab him.

Greg turned to face her.

"Hi."

"Hi." She smiled, darting her eyes away.

"You smell nice," he told her.

"Thank you."

"Perfume?"

"No, just me!" She laughed, embarrassed and knowing her face was flushed. Her throat muscles were so tight she could barely speak, nor could she look at him. She waited for him to touch her.

He did. He reached and took away the top edge of the sheet from where she had it wrapped around her breasts and under her right arm. He pulled it down and off her body.

The sheet caught beneath her waist and she moved her hips, helping him expose her. She watched his eyes as they swept her body.

"You're beautiful," he told her.

She closed her eyes. She wanted him to touch her. She wanted him inside her.

He reached and took her by the wrist and pulled her into his arms, smothering her face with kisses, tried to consume her at once with his lips. He moved down her body and across her breasts, sucking and biting her nipples until she gasped and moaned, hurt from his teeth.

He jumped up, frantic in his desire, and seized her slim body between his hands and arched her body, lifted her hips, and buried his face in the hot warmth of her vagina, darting his tongue into the thick lips of her soft sex.

She came, rocking the thin mattress, jerking her crotch into his face. Reaching down, Melissa seized him by his hair and pulled him away from her vagina.

Then, sitting up, she reached for his erection and sucked the thick tip into her mouth, raking her teeth over the taut skin.

He filled her mouth, and gulping, she choked down the come. In the deep recesses of her mind, the memory returned of her childhood, of Roland Davis forcing her to have sex with him. The trapped nightmare surged into mind, swept over her, made her dizzy with rage. She struck out, slammed her fist against Greg's face. She hit his nose and mouth, bloodied his lip.

"Mel, for chrissake!" Greg tried to duck her blow. "What are you doing?" He slid his head away from her swinging fists.

She hit his left eye and he seized her wrist, pulled her across the mattress, and slammed her down, leaping up to straddle her with his legs. He pinned her arms over her head. He kept swearing, trying to subdue her. Melissa kept fighting, struggling under his tight grip, crying hysterically. The blood from his nose and mouth dripped onto the sheets, onto her flushed face, her wet cheeks.

"What the fuck!" he swore, panting and out of breath. He leaned forward with his arm braced across her chest. She snapped at him when he was within reach, bit him hard in the bulging muscle of his right shoulder.

Now he hit her. He slammed her face and, seizing her by the shoulders, shook her body. When her hands were loose, she punched him low in the stomach, and then tore into his back with her nails, drawing more blood.

He yelled out in pain and hit her hard this time, furious, and in his own rage. He caught her in the nose, breaking a vessel. The warm blood from her nostril sprayed his face and chest, smeared her sweaty face.

He kept swearing at her, yelling in the silent house. He pushed her back into the soft mattress, held her down with his strength, forced her to surrender. She kept trying to free her legs, to bring one knee up and smash his groin, and all the while realizing that she had never been so excited in her life.

"No you don't," he told her, seeing how she planned on attacking, and he spread his own legs, blocking hers, as she kept bouncing up, hitting him in the crotch with her pelvis. "Now it's your turn!"

Without letting her go, he shifted his body and drove himself into her vagina. He wanted to rip her apart.

He was half kneeling, with her body trapped against him. He pumped at her, driving harder, furious at her physical attack, and also caught up in his need. For a moment, she struggled with him, fought against his rape. He felt her resistance slacken and her body relax. She became willing and pliable. She hugged her body to his.

Greg let go of her wrists and wrapped his arms tight around her body. They both concentrated on the steady, quickening rhythm that they had created between them.

Melissa turned her bloody face and sought his mouth, filled her face with his. She reached down with both of her hands and caressed his rocking buttocks. Greg slid his hand under her bottom and shoved his finger into her anus. They came together.

"What was that all about?" he asked, panting in her arms.

Melissa shook her head and tentatively touched her mouth, felt her bloody lips.

"I'm sorry," he whispered and went to kiss her.

She turned her face away, saying, "It hurts." She touched his face and said, "I'm sorry."

"Does this happen every time you make love?"

She smiled sadly, shaking her head. "No, never." She ran her hands through her head and pulled herself into a tight ball. "I had this sudden vision that you were Roland Davis."

"The guy your mother married?"

Melissa nodded.

"You hate him!"

Melissa nodded. "I hate him because he raped me. Raped me lots of times. Week after week in our little trailer home. I know I told you once that he never did, but he did. I lied to you. I'm sorry. I couldn't..." She started to sob and choke on her tears, and Greg sat up and took her into his arms, cuddling her close, as if to squeeze out her pain. He let her cry and when she had, she nodded that she was okay, and reached across the floor and pulled several tissues from a box, saying, "None of this has anything to do with you. I'm sorry how I behaved this way. I couldn't stop myself."

"Why didn't you tell me?"

"And what was I supposed to tell you? That my stepfather raped me when I was thirteen years old?"

"Yes, that's exactly what you should have told me. How else are you going to get rid of your demons?"

"I don't have demons. I had a stepfather who raped me."

"You're not the only person who had something terrible happen to them when they were a child. You learn to share..."

"And your father raped you?" She raised her voice.

"No, not that, but..."

"Then you don't understand what I'm talking about." She was angry with him, and he had disappointed her, which made him feel even worse. He had always been someone she could turn to. She moved to get up and he held her arm.

"You can't live your whole life with this nightmare."

"I'm living my life with this nightmare."

"When I was two years old my mother committed suicide," Greg said quietly. "She took me into her bedroom, propped me up on pillows, and then sat down beside me and blew her brains out with a small revolver. When my father came home five hours later, I was sitting in her blood and my own shit screaming out my lungs."

His sudden confession stunned her.

"I didn't remember, of course. I was only two. Still, I guess, I knew something and had repressed it. Years later, when I was in high school and had come to believe that she had died of a heart attack, I dropped some acid one afternoon with a couple of guys and it came back to me.

"I saw my mother. I saw her carry me into her bedroom. I watched how she carefully propped me up so I wouldn't fall off the bed. I watched her take the pistol and sit for the longest time beside me. She was holding this small silver object and talking to me. I was fascinated by the shiny object. I couldn't take my eyes off of it. And she talked to me for the longest time. I have no idea what she was telling me. No recollection at all of that. Just the shiny gun. Then she just lifted the pistol and stuck the short barrel into her mouth and pulled the trigger. The blast terrified me. I screamed and screamed. Her head popped open, exploded, and all her brains and blood and blond hair went flying."

"Oh, dear God." Melissa's hand went to her mouth and she bit down hard on her knuckle.

"We all have demons, Melissa."

"I never..." she whispered. She reached out and touched him.

"Neither did I, until I dropped the acid. But, of course, I did know! That's the point. Having it out in the open, exposed. It took a giant weight off me. I was a kid with a great secret, but I didn't know what my secret was."

"Why didn't your father tell you?"

Greg shrugged. "I guess he was trying to submerge the truth

himself. And, I guess, he was trying to save me from being scarred. He remarried when I was three. I don't think Mom—my second mom—even knew." He shook his head, staring at Melissa. "Everyone has dark, deep secrets, darling. You and I have ours, too."

"I can't live with any more secrets."

"You have more?"

"Only that I love you."

They made love again, quickly and silently, and then both fell asleep in each other's arms. When Melissa woke, she could tell by the light outside the small porthole window that it was late afternoon. The sun had already dropped over the side of the house and there were shadows on the lawn. She felt hot and sweaty and wonderful.

She needed a bath, but she didn't want to leave Greg's arms. It was enough for her to watch him sleep, enjoying the pleasure of spying on him.

She had dreamed of Adam, of being with him in New York. He had been able to talk, and they were happy, just the two of them. A mother and son, living a life together.

She knew what the dream was all about. She must have a child of her own. She would marry Greg, she decided. They would have a little girl, and she would be happy for the rest of her life. It was all she needed. A family of her own. It was all, she realized, that she ever wanted in her life.

She smiled, dreaming of her future, and carefully slipped her arms from Greg, untangled her legs, and moved from him. He turned on the mattress, sought warmth, and she pulled up the top sheet and tucked it in around him. Then she moved off the mattress and, still naked, climbed down the ladder.

She was halfway across the open space when the man appeared, stepping out of Adam's room. As soon as she saw him, she realized that the side door of the schooner-house was open. She had forgotten to lock it. The man was wearing a gray suit and tie that was too big and the wrong color. He looked out of place standing in the house, being there at all. She remembered then who he was, and where she had seen him.

The man said quickly, "Ms. Vaughn, I've come for Adam." His eyes never left her face.

"You can't." She tried to cover herself.

"I have a warrant for his arrest," he went on, speaking gently. This time his eyes did falter and swept her body.

"Adam is missing," she answered, standing straight, using her total nakedness as a show of defiance.

"Your life is in danger, Ms. Vaughn. I believe that Adam is going to attempt to kill you."

Nick Kardatzke had brought with him a dozen eight-by-ten black-and-white photos. After Melissa and Greg had dressed, he sat across from them in the living-room space and laid out the police photos on the hand-built coffee table. All of the photos were of naked corpses, boys and girls, men and women. All of the victims had their hearts ripped out of their bodies, or had been brutally mutilated in some way or the other.

"Adam couldn't have done all this!" Melissa stated, staring at the bodies.

"He's a suspect," Kardatzke answered calmly. "This is the real Adam Chandler. He was found a month ago in the Bronx." He tapped the glossy print with his thumbnail. The detective sat back and looked at Greg, "After I spoke with you, another white male, age about forty-five, turned up in the tunnels. The computer finally spit out a match. Same MO. Body mutilated."

"Was he sexually molested?" Greg asked, speaking quietly, as if this was all clinical and had nothing to do with real people.

"We don't think so. No semen was found. There're no marks on the body. Besides the missing heart."

Melissa turned away from the photos. She thought of Adam, the way he looked up at her. Silent and trusting, and never a sign of violence.

"That's the MO," the detective said once more and shuffled his photos together. "That's why we have to speak to your Adam."

The city detective was an old man, Greg realized. A man pressing retirement. He had the sad eyes of someone who could no longer be surprised by what he saw or heard. He had registered no emotion when he found the two of them naked in the house.

"You think Adam killed them all," Melissa said, angry at the cop's indifference. "I mean, why fly all the way down here if he isn't the murderer."

The cop nodded, staring over at her. "I came because of the kid."

He kept watching her across the coffee table. His thick black eyebrows hooded his eyes. He looked like a sad dog, Melissa thought.

"And?" she asked.

"I have a warrant for his arrest."

"How can you be so sure?"

"I talked to the sheriff's office in Marian. The same MO turned up with those women in the tent. Also, that guy Batts who allegedly offed his family."

"I didn't hear this!"

"They ain't saying anything in the sheriff's office. They don't want a fuckin' riot up here. Excuse me, ma'am." He talked like a cop on television, Melissa thought.

Kardatzke shuffled his crime photos together and then sat back in the old sofa chair and, brightening, asked, "Could I get a glass of water or something?" His eyes went from face to face.

"How 'bout a beer?" Greg offered. "You have beer, Melissa?"

"That would be just great." Kardatzke smiled, pleased by the offer.

Greg was up at once. "Melissa?"

Melissa shook her head, not taking her eyes off the cop. He seemed to be sinking deeper and deeper into the old sofa.

"Who do you think then . . . I mean, do you think Adam killed all those people?" She nodded toward the stack of black-and-white eight-by-tens.

The detective shrugged, seeming to be genuinely sad that he didn't know. He said softly, as if to keep the question just between them, "Why did you take that kid, Ms. Vaughn? Why did you bring him here to this place?" He gestured, including the house and the hills.

Melissa wondered how much she should tell the man. She was so tired of holding back, keeping secrets, even from herself. Her whole life, she knew, was built on lies. She wasn't Melissa Vaughn. Her name was Gross. Mary Lee Gross.

She was about to tell him, as she had told others, of how she had decided when Adam was brought into her office that this child would not be turned over to the welfare system. He would not be sent from foster parent to foster parent, a victim of a city that had no place for small children, for kids who couldn't defend themselves.

Melissa leaned forward, placing her elbows on her bare knees, and looked across at the older man.

"When I first came to New York, I was just out of college. I wanted to be an actress, and I was taking some classes, and working in whatever little acting bits I could find. I was twenty-one. I had no money. No family to support me.

"I got this part-time job with the city, working as a counselor in one of the foster-care places. You know about them?"

The detective nodded.

"Well, excuse me, but you don't, Lieutenant. You really don't, not unless you've lived in one, like I did, and saw those kids they bring in. They're called 'overnighters.' They come from all over the city. All children, little kids. Some of them are brought there because they're being beaten by their parents, others are found wandering around the city, homeless kids."

"I've been to those places," the detective told her.

Melissa nodded, but didn't reply. Greg returned from the kitchen with the detective's beer.

"The kids were always in terrible shape, coming to us. They'd have head lice and fevers and strep throat. Plus diseases you never heard of.

"We'd clean them up and try to get them to sleep. But they never could sleep. I remember trying to talk to them when I first started. I thought I should do that at least, make some sort of human contact, show them that this adult wasn't all bad. I would care for them. I was remembering myself when I was that young, and how lonely my life had been.

"Also, I was curious, you know, about them and who they were. How could their lives be so terrible? I started to ask questions and be friendly, and one of the other counselors, a black woman who had been with the city forever, she told me not to get to know these kids. She told me it would break my heart. I thought she was hard and callous, a terrible bitch." Melissa smiled sadly, remembering.

"One night they brought in a little black girl. She was only seven, and a deaf mute. She didn't know how to take a shower or brush her teeth. She had been dipped in scalding water, I was told, and was terrified of water. Another night there was an eight- or nine-year-old girl who had been attacked by a gang of kids who lived in her welfare hotel. Then there was a boy of six who had seen his father stabbed to death and he had such terrible nightmares that he'd scream out and throw himself down onto the floor."

"Melissa, easy," Greg whispered, reaching over to touch her.

"No one was taking care of these kids," Melissa kept talking. "I certainly wasn't. I mean, I was just another part of the system. I was processing them. None of these kids knew what was going to happen to them next. No one cared, really. The kids were nomads who couldn't defend themselves. We'd have them for a night or two, then they would be put into a foster home. I remember one girl that summer. A cute little white child. She had gone off to a foster home and a week later was back with us, her face and back and arms covered with bruises. She told me that they had beaten her with a baseball bat at the foster home."

"It's a tough world out there," the cop said.

"Yes, isn't it," Melissa answered dryly, staring at him. Then she said, "So you asked me why I took Adam home. That's why. Because of that summer job I had when I was twenty-one. I couldn't go back to acting. I enrolled at Hunter instead and got a masters degree in social work. I was determined to change the system, to take care of these children, to see that this shuffling them around in the middle of the night would stop."

"And you found out quick enough that you were just another cog in the wheel, didn't you?" the cop said.

"Fuck you," she answered back.

The cop sat up, jabbed his finger at her.

"Easy," Greg said to both of them.

"Listen, lady, I came down her to this ass end of the world to get you and that kid. You broke the law, taking the boy out of state."

"Why don't you read me my rights! Arrest me!" She stood, weary of dealing with the man. The phone rang as she walked away from the detective. Without pausing, she went to the telephone hanging from the center tree-post and picked up the receiver.

Greg looked from the detective to her, watching to see if she was okay. There were times at the agency when she would become so overwhelmed by work that she would get hysterical and start sobbing uncontrollably in her office.

He saw her raise her hand to her forehead, press her temples with her thumb and forefinger. She was saying yes in a soft voice, responding to questions, and without saying good-bye, she hung up the receiver.

"What is it?" Greg asked at once. Melissa had not moved away from the phone. Her hand was still on the receiver.

Without looking at either of them, she said calmly, "That was Connor. He said that there has been another killing. Up at the school. It was the director, Gene Martin."

She turned around and looked at Greg. The fear in her eyes spread over her pale face. Her body was trembling when Greg seized her by the shoulders. She kept talking, "He said it looked like the man's heart had been yanked out of his body. As if a ravished dog had done it, had bitten out the man's heart."

20

GREG DROVE AND MELISSA sat beside him in the front bucket seat of the van. They made the detective sit in back, and now he leaned forward talking as Greg raced the van up the bumpy road into town. The detective was telling them about a case he had read about years before. It had happened in Wisconsin.

"Sometimes a place, you know, breeds a killer. There was this local farmer, Ed Gein—they based the movie *Psycho* on him—who had a mother who railed against women wearing short skirts, perfume, or lipstick. The boy never dated, hated women, just like his mother taught him.

"When she died he was living alone in a farmhouse with no electricity, no plumbing. Nothing at all. Then women started turning up missing. For twelve years they kept turning up missing throughout southern Wisconsin.

"When the locals moved into Gein's farmhouse, they found a body strung up by the heels in a summer kitchen. It had been eviscerated and dressed out like a deer. The woman's head we found in a cardboard box; her heart in a plastic bag on the stove.

"Around the farmhouse there were the skins of ten other women, all neatly separated from their bodies. The cops found skin between the pages of magazines. Some used to make belts. He had upholstered a chair seat with more. And one large section, the front of a woman's torso, was rolled up in the living-room corner. There was a box of noses in a hall closet."

"Stop!" Melissa ordered.

The detective kept talking. "The psychiatrists who interviewed Gein said he was a victim of a common conflict. While consciously he loved his mother and hated other women, unconsciously he had hated her and loved other women. The reason he cut up his victims and saved their parts, according to the shrinks, was to try and bring back his mother at the same time he wanted to kill her. They had never seen a schizophrenic like him."

The detective paused and stared out the window, then added, "If you ask me, it's the place. The land creates an atmosphere and triggers people. A place like this, remote, played-out mines, no work of any kind, and all cut off from the civilized world. It breeds killers. The same's true of New York. Down in those subways, that's where the real psychos live and breed."

Melissa could see through the front windows the beautiful mountains in the far distance, now all shrouded with storm clouds. There would be rain that evening, she guessed. Without turning around, she told the detective he was wrong. She disliked the man so much, she enjoyed disagreeing with him.

"Hang around a city housing project and tell me it doesn't breed killers, rapists, druggies. Those places are infectious," the cop answered back.

"So is Park Avenue," Greg interrupted. "Where do you think white-collar crime comes from, not slums. All those guys stealing on Wall Street are Harvard and Yale grads. The best schools."

"The best and the brightest," Melissa added.

The detective snorted, but shut up. He leaned back in the rear seat and asked, "Where're we going?"

"To church," Melissa told him. She pointed ahead to the cutoff road, the narrow tarmac that went up the mountainside to the top of Simon's Ridge and the New Land Tabernacle Church. Greg downshifted to take the van up the steep rise and Melissa turned around in the bucket seat and shouted over the engine, "You want to find Adam. This is where he's been hanging out."

"What about this school? I thought we were going to see this director?" The detective's eyes shifted between Greg and Melissa. He looked worried, as if he were losing control of the situation.

"He's dead."

"I know he's dead, for chrissake! I want to speak to local law enforcement. Take me to the school," he ordered.

"I'm looking for Adam," Melissa answered, "and this is my van." She turned her back on the detective.

"I'm going to get the both of you for obstruction."

"Fine, you do just that."

The van burst out of the wooded drive and onto the crest of the ridge, which was flat and open and the site of the pretty white church. A gravel parking lot opened onto the graveyard, shaded by trees and protected by a low stone fence. Melissa thought how pretty it all looked, the white building silhouetted against black storm clouds and the wide sky. She was distracted, however, by a crowd of people, all surrounding a caravan of cars and pickups, and two old yellow school buses.

"What's this about?" Kardatzke leaned forward again.

Melissa said nothing, though she had no idea. She kept scanning the crowd, searching for Adam.

"See him?" Greg asked, stopping the van.

"No. I'll go ask." Opening the door, she spotted several men cradling rifles. She forced herself to jump out of the van and walk across the gravel yard to the caravan of vehicles. Coming closer, she saw the beds of the pickups were filled with suitcases, kitchen utensils, even furniture. She thought of the old black-and-white photographs from the dust bowl, farmers leaving the barren farms of the Great Plains.

No one stopped her from approaching. She was aware of everyone's silence. Even the children were behaving. They stood aside or sat motionless in cars, watching the adults with their dark saucer eyes.

Melissa kept searching for Adam. Not seeing him, she looked for a familiar face. She saw the man who had led the church service. He was standing on the front stoop of the white church. She went to him and asked about Adam. She knew they recognized her.

"He done told us to get out of here, ma'am."

Melissa shook her head. "Adam can't talk. He's mute." She looked from the preacher to several other men standing close by. They were all watching her.

"He talks well enough," another man replied. He had a child's small and soft voice.

The man was afraid, Melissa realized. She glanced around and saw the collective look of fear on all of their faces.

"Where's Adam?" she asked, feeling herself tensing.

The men moved off the stoop and went wordless toward the parked cars and trucks.

"Please," Melissa asked. "I'm Adam's mother. You must tell me."

Tyler Donaldson stopped on the walk leading to the cars. Without looking back, he said, "The boy told us to get. Told us we're too far down in the valley to be saved. We're going onto Grand Father Mountain. They got themselves a big tarmac parking lot. Ain't room enough here for a fiery chariot." He gestured toward the gravel yard.

These people were all crazy, Melissa realized. She had come into the mountains and stumbled on a mad world.

"Where's Adam?" she asked again. "Is Adam going with you?"

"Adam has gone to slay the dragon," the deacon told her.

"Slay the dragon?" she asked quickly, falling into step with the tall man.

"He's gone to slay the dragon," the man said again. "God be his judge and guardian."

"What are you talking about?" Melissa demanded.

Her sharp question stopped the man. He turned to her and still without looking into her eyes answered, "You're the dragon. You and the likes of them." He jutted his leathern chin toward the van and the two men.

He had milky eyes, Melissa saw, and as he talked about them, the outsiders, his eyes hardened. His jaw and cheekbones tightened. "They're all dragon," the man continued. "If you ain't saved; you're damned. God Almighty, it's as simple as that." He turned away from her and stomped off, his boots scraping the gravel.

"God Almighty," Melissa whispered. She stood still watching them leave, piling quickly into their cars and pickup trucks, scrambling for seats where they could find them. One after another, in quick procession, the vehicles spun out of the churchyard and roared away.

She saw that the detective had opened the side door of the van and was coming after her. His suit jacket was open and he was hoisting his trousers as he walked. She spotted the cop's revolver tucked up under his left armpit. He would kill Adam, she knew. It was a clear and certain image that she had of the cop shooting down her Adam.

She started walking, then running, back to the van, while Kardatzke peppered her with questions. She reached the van and jumped in beside Greg, making the detective chase her. All she could think of was that she had to find Adam before he was hurt.

"The school," she calmly told Greg. "Let's try the school."

"There's Connor," Greg said, pulling into the crafts school.

Connor was standing on the open front porch of the main school building, a giant log cabin, that served as office and class-rooms for several crafts.

"Who's Connor?" Kardatzke asked at once. He had already pushed down the latch on the back door and shoved it open. This time, he wasn't letting the woman go off alone.

"He's the man who called me about the director," Melissa answered, jumping from the van and going up the hill to the building and Connor.

"They're gone," he called down to Melissa. "The cops took the body, and Crazy Sue." He sounded enormously relieved.

"Crazy Sue? Jesus, who the fuck is that?" Kardatzke asked, reaching the wooden porch. He immediately pulled his shield out and flashed it in Connor's face. "I'm looking for this kid. This bald-headed kid, Adam?"

"Crazy Sue," Melissa whispered, and realized the sense it made. The old woman had finally snapped. "Of course!" She leaned against the thick log pillar of the wooden porch. She felt deliriously happy. It wasn't Adam. All of these deaths had nothing to do with her boy.

Connor kept talking, explaining how the cops had found the old woman. "There was blood all over her dress, matted in her hair."

He had to keep backpeddaling with his story to fill in for the detective, giving Kardatzke a capsule history of Betty Sue Yates's life in the hills.

"The kid?" Kardatzke demanded, cutting through Connor's long story. "Where's the kid?" Now in the late afternoon, after the long trip, and dealing with the two social workers, his temper flared at any interruption. He had to find the bald-headed boy. It had become a point of honor with the man.

Connor stared at the small detective, puzzled by the question, and surprised by the rage of the cop. He shook his head while glancing at Melissa, as if she might know the answer, and had kept it a secret.

"We can't find him," Melissa reported. "This man, Lieutenant Kardatzke, wants to talk to Adam."

"But he can't talk."

"Jesus Christ! If one more fuckin' person tells me that fuckin' kid can't talk..." Agitated, the detective paced the porch, his shoes stomping the wooden porch.

Melissa glanced at Greg, grinning for the first time that afternoon. Kardatzke looked so out of place in his cheap suit, she thought, and standing next to Connor with his long blond hair pinned into a ponytail, and wearing cutoffs, tire sandals, and a T-shirt with Hemingway's photo. The cop looked as if he had just stepped off an immigration boat, a refugee from some obscure East European country.

"I have no idea where Adam is," Connor said, silencing the cop.

"How come no one knows where he is?" Kardatzke's dark eyes darted from face to face, like a hungry dog.

"He's been on his own since I came into the mountains," Melissa answered. "That's why I came here. I wanted him to have a backyard, a place to play that was more than city streets and the park. He plays in the woods, you know, just like any other normal boy."

"Why do you want Adam?" Connor asked.

"He's wanted in New York for questioning," Kardatzke snapped back, realizing that all the events of the day had somehow gotten beyond him. In New York this would never have happened and he was furious at himself for letting it happen.

He had tried to be friendly and low-key, almost neighborly to these social welfare people, and they had spun him around, filled him with bullshit, and outright lied to him. Jesus Christ, he swore to himself. He was too old for this crap.

And now, dismissing the two, he asked Connor where there was a phone. He was cutting these two loose. His cop instincts told him they weren't hiding the kid. They had fucked up their lives, having an affair, but it wasn't his problem. He wasn't into social welfare.

He needed to get in touch with the county sheriff, he told Connor.

Connor led Kardatzke into the office and showed him the phone. When he went back onto the porch, Melissa was waiting with a question.

"Where did the cops find Crazy Sue?" she kept her voice down.

"Walking down the road, over there." He pointed to where the mountain road bypassed the school. "She was walking along, singing out loud. They should have locked that crazy bitch up years ago."

"Jesus Christ," Greg whispered. He was thinking how Melissa had fled the city to find a safe haven for Adam and ended up neighbors to a homicidal lunatic. The whole country, he thought next, was full of nuts.

"What do you think?" Melissa asked. "Greg? What do you think?"

"I'm sorry." He shook his head, indicating he hadn't been listening.

"Do we leave? Go back to the house?" She was frowning, watching Greg, and unexplainably she felt a sudden, sharp thrust of pain in her chest, as if a thin sliver of glass had been driven home to her heart. She gasped and clutched her chest.

"Mel!" Greg grabbed her shoulder. "Are you okay?"

She shook her head, still gasping. Her legs were weak and she fought for a breath.

"Sit her down," Connor ordered. He grabbed a wooden rocker and slid it behind her, easing Melissa into the chair.

"What is it?" Greg asked again. He was kneeling beside her.

Melissa shook her head.

"She's been through hell," Connor said. "That damn kid has been spinning her for a loop."

They kept talking about her, trading information, telling incidents. Melissa didn't bother to listen. She lowered her head between her legs and rushed blood to her head. The fainting spell was caused by nerves, she knew. She knew how her body reacted to too much pressure.

She had to stop worrying about Adam. She had to stop being

terrified that he was a killer. Her nervous system was overloaded. She'd be a basket case herself if she didn't take care.

Melissa raised her head and saw both of the men staring at her. Greg's face had tensed up, as if he feared he couldn't really protect her. She yearned to embrace him. Connor watched them both, his eyes jumping from face to face.

Melissa glanced at Connor, telling him, "I'm going back to the schooner-house. Call me if Adam turns up, okay? If he's not back by tomorrow, I'm packing up and leaving." She nodded toward the office. They could see Kardatzke through the windows. He was still speaking on the telephone. "Let him find Adam."

Melissa shocked herself with her honesty. She wondered how she could suddenly be so cool and indifferent about Adam, and she guessed it was simply her body's way of protecting her, telling her enough was enough. At some point, she had to shut down her emotions and close him out; otherwise, she'd kill herself. He wasn't her child. She had never really bonded with the boy. If Adam was happy with these rednecks who thought he was God, fine. At least they'd take care of him. It was more than she could do. She had failed as a mother, she realized.

"His painting...? All his work...? I telephoned a friend in Washington...?"

"You can have his paintings. All of them except the ones of me. I don't care what you do with them. I know what I'm going to do with mine." She stood, feeling as if she were closing out a chapter of her life, a brief bizarre episode that lasted no longer than a summer vacation.

"Hey, Melissa, wait, I mean." Connor fell into step with them, leaving the wooden porch. "This kid has great talent. I mean, everyone agrees, right?" He glanced at Greg, then back to Melissa, who had focused her attention on the path, striding ahead, rushing to leave the crafts school.

"I can't handle him, Connor. I accept that failing of mine. I made a mistake. I thought I had more strength and I didn't."

"Mel, you're being too hard on yourself."

"Okay," she answered back, "the fates were against me. Whatever."

Greg wrapped his arm around her, and she slid down into the

nest under his shoulder. Greg nodded good-bye to Connor and turned Melissa toward the van.

Connor watched them leave. Greg was driving and he kept missing the gears. The big van lunged and jerked, then sped off down the hill, tires squealing.

"Shit," Connor swore, kicking up gravel. It was all going wrong. He would lose the woman without sleeping with her, lose his rent money, lose his job. Martin was right. No one would come up again to the mountain crafts school, not when they heard how these people had been murdered in the hills.

"Goddamn fucking shit!" he shouted, just to hear his own voice.

He turned around and moved toward the crafts house office when he spotted the boy hidden away in the long grass and weeds behind the parking lot. The boy grinned at him.

"You little shit!" Connor ran for the kid, jumping Adam before he could flee.

Nick Kardatzke had to spell out his situation to the local police. They were overwhelmed with calls from all over the hills, and even the national news. "Dan Rather called me," the Beaver Creek police chief declared. Kardatzke made his case, how he had left his rented car at the schooner-house, and now he "needed wheels."

He called New York next and reported in, telling them about the killings.

"It could be this crazy bitch," he told New York, "but I'm getting the kid, and getting out of here."

When he hung up, he glanced around the crafts school offices. The downstairs rooms were empty and the big building was silent. He had a sixth sense about knowing if a place was empty, and he knew that this place wasn't. His pulse quickened.

He reached under his suit jacket and pulled out his small Smith & Wesson .38 and stepped out into the hallway. There was another set of rooms across the hall with both doors open, displaying pottery and hand weaving art objects.

He glanced around, then moved slowly and softly toward the back of the building and looked outside. The parking lot was empty. The van was gone. It didn't surprise him. He had given the description of the van to the local police. If the girl tried to leave the mountains, she'd be stopped.

The detective turned, walked back down the hallway, and looked out the front screen door onto the open front porch that overlooked the valley. He was momentarily distracted by the sight, by the long lingering summer sunlight that swept the fields and turned the grass golden. Pretty, he thought. His wife would like it.

He saw the crafts guy, Connor, still there, sitting in a rocker with his sandaled feet propped up against the wooden railing. Kardatzke took a deep breath. It was Connor's presence that he felt.

He put away the Smith & Wesson and pushed off the screen door.

"Okay," he announced, "we're in business."

He took two more steps and realized he was wrong, realized there was trouble, and pulled out his .38 in one quick, smooth action. Crouching at once, he spun around on the open porch. His heart pumped against his chest and his mouth dried up.

He was excited, and he was happy. Something was finally going down. He was ready. He kept turning, watching his back, and approached the rocking chair, moving so he came up from the front and could see if the man was alive, though his instincts told him Connor had already bought the ranch. Violence, the cop knew from experience, left its own odor.

Connor looked fine. His head was propped artfully up against the palm of his right hand, and he was gazing off, looking at the pretty mountain sunset.

There were no violent marks on his face or arms, Kardatzke saw, and nothing was missing but his heart. The cop whistled, as he always did when he was really frightened.

The heart had been ripped clear from his chest, pulled out through a gaping bloody mass of muscles and tissues and rib cage. It was as if someone had done a bad job of gutting a human being, Kardatzke thought next, and thought, too, how what had just happened to this Connor had happened to a dozen others in the subways of New York.

"Shit," he whispered. He knew he was alone, without a backup team. He could almost taste how much he was alone. There was no traffic on the nearby mountain road, no voices. Nothing. He felt his bowels loosening.

"Shit," he said again, remembering Korea and his first fire-fight.

He realized next that it would take more than the local cops to find this killer. He wondered how long it might take to mobilize the National Guard and get them into the mountains. Then he thought, and this was the final thought of his life, that he shouldn't have let the two of them drive off in the van, that they were nothing but trouble, he knew, but at least there were two of them, and there was always safety in numbers.

The bald-headed boy was up on the side of the mountain cliff behind the schooner-house, sitting perched like a great big owl in the first dark of the mountain night. He was watching the house, shrouded some by the cold mist off the creek, which was spreading and closing in around the building.

He sat roosted on top of a flat boulder, more like an animal of the woods, without a thought, or reason why, and just the barest of memory, watching the woman and the man inside the glass house. He sniffed the air, smelled meat being fried, and that stirred him, made his mouth water. He was hungry. He blinked his eyes, and waited, though he did not know why he waited. Soon, though he didn't know it, he would be stirred into desire and need. He yawned, curled down close to himself, and wrapped his thin arms around his body. He waited in the dark woods.

Melissa hung up the telephone, stepped back to the stove, and pushed the pieces of frying chicken on the skillet. She had telephoned the school and Connor's house, but couldn't reach him.

Perhaps he was driving over. He liked to drop in unannounced. But he wouldn't do that, not with Greg here. She had seen how upset he was that Greg had arrived. Well, it was her fault. She hadn't handled the two men well. She had let Connor come on to her, and dropped him when Greg arrived. She felt rotten at the way she had treated him. Connor wasn't a bad guy, and she had been attracted to him. Or had she just wanted to get it on with him to stop herself from obsessing about Greg? She shook her head, marveling at how she had screwed things up.

"Melissa?" Greg called.

She turned and looked across the open space to where Greg was standing in the middle of the living-room space. He had been looking at Adam's paintings when she started dinner, and she saw he had displayed them around the room.

He nodded to her, indicating that she should come to him. Melissa turned down the gas under the chicken pieces and walked around the counter that divided the two sections.

"What do you see?" he asked.

Melissa scanned the paintings as a group for the first time, all the different sizes and shapes, the different techniques.

"Study them," Greg said.

Melissa glanced from the paintings to Greg, who was pacing the length of the long room, as if this were a SoHo loft. She wondered what he was driving at. Greg was that way. He would toss off a comment, let it float into the room, and watch others decide what he meant. At the agency it drove her crazy, his little games.

"What do you want me to say, Greg?"

"I don't know!" He shrugged, defending himself against her quick comment. "Don't they tell you something?" he asked, gesturing to the twenty odd pieces.

Melissa kept frowning, thinking that Greg had discovered some truth about the paintings, about Adam, and he wanted her to guess it. She hated it when he behaved like a shrink.

"I don't know anything about art."

"We're not talking art here. We're talking a crazy person. Do they tell you anything about Adam? Come on, you're the one with courses in art therapy."

She concentrated on the paintings, going systematically from one to the next, glancing at the pencil sketches, the charcoal drawings, the two large oils, and the other smaller drawings she had found in his sketchbook.

"They have nothing to do with Adam," she finally said. "These paintings are about me. I'm in every one, in some way. Look!" She drew Greg's attention to a small sketch of the New Land Tabernacle Church, showed him how Adam had drawn her in the congregation, a frightened face hidden among the mountain believers. "I hadn't even been up to the church," she told Greg, "but, you know...he knew." She looked at Greg, letting another wave of fear sweep her body.

Greg drew her into a tight embrace. She closed her eyes, frightened by the art.

"It's a crazy puzzle, you know," Greg said, looking at the paintings over Melissa's shoulder. "I keep searching for clues, as if I can figure out these drawings, then I'd understand him and know what to do."

"He knows me. He knows what I'm going to do. He knows where I once lived as a child. He knows my nightmares." She was trembling in Greg's arms.

"You need a drink," he told her.

"I need to look at the chicken." She smelled the meat burning on the stove and pulled from Greg's arms, thinking that if she kept busy, she would be all right. "I want to get out of here right away," she told Greg. "Right after we eat, let's get packed and go."

"What about Adam?"

"I don't care."

"The cops might want to talk to you," Greg said, coming into the kitchen. He was looking for the liquor.

"It's here," she told him, pointing to the bottom shelf, as she kept turning the chicken. "If the cops want to talk to me, they can do it back in New York. I'm getting out of here. I'm scared to death in these mountains."

She glanced out the window as the thick mist off the mountain creek encased the house. Just a few weeks ago, she had thought how beautiful and romantic the mist looked, how much like a sailing ship the schooner-house really was. Now it frightened her. Everything outside, beyond the safety of floodlights, frightened her.

"You're not alone," Greg told her. He was crouched down, looking through the lower cabinets. "Why does this Connor have all these small plastic bags?" he asked, holding up three boxes.

Melissa shook her head, not paying attention. She was thinking of what might have happened if Greg hadn't come down. "I'd be dead, you know," she told him.

Greg stood up, holding a bottle. "Scotch?" he asked.

Melissa nodded.

Greg poured two drinks, then swung around, and jumped up

onto the kitchen counter beside the stove and watched her finish cooking the chicken. "Did you keep an old diary around your Brooklyn apartment, something Adam might have read, something that would have told him about what happened to you as a child?"

Melissa shook her head, still not looking at Greg. She concentrated on the chicken that was sizzling on the hot stove.

"Is there something you want to tell me?" he asked softly. Greg was aware of the silence of the house, and the water rushing over the pebbles in the stream outside, the hard gushing sound of the cascading water. He watched Melissa breathing. He saw her chest labored with tension. He resisted an urge to go to her, wrap her up tightly in his arms. He thought of his wife in labor, remembering her pain at the moment of delivery. He had never loved his wife more than at that moment, and now he loved Melissa totally, watching how she was forcing herself to speak.

"I had a sister," Melissa said slowly. "Her name was Stephanie. She died when I was eleven. I tell everyone that she died of meningitis. But she didn't die of meningitis. She was six years old and we shared a room on the second floor of this house. We were living in Arizona. It was summertime and very hot. I had wanted to go to the public pool, but Mom wouldn't go. She was waiting for some guy, I guess. She had sent the two of us upstairs to play, while she sat alone in the backyard, having a drink, getting a tan. I was supposed to look after Stephie.

"We got into a fight over something. I don't remember what now. We were always fighting, siblings you know. I remember I was always very possessive of my things. I didn't have many toys, and everything I owned was incredibly important to me.

"I don't really remember what happened next. I was playing with my things, I guess, but when I looked up, or something, I saw that Stephie had gotten out onto the window. There was this ledge there, like a window seat.

"I guess I yelled at her. Told her to get down. But she wouldn't. And I remember thinking: Why don't you fall off the roof and kill yourself. That thought is the one clear memory I have of that moment in my life.

"The next thing I knew she was tumbling down the roof. She hit the gutter and flipped off, disappearing. I didn't even hear her hit the ground. All I heard was my mother screaming.

"I never left the bedroom. I just climbed into my bed and tucked my dolls around me. They came for me about ten minutes later, after the ambulance arrived, and the police, and all the noisy neighbors.

"My mother never asked me what had happened. She just tore into the bedroom and slugged me with her fist. I was supposed to be watching Stephanie."

Melissa stopped talking. She was leaning over the stove and her tears fell into the frying pan, sizzling as they hit the hot iron.

Greg held his breath.

"I'm not sure why I killed her. I was in a rage, of course, because of my doll. I had had it since I was an infant. My father had given it to me."

She took a deep breath, lifting the chicken parts from the skillet.

"They had me tested at school, and there was a lot of trouble. I was given dolls to play with, you know, and asked to imagine one was my sister. They asked me what I would do with the doll. I kept putting her to bed, tucking her in, kissing her good night. I knew what I was doing.

"I wasn't crazy. They hoped I might be. It would have made it easier for everyone, given all of them some sort of explanation. They couldn't just believe a little girl got mad one day and killed her baby sister. They didn't want to believe it. And finally, they didn't believe it. They called her death an accident."

Melissa stopped trying to lift the chicken parts from the stove. Her hands were trembling. She looked up at Greg, her eyes brimming, and she shrugged, helpless in her plight.

Greg took her into his arms, smothered her against him, and squeezed her tight. She wasn't crying and she didn't respond to his embrace, but she needed to be held and comforted. She could never remember being comforted as a child, of having the luxury of cuddling with her mother, of feeling protected from life.

"It happens," Greg whispered. "Things like that happen and they are terrible. It wasn't your fault. You didn't know."

"Oh, I know," Melissa told him. She pulled free of Greg. "I wanted to kill her. I remember that moment clearly. There is no denying I wanted to shove her off the ledge, get her out of my sight. I hated Stephanie. She had taken my mother away from me. I was jealous of her. And in my adolescent mind, I blamed her because my father had left us."

She started to cry, sobbing from the depths of her body. With one hand she clung to the counter, but she kept explaining, telling Greg how she should have been helped, given treatment, but no one wanted to admit that little girls kill their siblings.

"We know," she told Greg, reaching in her back pocket for some tissues. "We have seen the data from our shelters. But twenty years ago in this little hick town, they didn't want to know. It would have been too expensive to treat damaged kids like me, so they labeled Stephanie's death an accident and filed it away. No one gave a shit about me, that's for sure. They didn't care what kind of nightmares I was going to have for the rest of my life."

Melissa looked down at the fried chicken and said calmly, "This is done, let's eat."

They ate in silence, sitting together on the sofa and using the handmade coffee table. Melissa was famished. She hadn't eaten all day, and the tension had made her hungry. Greg picked at his food. No wonder he was so thin, Melissa thought. The man never ate. She knew this from work, from having had hundreds of luncheons with the man.

"Adam didn't draw that, Melissa," he said after a few minutes. "There's nothing here about you, you and your sister." He was holding a leg of chicken in his right hand and he motioned toward the circle of paintings that he had pinned to the schooner-house walls.

Melissa nodded.

"I mean, he knows everything else about you, why not that?" Greg turned sideways to look at her.

"He knows," she said.

"He knows?"

Melissa wiped the corners of her mouth with a napkin. She was nodding, swallowing the food in her mouth, then she said, "He knows everything about me, that's why he's after me."

"But he's not after you, Melissa. You and he have been together for what, a couple months, and nothing has happened."

"Something will."

"Why?"

"Because I killed my sister." Melissa continued to finish her dinner, carefully cutting up the pieces of chicken on her plate.

Greg leaned away, to get a better angle on her face, and was watching the sharp profile of her small face. She was frowning, concentrating on her food. Her cheek muscles were tense and tight, making her face dark and small. He was aware and irritated by the scraping of her silverware on the heavy pottery plate.

"Melissa," Greg said, still watching her. "You're letting this thing get out of control. Adam, as far as we know, hasn't done a goddamn thing. It's that crazy woman who's killing people. The cops aren't here, are they?" He was talking fast, like a man building a defense against a tide of evidence. "It's nonsense to think that Adam, some-how, in some way, has come to get you, like an avenging angel, to make you pay for what you did as a child."

"I wasn't a child."

"Melissa, please don't do this to yourself," Greg reached for her.

Melissa moved her arm away. She would not be comforted. Not now, she thought. She didn't deserve his love.

"You're mind-fucking yourself," he told her, angry with her sudden coldness. "You have gotten everything twisted around. You're seeing shadows and ghosts. You're making yourself into a victim." He raised his voice, compelling her to listen.

Melissa set her plate and silverware on the handmade driftwood table and sat back in the deep couch. She looked lost, surrounded by oversize pillows. She wouldn't look at him, but she didn't bolt away either. Greg kept talking, telling her to be logical, that she was right, they should leave, let Nick Kardatzke find Adam, but above all, she should stop doing this, making herself believe she was responsible for everyone's life.

"You do that at work, you know," he told her. "You're always taking care of people, me especially! You've got to start thinking of yourself, of getting your own life in order."

Melissa reached over and took hold of his hand, squeezed his fingers. She was smiling sadly, weary from the long day. She nodded once, as if agreeing, then said, "I'm tired, Greg. I can't leave. I don't have the strength to pack."

"We'll do it first thing in the morning, okay?"

"I was thinking about what Kardatzke said earlier, how a place can generate trouble. You know, that guy in Wisconsin."

Greg nodded, watching her.

"It's not true."

"Of course it's not true! It's psychobabble. You wouldn't think a New York cop was so existential."

"We cause our own trouble," Melissa went on. "We generate the evil. Look at John F. Kennedy. He was fooling around with all those women. He had Judith Campbell sleep with him in the White House. He attracted his assassination. He was killed with Jackie next to him. Poetic justice."

"Hold it!" Greg sat up. He clutched Melissa's fingers as if he thought she was slipping away from him.

"Greg, we are responsible for all our actions. Nothing is by chance. Don't you believe that?" She was staring at him, her eyes heavy with sleep. That one drink had broken down her resistance. All she wanted to do was sleep.

"I believe we are responsible for our actions, yes, but that doesn't mean someone—Adam, for example—has been sent to deal a deadly blow, to avenge another person's death. Melissa, if you are thinking that, then you're as crazy as those Tabernacle people who think Adam is the chosen one."

"Evil exists, Greg."

"Crazy people exist."

"There are people who simply are evil. Look at Hitler. Or that guy in New York last year who cut up his girlfriend and checked her skull into a Port Authority locker."

"The guy from Tompkins Park? He thought he was Jesus Christ...?"

"He was evil."

"He was crazy."

"And Adam?"

Greg frowned, puzzled by her argument.

"Some people are crazy, Greg, but they're harmless. Others aren't. Adam isn't harmless."

"What are you saying?"

She shrugged, looking off. "I'm evil. Or at least I attract evil people."

"I won't let you believe it. If anyone is a malignant pole, it's this Crazy Sue," Greg told her.

"I think it's much more complicated..." Melissa answered, pondering her thought. Then adding, "We all have the potential for good or evil. I should think that somewhere in our life we connect, you know, with someone. It's either a positive connection or it isn't."

"My connection with Adam wasn't positive. It was basically wrong. We were two negatives making a fusion. Two live wires that connected and blew apart. It was too much for him, I guess. The latent evil that is part of me connected with him, and..."

"Melissa, stop this shit! There is nothing evil about you. My God, you are one of the finest people I know!" He jumped up, upset by her conclusions.

"Then why am I sleeping with you? Why am I stealing you away from your wife?"

Greg kept shaking his head, fighting off her questions.

"There is like original sin, Greg," Melissa reminded him. In her mind, the question had been answered.

"Oh, for chrissake! You said you were baptized."

"I was, but there are some sins that can never be forgotten, even by God."

"Melissa, I can't discuss this with you. You're not being logical." He paced away from her, asking as he walked into the kitchen space, "What about me? What does someone who happens to be Jewish do? I wasn't baptized, for chrissake!"

"You were circumcised."

"Mel, this is nonsense!" He looked back at her. Melissa did not look away. She seemed so small and lost, he thought. He ached to take care of her. She needed him more than ever. If he could get her away, back to New York, she'd be all right.

He shrugged, letting her have her way. This was not an argument that needed to be won.

"I know you don't believe me," she told him. "I know you're just humoring me. That's okay." She was not offended. "But I know I'm right." She nodded again, drawing her lips tight.

Greg came back to sit beside her, leaning forward and resting his elbows on his thin knees. He could not let go of this, he realized, cursing himself for his own stubbornness.

"Mel, I agree there's evil out there, okay!" He waved toward the darkness of the hills. "There was Hitler, Idi Amin, and Qaddafi, okay; they're evil. And that killer out in California who shot up the school yard. The guy with the AK rifle? Yes, I agree. They're evil. And maybe Adam is, too, but you don't know. I don't know! We don't know whether he killed anyone or not. But Melissa"—he was shaking his head, frowning, and seemed in pain—"you are not evil. You are not responsible for any of this. It doesn't matter whether you were baptized as a child or not. It just doesn't matter."

He leaned forward and kissed her on the cheek.

When he pulled back, Melissa was watching him. Her eyes were bright with the excitement that comes when one has discovered a truth.

She held up her two forefingers, inches apart, watching Greg as she spoke.

"This is me. This is Adam. All right?"

Her eyes darted from Greg's face to her own fingers. Slowly, as she spoke, she moved her fingers closer. Greg found he was holding his breath, waiting for her explanation.

"Dallas prepared Lee Harvey Oswald to kill Kennedy. There was hatred for Kennedy in the air. That hatred ignited Oswald. He was a bomb. A tragedy waiting to happen."

She moved her fingers closer.

"If you have two evil forces coming together, two people who are connected somehow, maybe they're related, maybe they share the same star, or have some sort of biological connection, something cosmic that sets off a spark. I caused that spark. I triggered Adam."

"Why didn't it happen in New York?"

"Perhaps the place was wrong. Kardatzke might be on to something. You need the combination of place and people; it sets off a killer, as it did with that Gein guy in Wisconsin." She carefully moved her forefingers together, letting the soft fingertips touch. She looked over at Greg.

"I don't believe it," he told her.

"I'm afraid not to believe it."

She leaned back in the soft cushions and stared ahead, not

focusing on any of the drawings, but thinking how bizarre it was that Adam had been able to read her mind, to recall the nightmares of her life.

They fell asleep together, in each other's arms, stretched out on the long sofa. They were nestled together like spoons, with Greg's arms wrapped tightly around Melissa, holding her close.

The moonlight woke her. She stayed where she was, nestled in the strength of Greg's arm, thinking first how lucky she was to have Greg, but all the dread that waited for her with the reality of daylight came rushing back, and she felt her body tensing. Greg stirred in his sleep. She closed her eyes and concentrated on the warmth of his body, her own pleasure.

When she opened her eyes again the moonlight was brighter. It poured through the high stained-glass window, creating a mosaic of shapes and shadows on the bare hardwood floor. She lay still, thinking she should try and get back to sleep. She was wondering what time it might be when she spotted them.

At first she thought they were only shadows from the windows, a high tree branch reflected in the moonlight, but there were too many shadows, too many shapes, too many smooth, dark shadows slipping across the bare, bright hardwood floor.

Melissa shot up, pulling out of Greg's embrace, and grabbed his shirt.

"What! What is it?" He sat up, trying to rouse himself from the fog of his sleep.

"Snakes," she whispered, "the house is full of snakes." She moved to get off the sofa, but thought better of putting her bare foot on the floor. "Greg, what are we going to do?"

He moved out from behind Melissa on the sofa and, awake, saw the snakes. They were everywhere in the bright moonlight.

"Jesus," he whispered, stunned by the sight of the waving shapes, their thick, long shapes.

"Look!" Melissa shouted. She pointed into the dark corners as a half-dozen snakes curled around the feet of chairs, then went racing across the open expanse of floor.

Greg reached up and turned on the standing lamp beside the sofa.

The light blinked on, briefly blinded them, and Greg, squinting into the room, started to count the snakes. At thirty-five, he quit.

"Adam!" Melissa said. She was sitting up on her knees. "He got them from the church."

"Snakes?"

"It's part of their ritual," Melissa explained, realizing that Greg knew nothing about the Tabernacle Church and what she had seen.

"Serpent-handlers," Greg said.

"He's let them loose on us." At that, one of the dark shadows slipped loose from a cluster and crossed the floor in a quick wave of golden color, slipping out of sight just as suddenly as it had appeared.

Melissa screamed.

"We got to get out of here," he announced.

"How?"

"I don't know, but we have to," he shouted back at her, and then realized that he couldn't get hysterical. He forced himself to be logical, trying to remember his teenage years at camp, what he had been taught about snakes. Both of them were standing on the sofa. In one part of his mind he was thinking how silly all of this was, thinking that someday they would look back and laugh at how they had behaved.

"Where are my shoes?" Melissa asked. She knelt down at the end of the sofa and quickly grabbed one sandal and then the other. She wished she had real shoes to wear.

"We got to go," Greg said again, reaching for his own sneakers.

"How?"

"Get outside. Run for the van."

"My stuff?"

"Leave it."

"I don't want to come back to this place, ever."

"Okay, you stay on the sofa. I'll pack for you."

"No, I'll get my stuff. It's upstairs. There are no snakes up there. It's impossible." She glanced over at the ladder, tried to judge how many steps it would take her to reach it safely.

"If we could get them into that box," Greg said, wondering.

"What box?"

She saw then the New Land Tabernacle Church box with the lid open. Adam had come into the house and set the box on the counter, opened it, and let the snakes crawl away on their own. Some, she saw, had escaped to the tree trunk in the center of the building, had slithered out onto the bare limbs. Looking up, she spotted the rattlers and copperheads above her, their puffy white bellies wrapped around the thick branches. "Oh, shit," she whispered, realizing they could already be in her loft bed, snuggled down into the warmth of the mattress, or nested in her nightgown, in the drawers where she had stacked her underwear.

"Come on," Greg urged.

"I can't," she said, thinking of going upstairs, of opening a dresser drawer and finding a rattler curled down in a tight ball on her silk panties. How could Adam know she was pathologically afraid of snakes?

"We'll do this together," Greg said, trying to sound in control. "Where are your bags?"

She pointed to the ladder.

"Get a broom. We'll need a broom to keep them away." He spotted the broom in the far corner, near the side door. He saw that two or three snakes were wiggling across the bare floor, moving with a speed that impressed and terrified him. "I'll get the broom," he said, trying to build his courage. He did not move. He tried to judge the distance between where the broom was and the sofa. "This is ridiculous!" he shouted, angry at himself for his fear.

Melissa grabbed his arm and dug her nails into his flesh.

"Can't we call the super?" Greg asked, trying to cut the tension.

"We're going to die here," Melissa stated. "I'm going to die here."

"We're going to starve to death if we can't get off this sofa, that's for sure. Unless Connor shows up." The thought of Connor finding him frightened and marooned on the sofa made him more angry at himself.

"They'll go away at daybreak, won't they?" Greg asked.

"How do I know! You're the Boy Scout, remember? What were all those stories you told me of camping on the Hudson River?"

"The Hudson doesn't have copperskins."

"Copperheads."

"Okay, copperheads, whatever!"

"Connor would know what to do," Melissa stated.

"Fuck Connor!" Greg reached down and banged the floor with his fist and the snakes scattered, frightened by the bounce of his hand on the barn board.

"That's it!" Melissa exclaimed.

"What is?"

She looked hopefully at the counter, to where she had set her portable Sony radio.

"Music," she told Greg. "Lots of loud, god-awful country music."

"I can't believe this!" His fear was making him giddy. "Willie Nelson coming right up!"

"You betcha! Watch!"

She summoned up her courage to jump from the couch and as she did, a heavy rattler slipped off the bare branch overhead, and tumbled down in a thick disjointed arc, like a loose belt, and dropped onto her head, fell across her thin shoulder, and into her lap. She screamed at the touch of the heavy, cold snake, and tumbled off the sofa, throwing up her hands, as if to bat away the snake.

Greg jumped over the end of the sofa, escaping the reptile. He was yelling, damning the snakes and the mountains.

Melissa ran for the counter, saw this as her only hope, and blocked the fear from her mind. She forced herself, as she had as a lonely child, to save herself.

She hit the small radio with her fist and fumbled with it, until she pressed the ON button.

Loud, scratchy electric guitar music blared into the schooner-house.

Melissa jumped back, jumped away, as the snakes, over fifty, she guessed, slithered over the floor, lifting their poisonous and fanged mouths to reach the top edge of the box, and slid down into the deep, warm safe box.

Melissa, dancing out of the way, kept her distance until the last of the bright wavy snakes found its way home.

She reached out with her foot and flipped the lid over, on top of the box, slamming it shut.

When she turned, she saw Greg standing on a kitchen chair. He was pulling up his pants legs.

"Girl Scouts," she said, and fell back against the tree-post. She shut her eyes and listened to her heart pounding her chest. It made her breasts hurt.

21

THEY FINISHED PACKING IN the hour before daybreak. It was not
so much packing, as simply grabbing everything that she owned and
taking it from the house, throwing it into the back of the van. She did
not bother with Adam's things, leaving them all in his bedroom. She
could telephone Connor later, and let him deal with Adam, if the
boy did return. Now she did not care whether he did or not. All
she could think of was getting off the mountain and out of the
state.

When they left the schooner-house, she didn't lock the doors,
only left her keys and a note for Connor on the kitchen table.
She guessed he might come by later, on his way to the crafts
school.

Leaving in the dark fitted her mood. It had only been a nightmare for her, coming south to the mountains, and what disappointed
her the most was that she had had such hopes for Adam and herself.
She had let her dreams once again get her into trouble.

Now, sitting beside Greg, letting him drive, she looked straight
ahead, not even giving a backward glance to the strange handmade
house, which once she had thought was so wonderful and creative,
and now she realized was just silly and stupid, and no way at all to
build a house. She should have known, she told herself, that the
house was all wrong, that the whole idea of creating a family
with Adam was more of her sickness. Greg had been so right about
that.

Greg stopped at the light on Store Front Street. The main street was empty. Lights were on across the intersection at the Mobil Station, but it, too, was empty. Nothing was open in the mountains. Go ahead, she told Greg. There was no need to wait for a green light. But Greg waited.

She shook her head, smiling to herself in the dark cab. It was so like him. He did everything by the books. They weren't at all alike, she reminded herself, and once they were safely in the city she would have to tell him that it would not work. She could not take him away from Helen.

She would get out of his life, leave the city and head west, perhaps she would go to California and try again, start another life. She could change her name. She had been Melissa Vaughn for over ten years. It was time for a new identity. She was like one of those rattlers, she thought, all she needed was another skin.

The light changed.

"Which way?" he asked.

"Oh, past the school. No! Don't go that way. Turn left anyway, but don't take the fork. Follow the main road. It's longer and goes around Buck's Landing, but there won't be any traffic, not at this hour."

The road was wet from overnight fog, and still shrouded in patches. Greg drove slowly, unsure of the road and the big van. His caution made Melissa nervous. She would let him drive for another half hour, then take over the wheel. Otherwise, she realized, they'd be in North Carolina all day.

It was quiet and cold in the van, and Melissa was thinking that she should have made coffee for the trip, and then tried to remember where there might be a diner open at this time of the morning, and this high up in the mountains. They would have to reach Johnson City, she guessed, before they could get any breakfast, but, as least, she thought, they would be out of the mountains.

"Well, they didn't get far," Greg said. He pointed ahead.

Melissa saw through the misty and half-light of morning, the New Land Tabernacle Church buses and a half-dozen other cars and pickup trucks parked in the small lot of Buck's Landing. The congregation had put up tents in among the trees, making the rest stop at the edge of the river resemble a makeshift camping site.

"They didn't go up to Grand Father Mountain," she said out loud, but speaking more to herself than Greg. "I wonder why..."

Greg had slowed the van to a crawl as they passed the campsite.

"Lower the window," he said to Melissa, and when she did, he asked, "should we stop?"

"No! Why would you want to stop?"

"Adam might be with them."

"I don't care."

"Yes you do!" He glanced over at her, then impulsively, he swung the van into the gravel parking lot.

"Greg! I don't want to talk to these people."

"You won't have to."

"They're asleep. Greg, it's not yet five o'clock."

Greg parked the van and turned off the engine.

"I'll run and see if anyone has seen Adam, or if he's with them; then we're gone, okay?" He smiled at her.

"Why are you doing this? You don't even like Adam."

"I love you, that's why, and I know how you don't leave anything unfinished. It's not your way."

He jumped from the van and stepped into the cool morning. "I'll be right back."

The fog was lifting. Melissa could see most of the campsite, and saw that there were people scattered across the grass, as if they had fallen asleep there between the picnic tables and in among the parked pickup trucks.

She sat up and leaned out the window. The cold breeze off the river chilled her cheeks. She was about to call out to Greg to ask him what was wrong, why were these people scattered like this in the parking lot, and then she saw there were more, children, men and women, back by the tents. It seemed as if they had in some shotgun fashion come running from the tent, then tumbled over in odd ways onto the lawn, falling into deep and motionless dreams.

But they weren't dreaming. They weren't asleep. Melissa opened her mouth to shout after Greg, to stop him from approaching the closest figure, a man who had fallen onto the gravel parking lot, and had somehow flipped over on his back, so his arms were raised, reaching up, grabbing at the thin air. She screamed, but no sound came from her choked throat. Her terror had squeezed the breath from her lungs. She pushed at the door, opening it, fleeing the cab.

She wanted to stop Greg, to save him from whatever it was out there hiding in the tent, or might be lurking down by the river. A monster, she realized with a certainty that was brilliantly clear, who had killed these people and shattered them like picnic litter.

"Greg!" she screamed again, and this time a thin whistle escaped her throat.

Greg had reached the body and approached slowly, puzzled by the figure. He had thought at first, jogging across the gravel parking lot, that it was just a bundle of rags, and not human at all.

But this was a man. He lay with its arms thrust up, and he was not sleeping out in the cold. Greg spotted the pale green fingers of the dead man. He had been reaching out, Greg thought, as if seeking help from the heavens. But there was no help. Greg studied the man's face, saw the puffed-up lips, the bloated cheeks. He recognized the caked white powder at the edges of his mouth and realized at once that the twisted and distorted face was frozen forever by strychnine.

Melissa reached Greg and threw her body against him.

"Strychnine," he said, not taking his eyes from the scattered bodies, and quickly, unaccountably, began to count all the fallen victims, realizing there were women and children, too, littering the lawn.

Melissa moved, as if to approach this ejaculated figure.

"No," Greg told her.

"They're all dead," she whispered, stunned by the fact. "They were going up to Grand Father Mountain," she added, not fully grasping the tragedy. She had spotted two little girls dressed in thin cotton summer dresses. They were embracing and had fallen together beside a picnic table, dying in a death hug. She raised her hand to her mouth and bit down hard on her knuckles to keep herself from screaming.

"Why...?" Greg asked, and then in the same breath, "We have to get the cops." He pulled at Melissa, wanting to flee the place.

"No, wait!" She stepped away and cautiously moved toward the main tent, which was set closer to the river.

"Melissa, don't," Greg said, and saw she was scanning the bodies, looking for Adam. "He's not here," he told Melissa.

"I have to be sure." She stepped to the open flap of the tent.

It was light enough inside the tent to see the remaining dead bodies, who had died within the canvas, falling over in a jumble of distorted arms and legs, in a junk pile of bodies.

Melissa skirted the bodies, hugging the edge as she went to the front of the tent. She saw the man she had spoken to the night before, the man Connor called Tyler. He had died while on his knees, had toppled forward and smashed his face against the hard dirt. She was thankful she couldn't see his face.

There was so much pain in the other faces. She was horrified by the sight, but couldn't look away. The faces were fascinating in their distortion of shapes and flesh.

"He's not here," Greg told her. "We have to get the cops."

He glanced around again at the carnage. It seemed almost that they were sleeping out in the cold of the early morning, except for the twisted shapes of their bodies, and the strange looks of horror on their faces as the strychnine squeezed the life out of them.

What madness, he thought, what goddamn terrible madness. In a few minutes the sun would clear the mountain and reach the river. It would burn off the morning dew and heat up the bodies. Bake the flesh. In another few hours, no one would be able to walk among the dead without gagging.

He spotted a little boy, a five-year-old, the same age as his son. The boy must have tried to escape the burning on his lips. He had run for the river to wash away the taste and had stumbled over, falling headfirst into the long grass, the cattails, and the lily pads, to die like an amphibian, half in and half out of the muddy river.

"Dear sweet God," he whispered, beginning to cry, and thinking he should pull the child from the weeds, but remembered this was a crime scene. He had to drive to town and find the police station. He had to tell them what had happened to the people of the New Land Tabernacle Church.

"He was here," Melissa whispered. Her eyes were wide. Now she could not see enough of their faces. She thought of the intense and sudden pain they had endured, and knew the distortions of their flesh, the freakish expressions on their faces, were not because of poison, but the story of their lives. All the suffering they had endured, the sins they had committed, were displayed on their faces.

"Come on." Greg pulled on her arm.

She did not move.

"Melissa!"

"I'll never escape my past," Melissa told him. "It's silly for me to think I could grow up, move away, change my name, and not have to pay for what I have done. I have to pay, Greg. Everyone does."

Telling Greg gave her a sudden and profound sense of peace. She felt as if she didn't have to run anymore. Her time had come.

"Melissa, you're wrong. This is something else, something evil."

"I'm evil. I killed my little sister. I never paid for it. Now I have to pay. Adam has come to get me."

"Melissa, don't do this to yourself. You were a victim. Whatever is wrong with you, you can blame on your mother, or your father. You weren't born evil!"

He was sweating, afraid he was losing her. He had Melissa in a tight embrace, but he felt her slipping away. "Melissa, please," he asked. "Don't do this to yourself. Don't do this to us."

"I'm saving you, Greg," Melissa told him. "I'm saving you. Go home to your family before it's too late. Take the van, please."

"Honey, you're not making any sense. This crazy bald-headed kid isn't a messenger of God." He was whispering, trying to make her believe him, but he saw her eyes glass over.

A semi came roaring out of the mountains, swept by on the narrow, twisting two-lane road. Greg turned and waved, tried to signal the man to stop, but the driver, high in the rig, only waved back and downshifted, roaring off.

"Shit!" he swore, realizing how alone they were, and thought next about Adam and wondered if the boy was hiding in the woods, watching them, waiting to strike.

"Melissa, we've got to get out of here."

She let herself be led away and he hoped no one would drive by. He wanted to get away from the tents and the dead congregation.

She had fallen silent in the van and he had a brief moment of fear that the stress and her physical exhaustion would be too much, that she'd flip out, go off on her own to look for the boy.

He had to get her off the mountain, but if he stopped by the police station, there would be more questions and delays. He was afraid now of what Melissa might say to the cops. If she started to talk about Adam and how she was responsible for these brutal murders they would never let her go.

At the stoplight and the Mobil Station he stopped, then swung the van onto Creek Drive and drove back to the schooner-house. She didn't react. She was staring out the front window, not registering where he was driving. He would get to the house, he decided, leave her there, and go up to the police station, tell the cops himself what they had found. He wouldn't ever mention Melissa. He would keep her out of the picture altogether.

Swinging into the backyard of the schooner-house, Greg just halted the van and told Melissa that he'd see the police and then come back to get her. Melissa nodded, opened the side door, and jumped out. She didn't look back.

Greg waited and watched while she walked across the lawn and into the house. He shouldn't leave her, he thought, thinking of Adam, that the kid might be waiting for her inside the house. But she didn't seem afraid of the kid, he reminded himself, and also, he told himself once more, the boy wasn't wanted by the cops. They had caught the killer. It was only Melissa who believed the boy was inherently evil.

He saw the lights flicker on inside the schooner-house and that reassured him, then he waited a few minutes more, letting the engine of the van idle, and when he realized Melissa wasn't coming screaming for help, and hadn't come racing out of the house, he threw the gear into first and pulled out of the yard, went bouncing over the washboard dirt road and back up the small hill and into town.

Adam had been there, she realized, turning on the lights. All of the paintings had been ripped from the wall. She saw smoldering ashes in the fireplace where he had stuffed his art work and set it on fire.

"Adam?" she called, standing by the door. She was too frightened to go into the rooms. She guessed he wasn't in the house. He had burned the paintings and left, she hoped.

But he had been there the night before. He had let loose the snakes. She had no question about that.

That thought chilled her. Had he been waiting until she came back alone to the schooner-house? She heard the van engine start up and grabbed the doorknob, started to pull open the door and run for Greg, and then she stopped. He wouldn't surface unless she was by herself. She would have to deal with Adam alone.

"Adam?" she asked again, struggling to keep her fear from quivering his name.

It was now bright in the high-lofted rooms of the house. The lights were not necessary. She stepped a few paces into the room, moving into the center, so that he couldn't surprise her, turning around as she stepped into the living-room space, glancing toward the open doorway of his room, glancing up at the small crawl space of her tiny bedroom. The house was so open that there was nowhere to hide.

"Dammit," she whispered, angry at her predicament. "Adam, where are you?"

She stood very still listening for him. The silence of the big strange house frightened her.

"Adam, we have to talk." She had softened her voice, as if her sudden gentleness might help him respond.

And then she saw him. He was sitting on the bare boulder behind the house, but seeing him startled her, and her heart leapt to her throat.

"Oh, God," she exclaimed, frightened more by the sight of him. If he wasn't there, if he had not been waiting for her, she could have gone away knowing she had tried, and whatever else happened would not have been so much her fault. Now she had to deal with him. He was her responsibility.

But seeing him calmed her somewhat. He was in his familiar pose, sitting with his back to the house. She could see the top of his round, perfectly bald head. And from the way his shoulders moved, she knew he was tossing pebbles into the creek. He knew she was there, too, and was just waiting for her to come get him. She did not call for him. He wouldn't respond, she knew.

She glanced around the house impulsively thinking that she might take some weapon with her. One of the irons from the fireplace, or perhaps a kitchen knife, and then in the same thought realized she could not use a weapon on the boy if he did attack her. She would have to deal with him in some other way, though she did not know how or what way.

Leaving the house by the side door and walking around to where he was sitting, she made as much noise as she could, scraping her feet on the gravel walk, calling his name.

Outside, she was less frightened. It was a warm morning, and bright. A wonderful day, she thought, to be in the mountains. She turned the corner of the schooner-house and saw he was gone.

She ran to where he had been sitting on the boulder and caught sight of him. He had jumped the creek and was walking deliberately up the side of the hill, disappearing into the trees. Melissa shouted after him, knowing he wouldn't stop, seeing him stride away. He wanted her to follow him.

She glanced back, looked at the safety of the house, thinking she should go inside and wait for Greg. She should call the station, she thought, and tell them she had seem Adam go off into the woods. But even as she thought this through, she knew she would go after Adam. She had to deal with the boy.

She jumped the creek and walked up the narrow deer path into the trees, climbing the hillside, which was still damp with dew, and also cold, once she was out of the sunlight.

She could not see Adam. He had crested the hill and gone off, she guessed, across the level, open pastureland. Still, she kept glancing around, looking into the dark underbrush, watching thick trees, half expecting that Adam had lured her up the hillside and was crouched in the shadows, waiting until she came closer, and then he would jump her.

Just thinking that frightened her, and she raced ahead, up the steep hill, running toward the daylight and stumbling into the warm sunlight and gasping for breath. Adam was not waiting for her. She scanned the meadow and spotted the top of his bald head, saw that he was moving toward the woods beyond, in the same direction she had crossed earlier, toward where she had found the body of the dead student.

"Adam, stop!" she shouted out, realizing he would not stop, and not even sure if he could hear her. Here, in the bright open field, her voice diminished, as did the threat to her life.

She was just imagining all of this, she thought, following him again, making a path through the long grass. In the daylight, he seemed harmless, just a boy out exploring.

Then she remembered the dead at Buck's Landing, pictured all of the bodies, the violent strychnine deaths. She heard police sirens next. Their distant wail echoed through the hills, bouncing off the far mountain ridges. The bodies had been found. And Greg would be driving back to the schooner-house to look for her. She had forgotten to leave him a note and momentarily thought of turning around, of going back and getting him, but then the boy slipped out of sight, disappeared into the edge of trees, and at once she picked up her pace and jogged after him in the bright early morning sun.

Reaching the cool woods, and the damp path that went downhill toward the creek where she had found the boy's body, submerged with rocks, she stopped walking. She could not see nor hear Adam. The woods were cool after running across the hot field. She stood very still and listened for him. There was no doubt that he knew she was pursuing him, and that angered her. She thought of everything that she had done for him, how she had saved the boy from death in the subways, and then she reminded herself that she wasn't dealing with a normal child, that Adam was a strange aberration, a savage child who had come to kill her.

She plunged down the path, picking up speed on the slippery dirt and ran toward the creek, jumped it, and went on running downhill, heading, she knew, for the school road. He would catch her there, she thought, running full speed. He would leap out from behind one of the thick trunks and seize her, knock her off stride. She wondered if she was strong enough to defend herself. He looked like such a thin, helpless child, but if he was truly mad, she could not defend herself.

She burst into the open at the base of the hill, running full stride onto the mountain road, stumbling and grabbing onto low branches to break her stride, to keep herself from falling. She spotted Adam at once. He was walking leisurely up toward the crafts school.

"Adam," she shouted, furious once again at this cat-and-mouse chase.

He halted then, and, turning, waved to her, signaled that she should follow him. He was smiling, she saw.

"What is this?" she murmured, taking several deep breaths and following. She was too exhausted to run and catch up, and Adam wasn't waiting.

The crafts school was deserted, she saw, approaching the buildings. The parking lot was empty except for Connor's Jeep. She wondered where the detective had gone, and then she spotted the cop. He was on the front porch of the school, sitting with Connor. She knew at once, when she was more than fifty yards from the school, that something was wrong, that this didn't make sense. The men were motionless, sitting together in the early morning on the deserted school porch.

"Connor," she shouted, hoping he was all right, that she would get his attention.

Neither man stirred. They were grouped together in an awkward setting. Connor, with his back to her, was sitting on the rocker. And the New York detective was stretched out on the long wooden bench. She thought at once of the bodies at Buck's Landing and the silence of the scattered dead.

"Oh, God," she whispered, needing to hear her own voice. "Oh, dear God."

Adam had done this on purpose. He had brought her to the school. He had wanted to show her what he had done to Connor and the cop. She saw even from a distance of ten yards that the bodies had been mutilated. She saw just enough of the bloody mess to look away at once, to take a series of quick, deep breaths to keep from getting sick. Then she ran by the bodies and went into the cool, dark interior of the school and stood alone in the front hallway. She needed to telephone the police, more murders in the mountains, she thought wryly. The number of bodies that she had seen that morning had numbed her reaction. All of her emotional responses were frozen. She just had to get through the day. She had to deal with Adam, and stop him before they were all dead.

She phoned the town's police and told them two more people had been murdered at the school. When she was assailed by the operator, and asked more questions, she hung up the phone and left the office, went looking for Adam.

He was in the building, she guessed, and immediately she mounted the wide wooden stairs to the third floor, knowing it was the art studio where he had gone. And she found them there, working on his last painting.

When she saw what he had done, the vast oil paintings that filled the four walls of the large art studio, she knew it hadn't been the bodies on the porch that he wanted her to see, but that he had brought her back through the woods to see this piece of work.

She guessed he had worked on it most of the night, drawing it after he had killed Connor and the cop, perhaps after he had led the congregation of the New Land Tabernacle Church in their mass suicide. It had taken most of the night, she knew, and seeing it, without implication of what it meant, she was impressed by the size and detail, the richness of the world.

She thought of when she had gone to Florence and visited the Uffizi, and how Michelangelo had used members of the Medici family as models for the three Wise Men in his masterpiece the *Procession of the Magi,* while Botticelli used the mistress of another Medici as his model for the *Birth of Venus*.

Adam had done the same here, though the work on the wall was not of his brief life, but, she saw, of hers. He stood in the middle of the room, holding a paintbrush, still wet with paint. He was still working, Melissa realized, and as she scanned the four walls, he went back again and again to touch up some point, or redefine a detail.

She pivoted on the heels of her feet, trying to take in the whole mural with one glance, as well as trying to understand what it all meant.

She saw herself again as a child, saw herself in Kansas City and Texas, saw memories from her childhood that she could not remember, but which she guessed were true. Had she been so frightened by a teacher that she wet her underwear?

What she knew was that the shy little girl with the mousy brown hair that he had sketched in dozens of oil portraits was her. She did not question the art, only the meaning.

Without taking her eyes from the wall, she asked Adam, "Who are you?" She half expected he might answer her, but when he didn't, she asked next, "What do you want? Why are you doing this to me?" She was so ashamed for the humiliation he had caused her, for all the pain she had endured, for the deaths she had witnessed that she only wanted it done with, to have it all over and finished. "Tell me!" she demanded, screaming at him. "What is it that you want?"

He went again to the wall and started to paint quickly in one small corner, which, she saw now, had not been used. She moved closer, knowing she would have her answer. He would paint his reply, he would finally tell her the truth.

He worked quickly, using the oils from a dozen small cans, and drew a woman, a beautiful woman, who was standing by the seashore looking west into a storm cloud. The painting was lush with color, a lovely, slim woman in her twenties, with golden hair, beautiful skin, and holding a white sun hat. She was watching sailboats that tossed on the waves, and Melissa knew, too, from the smile on the woman's face that she was watching her lover.

"She's lovely," Melissa whispered, "but who is...?"

Then she realized who it was. He had drawn her sister Stephanie as she would have been. Stephanie as a beautiful, wealthy woman, if she had lived, if she had not been pushed off the window ledge and sent tumbling down the shiny shingles to fall with a deadening thump onto the grass beside their mother's reclining lawn chair, sipping her gin 'n' tonic as her daughter dropped to her death.

She went for Adam. She leapt across the room and tried to grab him, to rake her nails down his face, to harm the child, to kill him before he drove her crazy with his paintings.

He spun away as she dove and swept the thick brush through the air, showering the room and Melissa with dabs of paint. She kept coming, jumping to her right, and wedged the small teenager in the far corner of the room. He was grinning at her, enjoying this. He jabbed the brush into the bucket of red paint and then held it up like a club. The brush dripped paint onto the floor.

Still enraged, Melissa jumped him again. She was small and quick and her speed surprised him. He got his arm halfway up, was ready to swat her with the heavy brush when she caught him on the shoulders, knocked him against the wall.

He bounced off the wall and tried to dart past her, but she seized him at the waist and held on, only to lose her balance on the slippery floor and slide to her knees. She pulled Adam with her.

He jabbed her in the back of the neck with his elbow, then

whacked her in the face with the brush. Melissa ducked her head, trying to avoid the blows, and held on. If he got away, she knew, she would not have the strength to go after him, but now she wasn't certain she had the strength to hold him.

She reached back with her feet, trying to get some traction, but her feet kept slipping on the wet paint. Then, wrestling him under her, she shifted her slight body and braced her feet against the wall, and just as quickly she raised up, lifted the boy in her arms, and tumbled him over, slammed him down, and jumped on top, saddling his body with her legs, tramping his arms under her legs. She forced him back so he lay spread-eagled beneath her.

"Who are you?" she screamed at him. "Why are you doing this to me?" She could barely talk, and her questions were forced out between gasps of breath.

Outside, dimly at first, and then increasingly, she heard the sound of police sirens as cars came up the valley road to the school.

The bald-headed boy grinned up at her.

"I hate you," she shouted, striking him, swinging her small fist at his smooth pale face.

He did not stop grinning, even when she cut his lip with the ring on her finger. The blood ran in a bright color down his chin.

"Goddamn you!" She grabbed his throat, drove her nails into his throat, squeezing his Adam's apple. He kept grinning at her, watching her with his silvery gray eyes. She kept squeezing, trying to wipe the smile from his face. "Stop it!" she shouted, tightening her grip, feeling the life of the child being forced out of his throat. Her nails punctured the skin of his neck.

She watched his face as she squeezed, waiting to see the realization of death cross his eyes. She saw a flash of pain shine in his glassy stare, and tears bubble up in the corners of his eyes. Still, he kept smiling.

He was enjoying this. He did not struggle beneath her grasp. He wanted her to kill him, to choke the life out of him.

She loosened her grip. She took her hands off his throat, leaving the fresh imprint of her long, thin fingers on his white flesh, and a thin trail of blood. Adam gasped and choked, regaining his breath. Momentarily his round hairless head was bright red as blood and oxygen flooded his brain. She let him go.

She moved off his body, freeing his arms, and standing; exhausted from chasing him, from trying to kill him, she stumbled away and found a chair. Sitting, she lowered her head between her legs to regain her strength. She was aware the boy might attack her and she almost wished he would. If he did attack, she might feel outraged enough to defend herself and kill him. She knew it was wrong, letting him live, but she could not kill Adam.

She remembered Stephanie, the startled look of hopelessness and fear as the little girl went tumbling away from her and down the bright shiny shingles of the roof.

There were now a stampede of footsteps on the wooden stairs of the crafts school, and she heard Greg, shouting her name. She looked up. Adam was watching her. He stared at her with his familiar accusing eyes. The same way he had looked at her when he came up from his subterranean darkness. The smile was gone from his eyes. He seemed disappointed to be alive.

She closed her eyes, knowing that when she opened them again Greg would be beside her, holding and comforting and protecting her.

She heard Greg's voice beside her, whispering that she was okay, that she was safe, and then he gently took her into his arms. She opened her eyes and saw she was right. She was alone with him in the third-floor studio.

She stared at the great canvas of her secret life, all of the places and events of her childhood. She saw Adam had painted as well the bedroom she shared with Stephanie in Arizona, the bedroom where Stephanie had tumbled to her death.

There was an open window, too, with white lacy curtains blowing into the breeze. The window was empty, the tragic accident had occurred, Stephanie had fallen to her death. And then Melissa saw Adam had sketched something else, a small stuffed animal, a child's toy, abandoned on the roof and beyond the reach of the window. It was only then that Melissa remembered her tiny toy, and why it was on the dangerous ledge of the roof. It was only then that she realized why she had been unable to kill the bald-headed boy.

Melissa lay on one of the dormitory thin single beds. It was very quiet in the big building, though she could hear voices outside, and footsteps on the gravel path, and now and then a police car would leave, and a siren would fill the clear mountain air. Greg had been with her, had brought her to the dormitory room to rest after she had washed off the paint.

It was peaceful in the second-floor dormitory room and cool after the heat of the morning, and her exhaustion. She wished she could sleep, but she knew she couldn't and she tried to keep from thinking at all, tried to let her mind just drift off into space. She wished she knew how to meditate.

Greg came back into the room, walking softly so as not to disturb her.

"Did they get him?" she asked, opening her eyes.

"Not yet." He sat beside her on the bed. "They will. They've got every good old boy in the county looking for him. The parking lot looks like a used pickup lot. The word, I guess, went out on the CBs." He was smiling, trying to be positive. "They must have a half a hundred mountain boys down there, and everyone is carrying a shotgun." He reached over and took hold of her fingers. "Are you okay?" he whispered, touching her. Her fingers were dry and lifeless. He waited for her to respond to his gesture.

"I don't know if I'm okay or not," she told him. At that moment, she wished she could stay there forever in the coolness and quiet of the second-floor dormitory.

"He would have killed you, Melissa," Greg said, "if we hadn't got there. I don't know how in hell he got away. I saw him, you know, for just a second. He flashed by me. I didn't know who, what it was."

Melissa did not answer. She knew Adam would not have killed her.

"What will they do with him? If they catch him?"

"Lock him up. He killed Connor and the detective." He stopped talking and studied her, puzzled, and feeling bewildered and overwhelmed by everything that had happened to him and Melissa since he arrived in Asheville. "Are you really okay, Melissa?" he asked, meaning himself as much as her.

"I don't know." She shook her head, not stirring from the bed. "Can we leave this place?"

"I guess so. The bodies are gone."

"I want to get away from here."

"You're right. Let's go before the television people get here. They should have heard what happened down by the river. Tonight, Buck's Landing will be on every news program in America. It's just like Jonestown." He stood up then to give her room to get off the narrow bed.

"Are they blaming him for that?"

"Who else? They'll pin all these murders on him."

"No they won't." She swung her legs off the bed.

"Of course they will."

"Adam didn't kill those people. They killed themselves. Some smart detective will figure that out."

"Melissa, what is this? You can't go on defending him."

"I'm not. He didn't do it."

"What about Connor? Who killed him?"

Melissa stood, straightening her skirt. She caught a glimpse of herself in the small mirror on the dresser. She looked like her own nightmare. Her hair needed combing, and she needed makeup. Melissa turned from the mirror, embarrassed at what she saw.

"Adam killed him and the cop," Greg said, making his point.

Melissa put her hand on Greg's shoulder, and using him to balance her, she slipped her bare feet into her sandals, "Adam doesn't kill people. He lets other people kill themselves, or causes people to kill others. That's his way." She thought of herself saddling him, how she had dearly wanted to kill him.

"You told me. He's evil."

"That detective was right, you know," Melissa said, staring up at Greg. "There are places that breed killings. Dallas was one. Dallas killed Kennedy. Oswald only pulled the trigger."

"And New York is another?"

"Yes, New York is another. Everyone knows that." She was trying to do something with her hair, and having failed walked out of the room, expecting Greg to follow after her. They were alone in the crafts house. She could feel the silence of the place, and immediately she became tense. "Let's get out of here," she said quickly, and went rushing down the wooden stairs that led to the main front room, and then outside. They walked onto the front porch where there were still cops in uniforms, and in the distance, kept back and across the road, dozens of local people standing together in small clusters.

She glanced over to where she had seen the two bodies and saw that the cops had sketched in white caulk the positions of both bodies. The markings looked like stage directions.

Greg had come up beside her, and lowering his voice so the others wouldn't hear, he finished off his statement, "If they get Adam alive, they're going to find out he is nothing more than a psycho. He would have killed you. He just likes it. He gets a thrill out of murdering people, ripping out their hearts."

Melissa looked at Greg. The pain and terror of the last half day had given her a new sense of security. She knew what to believe. When she hadn't been able to kill Adam as he wanted, she had learned a secret truth about her own self. It gave her confidence that she had lacked all of her life. She felt again like that little girl deep in the greenish blue pool in West Texas. She knew she was alone in the world and that it was okay. She was going to be all right. She could take care of herself.

"But you don't understand, Greg. Adam doesn't exist. He never really existed."

"Melissa, please."

She recognized that tone in his voice. He was exasperated with her, and in a moment he would become patronizing, as he sometimes did with her at the agency.

"Adam exists. I saw him. You lived with him. He lives, and guess what? He kills people, too."

Melissa stared at Greg, not backing off. "We kill, Greg," she said calmly. "We want to kill, too. It's in our hearts. Adam just acts out our passions." She stepped off the porch, leaving the school. "He's nothing more than the medium. We're the message." She tapped her heart. "It's all in here."

"You told me, negative forces, or was it impulses?" He was following Melissa. Who was walking toward where he had parked the van on the side of the county road.

"I was wrong. I thought I was the link with him. But it wasn't me." She stopped at the door of the van.

Greg came up behind her, reaching for the van keys. He waited for Melissa to continue, to explain herself, but she jumped into the front seat and waited for Greg to start the engine.

"Okay, why wasn't it you?" Greg asked, turning the van around on the narrow road.

"Because I couldn't kill him. He wanted me to, but I wasn't able. He's tapped another vein of my subconscious. He found all my hidden, secret nightmares from my childhood. He thought I was someone who kills."

"What about your sister?"

"I saw in the paintings upstairs something I hadn't remembered. Something that Adam hadn't drawn until I came into the crafts house."

Greg was trying to drive as he kept glancing over at her, watching her face as she explained. Melissa was staring straight ahead, concentrating on her explanation.

"He showed me Stephanie as she would have looked as an adult."

"I saw that!"

"But also, in the corner of that scene he had drawn something else. Did you see?" She glanced across at Greg, then continued, "There was a small teddy bear sitting on the window seat, below the window. I had forgotten about it. The teddy bear was mine. His name was Mike. I had him since birth. My daddy gave him to me, I was told.

"That afternoon Stephanie had crawled up to the window and I had told her to get down. I remembered as soon as I saw the painting. She had taken Mike with her and I got hysterical. I ran to grab it, but she was too quick. She took the teddy bear and tossed it out the open window. It was sitting on the ledge and I reached for it, but I couldn't reach the doll, and she had blocked my way. I started to cry hysterically because I couldn't get hold of the little stuffed bear. You have to understand how much that bear meant to me. It was the only toy I had from my daddy. It was all I had to remember him by, his little gift to me.

"Stephanie went for it. She was always after any toy of mine, and I started screaming, telling her to get back inside, knowing she could fall, and also I didn't want her to get my bear.

"She kept crawling, going after the bear and having no idea, of course, that she was in danger. I remember thinking I had to stop her, that she would fall, and also I remember thinking how much I hated her for taking my bear, tossing it onto the roof. But I made a decision then. I had to help my sister and I grabbed her leg, and, she, of course, thought I was trying to keep her from getting Mike and she flared out at me with her leg, kicked me away, and she did catch my face and knocked me back. I lost my grip on her leg, and pulling herself free, she went tumbling down the side of the roof."

"You didn't kill her!"

"But my mother blamed me nevertheless. I was the older child, I was responsible, and I've carried that recollection with me until I saw Adam's painting." She smiled wryly. "It's funny, but he's freed me from that memory."

They had reached the main highway. To the right was a sign saying that Johnson City was thirty-two miles. Greg turned on his blinker and looked for the oncoming traffic.

"No," Melissa said, "take me to the schooner-house."

"Mel, what are you talking about?" He hit the brakes.

"I'm going to wait for them."

"Who? The police? Melissa, we've given our statements."

"No, not the police. I want to wait for Crazy Sue and Adam."

"Betty Sue was picked up. Connor told you! Let's get out of here."

Melissa shook her head. "She'll be let go. These are her people. It's Adam that they want, not her. And those two both want me."

"Why? You said he wouldn't kill you; he had his chance."

"She will. She is like an idiot savant and will do what he wants. They have a sick symbiotic relationship."

"We'll get the cops. We'll wait for them." He had returned to town, which was filled, he saw, with cop cars, and more traffic. He spotted two television mobile vans parked in front of the diner as he turned onto Creek Drive.

"No," Melissa told him. "I want you to just leave. They'll never come if you're around."

"Melissa, I can't just leave you," he told her, frightened at once. He knew that tone of her voice.

"Yes, you can. And you've got to. Besides, it might be dangerous. I don't want you getting killed. Take the van and drive to New York. Call me on your way. If I don't answer, well, then..." She shrugged.

"Mel, if you weren't able to kill Adam back there, at the crafts school, how are you going to kill both of them here?" He slowed the van. They were nearing the schooner-house. "They could be there already, for chrissake, waiting for you."

"Maybe." She sounded almost glad.

"Melissa, I won't leave you." Greg stopped the van.

"You have to, Greg. He—now both of them—are my responsibility. I brought Adam here. I exposed him to this Crazy Sue person and I have to deal with the consequences. If I don't. If I leave them both..."

"The cops will find them. They'll run them both down in the hills."

"They won't find them until more people are killed." She opened the cab door, and looked over at Greg. "You aren't leaving me to the wolves, Greg, I know what I'm doing. You warned me about Adam and I didn't listen, and I won't have you put in danger. Not with Helen and the boys. They need you. I don't."

"Melissa, I love you."

"And I love you. I love you enough to know that this is my fight. I have nothing to lose."

"Holy shit, I don't believe it." He shut off the engine.

"Greg, don't make this worse. I have to do this my way." She reached over and touched his hand. "I know what I'm doing."

"No you don't. This is as crazy as taking the kid down here in the first place. Only now, we know you can get yourself killed." He was so angry that his vision began to blur. He stared across the bare backyard. It was almost noon and the sun was high and hot on the clear day.

"I have one chance, Greg," she answered calmly. "I stay here and let him and Crazy Sue find me. And then I deal with them."

"I'll give you a couple hours and if they don't come back, we leave."

"I'll be okay." She forced a smile.

"I'll go up to town and have a cup of coffee and then I'm coming back and we leave. If you're still alive."

"I'll be alive. And that's a deal."

"Goddamn fool," Greg swore, turning over the engine. She would be dead and it would then be his fault. He drove up Creek

Drive, realizing he might be watched by Crazy Sue or Adam, who could be hiding off anywhere in the woods, eyeing the house.

In town he pulled into the parking lot behind the general store and went inside and bought the biggest hunting knife he could find, fifteen inches of thick Winchester steel, in a heavy leather holster that he strapped to his belt at the small of his back. Then he walked across the street to have a quick cup of coffee at the crowded Bonnie & Clyde's, which he saw, from the sign in the front window, was under new management.

22

MELISSA PUSHED OPEN THE side door, letting it bang against the wall, and called out, "Hello?" as if Adam might reply. The house was silent.

She searched the door frame looking for snakes, half expecting to see one or two curled up in the coolness of the doorjamb. If she could see a snake, she wouldn't be half as frightened. It was when they startled her, came dropping down off the tree branch, or suddenly slithered between her feet. She shuddered, and made herself concentrate on what she had to do. The snakes, she knew, wouldn't kill her. But Crazy Sue and Adam, together, they could.

She stepped into the house and said hello again, louder this time. No one was there. She felt the emptiness of the place. That gave her a sense of security and she took a deep breath, realizing she had been holding her breath, expecting the worst.

She walked farther into the schooner-house and glanced around. She saw the snake box was where she had left it, still with the frying pan holding down the lid. She relaxed some. She scanned the corners of the big room, looking for curled rattles, just in case. The floor was empty.

Moving through the room, going into the kitchen she kept to the center of the floor away from the closed wooden box on the counter. She wanted a cup of tea and her desire for that helped her overcome her fear. She checked out Adam's room as she passed. The room was as she had left it that morning. No one, she thought, relaxing more, was hiding in it. She took the kettle off the stove, filled it with cold water, and turned on the gas. She stood staring at the flame, briefly mesmerized by this simple task. There had been so many killings, so much violence and slaughter, that the simple wholesome act of making a cup of tea seemed marvelous to her.

She looked out the kitchen window at the huge boulder, half expecting to see Adam perched there, but the boulder was bare. She couldn't decide whether that was good or bad. She opened the utility drawer and looked down at wooden spoons, several peelers, measuring cups, and a selection of knives. She picked up two before she settled on one that felt comfortable in her hand. She slipped the knife into the waistband of her jeans. It hindered her movements. She took the knife out and placed it on the counter within reach. Then she took down a mug from the open shelves over the counter and opened Connor's tea canister. There was a cottonmouth stuffed inside the tea container and it flopped out when she lifted the top, slid across the counter as Melissa, shrieking and stumbling away, dropped the can.

She grabbed the kitchen knife in a rage and whacked down on the thick brown snake, catching it just behind its blunt head. The heavy sharp blade cut cleanly through the thick skin and flesh, severing the snake's head. Its open and pink mouth and tongue darting, the head flew off the counter. The long length of the snake's body twisted and jerked, flipping over in agony until it lay with its milky smooth skin exposed and shivering, blood dripping from its severed body.

Melissa stumbled away. She had the bloody knife in her hands, and she realized then that she had swung at the snake with both her hands, as if she were trying to make some impossible backhand at tennis. She threw the knife down, sobbing and gasping for breath. This lack of breath frightened her more than the snake and she grabbed the sink to hold herself steady.

She was thinking of Adam. He knew she would want a cup of tea. He had watched her silently with his gray stale eyes as she routinely had tea just before dusk. He had stuffed the snake into the canister, knowing her habits. That little bastard, she thought. It was not a silly, childish trick, an adolescent way to scare an adult. Stuffing that cottonmouth into the tea canister was vicious. He had wanted her to be bitten, to die in agony.

She stepped over to the counter and opened the utility drawer and took out another knife. This one was longer, with a thin blade, a knife for cutting up a turkey or a Virginia ham. She walked out of the house to sit in the sunny backyard that looked west, and would be the last section of the property to lose its sunlight. She would wait for Adam, outside, in the open, where she knew they couldn't surprise her. She had her fill of Adam's surprises.

Sitting down in a tractor's seat that some iron worker had made into a craftsmen's lawn chair, she lay the long kitchen knife beside her, thinking she had at least an hour to wait. He wouldn't come until it was dark.

She sat facing the house and the woods behind, guessing Adam would come out of the trees and come down the rise, following the deer path she had used earlier to go up onto the high, level meadowland. She purposefully sat in the sun, realizing how little time she had spent outside and relaxing. She closed her eyes and let her body relax. After the long day, she was finding a few moments of peace and quiet in the warmth of the mountain sun.

The fading sunlight awoke her. Melissa blinked her eyes open and sat up, terrified at once. She reached for the long kitchen knife, grasping its handle as she stood, upset with herself for napping. The sun had disappeared behind the ridge, and she realized she had been asleep at least an hour. She could have been killed, she thought. Adam could have caught her there and cut her throat.

She spun around, searching for him. The yard was empty. She turned toward the house and now, with the approaching darkness, saw that several lights had been left on in the place. Had she left them on that morning when she fled the place? Or had Adam come back and gotten inside while she slept?

Dammit, she thought, approaching the house.

She circled the schooner-house and came back to the terrace that faced the boulder and wooded hillside. Standing there she could see most of the downstairs living area as well as part of the kitchen. Everything seemed as she had left it earlier.

She opened the old barn doors Connor had made into makeshift French doors and stepped inside. The living room was warm, having been lit all afternoon by the sun. She closed the doors, hiding the kitchen knife behind her.

"Adam?" she asked, speaking calmly, needing to hear her voice in the big open space.

He appeared from his bedroom at the mention of his name and Melissa jumped, startled by the sight of him.

He smiled at her.

"You came back," she said, regripping the black-handled knife.

He stepped clear of the bedroom door and Crazy Sue followed him from the room. She glanced from Adam to Melissa, her head lopped to one side. She had both of her hands behind her, and Melissa saw the dark stains of blood on her old cotton dress.

"Sue, why are you here? They said you were taken by the police."

"The police, they got Rufus, ma'am, not me." She kept grinning, the dark gums of her mouth filled with misshaped and missing teeth.

"Why Rufus?" Melissa asked next, realizing she had to keep breathing, and that if she didn't speak she would lose it.

"He killed all those people, Rufus did."

"What people?" Melissa asked.

Crazy Sue glanced from Melissa to the boy and shook her head, shrugged. She was standing on one foot like a schoolchild, and hooked the other foot behind it. She teetered back and forth.

They were both crazy, Melissa thought, and realized the foolishness of her idea. They would kill her, she thought. She wasn't a match for two crazy people.

"I found your snake, Adam," she said, needing to keep a conversation going as a barrier between them.

Adam and Crazy Sue grinned at each other.

"I killed it," Melissa said calmly. "And I'm going to kill you, too." She smiled.

Melissa suddenly felt better, more at ease. She stepped into the room and moved several steps closer. She thought that perhaps it was true that once you kill anything, a snake, a deer in the woods, you harden to death, and the next murder is not so difficult.

"We're going to kill you," Crazy Sue answered back.

"You're going to kill me, Sue?" Melissa taunted her.

"Me and Adam here." She nodded at the silent little boy, quite pleased with herself. Her old face was bright with a smile.

"Why are you going to kill me, Sue? Why did the two of you kill the others?"

" 'Cause," she said.

" 'Cause why?" Melissa asked calmly, amazed by her calmness.

"He said so." She glanced over at Adam.

"But Adam can't talk, you know that." She stared at the boy, wondered if he had fooled them. What if he could talk, the little fucker?

"He talks well enough, if you listen," Crazy Sue answered, smug and deranged, bouncing up and down on her feet.

"And you know how to listen, do you?"

Crazy Sue grinned.

"What's he telling you, Sue?" Melissa believed the two of them could communicate in some crazy way. There was so much craziness between them that they didn't need language. Adam had been able to read her nightmare dreams simply by sleeping on the couch in the next room.

"He's telling me to kill you, too."

Melissa kept watching Adam, watching his pale silvery eyes. He was a beautiful child, she thought, but she realized Adam was worse than crazy. Adam was evil. She thought of the saying she had heard up at the Tabernacle Church, "Evil all around us. In the hills. On the street. Right beside you in your seats."

"Where does Adam come from?" Melissa asked Sue, not taking her eyes off the boy, though she knew it wouldn't be Adam that tried to kill her. It wasn't his way. He'd let a damaged soul like Crazy Sue do his bidding.

"He didn't come from nowhere," Crazy Sue answered, not understanding what Melissa wanted. "He came with you in your big van. I seen you."

"Is he the devil, Sue?" Melissa asked, as if to lead the old woman through a maze of questions.

"No, he ain't no devil," Crazy Sue shouted back. "I know the devil. He has horns, pointed ears, and carries a pitchfork." She grinned again, pleased with her answer. "I've seen a colored picture of the devil once in a church book."

"No, he isn't the devil," Melissa said calmly, approaching the child. She regripped the handle of the kitchen knife, surprised that her fingers were so dry. "Adam is really a victim, isn't he? You don't understand this, Sue. You're a victim, too, in your way. You both have a kind of sickness...

"But Adam is—was—a nice normal thirteen-year-old boy who might have run away from home, or was abducted. I'm not sure. We'll never know. But I do know that somewhere—and I guess it's in the subways of the city, something happened to this innocent little boy. You don't understand, do you, Sue?" Melissa had stepped within two feet of both of them, positioning herself so she needed only to leap forward and strike. She saw Adam was alerted. The sickness of his soul had been warned. It knew its existence was in danger, that this safe harbor within the mind of the poor child was being threatened. She knew, too, that she couldn't save the boy, but that Crazy Sue might live. Once the link was broken, the old woman would be harmless.

"My mommy gone sick and died when I was just a baby."

"That's right, Sue, but that's a different kind of sickness, and there's no cure. No way to stop it. It seeks out people who aren't well, who are filled with hate. It corrupts them. And it causes an infection. Not a physical infection, but an infection of the spirit."

Melissa realized that she had lost the old woman, that Crazy Sue didn't understand her, but she kept talking, explaining how the sickness had reached this boy. She wondered what the child had done in his brief life to have been such a receptive organ. She wondered, too, where the child had been contaminated. Even as she wondered, she knew it was the city, somewhere in the depths of the subway, lost perhaps in the dark tunnels under Grand Central. He had stayed too long with the scum of the earth and had been corrupted by them.

She saw Adam glance at Crazy Sue, as if to signal the old lady. And in the damaged, childlike mind, Melissa realized the seeds of death were taking hold. Crazy Sue whipped a knife from the folds of her cotton dress and, raising it high, slashed it through the air, driving down toward Melissa, who struck at that moment herself. She jumped forward and pierced the blank face of the small mute boy.

Melissa drove her long blade deep into the cheek of the child, pierced his face with ten inches of steel. She severed his tongue and cut through his lower jaw so that his face resembled nothing more than a butterfly pinned by an enormous knife.

Adam turned away from Melissa, dancing a silly little dance into the center of the open living room. His life was spraying out in a thick shower of warm blood. Both of his hands gripped his face, tried to pull out the enormous knife. He seized the knife with his small hands, but they slipped off the bloody slippery black handle.

Melissa screamed, stunned by the sight of Adam dancing to his quick death on the hardwood floor. She forgot about Crazy Sue, who had tumbled over as she slashed at and missed Melissa.

Betty Sue regained her feet, saw Adam spurting blood, and, screeching at the sight of him, turned and ran, frightened that her aunt would catch and box her ears for getting little Adam hurt.

Crazy Sue ran with the knife, ran away from Melissa. The old woman ran through the side door, ran into Greg and knocked him back. He had pulled out his new knife and was running to help, hearing Melissa scream, when Crazy Sue came tumbling out of the schooner-house. She ran onto his blade. Her thin chest consumed the thick steel.

Greg tried to pull the knife away and stumbled over the two cinder blocks Connor used as a makeshift step. Crazy Sue came tumbling over him, falling on top of Greg in an awkward embrace, soaking him with her blood.

He shoved her off and rolled away from her long, thin limbs. Lifeless, she weighed slightly more than air. Melissa had come to the schooner-house door and vomited into the backyard. She bent over, clutching her side. Greg reached her, damp with Crazy Sue's blood. He seized her by the shoulders and asked where Adam was, terrified that the boy was still loose. He had left his knife in Crazy Sue's chest.

"Where is he?"

"I killed him," Melissa managed to say. She had braced herself against the wheelbarrow. "...with a kitchen knife."

Greg turned around and tried to see Adam through the open doorway.

"Thank God," he whispered.

She kept shaking her head, too sick to speak.

"It's okay," he told her. "Everything is okay." He walked to the doorway and peered inside. Adam lay in the center of the room, inside a spreading pool of blood. Adam was curled up with his back to the side door. Greg could not see his face. He stepped inside, stunned by the sweet smell of blood in the hot house, and circled the body, knowing he had to see Adam's dead face to be sure.

"Don't," Melissa called. She was standing in the open doorway, afraid to come closer. "Let's get out of here," she pleaded.

Greg saw the black-handled kitchen knife, saw how Melissa had jammed it into the boy's face, pinning his silent tongue to the inside of his gasping mouth, leaving him bloody and unrecognizable.

He saw, too, with mounting fear, that the strange child, the bald-headed boy who had been brought into their office, lay dead and butchered on the bright floor.

Greg looked over at Melissa. She stood, hovered in the fading sunlight at the open door, and he whispered, "Who is he, Melissa?"

23

MELISSA CAME UP OUT of the IRT subway and walked down the short marble corridor and into the high-vaulted and beautiful main concourse of Grand Central Station. It was not yet five A.M. There were a few early morning commuters rushing through the station, but Grand Central was filled nevertheless with sleeping men and women, all of the homeless who spent that winter night in the vast public building.

Passing them, seeing how they slept curled up in rags and blankets, and bedded down on pieces of cardboard, she marveled at their ability to sleep regardless of the noise, the cold, and any lack of comfort. She also knew from experience that they were always tired, but it wasn't from lack of sleep. They were simply exhausted because of hunger.

She glanced at the clock over the information station and checked the time, making sure she wasn't late, and then she scanned the concourse for Greg. They had agreed to meet at the information booth at five A.M.

This was the third week of their search, and the weather had turned colder. She knew how hard it would be for Greg to get out of bed, knowing he had to leave the warmth and comfort of Helen. But then, he had wanted to help her. She wasn't forcing him out into the cold.

That morning, however, when she woke, she almost telephoned Greg to tell him to stay in bed. She might have called, but the thought of waking Helen, of having to speak to her, stopped Melissa. She had the courage, she told herself, to go down into the subways of New York and seek out a killer, but she didn't have the guts to talk to Helen, not after having slept with Greg.

Instead, she had tossed off the blankets and forced herself to get up, shower, and dress for a morning down in the city subways.

She yawned and saw her breath fog over. It was colder than she would have thought, even in the center of the station. She would get a cup of coffee and a donut, she thought next, seeing one of the small shops off the grand concourse was opening. She had to keep busy, otherwise, she'd realize what a crazy and dangerous idea this was, searching for the killer.

She crossed the enormous concourse, looking for Greg in among the few dozen overcoated men she saw hurrying through the building, rushing for work, or really, she knew, rushing to get away from Grand Central and the homeless huddled in every dark corner.

They should have come into the city together, she thought next, and then he would have had to go farther out in Brooklyn to meet her, or she would have had to stop by his place, and she didn't want that.

She hadn't told Greg not to say anything to Helen, but she was half afraid that in his need to be honest, he had confessed they had made love in the mountains. Men, she knew, weren't very bright when it came to such matters.

She bought coffee and a donut and stepped over to a section of the ticket counter that was closed, and used the marble counter as a makeshift table, putting down her coffee and unwrapping the wax paper around the sugary donut. She had barely opened the paper when a homeless man, wrapped up in a blanket, approached her, mumbling something. He held out his hand, begging.

Melissa tensed, preparing to defend herself. She studied the black man's face, searched his eyes, and relaxed. It wasn't him. Still, she guessed, she couldn't really be sure. Who would know what his identity might be? She wondered again, how in the world they would ever find him, but then she thought, as she always did, that he would find her. He needed to kill her. That was his great need, his only desire.

Melissa coldly shook her head, and the stoop-shouldered man

shuffled off, leaving in his wake the rich odor of an unwashed body. Melissa saw the black man was barefooted on the cold winter day, and that he was naked under his heavy blanket. She was getting good at this, she thought wryly. It no longer hurt her to turn down beggars. She was getting good and tough, just like every other New Yorker.

A year ago, Melissa realized, even four months ago, she would never have been able to do that. She would have given the man money, as well as a printed card with information on where he could go to find a warm shelter. She would have intervened in this man's life. She would have encouraged him to seek help from her agency, or any of the other volunteer groups. Now the homeless man was no longer her business. She had left the world of social work. She walked down the streets of the city and never noticed the homeless.

Besides, she guessed, thinking of the black man, he wouldn't have listened to her. He wouldn't have gone to a city shelter. He knew, better than she did, how dangerous shelters were.

And he wasn't alone. She had seen how the number of homeless on the city streets was growing with the cold weather. Every day she spotted more and more men and women sleeping in the corners of public places, at the entrance of buildings. They were making New York a third world city. And there was nothing she could do to stop the tide of human misery.

Coming back from the south, she decided she couldn't return to the agency. She knew she had to give up her job, get away from all the poverty, and get away, too, from Greg.

She had found a job at a travel agency with an office in midtown Manhattan, two blocks from Grand Central Station. All day, all during the fall, she helped people escape New York and fly off to warm and exotic places in the sun. She never thought twice about her work. At the end of the day, she walked away from it. She was, she realized, doing what most people did. Work was something they did to make money, and had no other importance in their lives.

They weren't like her, she realized, out to save the world, needing to help people. In fact, she had come to see, most people thought she was naive for spending her life helping others, being a social worker, and earning so little money. Well, not any longer.

She gave up reading the newspapers and watching the news.

She did not want to know what terrible things were happening in the city. At night, at home, she read thick romantic books, of life long ago in faraway countries. She took dance classes and worked on her French. In the spring, she had thought she might fly to Paris and spend a month sitting in the sun.

And she made herself get over Greg. Coming back to New York, she had told him that they couldn't continue. She wasn't going to break up his marriage. "I can't do this to the boys," she said, remembering her own fatherless childhood. "And Helen hasn't done anything to me. I'm not going to steal you away from her."

It had been hard to live with her decision, knowing, too, that Greg was only a phone call away. Greg loved her, Melissa knew, and he also loved Helen. And Helen was his wife, the mother of his children.

Adam had even been harder to forget. She had nightmares about the boy. She woke up screaming, terrified that he had gotten into her Brooklyn apartment and was coming to get her. She changed her locks several times and spent hundreds of dollars on an alarm system, even though she knew he was dead. She had killed him. She had driven a butcher knife into his skull. Still, she slept with the small pistol beneath her pillow. Nick Kardatzke's small .38. The one she had taken off Adam in the schooner-house. She had found it tucked into the small of his back. She had not told Greg she had it, but she knew she needed the gun, and she kept it with her at work, on the subway. She slept with the ivory-handled pistol under her pillow in Brooklyn, taking endless comfort from its smooth, cold metal.

Still, she could not fortify herself against her memories. She knew that everyone lived their lives with some nightmare from their childhood, that no matter how long they lived, how far away they fled from home, a shadow stayed with them. It waited to be remembered, waited for the moment to haunt. She had thought in the mountains, she had finished off her nightmare and rid herself of the memory.

And Greg had believed it, too.

It was five months after they returned from the mountains that Greg walked into the travel agency with the clipping from the *Post*. It was a small item, just several lines long, saying a body had been found in the East River. It was the body of a missing Latin American diplomat at the U.N. The man had somehow been involved with cocaine dealers. He had been a courier carrying dope to the United States in the diplomatic pouch. There was no mention of his body being mutilated.

Greg told her about the missing heart.

"The cops came to see me," he said, leaning close to her and lowering his voice.

Melissa had opened a Michelin map on her cluttered desk to imply that the two of them were planning this man's tour of Europe.

"They had questions about Adam. It was all the old stuff. They wanted to know if I had heard anything more, you know, from the South. Or from you. They were from Kardatzke's division, that special drug enforcement team."

"He's alive," Melissa whispered, feeling a surge of fear whip through her body. She stared at Greg, holding him in sight, so she wouldn't become hysterical. Wave after wave of fear kept cresting in her body.

Greg glanced off. "They told me finally this guy's heart had, you know, been ripped..." He stopped talking.

"He'll find me," she whispered, knowing it was true.

"He's after Helen," Greg told her, looking up.

The breath caught in Melissa's throat. Her eyes widened, waiting for Greg to explain.

"Someone tried to jump her the other night, coming home from work. It was early, you know, only five o'clock. The subway was crowded."

Melissa saw that his hands were trembling.

"She wants to leave the city," he said.

Melissa realized what it was. He was ashamed. He had brought this on his wife, his affair, his involvement with Melissa.

"Is she okay?" Melissa whispered, her body freezing up.

Greg nodded. "Yeah, she doesn't know. She thinks it was just some high school kids, you know, trying to grab her. She managed to spin away and escape."

"Did she see them?"

"One was fourteen, she thought. And bald-headed."

Melissa dropped her head into her hands. She had brought the monster back from the mountains, she thought. He had lived, somehow. They never die, she thought. They never die.

Greg glanced around. He saw the other agents were glancing at them. There was a lull in the office phones. The crowded room was quiet.

"Why don't we meet later, have lunch or something?" he suggested, seeing how upset she was. "I don't want you to get into trouble here at work."

Melissa shook her head. She didn't dare have lunch with him. She was afraid of being alone with him, afraid something might happen to Helen while they were having lunch. Enough was enough.

"I'll call you at the office." She folded up the clipping and slipped it into her desk, saying, "Do you believe me?"

"Believe you what...?"

"...that it's some ancient evil."

Greg's face tightened as always when he had to say something difficult. "It doesn't make sense." He looked at her, baffled and overwhelmed by what was happening to his wife.

Melissa nodded. "If I don't stop him Helen will be killed. You'll be killed." She said it calmly, but her face was frozen with fear. And as she said it, she realized it was true. Both of them would be killed.

It kills, she told Greg. "It hatches within one's body and when the time is right, or the place, as it was in the mountains, then it turns people into killers. It turned Adam into a killer."

"What about these mutilated bodies?"

Melissa nodded. "That's how it escapes. When the body dies it moves on. It needs another, what do doctors call it? Another compatible host?"

Greg stared at Melissa. His eyes widened, baffled by her, and then he said softly, "Melissa, you're crazy!"

"Am I?"

"Why in God's name would this thing come after Helen?"

"It's not after Helen. It's after me. Because of you, it went after Helen. It wants my corrupted soul."

"Why, because you killed Adam?"

"It knows I'm vulnerable. It knows I killed my little sister. I'm not a good person, Greg. Evil does not go unpunished."

"Jesus Christ, this is all nonsense." He stood and put back on his Paragon jacket. "You didn't kill your sister. You told me that yourself."

"I wanted her dead, Greg. I was thirteen years old, the same age as Adam, and I wanted her dead."

She was looking down at, but not seeing, all the paperwork on her desk. Having started to talk about it had made her tense. The phone was ringing, and she looked at the blinking light unable to concentrate.

"I killed an innocent child, the child that was Adam, but also the evil knows I was after it!"

Greg slipped back into the hard-back office chair beside her small metal desk.

"What you're talking about here is old-time religion. You are talking about the devil. Or a vengeful God." He was trying to make sense of Melissa's rambling.

She looked at Greg. "I don't believe in the devil. I do believe in evil. Corruption is a human condition. People are evil. I see it around me in this city. How do we know that evil isn't just growing in the subways of this city, in the dank and dangerous world under Manhattan? Why can't it spread from one person to another like the common cold? All I know for sure is that the evil is a living organism. And I know it wants me."

"And why you?"

"You know why. So far, I've fought it off. I've been lucky. Now it's coming after me through Helen and you!" She was leaning closer to his face, trying to keep her voice down, and hissing out her words, spraying his face. "It'll kill your wife to get to me. It will kill you to get at me."

He kept staring at her, as if evaluating what she had said, and then he answered simply, "I'll call you later."

When they did talk later that day, she had already decided what had to be done. That afternoon she bought all the city's papers and studied the news of the city.

She looked for reports of human mutilation, anything hinting that the victims in the city might have someway been cut up, ripped apart. She knew that even the *New York Post* won't tell the readers everything. Still she knew how to read between the lines. In the next two days, she found other suspicious deaths. She started to clip the articles and keep a file.

The police referred to a serial killer loose in the subways of New York. There was no public outcry. The victims were prostitutes from 7th Avenue, out-of-town kids with no family connections, more of the homeless.

A serial killer, Melissa thought wryly. It would have been a blessing. This wasn't a serial killer. At home, in her apartment, she charted the locations of the killings on a city map. In less than two weeks she had pinpointed the source. She knew where it lived. She called up Greg at work and told him where they had to begin to search.

That same day she was fired from her travel agency job, told that she wasn't paying attention to her job. Her boss even produced her file on the city's murdered victims. Told her she was spending too much time on this "craziness." Melissa saw the wariness in the man's eyes. He was afraid. Melissa didn't object. It was true. Her work meant nothing to her. She had bigger problems. Life and death problems. Her life.

Greg and she began to meet at dawn to search the tunnels under Grand Central. He was there, she knew, waiting for her.

Melissa spotted Greg crossing the concourse. He was bundled up against the weather and she stepped from the shadows so he would see her. He nodded, then motioned that they should walk toward the lower level, where the trains came into Grand Central. His face was wrapped in a bright red Christmas scarf. She was again annoyed that he wasn't looking at her, that he was denying her eye contact. Punishing her. He was still angry that she had broken off their affair when they came back to New York City. It was his small, angry way of getting even. His behavior disappointed her.

"Ready?" he asked.

She took a deep breath, trying to be understanding, and realizing, too, that he didn't have to help her. She was the one with the nutty idea that they would find it in the bowels of the city. "It was where he felt safe," she had tried to explain to Greg. "In the subway he is with his own kind."

"I would think that would be Trump Tower, with Donald."

"We'll go there next," she said, humoring him.

They went together down the marble slope of Grand Central Terminal to the lower level, and then across the waiting area, moving quickly toward the gates.

Trains were arriving. A tide of hurried commuters suddenly filled the lower concourse, rushing to work. Greg edged to one side and let the tide pass them as they continued to work forward, edging ahead.

Today, once again, they were headed for the subbasement of the terminal, deep underground. They had been stopped only once, and then Greg showed his city identification to the Metro-North police, explaining that they were surveying the homeless.

Melissa wasn't worried about the cops. It was the homeless that she feared. The homeless were the most desperate, the most deranged. She knew those this deep underground had retreated to this dank underworld because they were too crazy to survive on the streets. She guessed there were some who hadn't been above ground in years, but lived like rodents, surviving on the garbages they grabbed off the commuter trains parked overnight in the vast network of midtown tracks.

Melissa shivered. She wasn't sure if it was the cold whipping through the long dark tunnels or her own fear. She picked up her step, wanting to stay closer to Greg, and reached inside the pocket of her puffy down coat and felt the smooth, slippery handle of the small .38.

She should have told Greg she had the gun, she guessed, but she knew, too, why she hadn't. He wouldn't have let her take the pistol. "Bernard Goetz!" he would have screamed, warning her.

"Greg?" she asked, and her voice carried away from her, went echoing into the darkness. The sound of her own voice as always surprised her. In the subterranean tunnels, her voice echoed and echoed. It traveled away from her, endlessly.

A rat surprised her. It ran toward them on the long wet track, running on the cold steel railing as deftly as a ballerina. Greg's flashlight picked it out. The rodent was as large as a prairie dog. It was like the ones she had watched from the windows of her Texas motel, saw running across the empty brushland beyond the buildings. Its eyes were red in the flashlight.

Greg grabbed her arm.

"What is it?" she demanded, pulling free.

"We're lost." He couldn't control his fear. It had swept away his reasoning. He was behaving badly, he knew, but he couldn't stop himself.

"Look!" she said. "We've done this all before."

"I see lights."

Melissa looked ahead and saw a dim bulb.

"Okay," she said, "let's keep going."

"No!" he insisted. "Let's go back."

She pulled free and made him follow her toward the light.

He resisted for a moment, then fell into step.

He was afraid of falling into the mud and pools of water between the rails and cinders. The light might mean an exit, he hoped. He had a brief vision of being above surface, of seeing the sooty winter sky and crowded New York streets. These excursions into the depths of the city had ironically made him appreciate midtown traffic.

When they reached the light, he realized at once it wasn't an exit, but someone, a bundled-up homeless person, who had started a fire deep underground. The fire was built into a rocky urban cave, made of cast-off track ties and pieces of scrap. The flame was bright reds and orange and reflected off the wet stone wall. It looked, Greg thought, as strange as a prehistoric cave.

Beside the huddled figure were shopping bags of the woman's meager belongings. She was feeding the fire pieces of scrap wood, odd trash found in the underground. The flame sparkled with each piece of new fuel.

He thought how medieval the scene was. He tugged at Melissa's arm, to pull her away from the woman, to not let them disturb her. She was a Grimm character, the old witch in Hansel and Gretel. The shrouded woman looked up, grinning at the both of them. It was Crazy Sue.

Melissa squeezed her fingers around the smooth pistol.

No, it wasn't Crazy Sue. It couldn't be. It was just another homeless old woman. They all were strange-looking and crazy after months in the subterranean world of New York.

Her fingers relaxed on the ivory-handled pistol.

"Let's go," Greg urged. "Let's get the hell out of this place."

"No," she said. She kept staring at the woman, watching her. She realized she wasn't mistaken. It was Crazy Sue. She had come after her.

"You!" she growled, stepping forward.

"Mel!" Greg reached for her.

Crazy Sue grinned and in the leaping firelight, Melissa saw the same cold silvery gray eyes. Adam's eyes.

She pulled the small pistol from the deep pocket and fired at the old woman, hitting her twice. She saw her spin around and topple facefirst into the scrap-wood flame.

"Oh, Christ, Melissa!" Greg ran by Melissa, rushed to pluck the old woman from the fire.

Melissa grabbed the flashlight from where Greg dropped it and ran ahead, ran off into the darkened tunnel, running for the next shadowy lights.

Greg called after her, told her to stop. His voice rang off the walls. She did not answer. She knew he would be after her. She heard his foot crunching on the gravel base of the train tracks, and she spun her light around. The thin beam richocheted off the rock walls, then found Greg.

She caught his face in her beam. She saw his eyes. She realized in terror that she had made a mistake. She had left him alone. She had not thought...

Of course! Of course! The world around her slowed. Time lengthened. Crazy Sue had brought it to New York, to this subterranean world. It had trapped her.

"No," she said, reaching for her pistol. She tumbled backward, tripping on the wooden rail ties. The bag lady by the fire, she knew, was dead, her heart gorged.

Greg fell on top of her, seizing her throat.

She brought her leg up and hit him in the groin. She could see his eyes. They were Adam's eyes now. The same cold silvery eyes. The eyes of the evil.

She jammed the small pistol up into Greg's left side, aiming it at his heart.

"No, don't," he asked, reaching for her.

She tried to speak, to whisper that she was sorry. He was coming to kill her. She thought of Crazy Sue's verse, "Evil all around us. In the hills. On the street. Right beside us in our seat." She pulled the trigger and the small pistol exploded. It sounded muffled in the thickness of winter coats.

Greg's fingers jerked loose from her coat, giving her a moment's escape, and she rolled to one side and away from her dying lover, splashing through a pool of water, but free of the man. She was screaming, but nothing came from her throat. She pulled herself up on her knees.

She was freezing from fear and the cold, and clutching her body, wrapping her arms around her, she forced herself to look back along the track, to where Greg lay facedown in the mud and gravel.

"Oh, God," she whispered, "oh, dear God." She bent over, crying and in pain, and knowing she had to get out of the tunnel. The flashlight was within reach. Its beam turned harmlessly away, shooting off into the dark interior.

Melissa seized it, pulled herself up, and ran, stumbling away, following the track, running ahead to where she saw was a single red light, and, she guessed, a metal staircase that would take her up into the streets. She remembered reading how passengers were evacuated from stalled trains under Park Avenue.

Running, she knew she should have stopped to see if she had killed Greg, but she did not have the courage to look into his face, to see him dead. In time, she knew, this would all be another nightmare to carry, another memory to flee.

Melissa reached the metal stairway and slipped the cop's revolver into her pocket and climbed the circular steps to the manhole cover.

She had to use her back and shoulders to lift the heavy metal cover, but slowly, with great effort, and in her desperation, she forced the cover off the hole and came up into the bright winter sunlight. She was at 50th and Park, in the middle of the intersection. A car passed overhead, rattling the loose manhole cover.

Desperate, Melissa shoved the cover away and before another car could cross the street, she jumped up into the middle of the busy morning intersection, into the windy cold day.

She ran. Leaving the open manhole, she cut in front of cars and ran onto the sidewalk, disappearing into the rush of pedestrian traffic. She ran from Grand Central and the crowds of homeless.

She headed for Fifth Avenue, crossing Madison, and walking fast, matching strides with all the other harassed urban workers. Within a block, she saw people moving away from her.

She was crying, she knew, but she did not know why. Still she kept walking, rushing to reach Fifth Avenue, to get away from the dead bodies she had left under Park.

She turned onto Fifth, and headed downtown. The day was clear and clean and gloriously bright. Looking up, the tears in her eyes and the low morning made it difficult to see. She took some tissues from the coat pocket, wiped her eyes and blew her nose.

She slowed a bit, losing strength. She couldn't stop trembling. Her body was soaked with perspiration. She glanced into the windows of Fortunoff and caught her reflection.

She looked like a bag woman.

She stared at herself in the beautiful store window. She studied her own face, smudged with soot and streaked with tears. She looked at her own eyes to see if they were the telltale gray of evil. She decided at that moment she would kill herself if they were. She could not go on doing more harm to others, filling the world with more misery. Her hand gripped the revolver, safely in her deep pocket.

She saw herself. There was no image of death. The ancient plague had been stopped.

She turned away from the windows and took a deep breath. She was okay. She had survived. She had conquered the stalking scourge.

She passed a blind man standing in front of a Fifth Avenue store. He had a dog kneeling beside him and was selling pencils. She looked into his face. His eyes were open and sightless and innocent. She reached into her coat, took a handful of money and gave it to him, stuffing the bills into his small tin cup.

He mumbled his thanks and his cold breath fogged the air. She thanked him in return, and he frowned, unable to comprehend.

"Thank you for being you," she told him, not knowing how she could possibly explain what it meant to her to give help to a good human.

She stepped away briskly, feeling immensely better and passed Trump Tower as a rush of people swept out of the complex, hurrying for stretch limousines parked at the curve.

One woman wrapped in mink glanced over, frowning and apprehensive at the closeness of her. Melissa realized what she appeared like, all bundled up and dirty from the tunnels. She looked like another deranged homeless woman, like Betty Sue herself.

But she wasn't crazy, Melissa knew. Grinning, she thought of herself as an avenging angel come to wipe out the evil in the world. To rid the world of evil people, like Adam, like Greg.

She stepped around the rich woman and saw the woman's eyes, saw the cold silvery gray eyes of the woman react to her dirty face, her bundled up body.

Melissa caught, too, the faces of the others, saw all the rich men and women dressed in silk and suede and beautiful animal fur. Their faces differed, but their eyes told the same story.

She ducked her face into the thickness of her bulky parka and pushed through the rich residents of Trump Tower as her fingers tightened around the .38, and thought with pleasure how her real work in life was just beginning. Work that she would do in silence and in cunning.